THE FINAL

JOURNEY:

A DIARY OF SURVIVAL

"Choose To Survive!"

LARRY D. HORTON, PhD

WESTBOW
PRESS®

A DIVISION OF THOMAS NELSON
& ZONDERVAN

Scripture quotations taken from the New American Standard Bible® (NASB), Copyright © 1960, 1962, 1963, 1968, 1971, 1972, 1973, 1975, 1977, 1995 by The Lockman Foundation Used by permission. www.Lockman.org.

WestBow Press books may be ordered through booksellers or by contacting:

WestBow Press
A Division of Thomas Nelson & Zondervan
1663 Liberty Drive
Bloomington, IN 47403
www.westbowpress.com
1 (866) 928-1240

ISBN: 978-1-5127-8065-9 (sc)
ISBN: 978-1-5127-8067-3 (hc)
ISBN: 978-1-5127-8066-6 (e)

Library of Congress Control Number: 2017904483

Print information available on the last page.

WestBow Press rev. date: 03/29/2017

DEDICATION

To those who have gone before. For two thousand years, countless millions have chosen to accept death rather than compromise their faith in Jesus Christ. Today believers die at the hands of evil across the world. The future will call many more to stand for their faith and to die rejoicing in the hope of eternal life. This book is dedicated to those who have, who are, and who will die in Jesus Christ.

The Martyrs

CONTENTS

THE AUTHOR

Dr. Larry D. Horton, pastor, missionary, Old Testament professor, historian, cross-cultural scholar, business executive, and yes, former PGA golf professional, has spent his life studying and experiencing spiritual and professional survival in our increasingly chaotic world. A graduate of Grove City College, Asbury Theological Seminary, and Michigan State University, he has now turned his attention to practicing and sharing **common-sense life survival** knowledge and skills in our uncertain world. He lives with his wife, Jude, in Katy, Texas. They have three children, five grandchildren, and of course their four-legged children, Sadie and Sophie.

AUTHOR'S PURPOSE

My purpose is to present to you the fundamental philosophy that my wife, Jude, and I will use to prepare for a potential survival journey at some point in the future through a fictional diary. Our advice is to build your own philosophy of survival on the fundamental principles we have tried to identify. Always remember that if you prepare for what could potentially happen, you increase the odds that you will indeed survive. If you fail to prepare, you will find yourself at some point in time with nothing, and you will not survive.

Larry D. Horton, PhD, November 2016

AUTHOR'S INTRODUCTION

The fictional journal that follows presents a worst-case scenario. Events depicted represent a possible world that no one wants to become a reality. The possible events could potentially happen in any kind of man-made or natural disaster scenario. Key to understanding the purpose of this fictional writing is the fact that each of us must prepare for any potential disaster and be ready to do whatever is necessary to survive. As Christians, we must be prepared to deal with a world that has a very different perspective related to the efforts of humankind to build the kingdom of God on earth. We must do all we can to prepare for our Lord's coming again.

The political and social issues used to build a context for the writing are very possible. Will they occur? That is left to be seen. Is the writing predictive? It may be to some degree. However, events over the last few weeks of writing might lead one to think that the events may not be far-fetched at all. One example of what I mean by that: A situation was written into the fictional journal in which many, if not all, electronic communication portals and social media outlets and tools were hacked and shut down. That scenario was written early one week. On Thursday of that week the event actually happened in real life. External hackers actually shut down multiple social media sites in the United States for a short time.

Predictive writing is not difficult. One can just let the imagination go anywhere. However, writing predictively with a decent chance of that prediction becoming reality is much harder and more complex. History, both short- and long-term, within a particular country and back through the ages, international events, political realities, human nature, social and economic realities, and other influences must be put into some reasonable understanding of what might be possible. The writing that follows attempts to do that in a reasonable and believable way.

Again, my hope is that none of what is written will become a reality. But in all honesty, I believe there is a better than even chance that we as individuals, as a society, as a country, and as a world will face this terrible future. It could even be worse than what can be imagined. My biggest remaining question for you is whether or not you are prepared. Are you ready for a future that may take you back to a time like the beginning of the nineteenth century? If you are as ready as you can be, that is wonderful. If you are not ready, it is time to start preparing. Not to do so will mean your end. And that would be sad. Remember, we are all told that to fail to prepare is to prepare to fail. Which choice will you make?

Larry D. Horton, PhD
November 6, 2016

REFLECTIONS: THE END OF THE BEGINNING

Final Journey—A Day in the Future

"As the last sliver of the sun sinks below the hills to our west, I look into the dancing orange-yellow flames of the last open fire I will sit in front of after our four-month, 1,500-mile journey. With my wife, Jude, sitting beside me, and our two beagles, Sadie and Sophie, beside us near the fire smelling the lingering scents of our just-completed cups of hot soup, the weariness of the day sets in quickly. We know that just two miles remain to arrive at our final destination, and our overwhelming sense of relief is tinged with a grateful exhaustion that our journey's unimagined challenges will soon end."

What will the future hold for us? Only the living of those future days will show us. Days in which we will hope and wait for our Lord to call us to our final home. But I write not about that wonderful last homecoming but rather about the journey that led us to our final campfire.

Our hope is that, whoever you are, you are prepared, or soon will be, for your own final journey. May what we learned and experienced motivate you to be ready to survive and successfully complete the final journey that will change your life.

**Therefore be on the alert, for you do not know
which day your Lord is coming.
(Matthew 24:42)**

**But as for me and my house, we will serve the Lord.
(Joshua 24:15)**

THE FINAL JOURNEY

Planning and Preparation

THE JOURNEY BEGINS: THE CATALYST

I go to prepare a place for you. If I go and prepare a place
for you, I will come again and receive you to Myself,
that where I am, there you may be also.
—John 14:2–3

If it is disagreeable in your sight to serve the Lord, choose
for yourselves today whom you will serve.
—Joshua 24:15

No one should have been surprised. For eighty years, the country had
been fundamentally changing. Awareness of history, not just of our
country but of every great nation or empire that had ever existed, seemed
no longer to matter to those who were now leading humanity toward
the inevitable end of our world as we had known it. Political correctness,
fear, selfishness, greed, and covert and overt hatred appeared more and
more to be the motivators of words and actions. Courage, integrity,
ethics, honesty, and love of one's fellow human beings moved ever
further into the background. Fear was the ultimate motivator—fear
not of losing life but of losing possessions, status, power, and influence.

For the first time in my life it felt as if our country had started an
unstoppable downward spiral into a dark future. For decades, we had
looked to our political leaders to guide us into a secure future. Those
leaders had failed us and continued to fail us daily. It had become
increasingly clear that to survive, we would have to return to a time
when the individual and the family took responsibility for their long-
term well-being, their survival.

In the summer of 2016 the signs of impending turmoil were increasing.
The time had come to take charge of one's own future. Common sense
said to prepare and prepare now. The path down the slippery slope

would accelerate even faster after the upcoming national presidential election in November.

So, prepare we did, in earnest. The diary that follows is a record of the journey that was thrust upon us. Our mantra was now, not to prepare for the worst is to find oneself surrounded by the worst without being prepared.

THE JOURNEY BEGINS: PREPARATION AND PLANNING

Once we had made the decision to be prepared, our work was just starting. Beginning with only occasional experiences in backpacking and hiking, which required only short-term thinking, we now had to look at what long-term preparation meant. The time frame in which we would have to survive was unknown. It could last a few short weeks or extend into years. So we asked ourselves, what knowledge did we have to have? What skills did we need to gain? What criteria would we use to make our preparation decisions, purchases, and practice? How would we know when to put our plan into action? The list of questions was unending.

We quickly found ourselves out of step with the mainstream of society. Few if any of our friends and neighbors seemed even remotely interested in what we were contemplating. We were starting on a journey alone but knew it was a journey that we needed to take.

Knowledge

We purchased and read as many survival books as we could afford. We read and reread them while making lists from their suggestions as to what equipment, materials, and supplies were required to survive, not only for the short term but potentially for years of living in a different way.

Searching the Internet for articles related to specific topics, such as emergency and long-term health care, food, emergency first aid, and caring for pets, we built a significant amount of head knowledge of the many issues we could face.

Preparation Planning

As our head knowledge increased, it became clear from the experts we were tuned into that we needed a **preparation plan**. What did we need to accomplish in the first thirty, sixty, ninety, and 180 days of preparation? We knew that we might have to make our move in any of those time frames. So what would we prioritize to accomplish in an unknown time frame? Even if the trigger events that would put our plan into action were delayed, we knew that clearly defined action steps with constant vigilance for any trigger events would move us to action immediately. Quickly we realized that there were a few things that needed to be planned and ready to use upon a moment's notice.

First, we knew that our ultimate objective was to survive and journey to a point in the Allegheny Mountains in west-central Pennsylvania—a minimum 1,500 miles from our location. We knew that the shortest route would likely not be the final route we would travel. Alternative routes were planned with the understanding that we would likely travel more miles and take a longer time to reach our destination than expected. Although we hoped that much of the journey could be accomplished by vehicle, we knew that when things hit the fan, the supplies and materials necessary to support that travel would not be available.

How many alternative routes would be enough to prepare? Easy question to ask, but difficult to answer. We settled on **five possible routes**. Why five? No good answer, but that just seemed to be a good number. We identified a set of **route criteria** which would determine the ultimate feasibility of following any one of our planned routes. Common sense told us that even after a decision based on the following criteria, we would have to **adapt and adjust** that decision using what we came to know as **survival common sense** to enable us to see another day.

And what were our **route criteria? What route would expose us to the least potential for human interaction or confrontation?** We knew that when local and national structures fractured, the greatest threat to our safety would be from other human beings. As people became desperate for what they considered necessities of life, especially the food and water to survive, lawlessness would increase. Physical and armed danger would increase. Groups would take over access to main highways, bridges, town centers, and supply depots and demand, at a minimum, expensive bribes to ensure one's safety. The country in desperation would involve the military to try to keep social control. Local militia, legal or otherwise, would take control of swaths of geography. It would become increasingly difficult to move anywhere without confronting some kind of desperation control by others.

So our route plans were designed to keep us as safe as possible from these threats as well as to give us the simplest path possible. The plans involved staying on secondary or country roads; identifying major obstacles such as rivers, and locating bridges that were off main travel routes; studying and becoming familiar with geographic and topographic realities, knowing full well that we will likely have to set out on foot once fuel is no longer available; avoiding population centers at all costs, circling even the smallest communities, except where it is necessary for supply or health issues to risk contact with others; and finally, awareness of weather patterns for each time frame in which we will be traveling. Such awareness was critical to our preparations related to supplies, clothing, and emergency gear to enable us to cope with any weather contingencies that could occur. A last point of basic route preparation was to secure detailed road maps for each of the states we might find ourselves traveling through, realizing that most would not include the minor roads we would need to use.

Second was our own physical preparation. My wife's primary health issues were hypothyroidism, fibromyalgia, and lack of overall physical conditioning. Mine was a fourteen-year history of heart issues, including two heart attacks and quadruple bypass surgery, as well as overall physical conditioning. Both of us were on maintenance drugs that could only be secured through a physician's prescription. We had to do some serious study of alternative medications for our issues, knowing that any backup supply of medications was difficult to secure at best because of health care and insurance practices. Yes, over time we might secure a few backups, but we could not count on that, given the potential time frames we were looking at as well as the inevitable breakdown of traditional medical services.

Our physical strength became a consuming passion even as we were still involved in the planning stages of our efforts. We would not survive the physical and emotional stresses that we would likely face without being in the best physical shape, with the strength to handle the physical strain of potentially traveling by foot for days or months over a geographic landscape that we could not control. Our goal became physical health in spite of the issues noted, which would afford us a better quality of life even if the survival scenario was delayed or hastened.

Third, what criteria would we use to make the decision to begin our journey, and what decision criteria would we use during the challenging days that would be involved in our travels? We quickly adopted what we started to call the **Four *Es***.

1. **Evaluate:** Daily and weekly we would evaluate multiple issues. Prior to deciding that we needed to head for the hills, we would keep a close eye on the political, social, international, and local environment to determine whether things were reaching a point where our only possible guarantee of safety was to start our journey. Once the journey started, we would constantly be evaluating our environment related to safe travel routes, observations of what other people were doing, the safety of travel given current and expected weather conditions, the availability of safe locations to hunker down if necessary or spend a night, physical threats posed by humans or animals, and many more issues that we might not even foresee. This meant keeping our eyes and ears open to everything that was happening around us, or that might happen, and evaluating our next steps based on what we earlier called **survival common sense.**

2. **Escape:** When circumstances warranted, we would use a simple set of decision criteria to move away from danger as quickly as possible. From the initial decision to start our journey to the

day-to-day decisions related to physical safety, we would act without hesitation, never second-guessing ourselves but moving constantly forward, even if that meant going backward for a short time.

3. **Evade:** When we sensed any kind of danger, we would avoid it at all costs unless it was humanly impossible to do that. And only when it was impossible to avoid would we confront any dangers presented by other humans, animals, or the environment. With our long-term goal of reaching our destination always in the back of our minds, we would always strive to be invisible within our surroundings.

4. **Endure:** A sense of realism would be critical to our desired success. We had to believe that we would successfully reach our final destination, a **constant hope**, as others have written (Hawke, MacWelch, Towell). No amount of hardship, struggle, danger, or hunger would short-circuit our belief that we had the ability to end our journey successfully. Probably more than anything else, the belief in ourselves, our knowledge, our skills, our abilities, and our common sense were critical to what we knew we had to do. That, combined with an unending faith and trust in the Lord's guidance and protection, gave us **hope**. The moment we gave in to doubting the Lord and doubting ourselves or our ability to deal with any event or circumstance— even feeling some situations were impossible to overcome—we would lose. Not only would we lose the achievement of our final goal, but more than likely we would lose our lives as well.

Each of the **Four Es** and our ability to stay true to them hinged on our strong faith that we would be led by an eternal plan and power that we staked both our earthly and eternal futures upon.

The Lord is my shepherd, I shall not want.
He makes me lie down in green pastures;
He leads me beside quiet waters.
He restores my soul;
He guides me in paths of righteousness for His name's sake.

Even though I walk through the valley of the shadow of death,
I fear no evil, for You are with me;
Your rod and Your staff, they comfort me.

You prepare a table before me in the presence of my enemies;
You have anointed my head with oil;
My cup overflows.
Surely goodness and mercy will follow me all the days of my life,
And I will dwell in the house of the Lord forever.
(Psalm 23:1–6)

Fourth, once our survival journey started, the moment we walked out the door of our home, what would our priorities be? As many have written, there would likely be four or five priorities at the very start of our journey. Whether one calls the priorities: shelter/protection, location, water, food (Colin Towell); shelter, water, food, fire (Mykel Hawke); or shelter/protection, water, fire, food (Tim MacWelch); or something else, a sequence exists as to what one's priorities should be in any survival situation or journey. Rather than debate the order of these priorities, we adopted a sequence that seemed to make the most sense based on what these above, and many others, named as the critical priorities that should always be on one's mind.

Shelter: The dangers inherent in living in the open are beyond number. Even if one is lucky enough to have a vehicle, it can be found wanting in certain situations. Protection from the elements would be critical in our journey. Possessing the ability to build or secure protection from weather, heat, cold, and animals would provide us with some level of comfort to conserve our strength and health, enabling us to cope physically and emotionally with the many other challenges we would face daily.

Protection: In any situation, we had to have the ability to protect ourselves from any and all predators. At the top of the list was having the capability to protect ourselves from other human beings who meant to do us harm or run off with our survival gear and supplies. As harsh as

LARRY D. HORTON, PhD

it might have sounded before, we had to have the equipment to fend off other humans should they want to do us harm. It started with gaining training in using weapons of many types, not just firearms. Our safety rested on our ability to effectively use man-made warning systems, knives, firearms, and our bare hands if necessary. Remembering that our underlying priority was to **avoid** threats at all turns, the **Four E**s, we were realistic enough to accept the fact that we might have to fight rather than flee if a situation became uncontrollable or unavoidable.

Water: A universally accepted fact of life is that without water, human beings cannot sustain themselves even close to their normal capabilities after three days. Even in the best possible scenario, in which we had prolonged access to a motor vehicle with sufficient fuel, no such vehicle would be able to transport the amount of water necessary to survive for the period we were anticipating. Only so much space would be available in the vehicle due to the need to carry other survival materials. When we considered that we might spend most or all of our journey on foot, the foolishness of possibly carrying a significant amount of water became very clear. We adopted a strategy that beginning on day one of our journey, we would have to have the skills and simple tools or materials to secure a daily water supply for both ourselves and our two dogs. We agreed that meeting our minimum daily requirements would be a top priority and that we would ration our water resources on a daily basis if necessary.

Fire: The ability to have a warm meal, the need for warmth during cold nights and days, protection from animal predators, disinfecting our clothing and potential physical wounds, and just the emotional sense that all was not as bad as it could be when we had a fire—many factors confirmed for us that we better had have the knowledge and skills to be able to build a fire in any conditions with whatever materials were at hand. We had to be able to use multiple methods to get a fire started. So, we secured as many backup fire starting systems as possible, such as waxed waterproof matches, lighters, flint and steel, a fire-starting file with flint, magnifying glasses, and others. They were all within reach 24/7. We knew clearly that there would be times on our journey when a fire might present us with danger. A fire might draw predators toward us. It could become a beacon on a hill telling other humans that we were there. We accepted the fact that there would be times we would have to go completely dark and be cold rather than have the warmth of even the smallest fire. But with that acceptance and a great deal of care and caution on our part in most locations, we would have the ability to see a small spark bring warmth and light into our daily struggles.

Food – We knew that our diet would have to change dramatically as we traveled. Securing basic food necessities that had a multiple-year shelf life quickly became a priority. Once those stores were secured, we had to make decisions as to how much we would need to carry, first in our vehicle as long as we were able to use it, and then on our persons should we find ourselves on foot. Those preparations were the easy part of our food priority. The only cost was just a monetary cost. We knew that in backpacks, at best we might be able to carry a maximum of six weeks of the very basic food items that we would need. Add the food needs of our dogs to the equation, and it quickly became evident that we would need to have the knowledge and skills to find food along our path. We quickly realized that the **hunter/gatherer/fisher** knowledge and skills of our ancestors would have to become our own knowledge and skills. We would be able to carry only a limited amount of ammunition for firearms. We would have to become adept at **scrounging**. We would need to know and be able to safely identify plants that were edible in each area that we would travel through. We would have to overcome the hesitation not to eat certain creatures that our society rejected as food. It would require that we prioritize the types of food we ingested: lots of carbs, proteins, meats, fish, and wild edible plants. We would not have access to the supplements mythically necessary for healthy living. We would have to learn how to successfully trap and hunt meat. We knew that food along with water would become consuming priorities. But we also knew that over time our tastes and requirements would adapt to our situation. Our hope and prayer became that we would have the ability and capability to apply the many skills that we worked so hard to attain. Our lives depended on it.

Communication: Reality clearly told us that the likelihood of our being able to communicate with loved ones during such a journey were less than slim. Yet even with that awareness we prepared to at least have the capability to pass messages between ourselves and those we were trying hard to reach. We secured capabilities to power up our communication devices, our cell phones, that had multiple redundant power supply sources. When everything hit the fan, we knew that major communication methods and processes required an infrastructure that needed to be maintained and powered on a daily basis. We knew that would end at some point due to the inherent chaos that would overwhelm every system except those controlled from some central point. We also knew that our survival depended on knowing weather conditions, so we secured NOAA capabilities. We knew that while radio broadcasts were still possible we could stay up-to-date on social unrest, political events, and areas of potential danger to avoid. Just knowing that we had the capabilities to potentially communicate and stay aware of events beyond our immediate location would provide a sense of hope and motivation.

> **Though youths grow weary and tired,**
> **And vigorous young men stumble badly,**
> **Yet those who wait for the Lord will gain new strength;**
>
> **They will mount up with wings like eagles,**
> **They will run and not get tired,**
> **They will walk and not become weary.**
> **(Isaiah 40:30–31)**

Fifth, what would be required to survive overnight, for a month, or for a year on our survival journey regardless of our location when the journey started? Borrowing initially from our military services, survival authors have identified a three-level structure of preparedness to give people the best chance of regaining and maintaining their survival potential no matter what type of situation or location they might find themselves in. The last major element of our **preparation planning** was to secure all that we needed to meet the requirements of each level that was the norm within the survival discipline and that fit our capabilities.

Individual Overnight Survival Kit (IOS): We asked our first personal survival question, "What would I need to survive for a day and night in whatever situation I found myself?" The answers to that question were found in the five previous preparedness categories. What materials would I need to have on my person, or at my side, 24/7 to enable me to make it to the next day related to shelter, protection, water, fire, food, and communication? We first had to determine what was the best method to carry basic minimal materials needed for at least twenty-four hours—the fundamental simple kit. We landed on **EDCs**, every day carry packs. There are many other equivalents to this pack, but for us it made the most sense. So we set about securing the necessary tools and supplies that we would carry in this small pack and never let it leave our sight. Even when traveling internationally, we never let them far from our side despite travel restrictions. This small **EDC** pack remained the foundation for our survival journey as a redundant backup to the more complex kits that follow. We got many strange looks as we walked around with our **EDC** packs on, but we did not worry about those looks. We knew that we were far better prepared at this basic level than 99 percent of the people who were staring at us. We also made sure that we had the most basic tools, a pocket knife, a Bic lighter, and small sections of paracord with us at all times in our pants pocket or purse. We knew we could always lose our **IOS** no matter how hard we tried to protect it.

Bug-Out Bag (BOB): This second level, borrowing the name from the military, included multiple bags and packs, all of which could be carried on our bodies. Multiple elements were included: a simple day pack for the bulkier items, a military surplus medical kit bag for each of us for obvious purposes, a surplus military waist ammo belt with multiple compartments, and utility belts for each of us with multiple Molle bags. Because there were multiple components to our **BOB**, we could share their use and carrying. The expanded materials were primarily concerned with five major areas. **The first**, a small supply of survival food. Three days of emergency food was identified and secured to enable us to deal with the initial short-term period immediately after a decision was made to begin our journey. These food resources could also be used during a short-term weather issue such as a hurricane at our home location. **The second,** resources to enable us to build emergency shelter. For example, a supply of paracord, space blankets, a hand ax, a survival knife. **The third,** a change of clothing for each of us, taking into consideration conditions we might find ourselves in. These would be changed as needed according to the time of year. **The fourth,** expanded medical supplies to cover a broad range of potential needs. And **the fifth,** expanded fire starting and water purification materials of various types, including supplies of materials for fire-starting tinder, multiple prepared small tinder bundles, fire tins, small candles, water purification tablets, and water straws. Our **BOBs** were always kept in locations from which they could be grabbed on a second's notice and put into our vehicle or on our persons if we had to move unexpectedly and quickly. Most of the time the redundant prepared resources were kept in both our vehicles, as we had no idea which vehicle we might be in. We prepared U.S. components as well as international versions. We prepared these full resources, or smaller versions of them, to always be available no matter where we might find ourselves. Combining these **BOB** resources with our individual **IOS** kits would provide us with significant capabilities during our initial journey that might last a day or as long as two weeks. Many of the resources were present in multiple forms. Redundancy would save our lives.

Long-Term Kit (LTK): Our individual **LTKs** were where the rubber would meet the road, so to speak. The materials, resources, and capabilities that were included would enable us to sustain ourselves with some sense of security for a minimum of ninety days. We were realistic enough to understand that in a best-case scenario we would hope to be able to travel for as long as possible, for the greatest distance possible, by vehicle. We also knew that at some point, on day one, on day ten, on day thirty, or even day ninety we would likely have to abandon our vehicle and continue on foot. We therefore prepared for the day we would be walking. We prepared our largest and most complete kits at two levels, which, when combined with our **IOSs and BOBs,** provided us with the most complete survival set of resources possible.

First, the level at which we would have to humanly carry. This meant preparing individual backpacks of sufficient size to carry materials that would address each of our six survival priorities. Reality said that such a resource would have to be appropriate to our ability to actually carry it. That capability was primarily weight related. A smaller pack would become my wife's primary responsibility. In the end, we decided that I would carry a larger backpack, an army surplus ammo belt, our primary long gun, and our longer cutting tools. My wife would have responsibility for the daypack **BOB** and a medical kit bag, a utility belt and a much lighter air rifle long gun. Each of us would have responsibility for our individual **IOSs** as well. In the end, it was our hope that we would be as self-sufficient as possible should we find ourselves on foot. The entire process would be even more complex due to the necessity of caring for our two dogs. For this additional complexity, we would have to have some materials and capabilities that would not be included if we did not have four legged travelers with us.

Second, the in-best-case scenario, the level at which we would be able to use a vehicle for our initial journey segment. The amount and weight of material we prepared and secured in our primary vehicle was of significantly greater weight and complexity. For example, a full 120 days of survival food, tarps to provide primary shelter, hand tools related to fire and fire starting, a complete tool kit for all imaginable scenarios, additional fuel for our vehicle, and other items would be prepared. The type of vehicle we would use was of obvious importance. A four-wheel drive truck was the vehicle of choice. Its only potential significant shortcoming would be fuel efficiency. All of this, when combined with our **IOSs, BOBs,** and **LTKs,** would provide the limit of what could be prepared and transported regardless of the actual situation we would face. As mentioned before, our **survival common sense** would underlie any and all decisions made as to what materials and resources to secure and prepare across these multiple kits. The bottom line was simple. Whatever was included had to fit together like hand-in-glove.

PLANNING AND PREPARATION: A FEW CLOSING THOUGHTS

To repeat, much detail has been left out regarding specific materials, tools, and resources up to this point. You have total responsibility for determining what you should include in your own personal preparations. There are countless wonderful resources and books out there to help you think through the detailed decisions that you will have to make if you take your own survival preparations seriously. Your future and the future of those that you love rest in your hands. The survival plan you create, the materials you secure, the skills you learn and practice, the efforts you make to think through as many possible realities as possible, constantly alert for the **triggers** that set your plan into motion, your survival priorities, and the preparation of your physical and emotional capabilities are your responsibilities and yours alone. You must depend on what you can do and how you prepare. Don't forget, others will be totally wrapped up in their own survival story. Don't delay to start to prepare. And don't delay when events or the actions of others make it clear that your survival journey must begin. **Take action now, be ready, and good luck. We will be out there with you, and if circumstances are right, we may find ourselves with you, walking into a new future.** It is our hope and our prayer that you will not have to walk this future path alone but that you will have put your faith and trust in the Lord Jesus Christ to walk beside you, guiding you, preparing your path forward, and giving you His wisdom and understanding to enable you to embark on the journey that may lie before you.

In God I have put my trust,
I shall not be afraid.
What can man do to me?
(Psalm 56:11)

THE FINAL JOURNEY

On the Road

THE CONTEXT

The following diary entries are fictional. They have been created to illustrate examples of the events and issues that may occur should our society, as we now know it, make it necessary to take drastic actions to survive in a world that will be much different.

Given the time frame that is identified, a minimum of 120 days or four months, it is obvious that such an effort would require a good deal of imagination to complete. As well, as is the nature of a diary, details will be left out of each diary entry because of the overwhelming amount of activity that will potentially be required on a day-to-day basis just to exist. However, an attempt has been made to identify as many examples of the types of things that would potentially be faced as possible.

Historical, political, social, economic, governmental, and international issues will be identified and used as catalysts for the actions described in each diary entry where relevant. It should be understood that the issues identified are conjecture to some degree. But given current realities in our world, they are a best guess as to what the total environment might be like should even some of the events identified became the reality we must deal with in our future everyday lives. The study of history, nations, and empires over the past five thousand years gives a significant foundation from within the history of mankind and civilization for the issues identified. Extrapolating history into our current world is not that difficult. Human nature has not changed over the centuries. There is a better-than-even chance that the speculations identified here will be experienced. How we plan for and respond to those events will have a lot to do with whether we actually survive their impact on each of us as individuals and as Christians.

But as for me, I will watch expectantly for the Lord;
I will wait for the God of my salvation.
My God will hear me.
(Micah 7:7)

On the Road Diary: Entry #1

Date: November thru January 20th

November: Likely the most pivotal election in recent memory is now history. A new president has been elected. The country is still very much divided. The weeks and months ahead will likely be the most confrontational since the civil war. A great uncertainty has settled over the land. Our preparations now begin in earnest for a different world.

1. Our full long-term survival kits (LTKs) are just inside our back door when home and in either of our two vehicles depending which one we are using at any given time.
2. Our BOBs are in our vehicles at all times.
3. Our Individual Overnight Survival kits (IOSs) are on our hip continually and within easy reach when we are at home.
4. Our truck's covered bed has complete survival materials that are not carry-friendly in place 24/7.
5. A three-month freeze-dried food supply is at our back door or loaded into our vehicle anytime we are out and about and kept constantly ready for use.
6. Additional freeze-dried and shorter shelf life food is within easy reach in multiple locations and ready for use should we decide to shelter in place for a time, including a full supply of food for our two dogs.
7. Optional bug-out routes have been identified and developed.
8. Primary communication of our potential plans has gone to all family members, and the only related step necessary would be to communicate the day and time we actually put our bug-out plan into action.
9. Funding is secured to pay forward all regular bills, e.g., mortgage for six months (180 days), in the form of account credit or payment of actual amounts due for that time period.

January 20: New president was sworn in today. Based on inauguration speech of primary objectives for first 100 days in office, we have made our decision.

LARRY D. HORTON, PhD

On **January 21st,** we are bugging out. **It Begins!**

1. Our initial objective will be to drive as far as possible on the target 1,500-mile journey using our primary vehicle for transportation. Our hope is to drive a minimum of 1,000 miles of our target distance and go as far east of the Mississippi River as possible.

2. We are fully prepared to begin our journey on foot from day number one, January 21, but hope that will not be necessary. We realize that at any point in the journey we may have to start walking.

3. Should we be walking earlier than the Mississippi River, we will track north to a point where crossing the river will hopefully be as easy as possible.

Our God forever and ever; He will guide us until death.
(Psalm 48:14)

On the Road Diary: Day #1

Date: January 21   Mileage: Approx. 375 mi.

3:00 AM: We climbed into our truck to begin the journey, the truck carrying all materials as identified, including four-emergency five-gallon cans of vehicle fuel.

3:00 AM–9:00 AM: Traveled east on interstate I-10. Traffic seemed pretty much normal. Able to refuel as normal. Lunch secured at a quick-and-dirty hamburger joint at interstate exit. Dogs traveled quietly as usual. We approached the Mississippi River crossing without incident other than some anxiety about crossing this large hurdle as we planned.

9:30 AM: Crossed Mississippi River. A big sigh of relief. As quickly as possible got off the interstate highway and headed cross country on primary and secondary state roads, navigating to the northeast as our primary target direction. In reality we drove in more of a zigzag pattern but always adjusting to northeast as soon as possible, always on the primary route identified months ago.

11:00 AM: Listened to radio news broadcast. Initial steps of new president have begun. Multiple pieces of proposed legislation have been sent to Congress for immediate action. By the way, forgot to mention new president's party gained control of Senate in recent election. Other party basically not an issue within the new government. Our new president also issued a set of executive orders effective in one week, on January 28, related to the following:

1. Immediate limits put on financial institution withdrawals by private citizens
2. Immediate rationing program related to items considered critical for national defense, fuel primarily
3. Immediate grandfathering of all non-legal immigrants into resident status

LARRY D. HORTON, PhD

4. Temporarily stopping all federal approval, fingerprint checks, required by individuals wishing to purchase firearms or obtain a concealed carry license of any type
5. Temporarily cease all military action related to Syria and ISIS conflicts
6. Pull all naval forces out of Persian Gulf, the Mediterranean Sea, Southeast Asian waters, and the Indian Ocean
7. Increase number of sanctuary cities so that one would exist in all fifty states

News also reported a series of Internet threats of possible ISIS and other extremist attacks within next forty-eight hours in major US cities.

3:00 PM: Secured campsite about two hours north of river crossing at a state park, Homochitto National Forest, near Knoxville MS. Decided to hunker down for two nights to rest and to gain some awareness of reaction to activities in Washington DC. At small store purchased hamburger and buns. Cooked for warm supper. Dogs enjoying exploring our little camping site.

8:30 PM: Bedded down for the night under tarp tent. Things seemed quiet, very tired.

On the Road Diary: Day #2–3 Hunker Down

Date: January 22 and 23   Mileage: 0 mi.

Day #2, January 22: Up at dawn. Oatmeal and coffee for breakfast cooked over open wood fire. Took dogs for a walk. Ventured into Knoxville MS to fill up truck gas tank. Fairly long lines. People seem to be starting the inevitable hoarding prior to the beginning of rationing in a few days. Lots of people filling up gas cans. Spent the rest of the AM checking and planning our travel route further north day after tomorrow and for next two days after that. So far, we have been lucky that we have been able to use the truck; have a gut feeling that won't last much longer. Soup for lunch and another walk for the dogs. Napped and did check of the truck. Trying to build up our energy which we will likely need sooner rather than later. Sandwiches for supper. A final short walk for the dogs. To bed early. Listened to all the sounds of nature and did some stargazing. Campground is full. A lot of people seem to be on their own journeys. Several interesting conversations prior to hitting the sack. People are very worried about the short- and long-term future. No one really opening up too much. Everyone is very guarded.

Day #3, January 23: Rain showers overnight. Cooled things a bit. Tarp shelter worked well. Glad we had covered firewood. Fire not too difficult to start. Everything a bit damp under gray sky. Looks like more rain all day long. Dogs not happy with rain. After warm breakfast of oatmeal and coffee, took the dogs for walk shortened by hard rain. Dogs then stretched out under tarp. Rain stopped around 10 AM. Turned radio on to gauge external events. Runs on gas stations, banks, and grocery stores started within hours of new president's actions. Over next few days, until the twenty-eighth, likely to get a lot worse, which will put our refueling at risk. Likely will see price gouging even though price controls will supposedly be in place. Small towns will be safer, but their supplies will be less available than in larger population areas. Gas may become harder to find, and when it is, will pay dearly for it.

After light lunch of crackers, cheese, and juice, walked the dogs. Rain held off during afternoon. Spent afternoon preparing equipment, sharpening knives, checking weapons, food inventory, and water supply, repacking packs and truck, medical supply check, and medications inventory. Make sure we had certainty related to what we would take and what would stay behind in truck when we made the inevitable decision to start walking. Thank goodness have hexamine stove and fuel. Started raining again while preparing supper of soup, dried fruit, and tea. Finished packing everything up not needed for sleeping. Dogs bedded down; no walk tonight. Listened to NOAA weather (light rain tomorrow) and national news. Government contemplating whether to post law enforcement at all gas stations, banks, and stores to control potential violence. Alarm set for 4 AM. An early start tomorrow will hopefully put us ahead of others. Prayers for continued safe journey.

**Be anxious for nothing, but in everything
by prayer and supplication
with thanksgiving let your requests be made known to God.
(Philippians 4:6)**

On the Road Diary: Day #4

Date: January 24   Mileage: Approx. 220 mi.

No one slept too well during night, anticipating the new day and the unknowns. Up and at 'em at 3:45 AM. Cold breakfast. Packed damp bedding and tarp into truck bed. Supposed to rain lightly most of morning. Hope to have drier weather this afternoon and evening to get rid of dampness in stuff. Plan for the day is shorter drive into northern Mississippi before setting up camp. Dogs a little cranky this morning. Things are just different for them, and they like their routines. Don't we all. Everyone in truck so we are off. Hopefully diary notes later today will be of a safe, peaceful day. Time will tell. Lord, guide us safely and watch over us.

Stayed on secondary roads for the most part today. Did stop in one small town to fuel up truck. Prices were gouged a bit. Paid in cash, no change. Chalked that up to the new reality. Found some cold sandwiches and drinks at station as well. Again, cash only. Doing well with our food supply in truck. Also, bought couple gallons of water which will help that supply.

Pulled into Tombigbee National Forest and found a small campground there. Able to find an unofficial spot to set up tarp tent and build fire ring. Again, cash only. Scrounged in forest for wood as dry as I could find. Had stopped raining around noon seventy-five miles to the south, so wood was in pretty good condition. Glad had packed supply of tinder in truck as part of our preparations. Dogs were glad to get out of the truck. Put them on their long leads tied to tree so they could move around a bit. Quite a bit of digging and barking. Must be some small game around. People in campground keeping to themselves. Think that will be our lot in life from now on, as people are looking out for themselves and keeping very secretive.

Tarp tent up as soon as pulled into campsite. Hung up bedding and clothing to dry as much as possible. Built fire ring, started small wood fire, and hung things up as close to it as possible to help in drying process. Heated up one of the gallons of water purchased earlier and washed ourselves. We were beginning to smell. Not unexpected. Dogs drank a lot of water. Thank goodness campground has wells. Refilled gallon jugs. Broke out freeze-dried pasta meal, fruit, and coffee. Tasted great. Topography is starting to change significantly. Shortly after we crossed Mississippi River, moved into rolling hills. Today into more elevation changes as we get closer to Mississippi–Tennessee border. Grateful still able to use truck. Once it is gone, will not travel more than three to five miles per day initially. We are going to take it slow. Our physical conditioning will have to catch up to us. Some tough decisions to come soon, as we have to decide what to carry and what to leave in abandoned truck. The real survival process will start soon. News is more of the same. Society is struggling. More incidents of violence. Up early tomorrow. Prayers said. Good night!

**And the peace of God, which surpasses all comprehension,
will guard your hearts and your minds in Christ Jesus.
(Philippians 4:7)**

On the Road Diary: Day #5

Date: January 25   Mileage: Approx. 215 mi.

Up early. Packed up sleeping stuff. Cold breakfast. Dogs not too happy with having to get back in truck again. No one slept very well. Haven't mentioned weather temps to this point, but need to. When left home, temps were pretty mild for January, low sixties during day, high forties at night. As we have traveled east and north, temps moving lower. No temp gauge, but likely in low thirties last night. High forties during day at best. Listened to NOAA weather broadcast this morning, and forecast is for temps averaging forty-two degrees and thirty-two degrees for time being. Also, heard that within forty-eight hours a front will be moving in from the north, bringing freezing rain, sleet, and possibility of light snow in higher elevations. As we drove northeast, made decision to hunker down in forty-eight hours and see what the weather held for us. Once we decide it's safe to move again, will take a more easterly direction before heading north again. Weather could be nasty for the next sixty days given the time of year we are traveling. Likely means we will be hunkering down at times to wait out bad weather.

Able to partially fill up truck's gas tank this morning. May be last time for that, as will have no gas rationing stamps after hunkering down. We could not forget gas rationing startup was on the twenty-eighth. Able to cross over the Tennessee River without much trouble. Arrived in Flat Woods TN area. Found no real campgrounds to stop at. Drove around area and found wooded area on back country road. Pulled off onto what appears to be a logging or mining road and went about a mile into the forest, where we were able to find a small sheltered valley with a stream and lots of tree cover.

Set up our tarp tent with windbreaks using small logs around perimeter. Built fire reflection wall near front of tarp. Gathered what we hope will be enough dry wood to last the night. Also, gathered as much material for tinder as possible for next couple days and beyond. Fire consisted of two six-foot-long logs with fire in middle. Likely won't get much sleep, as I will try to keep the fire burning all night to keep us a bit warmer.

Boiled water over hexamine stove, and cooked rice, beans, and hot tea for supper. Dried out clothing. Washed some that we would be packing up for walking. Filled up two plastic gallon jugs with water after boiling. Dogs were very hungry. They have no idea what faces us ahead—as if we do. Rechecked equipment, our packs, and made some preliminary decisions about what to carry in final packs.

Called our families to let them know our plans and how we were doing. Everyone is doing their best to get to a safe location. Cold as we went to bed. Fire going well. Dogs very curious about surroundings. Tomorrow will be last day of semi-comfort. Good night.

His delight is in the law of the Lord.
(Psalm 1:2)

Date: January 26   Mileage: Approx. 140 mi.

Cold night. Not much sleep. Everyone very restless again. Heavy frost on everything. Was able to keep fire going all night. Heated up some oatmeal for breakfast along with coffee. Dogs had leftover rice and beans from last night. Packed up truck. Enough gas for about 200 miles, but likely won't use it all. Headed across KY line to Rosewood area if all goes well. Another major hurdle related to rivers. The KY River, we will see if can cross. If not able, will head directly east around the TVA lakes. We are all getting tired, and sky is very gray, with light rain falling. Temps likely in high thirties or low forties most of the day.

Meals today were all warm. Stopped for quick and dirty lunch at a mom and pop store. Supper was hot freeze-dried stroganoff, pudding, and coffee. Have used up our seventy-two-hour bug-out supplies pretty much. Will continue to use other freeze-dried food while hunkered down, and pack what we can once we are on foot. Will have to start living more and more off the land once we are walking. Will be boiling water for next few days. Need to make sure all of our clothing and our bodies are as clean as possible when we strike out from this temporary location. We are hoping we won't have to hunker down again until we make some progress.

Studied maps to gauge best route east. We are going to be heading into the real mountains of eastern KY and WV soon. Will slow us down some, but will likely have more opportunity for temporary living sites because of forests. The next couple weeks will be tough on us physically as we get used to carrying our packs, walking, and coping with dogs. We are watching our health very carefully, using maintenance meds as needed. Big question will be what to do when we run out of those. Have natural medicines and natural food books in pack. I think those are going to become even more important as each day passes.

Able to cross the KY River and start in east-northeast direction. Arrived in general area of Rosewood KY early afternoon with about four hours of gray sunlight left. Off and on light rain all day. Settled down early, as had decided to hunker down for few days. Needed to set up a camp that will protect us from coming weather so we can wait out the weather front. Drove around Rosewood area. Very hilly, small farms, not many people out. Decided to approach farm homes to see if they would be willing, for a price, to allow us to camp on their land. At second farm was able to barter for a place to camp in small section of woods on back of their property for three five-gallon cans of gas that we had on the truck. Truck fuel tank at one-fourth full. Held on to last five-gallon can of gas should we need it for more bartering with the farmer.

NOAA weather predicts three to five inches of snow starting tonight and then couple days of freezing rain. Need a good shelter. Tarp plus natural materials to keep us warm and safe for next few days. Committed to spend five to seven days at this location if necessary. Decided to make a full report on how we set up for the days that lay ahead. Our temporary home away from home. Site located at back of the farm. About three miles from farmhouse in a small valley with lots of pine and hardwood trees. Found a small stream. Realized would have to go quite a way upstream due to potential farm animal pollution of the water.

Tried to get as close to stream source as possible. Found that to be a small spring coming out of the side of a hill. Was pretty frozen but able to break ice and get water. Built lean-to shelter. Enough room for the four of us. Cut large amount of pine branches. Covered lean-to frame with branches, then covered with tarp and another layer of branches. Built ground cover for sleeping with more branches covered with moving pad blankets from the truck. Last layer was our two sleeping bags zipped together so all four of us could crawl in and keep warmer with our combined body heat. Built fire reflection wall at front of lean-to, and built fire. Gathered as much dry wood as possible, even putting some in the lean-to. Used second smaller tarp to shelter additional wood gathered. If weather was to be wet, needed to stock up as much as possible. Took about four hours to complete all this. Just in time. Light flurries started as we finished gathering wood. By time we set about cooking supper, flakes were larger and coming down pretty seriously. Glad we had been collecting tinder and putting in truck for last few days. Used cotton ball Vaseline combination to get fire started pretty quickly. Dogs stayed close to the fire or in cover of shelter. Not too happy.

Stored food in truck. Glad we still have the truck for security. It has served us well and given us chance to have all that we needed for the past week. Will be hard to walk away from it in a few days, but we must keep moving forward at a manageable pace. Put out early warning signals, a rope encircling camp with a few cans filled with stones in them tied to the rope. Farmer said there are lots of critters in this neck of the woods. Inspected weapons and secured in shelter for the night with ammo. Last thing we need is some four-legged explorers to get in the middle of our stuff. Really dark other than light from fire. Trees overhead provide lots of cover. Very still and silent. So different than neighborhood back in Texas. Dogs sensed that there were other residents of the woods close by, so that made them restless. Keeping them on short leash so they don't go running off.

Had a thanksgiving celebration in our shelter after supper. Very thankful we have made it this far, approx. 950 miles without much trouble. Still another 500 to 600 miles to go most likely on foot. Three to five miles per day at best. But we are still in good shape considering. Dogs really wanting a lot of attention when we climbed into shelter to go to sleep. They have been so good and are such a comfort to have with us. They are so loyal and loving. We are just hoping they are able to cope with the days ahead. It will be tough on all of us. My job again tonight is to keep the fire going all night. Last look outside the shelter before trying to get a bit of sleep was beautiful. Subdued light from fire with snowflakes falling. Getting colder, but we are safe and pretty warm. Thankful for that. Good night, God bless us.

**Worship the Lord with reverence and rejoice with trembling.
(Psalm 2:11)**

Date: January 27–31   Mileage: 0 mi.

Day #1 of Hunker Down (Rosewood KY area): Woke up to three to four inches of new snow. Nothing leaked in on to us from top of lean-to. Going to work on reinforcing and closing down sides of lean-to today to stop drafts from coming in as much as possible. Glad we built it with opening facing downwind, which enabled me to put up a small cover over the fire to keep it as dry as possible. Smoke went around and over fire reflector so we got most benefit from warmth. Rebuilt fire from embers and coals first thing, and put on pot of water to boil so we could fix breakfast. A hot one, oatmeal and coffee. Dogs stayed in sleeping bags until food was ready. Boiled some rice to add to theirs for bulk, and they had a dog treat which we are rationing.

After breakfast sat down and planned out the day. **Priority #1** was to reinforce lean-to and do as much as possible to increase its ability to shed water. **Priority #2** was to forage for more firewood, which will be a challenge given snowfall, but will get that done. **Priority #3** was to get some rest, maybe even a nap if possible, to gain some strength. **Priority #4** is full meals to increase fat and protein intake prior to setting off on foot, including some freeze-dried beef and beans.

Lunch was hot soup and hot tea. Dogs got a little bit. Need to build up their strength as well. They, on long leashes, are having fun in snow and exploring everything within twenty feet of the lean-to. Shortly after lunch they came into lean-to and snuggled up to nap. While they were napping and after building up decent fire with additional wood from under the lean-to, started foraging out a quarter mile in all directions from our little home to gather as much decent wood as possible. Winds have picked up. Sky is still gray and occasional snowflakes falling. Left camp carrying lengths of paracord to bundle up wood for transport. Left wife with dogs and weapon within reach should she need me. Also, both had whistles and agreed upon signals should I need to hustle back to camp. Left camp about 1 PM. Thirty minutes into foraging discovered first sign of rabbit run. Found two more within next fifteen minutes.

Given planned length of our stay, decided to put out three or four wire snare traps overnight to see if we get lucky and have fresh meat for a meal. Know the dogs would like that.

After bringing five bundles of small, medium, and larger pieces of wood back to camp, gave up that task. Had enough to last through the night if all went well. Same task tomorrow. Spent balance of remaining daylight getting three to four snare traps ready to be put out for tomorrow AM. Boiled up drinking water and filled two plastic jugs. Cooked hot dinner, freeze-dried corn, lasagna, pudding, and coffee. Warmed up considerably. Got ready for bed. Hung wet clothing as close to fire as safely possible. Put boots on poles. Again, near fire to allow them to dry out some. We all hit the sack early. Going to be a cold night. Lots of layers for warmth. Good night!

I lay down and slept; I awoke, for the Lord sustains me.
(Psalm 3:5)

Date: January 27–31   Mileage: 0 mi.

Day #2 of Hunker Down (Rosewood KY area): Another couple inches of new snow overnight. Kept fire going all night. Short periods of sleep. Breakfast of hot oatmeal and tea. Dogs were really hungry this morning. Rice and beans for them. First task was to replenish water from spring. Boiled and put into two gallon jugs. Glad had fabricated gaiters a few months earlier. Put them to good use this morning. Before heading out to gather firewood for the rest of the day and tonight, fashioned two walking sticks for us. Snow will melt a bit today, then refreeze tonight. Will be slippery. NOAA forecast is for a warming trend in couple days, about when we have planned on striking out. Will be wet and probably muddy. Slow going until the next weather front arrives in about a week. Gathered what should be enough wood and then added about one half again. Didn't venture more than fifty yards in any direction from the camp. Worked before lunch and for couple hours after lunch on that. Lunch was rice, beans, and some hot cocoa that we have been saving. Was really good.

Early afternoon spent couple hours putting out four snare traps on rabbit runs I discovered while collecting wood. Also, saw tracks of some larger critters and a few deer tracks. Deer out of the question right now unless could leave it for farmer. Speaking of farmer, he visited us this afternoon to see how we were doing. Had a good visit. He and his wife are hunkered down as well. Have been preparing for a spell. He invited us to the farm day after tomorrow in afternoon for an early home-cooked supper. We are going to take him up on that offer. Ended visit with prayer and handshakes. Glad we lucked upon these folks.

Late afternoon spent tending fire and maintaining weapons and a few repairs on our lean-to. It is interesting how wind has a way of creating new holes in the sides especially. Prior to supper boiled some water and washed socks and ourselves a bit. Socks hung up by fire and will put them in bottom of sleeping bags tonight to finish drying process. Had a grateful supper. Dogs had some freeze-dried chicken with their rice tonight. They are doing really well. Decided to take them for a short walk before started cooking, and they were in heaven. They found couple rabbit scents not near where I had set up the snare traps. Had to pull them back to the camp. Gets dark really early this time of year, so the four of us sat in front of the fire and sang some songs, read another psalm, and hit the sack. Will be tending fire again tonight. Won't be quite as chilly, but as damp as it is and with the cold snow lying around the lean-to, will not seem that warm. Not much sunshine today. Lots of gray clouds, but the wind is down a bit. The Lord has been good to us. No real problems with the cold so far. Dogs seem to be healthy. Ready for new day in the morning. Check snares, initial prep for moving on, and finalizing direction of travel. Trust the Lord to be with us.

Offer the sacrifices of righteousness,
And trust in the Lord.
(Psalm 4:5)

Date: January 27–31   Mileage: 0 mi.

Day #3 of Hunker Down (Rosewood KY area): Seemed a bit warmer last night. No new snow. As day moves, hope some of what is on ground will melt. Sunshine when the sun came up over the hills. Don't have much direct sunshine where we are located, but hope in more open areas snow will diminish. Hot oatmeal and coffee for breakfast. Fed the dogs oatmeal as well with a little bit of dog food mixed in. Rationing dog food, as it has to last a good while. Out to check snare traps first thing. Nothing. More tracks, but no luck. Rebaited them with small pieces of dog food. Will see if that works. After checking wood supply, went out and got as much new stuff as I could. Decided to line reflection wall with space blanket to see if we got more heat into lean-to. It seemed to work pretty well by doing that. Took wife's air rifle out after lunch to see if could get a squirrel. Saw several. Took some long shots but no success. Think I need to practice a bit. Have to watch pellet ammo supply pretty carefully, but probably worth a bit of practice. Lunch was more hot rice and beans. Also, boiled more spring water and refilled containers.

During the afternoon did an inventory of our food supplies in the truck. Doing pretty well so far. Spent considerable time reviewing our supplies, and made some initial decisions as to what to take in our packs when we set out. Going to try to carry six-week supply of freeze-dried stuff and hopefully by foraging and more luck at small game hunting to expand diet. Will be OK for at least that long. Realize there will be some lean days ahead so we are going to manage rations very carefully. Lunch was more rice and beans for all with a little spice thrown in for the humans. Plain for the dogs. Was good to have more than bland rice and beans. Added couple cups of hot coffee to the menu, which warmed us up.

After lunch, everyone took a short nap. Need to begin to store up energy. Also, boiled quite a bit of spring water and washed up any stinky clothing we had. Also, washed up ourselves a bit, especially our feet, pits, and bodies. We have become quite use to the smells of camping and the outdoors. Checked dogs for ticks and other skin or fur issues. Didn't find much, but glad we brought their medications with us just in case. Spent afternoon planning on alternative route for next stage of our journey. Decided would be too difficult to head into mountains of KY and WV given time of year, especially in mountains. Will head in a more northerly direction and try to find a place to cross the Ohio River safely. Then track more north and cut over into PA, hopefully north of Warren OH. Realize we will be passing population concentrations by going that way, but with care will do our best to stay safe. Supper was freeze-dried beef, corn, and strawberries. Dogs liked the beef with a bit of rice. Pretty restful day. No problems with critters or weather. We have been lucky. Lots of prayers tonight. Snuggled up, the four of us in sleeping bags. Will tend fire all night.

In the morning, O Lord, You will hear my voice.
(Psalm 5:3)

Date: January 27–31   Mileage: 0 mi.

Day #4 of Hunker Down (Rosewood KY area): Sun woke us up this morning. Seems warmer than yesterday morning. Dogs are full of energy with sun shining. Put them on their long leashes so they could get rid of some of their energy. Hot breakfast, oatmeal and tea, sure hit the spot. Out to check snare traps first thing. Got lucky, one rabbit. Thanked the Lord for His provision. Cleaned rabbit. Back to camp with rabbit heart in bag. Cooked it up like a marshmallow on a stick and gave the dogs a special treat. They almost swallowed the chunks whole and looked for more. Cut hide off rabbit. Put in plastic bag buried in snowbank. Cut up meat. Going to take the meat to the farmers this afternoon when we go there for invitation to cooked supper.

Got after new supply of firewood for the night ahead. NOAA weather indicates that next 7–10 days will be a bit milder. Less chance of precipitation, so that bodes well with our getting under way on foot. Had to bring several larger pieces of wood back to camp. Hard work dragging them. Have scrounged all the smaller pieces in area out a hundred yards of so. Didn't lessen amount collected just because weather is going to warm up a bit. Snow seemed to be melting some, but in all the cover we are in, that didn't last long. The melting, that is. Light lunch of soup and coffee in anticipation of the larger meal to come this afternoon. We all bunked down for early afternoon nap.

Turned radio on and listened to newscast for a while. Not long, as news is pretty depressing. Initial government actions, the fuel rationing and price controls put in place two days before. After some initial violence, people seem to be dealing with it even with the regulatory checks at every station. Bigger problem revolves around food, as distribution has slowed down due to fuel issues. Some riots in larger cities as people are looking to find food after not planning to have a backup supply in their homes. Police intervened in most major population areas, with injuries and arrests. Several homes were invaded, and six people killed in their homes nationwide. Imagine it will get worse in the days ahead as the government tries to stabilize things. All of that will impact our safety as we continue our journey.

Drove the three miles from back of farm to farmhouse. Dogs were excited that we had them in truck and we were moving. Took their long leashes so they could play outside after we arrived. They barked constantly after arriving. Lots of new smells and sights. They were in pig heaven. Were welcomed by farmer, his wife, and their two dogs. They are in their mid-50s. No kids at home. A few cows, lots of chickens, and typical buildings you would find on small farm in the hills of KY. Wonderful smells when we walked into the farmhouse. Fried chicken, mashed potatoes, and some kind of greens. Farmer's wife told us she had made our dogs a special chicken soup using small pieces of chicken and stewing bones in broth. When they got it, they wanted seconds and thirds, which they got. Presented the rabbit we had trapped. They were grateful. Prayers before we started to eat. Full of thankfulness for their kindness and for all of us being blessed to be safe and warm. Big surprise was dessert. A real homemade angel food cake. Even the dogs got a couple small pieces. Our conversation over supper was very interesting and had a few surprises thrown in.

Quite a conversation over great home-cooked meal. Farmer reviewed events taking place in country as he understood them. Given we had no TV, we had missed a lot trying to conserve battery use on radio. Congress was split. Each major party had their own agenda and tactics. New president's actions, as communicated just after election, were all taken by executive order. Country was in an uproar, but little action taken to counteract events. Internationally, events in Middle East and in Southeast Asia have escalated to the point of small incidents of live fire. Threats are growing across the world from ISIS and other terrorist groups. Europe has experienced three major terrorist events over last ten days, with dozens killed. Several small incidents in the US in large cities: New York, Chicago, and Los Angeles. One isolated incident occurred at a small Christian college in Colorado. People are extremely stressed across the country. Food distribution continues but not at a pace that keeps up with the demand. Countless runs on grocery stores have happened across the country. Several state governors have called up their state national guard to be on hand should things get worse. Runs on fuel continue at an increasing pace. Travel has become more difficult. The US stock market has lost 20 percent of its value over the past two weeks. Bank withdrawals have increased to the point where a bank holiday, as in 1929, has been declared and will last for a minimum of two weeks. Things are rapidly unwinding across all elements of US society. We know we made right decision after hearing all of this and realize that our lives were never going to be the same, given the decisions we have made.

As we were getting ready to return to our lean-to camp, the farmer looked at us and said he wanted to help us reach our destination. He said to stop by late tomorrow afternoon. He is going to return the three five-gallon cans of fuel to us so we can fill the truck tank one more time. We are flabbergasted but so very grateful. He also said we should strike out toward Maysville KY to cross the Ohio River to avoid traffic and potential danger in large cities, like Cincinnati, at all costs. We prayed together again and headed back to our lean-to campsite, so grateful that the Lord continues to watch over us. Busy day tomorrow. Re-planning our travel for one more day of driving. Finalizing our packing. Getting as ready as we can be for an even tougher time ahead. It is now going to be very important that we are as cautious and watchful as possible. Ended our day watching the darkness set in. Temperatures were moderating somewhat. Will keep fire burning all night. Dogs bedded down with full tummies. They seem contented. Read another psalm and went to bed.

The Lord has heard my supplication,
The Lord receives my prayer.
(Psalm 6:9)

Date: January 27–31   Mileage: 0 mi.

Day #5 of Hunker Down (Rosewood KY area): Breakfast of homemade bread and jam that farmer gave us, with coffee. Rice and beans for dogs and some dried beef from farmer. Spent the balance of the morning gathering firewood for our last night in lean-to. Gathered up wire snare traps and repacked them. Lunch of hot soup and tea. Dogs on long leashes. Snow continues to melt a bit. Looks like road will be in pretty good shape when we head out in the AM. Leaving as early as possible. Went back to farmhouse and filled up gas tank with gas returned by farmer. Still have one five-gallon can left for emergencies.

Spent the afternoon repacking the truck, washing dirty clothing and ourselves. Packs are ready for traveling on foot except for one final review prior to actually walking away from truck. We have done very well with food. Big issue ahead in our packing is just how much we will be able to carry. Prioritized packs to clothing, medical gear and supplies, protection items, shelter items, water purification, communication apparatus, fire building, money, bartering supplies, identification papers, weapons with ammo, blades, and a small quantity of treats. Rechecked weapons to ensure they were in good order. Checked medicines to make sure we are not leaving any of those behind. Checked our physical condition such as blisters and cuts. Treated any that needed treating. Boiled enough water to fill two jugs for last driving push. Our packs are going to be pretty heavy starting out. Know weight will lessen gradually as we use up freeze-dried food. Tried to plan for six weeks of carried food, knowing that we might be able to add to that by trapping and quiet hunting. Also, realize that the days will soon be upon us when we will be eating off the land primarily. Tough days lie ahead.

Fixed full meal for evening. Dried pasta, dried chicken, freeze-dried veggie, and pudding. Building up our strength as best we can. Dogs ate more than usual. Maybe they know something is up. Good fire going. Will be up quite a bit making sure it lasts the night. Broke down as much of our little camp as possible. Dried any wet clothing and our boots by the fire. We had a little prayer meeting prior to hitting the sack. Listened to radio and NOAA to get latest news and weather report. Things look pretty good for tomorrow. Hugged each other and the dogs and bedded down. The adventure continues tomorrow. Lord, be with us. Guide our steps along the path You would have us take.

O Lord my God, in You I have taken refuge;
Save me from all those who pursue me, and deliver me.
(Psalm 7:1)

On the Road Diary: Day #12

Date: February 1   Mileage: Approx. 225 mi.

Plan for the day is to travel across KY, skirting all population centers, and cross the Ohio River at Maysville KY, stopping for the night at Adams Lake State Park near West Union OH. Hoping to take no more than six hours for the driving part of the day. May take longer should we run into trouble and may even have to abandon truck unexpectedly. Farmer and his wife up and waved to us as we drove by farmhouse. How grateful we are for folks who continue to live by values which made our country great. Asked Lord to bless them and keep them safe. Turned on truck radio and tried to catch up on news. Also, found a Christian station and spent quite a bit of time singing songs that made us feel watched over. Little did we know what we would face during the day when we set out. Ate wax-covered cheese and crackers as we drove. Dogs love cheese. They bedded down in backseat and slept quite a bit. Quick lunch pickup in a small town northwest of Lexington. Being in KY brought back a lot of memories of the days at Asbury Seminary many years ago. How different the world is today compared to those days in the early '70s. The one constant, an eternal one, is with us. The Lord will guide us in our minds and hearts, no matter what lies ahead. We are in His hands.

Was able to charge phones using truck. Saving batteries in NOAA radios. Contacted all of our family that we could. All OK at this point. West coast kids were setting up for uncertain future. Indiana family was OK. All were gathering with their extended family. Extended PA family at their final destinations hoping their kids could join them but not sure of status. Let them all know where we are. Told them to stay safe. Same message to everyone. Cried some tears when we had to hang up with each of them. We have put them in the Lord's hands and trust they will find the path that will guide them safely into whatever the future holds for them. All we can do.

Trip northeast pretty uneventful until we approached area north of Georgetown KY where we needed to cross over I-75. Had targeted to cross I-75 near Sadieville KY. As we approached, saw several police cars and what seemed to be a checkpoint or roadblock. Backed up a bit but eventually was our turn to answer questions. We had put whole thing into Lord's hands but were still very nervous. Stopped twenty minutes. Afterward, figured that long because we had TX plates on our truck and were a long way from home. Truck was thoroughly checked. Lots of questions about weapons. Had to present CCL and give them count of weapons and ammo. Not much concerned with food and other supplies. Explained to them we bugged out from home in TX and are trying to reach friends' farm in PA to hunker down for long term. Most of officials were pretty nice. Just doing their job. One, however, seemed to be watching us very closely. They explained that there had been an incident in KY capital city of Frankfort, and they were looking for a red truck that was used. After a full inspection, they let us continue on our way with the warning to prepare to be stopped again because of the search for the red truck. We set out slowly, saying a prayer as we did. Thanked the Lord for watching over us. Next was Maysville.

As I sit here and write this fictionalized account, today, Sunday, September 11, 2016, the fifteenth anniversary of the attacks on the US, I must break in with a few comments. On that fateful day, a Tuesday, as I sat in front of a small TV in my employer's offices in Houston TX, the world changed. It was a dangerous time. It is even more dangerous today. Enough time has passed that a new generation has grown up without direct memory of those events. People are fearful. They live with higher levels of stress, yet live each day as normally as possible. But what is normal now? The world that I grew up in will never be repeated. We look to our leaders to give us hope for a better future. But little hope exists. Our country is sliding down a path of mediocrity that will forever change us. We need another George Washington or Abraham Lincoln. But those types of leaders don't seem to be available to us. We are left, so to speak, with second and third best options. The future is constantly on my mind. My remaining task in life is to do all that I can to insure the safety of my wife, my little children (aka dogs), and as much as possible our children and grandchildren. We hope that the Lord will return soon, but the timing of that is unknown to us, as it should be. In the meantime, the situation will get steadily worse, and we can only do all that is humanly possible until the Lord does return. So, we plan and prepare for those tough times to come. It is our hope and prayer that others are doing the same. Few likely are but for those of us who will make the effort this fictionalized journal is an attempt to let you experience what will be necessary to survive in the tough times that lie ahead.

Journal Diary Day #12 cont.: Uneventful travel to Maysville area. Fuel in truck is holding up. Should have enough to reach our target destination of Adams Lake State Park near West Union OH. Arrived a mile or so from the bridge over the Ohio River, and traffic was lined up moving very slowly. As we approached bridge, we saw another checkpoint. When it was our turn, we went through a similar inspection and questions that we had heard near Sadieville KY. Same reason for checkpoint. Authorities looking for a red truck. After ten minutes, were allowed to cross over the bridge to face a second checkpoint entering Ohio. Similar questions but also something new. Our out of state truck tags brought another set of questions. We are thankful that we packed as many forms of identification as possible. Especially our passports. Producing those enabled us to proceed. We breathed a sigh of relief as we pulled away as well as a prayer of thanksgiving. We have crossed another major natural hurdle on our way north. The last major river. Our plans forward are to travel on a route that will allow us to cross other secondary rivers, etc., at points where they were narrower and shallower. The only potential problem we can see at this point is that, as time passes and the weather warms, meaning spring thaw, water levels will likely be up. Decided that we will deal with those potential circumstances when they present themselves. Remaining drive to Adams Lake State Park was uneventful. Knew when we arrived we had a lot of work to do.

Arrived at campground shortly after 3 PM with barely two hours of daylight left. Weather was cooperating but cold. No snow even with gray cloudy skies. Typical Ohio winter weather. Campground was closed. No surprise given it is the first of February. Quickly decided since we are setting out on foot tomorrow and abandoning the truck, we will not expend any extra energy this evening. We will spend the night sleeping in the truck. Primary task was to get a good fire going to cook our supper. Took a bit to collect enough wood for a fire, as campgrounds tend to be picked over so had to go outside park boundaries to find enough. Took three trips to gather enough dry wood for supper. Once got fire started, cooked warm supper of pasta and freeze-dried veggies. Dogs liked it all. Warm cup of coffee also helped us. Spent what light was left doing final inspection of our packs. We are committed to what is in them and will deal with anything else as we come upon it.

We know that we will be crossing a line in the morning by leaving the truck behind. But we are grateful that even our best hopes for its use have been exceeded. We have traveled around 1,200 miles when we might well have only gotten one day's drive away from our home in Texas in it. We still have 400-plus miles to go on foot. A likely 100-day walk at best. We know we have been very lucky. We will take each mile ahead as it comes.

One last thing before we bedded down uncomfortably in the truck. I made sure that we had OH, PA, and WV maps in my pack. Making sure that we had reasonably detailed folding maps of each potential state we might travel through in our packs was something that made great sense, and we are glad we have them. Traveling three to five miles at best by foot each day will make those maps critical. We closed the day with the radio on, listening to Christian music. A reading from the Psalms, which has become our evening habit and a prayer of thanksgiving. What's next? Only the Lord knows, but we trust that He will guide us on the right path to the destination He has prepared for us. Good night!

O Lord, our Lord,
How majestic is Your name in all the earth!
(Psalm 8:9)

THE FINAL JOURNEY

Cross Country on Foot

Date: February 2   Mileage: Walk, 4 mi.

Woke up after uncomfortable night. Our goal for the day was to end up in vicinity of Dunkinsville OH, four or five miles northeast. Heated up some water and made hot oatmeal for all, using hexamine stove. First big task of the day was to unpack what we called our Travel Trekker. Knowing that we would be traveling with dogs and heavy packs, I had spent several months before starting our trip fabricating a small two-wheeled vehicle to carry our loads and the dogs if necessary. Knew from beginning of our planning that such a device would be useful in relatively flat terrain or on some form of roads or trails. Would determine what routes we would take to some degree. Also, knew that there would be times when terrain would dictate up and down over hills. Our plan was to cross these types of hurdles with Trekker when the time came. Trekker is a vehicle a bit larger and taller than a wagon or wheelbarrow running on two twenty-four-inch fat tires, the kind used when riding in sand on beaches. The frame is made out of lightweight metal in the shape of a rectangle with support posts rising thirty inches above the box frame and covered with a thick tarp made of very strong material. It was built to carry up to 200 pounds of freight, though we hope to never have more than 120 pounds in it at any given time. Spare tires, a patching kit, and a small manual pump were included as well in case of the flats that are certain to happen. Sticking out forward and extending to the back of the box frame to add rigidity to the entire device are two five-foot by two-inch poles rounded off at the very front end into a type of handle for each pole. A waist harness and shoulder harness were attached to each pole within which I would step to enable me to pull the entire operation. Padding was added to all the harnesses to help avoid sores. When you look at it, the entire thing looks like a small version of a horse cart from past centuries, but in this case I am the horse.

After a quick hot breakfast, we loaded up our gear into the Trekker, locked up the truck one last time, and said a prayer for traveling guidance and safety. With that we took our first step into the unknown. We agreed that with the short days for the next couple months we will stop at 2 PM each afternoon and set up camp for the night, no matter how far we have walked, one mile or five miles. Shelter, protection, fire, water, and food will be our priorities after 2 PM each day.

Our little wagon train started on our way at 8:30 AM, me and the wagon first with my pack, the dogs, and our extra food supplies on board. My wife followed, carrying her pack and air rifle slung over her shoulders. We started along OH Route 41 but quickly diverted off onto more secondary roads. Our travel direction zigged and zagged from that point on but generally in a northeasterly direction. We stopped every twenty to thirty minutes for me to take another compass reading and to consult our map. We don't want to wander too far off in any one direction and have to do any backtracking if it can be avoided. If and when vehicles passed us on the more main roads we got a lot of stares and a few horn blasts but didn't let that bother us. Once we started to use secondary roads, those events grew few and far between. Lunch was cold cheese, crackers, and water. The weather was cooperating, probably in high thirties or low forties.

Given the load I was pulling, had to be very careful not to overheat even in cold temperatures. To avoid that, we tried to stop for five minutes out of every twenty to cool down. Also, was smart enough to dress fairly lightly and add temporary layer of clothing as needed to heat up. Avoiding hypothermia is very important to us. After the first hour of walking our lack of conditioning started to show up, and I placed my wife's pack in the Trekker. It will take us a couple of weeks, if not more, to get our land legs under us. This is something we knew we might face. Our pace slowed accordingly. We had both practiced months ago with step counting to help us get some sense of how far we were walking. We knew that slopes and grades would add to the number of steps required to travel a mile. We also knew that elevation gains and loss would slow us as well. So we had agreed that our target step rates would be higher for each mile traveled.

When we reached our agreed afternoon stop time of 2 PM, we figured we had walked about four miles. We were tired but felt good with even that small amount of progress. Being in southern Ohio, we knew that our pace would be slower given the hilly topography that we were traveling through. Those hills will be with us until we reach our final destination in PA. So our daily objectives have to be realistic. The Trekker worked just fine. The dogs seemed to like riding covered up and warm. Our last point of reference was a four-way crossroads at OH Route 41. We saw a mileage sign indicating vehicle speed was to reduce to thirty mph in 1,000 feet, the outskirts of Dunkinsville, our first target. Crossing OH Route 41 we saw a wooded area a few hundred yards down the secondary road we had been traveling, and decided we would set up camp in those woods for the night.

Using Trekker as base for our camp for the night, set up tarp tent between some trees. A kind of quick and dirty lean-to. Cut several saplings to form frame and many pine branches for three sidewalls of the lean-to. Pine branches also cut to build sleeping cushion to keep us off the cold ground. Layered space blankets on top of branches with sleeping bags on top of those blankets. This will likely be our nightly arrangement until we have to hunker down again. Gathered enough firewood for cooking evening meal and keeping fire going through the night. Weather continues to cooperate quite a bit. NOAA forecast says light rain in a couple days. Then likely cold front about eight days out, with snow. Dried boots, socks, and other clothing by fire. Washed ourselves after boiling water.

Was lucky to find another stream nearby to get water. Went upstream about half a mile to make sure there was nothing contaminating the supply. Still boiled water when nothing found. Filled up two jugs we had in Trekker for tomorrow. Dogs were pretty thirsty. Supper by 6 PM. Pretty tired from our first day afoot. Grateful had safe day. Dogs had supper of dog food and rice. They wolfed it down. Ours was pasta, freeze-dried veggies and coffee. Planned our next journey segment, a target to reach prior to weather turning sour again. Goal is to reach Pike Lake State Park near Morgantown OH, approx. thirty-six miles in seven to eight days. Some of that trek will likely be on small secondary roads and maybe even some cross-country miles. At the worst, we needed to arrive at our goal in nine days to let us prepare for a second hunkering down session during next cold front. We will do our best to avoid contact with anyone else during those miles but there will always be a chance of that.

Finally bedded down for the night, tired and sleepy. Was a tough first day on foot testing everything out. Hopefully it will get easier day-by-day. Said our prayers and climbed into our sleeping bags. Knew would be up every few hours to check on fire and keep it going until morning. A blessed day.

I will give thanks to the Lord with all my heart;
I will tell of all Your wonders.
(Psalm 9:1)

LARRY D. HORTON, PhD

Date: February 3–11   Mileage: Walk, Approx. 36 mi.

The next nine journal entries will be pretty short unless detail is needed. Our daily routine will be much the same each day. Priorities will be to walk at least four miles per day, shelter, protection water, fire, and food each day. As we travel we are hoping to build a bit of routine in our activities. Also, we hope our last day of walking will end pretty early so we can build a more substantial campsite for the coming cold front that NOAA has predicted. How long we have to hunker down again will depend on what the cold front produces.

Day #14, February 3, 4 miles: Up at 6 AM, warm breakfast of oatmeal and coffee, dogs had oatmeal and rice. Uneventful day on secondary roads. Crossed Ohio Brush Creek and headed northeast to pass south of Jacksonville OH. Simple lunch of cheese and crackers with a bit of hard candy thrown in as a treat. Triangulated our position with compass about every thirty minutes. Stopped by 2 PM just southeast of Jacksonville between and near junction of OH routes 781 and 348. Set up camp in wooded area on south side of a small hill for shelter from the wind. Built same lean-to configuration with Trekker as yesterday. Set up campfire and gathered wood for cooking and the night. By 8 PM we were ready to call it a day. Dogs rode in Trekker half the day. Our little system seems to be working OK, but very cautious as always concerning overheating. Another night of short segments of sleep and keeping the fire going. Prayers and a few minutes listening to news and weather forecast on the radio. So far batteries holding up. Glad we have a good supply of spares, given our several-month journey that lies ahead. National news continues to report on areas of unrest in the country and internationally. We have a feeling it will only get worse.

O Lord, You have heard the desire of the humble;
You will strengthen their heart,
You will incline Your ear.
(Psalm 10:17)

Day #15, February 4, 4–5 miles: Up at 6:15 AM. Today was very much a repeat of yesterday. Reached vicinity of Locust Grove OH by our 2 PM objective. Warm breakfast, cold lunch and hot supper. Set up Trekker lean-to system in wooded area just east of Locust Grove. Terrain pretty hilly so stayed on secondary roads. Not too much traffic the entire day. Mostly farmland between hills and valleys. Had camp set up, wood collected, and supper by 6 PM. Spent what time left that evening checking equipment, the Trekker, packs, and our supplies. Boiled water supply for the day tomorrow. Glad we have the hexamine stove but need to be careful in its use due to fuel supply. Need to maintain it for emergencies if at all possible. Prayers and to bed.

In the Lord I will take refuge.
(Psalm 11:1)

Date: February 3–11   Mileage: Walk, Approx. 36 mi.

Day #16, February 5, 4 miles: Up at 6 AM. Today was mostly a repeat of yesterday as far as our walking, meals, camp preparations, and bedding down for the night. We set up camp about two miles southeast of Sinking Spring OH. When we finally finished supper tonight, turned on radio to check NOAA weather forecast and news. That is when the day changed from all the days over the last few weeks. Weather forecast is still the same for the next six to seven days, highs in low forties and lows around freezing at night. News is very different and we had a long conversation about it before finally settling down for a fitful sleep.

Shortly after 9 AM this morning there were multiple apparent coordinated attacks within the borders of our country. First, a truck full of explosives blew up at the main gate into the naval facility in Groton CN. Death toll and injuries were minimal due to in place security. Second, a national guard armory was attacked in Salt Lake City UT again using an explosive-laden vehicle. Thankfully, only a few injuries at this location. Third, at the Mall of America in MN five individuals with weapons stormed one of the entrances and opened fire. Thankfully the mall was not especially crowded so early in the morning, but it took several hours to ferret out the gunmen and only after several of them had used explosive devices. The death toll is growing hourly from this attack, and a final number will not be known probably until tomorrow morning.

Three additional attacks took place that are having both immediate and potential long-term impact. One was in the Denver CO area where a truck loaded with explosives was driven into a fertilizer plant. The resulting explosion created a noxious cloud compounded by the material in the plant itself. The cloud is drifting to the southwest and will eventually cover the entire metro Denver area. Emergency crews are streaming into Denver from across the west coast and mountain region. The second and third attacks were similar. Explosive-laden trucks were detonated. However, the targets were very different. Both attacked the petrochemical industry, one across the Delaware River from Philadelphia, the other in the Pasadena TX community. Both are burning out of control and will for several days. Deadly clouds are traveling across large population areas. Philadelphia and southern New Jersey have been declared disaster areas. Fires rage out of control in Texas, and a similar cloud of potentially deadly materials is spreading west across the entire city of Houston and its southern and western reaches. The immediate death and injury totals from the explosions are pretty high, but both will likely increase as the noxious clouds spread across large unprepared areas.

Reports from all of the above indicate that panic has risen in the targeted areas. The president has called up the national guard in each target area, and emergency crews are descending on each on a region-by-region basis. Panic buying has set in across the areas for supplies, food, and fuel. Government officials are advising people to stay at home and let authorities do their jobs. We called our family members to assure them we were safe and to tell them to be careful.

Our hearts were very heavy concerning all the events of today but particularly about the situation in Houston TX. We left there less than three weeks ago. We have countless friends and some family members in the metro Houston area. We attempted to call the family members in particular but were unable to get through, which should not have surprised us. We will have that uncertainty with us until we are able to connect again, hopefully soon. We could only lift them up in our prayers as we bedded down for the night. My wife was especially upset with the whole situation and the unknowns.

Finally had to turn the radio off to conserve batteries and had a long talk about what we had heard. We are grateful we were not in any of those situations but also realize the days ahead are going to be very different. The likelihood has grown that we will face new dangers related to our supplies and personal safety. People are going to be cautious. We have to be much more vigilant then before, avoiding contact if at all possible, and very cautious on the use of roads as well.

LARRY D. HORTON, PhD

We said a lot of prayers tonight before finally trying to get some sleep. We did our best to keep our small fire concealed and bundled up even more for the cold night ahead. It's now real. We will have to go dark more than before, but we were prepared for that eventuality. It is just going to be cold. The dogs seemed to sense that things had changed. Our last thoughts were with those who were suffering much more than we. Prayers said, we tried to sleep.

The words of the Lord are pure words.
(Psalm 12:6)

Day #17, February 6, 4 miles:
Up at 5 AM; not much sleep during the night. Lots of thoughts about yesterday's events at national level and from being cold. Fire died during the night. Restarted it and cooked hot breakfast. Since we have decided to go even darker on our travels, we plan on shadowing roads, staying off them if at all possible, only using them when we have no alternative. Land is getting more-hilly as we head east. Elevation is going up, so valleys are our best bet for travel. Will require a lot more use of compass and map.

As we have done since starting out on foot, covered the Trekker with tarp from our temporary lean-to, to keep our stuff dry should we run into any rain or snow showers. Temps not too bad. High thirties probably during the day. The day passed with the same routine as the last couple days, cold lunch, frequent stops to rest, care that we didn't overheat, and constant vigilance for any dangers. We know we are in the land of dangerous creatures, including humans, so watched and listened for anything that might pose a threat to us. Our travel goal for the day was to travel four to five miles northeast toward Pike State Forest area. We made it to the very edge of the forest by 2:30 PM and found a wooded area where we set up camp. Camp was the same as previous days, temporary lean-to, gathering firewood for meal and the night, filling up our water supply, and feeding the dogs.

After meal, we turned on radio to get news. All fires are now out, clouds of deadly materials have dissipated somewhat, casualties are increasing by the hour, and thousands are suffering serious issues because of exposure to toxic materials. National guard, FEMA, and Red Cross swamped with work. Incidents of panic and lack of control are lessening. Continued calls for calm, but population across the country is up in arms about how so many things could have happened when they had been told we were safer than before. Leaders at all levels of government are meeting around the clock to identify steps to take moving forward. Not the kind of news we wanted to hear. Our being cold seems less important compared to what we imagine others are experiencing.

Our goal for tomorrow is to get as close to Bainbridge OH as possible. We are surrounded by large hills, many over 1,000 feet in elevation. Our path tomorrow will be along valleys and streams using logging, mining, and dirt roads for the majority of the day. We know that at times we will have to strike out across land to maintain a northerly direction as well. That will be tough, very slow going. Prayers said, a short listen to NOAA weather, still predicting large cold front with heavy snow around the eleventh or twelfth which means an extended hunker down period for us. 8:45 PM turned off radio and tried to sleep, knowing will be up during night to tend fire if possible. Good night.

**I will sing to the Lord,
Because He has dealt bountifully with me.
(Psalm 13:6)**

Day #18, February 7, 3 miles:
Was awakened last night by dogs going crazy. They sensed some type of animal was close to our little camp. Thank goodness for the dogs. Had slept with firearm at my side. Immediately built up fire big time. Could see two pairs of eyes about 50 feet from us. Fire and dogs seemed to scare off whatever it was. At first light looked for prints. Found two sets of what seemed to be very large dog or coyote prints. The mountains around us were showing us what was out there. Again, security became an even more important priority. Today heated up water, hot cereal, and

coffee for lunch. Dogs got their food and some cereal as well. Very glad that, from first day on foot, have been hanging all food supplies eight feet off the ground for the night and that we eat our meals away from our lean-to. Meal prep cleanup now even further away from the lean-to. Probably 50 feet at a minimum. No food where we sleep.

Shorter mileage today as we had to go cross country up two shallow wooded valleys and down the other side. Was very difficult pulling Trekker. Twice had to relay everything up the steepest parts of the valleys. Overheated both times and had to shed clothing layers and dry them out by small fires. Since we got a little earlier start, 5:45 AM, we were able to make the three miles by 2 PM, our shut-down time. Beginning to dawn on us that southern Ohio will be an ordeal. Breakfast, lunch, and supper were the same as previous days. Some cold food, but made sure we had a hot evening meal. At best, we made it halfway to Bainbridge OH. Looks like we will have more of the same type of travel tomorrow unless we find a backwoods road or logging road.

Set up camp as usual, temporary lean-to, lots of firewood, food supply hung up in trees, and water refilled. Fire is larger given last night's run-in with some local critters. Finished the day with news update and NOAA weather forecast. Nothing has changed much in either case. Only piece of good news is that toxic clouds in Philly and Houston areas are dissipating a bit. One other thing was reported, that authorities are pretty sure all the attacks of a couple days before were coordinated from outside the country. That is not a surprise.

A bit of addition tells us that we have probably traveled around 15 miles out of our goal for the ten-day period, 36 miles. Slow going. It is going to take us much longer than we thought to travel any distance. But we should not be surprised given the country we are traveling through, the weather, the means we are using to travel, and our physical conditioning. We are hoping all those will improve as the days and weeks pass. But in spite of slowness of travel, we are safe.

Bedded down with firearms close at hand. Dogs are pretty skittish, and was hard to get them to settle down. They were on high alert all day as we crossed many signs of animals during the day. We are very careful when we choose our temporary sites to scout the area for animal tracks, caves, or openings in the hillsides that bears like, and of course streams near our campsite that might be used as watering holes for all those potentially nasty critters. Read from scripture and said prayers. All four of us bundled up close together to stay as warm as possible. Good night.

The Lord has looked down from heaven upon the sons of men
To see if there are any who understand,
Who seek after God.
(Psalm 14:2)

Day #19, February 8, 3 miles:

Day's events almost a carbon copy of yesterday. Some cross-country walking, up and down as little as possible, but still had to do some relaying movement of our stuff. Crossed under US route 50 using underpass where road went over what we think is Brushy Creek just east of Bainbridge OH. Quickly found a nice stand of pine trees and oaks and set up our temporary camp, repeating again our daily tasks related to shelter, fire, water, and food. Dogs seem to be getting the hang of everything. For most part, they just sit and lie around watching us set up camp. As soon as fire starts, they get excited about eating, and once that is done and they have smelled everything in sight, they head for the lean-to. Every now and then they jump up and start barking just to warn everyone and everything that they are standing guard. They are priceless.

A quick listen to NOAA weather and forecast is still pretty much the same. Predicting heavy snow about four days out and colder temps, and high winds, which is not what we need to hear. We are tired. After simple hot supper of soup, rice, and coffee hit the sack. Ready for visitors but hoping none show up. Read Psalm, said prayers, and will try to get some sleep. Know again that will be up during night to tend fire, but that is now a routine.

O Lord, who may abide in Your tent?
Who may dwell on Your holy hill?
He who walks with integrity, and works righteousness,
And speaks truth in his heart.
(Psalm 15:1–2)

Day #20, February 9, 4–5 miles:
Near Bainbridge OH and northeast of that small town is a fairly decent valley. Turns out to be easier traveling as the valley followed the course of Brushy Creek. Able to travel on some secondary dirt roads that are little traveled. Terrain is still very hilly around us, so sticking to flat land as much possible. No relaying required today. Saw lots of animal sign including a small group of white-tail deer. Rabbit sign was everywhere. Some open fields, small farms, and some cattle and horses. Trekker seems to be handling the trip OK, but it will need a few repairs soon. Is beginning to sag a bit due to combination of heavy loads and the rough terrain we have encountered last couple of days. But all-in-all still in pretty good shape.

Day was a repeat of the previous five or six. Walking, shutting down at 2 PM, setting up shelter, firewood, security, water, and food. Got it done a bit quicker due to familiarity. Settling down under a small grove of oaks with good sight lines in all directions. Quick radio and NOAA updates. Nothing much has changed. Beginning to think that couple more days of travel only before we set up a more permanent site to sit out coming storm. Dogs still on alert. We are all losing a bit of weight and are tired but happy to be together. Prayers, scripture, and turned in to get as much sleep as possible.

Preserve me, O God, for I take refuge in You.
(Psalm 16:1)

Date: February 3–11   Mileage: Walk, Approx. 36 mi.

Day #21, February 10, 6 miles:
Passed to the west of Bourneville OH and headed straight north toward Lattaville OH. Easier day of travel today, so mileage went up. Stayed on dirt country road for most of the day. Had to leave valley we had been traveling, but elevation gain and loss not nearly as bad as a few days ago. Found one road that helped. Routine for the day was much the same. Only had to get off the road a couple times to avoid other travelers. One thing I need to mention is that for past five days, once we heard of upcoming storm, we have been collecting dry tinder and putting it in one of our large plastic garbage bags. When storm hits, finding dry tinder will be an issue. Decided that we would continue this practice for the duration of our journey. Will help us only have to use hexamine stove and fuel when absolutely necessary.

Were able to shut down at 2:30 this afternoon. Given we had gotten a bit quicker in setting up temporary camp figured we could walk for an extra thirty minutes. Meals, camp setup, shelter, security, fire wood, fire, and water processes much the same. Found a nice grove of oaks and pines to set up camp again with a good line of sight in all directions. A bit up the side of a hill from our travel path. Again, lots of wild animal sign including the howls of a few coyotes in the distance. Will be extra vigilant tonight. Dogs on the alert. Funny to watch. Hair on the back of their necks and shoulders often standing up. They are a great comfort. Prayers said. Scripture read. Lots of work ahead in next forty-eight hours. One more day of travel and then task of establishing hunker-down location to get through coming winter storm. Good night.

> **I have called upon You, for You will answer me, O God;**
> **Incline Your ear to me, hear my speech.**
> **(Psalm 17:6)**

Day #22, February 11, 2 miles: Listened to NOAA weather forecast first thing. Storm to hit our area after 3 PM tomorrow. Decided to travel carefully and look for a good location to set up storm camp. Broke down temporary camp. Hot breakfast of oatmeal and coffee. On our way by 8 AM. After ninety-minute walk down a dirt road, spotted a low hill in distance covered with pine trees with a few oaks and maples mixed in. Got closer to the potential site and noticed a nice stream at its base. Also saw that timber had likely been taken off the hill not too long ago. That likely meant lots of potential firewood. Hill lies in an east-west orientation. So setting up our camp on lee side gives even more protection from the coming winds and storm out of the north-northwest. We made for the hill. Our decision was made. Cross the stream and stop. Lunch at the base of the hill on stream bank. Dogs smelling everything. Observed some animal sign, primarily rabbit runs. After lunch, I scouted both upstream and down for possible animal use. Downstream about one-half mile saw sandy dirt shoreline with lots of critter prints, a watering hole. Upstream about a mile came to a fork in the stream, took right fork which headed up a small draw between our hill and the one next to it. No animal drinking signs for the first few hundred yards. Then, scouted our hill near stream to find hunker-down location. About a hundred yards up a very gentle slope, maybe two degrees, came to a large stand of pines sitting on a nearly flat area on the hill. Probably 100 square yards of flat and trees. Has not been touched by loggers but is surrounded by areas that were cut. Back to family and decided to move closer to right stream branch. Used old logging road to vicinity of our chosen site. Took about an hour to actually get to the pine grove. Walked into center of grove and found two formations of eight trees, four trees in each formation more or less in the shape of a square each about eight feet on a side. Perfect for securing our coverings per our plan. Cold lunch, then to work. Because so much to do, not going to go into detail of camp setup until finished completely with that tomorrow. Got to get at it. We had about four hours until the sun would set and there was a lot to get done. Built fire pit area first so we could have hot supper. Continued to work on our site after supper. Glad we have LED headband lamps to work by. Bedded down, prayers said, and scripture read. Lots of work tomorrow. Last check on NOAA weather indicates that snow flurries and increased wind should start around 3 PM tomorrow afternoon. Up and at 'em early tomorrow morning.

I love You, O Lord; my strength.
The Lord is my rock and my fortress and my deliverer,
My God, my rock, in whom I take refuge;
My shield and the horn of my salvation, my stronghold.
(Psalm 18:1–2)

The next section of this diary records our planned hunker-down to wait out large winter storm that is to arrive. We hope that we will not be stationary more than five to seven days. Will plan for seven but if possible leave earlier if weather permits. Primary task during that time frame will be shelter, security, and rest. We will be off the beaten path as well. Hope to add to our food resources through snare trapping. Time will tell if that works. Will do a complete evaluation of our materials, equipment, and food while we sit out the storm. Make any repairs and adjustments as needed. Rest is going to be very important as we have been on the move for over three weeks since leaving our home in Texas. Last week of walking has been tough on us. By our best measurement, we walked between twenty-seven and twenty-eight miles. A bit short of our goal of thirty-six miles but acceptable as we really are not on a timetable. As each day passes, we get closer to the start of spring rain and slowly warming temperatures. Trek will not get any easier, as geography and weather will dictate the amount of progress we make on a daily basis.

Date: February 12–18   Mileage: Hunker Down 0 mi.

Afternoon & Evening, Day #22, February 11

Hunker-down camp setup was our primary task from arrival at site at approx. noon until had basic camp set up. As noted earlier, had fire location set up and working first thing. Used the time during afternoon to hang bedding and other items by the fire to air them out as much as possible. Things were going to get damp and much colder very quickly so did best to prepare the stuff. Likely not much chance to do it again for a few days.

We had several primary tasks to complete as much as possible and as quickly as possible after initial fire going. **First,** cleared out all pine tree branches up to six or seven feet high at our primary site. Those branches will be part of the layered wall structure of our primary shelter and part of our sleeping platform mattress. Checked for deadfalls above our campsite and found none. **Second,** found two trees approx. ten feet apart about fifty feet from primary site. Cleared off branches to about ten feet from ground. Scrounged for a pole eleven to twelve feet long. Placed pole between two trees, laid on strong branch in each tree, and secured with paracord. Will hang our food supplies from the pole a minimum of eight feet off the ground in large garbage bags. **Third,** gathered enough firewood, plus 50 percent, for the next two days and nights. Wife arranged wood by fire to dry it as much as possible.

Fourth, at approx. 3 PM started to work on primary shelter in earnest. Scrounged for and cut main structure supports, both vertical and horizontal, each approx. nine feet long. Dug four main vertical support holes twelve to eighteen inches deep at corners of eight-foot square. Set poles into holes and pounded noggins, three inches in circumference, on both north and south sides of vertical support poles. Prevailing winds were going to be from the north so wanted to reinforce vertical supports to avoid blowing down in wind. Filled in holes with compacted dirt topped off with large rocks to add additional weight to secure in ground. Next built sleeping platform within vertical supports at about eighteen inches off the ground. Lost bit of that gap at back of structure due to slight angle of ground at site. Buildup was to get us off the ground so we could stay warmer. Secured these supports to vertical poles. Then added four same-size poles in north-to-south direction to east-west platform poles. Wove one inch poles horizontally to the additional support poles to add support for sleeping and sitting. Then attached a second set of same size poles, two north-to-south, two east-to-west approx. four feet above sleeping platform to four corner poles. Built sloped roof support system by building an A-frame structure attached to top four cross members. Added six roof supports to each side of the A-frame roof. Bound all of this structure together with paracord. Using pine branches cut earlier when clearing site, built up a type of mattress on sleeping platform. Final step for the evening was to stretch one of our tarps over the roof structure for temporary cover during the night. Worked two hours into the darkness to complete shelter to this point. Time to hit the sack. Will not sleep much. On alert for critters and to keep the fire going. A lot accomplished in about seven hours, but a lot remains to be done to be ready for the upcoming storm.

Day #23, February 12: Up early, 6 AM. Hot breakfast of oatmeal and coffee for us. Dogs had their food with some rice mixed in. NOAA weather report indicated that snow flurries would start around 3 PM this afternoon. Immediately started on completing camp build-out. Wife started securing and boiling water supply for the day. Dogs on long leashes exploring site underneath pine trees. **Fifth project,** dug a trench latrine. Located it west of campsite on outer edge of pine tree growth. Fashioned simple walls around it using limbs cut from pine trees. **Sixth,** completed build-out of sheltered area for Travel Trekker and firewood storage. A very simple design. Fashioned center pole from small log four inches in diameter. Laid second tarp out on ground and found center by measuring equidistant from each grommet. Reinforced ten-inch area in center of tarp with eight layers of duct tape for additional strength where center pole pushes tarp upward. Tied off four corners of tarp to adjacent trees, running paracord from four corner grommets to individual trees. Did best to create same slope angle for each side of the tarp and drew into as tight a slope as possible. Moved Trekker under this shelter.

Cleaned off junk from ground where we would stack our wood supply. Early lunch of hot soup, pudding, and coffee.

Back at it as quickly as possible. Wife busy cleaning all junk out from under sleeping platform and in a ten-foot circle around fire location. My **seventh project** was to build walls on three sides of our shelter. A stout wall facing the wind on north and northwest sides as well as woven walls using pine branches on east and west facing walls. Started work around 11 AM. Secured multiple nine-foot-long three-inch diameter poles from brush left by loggers just to the east of the pine tree grove. Cleaned them and hauled back to camp site. Cut one pole in half and secured in ground by two northern corner support poles of shelter, leaving a three-inch gap between support pole and shorter pole. Then placed three-inch diameter poles in between shelter and second poles building up as solid a wall as possible about five feet high. Tied off the ends of each pole to a corner support pole using paracord. Then completed remaining east and west sides of the shelter by placing five vertical poles about one and a half feet apart between the shelter corner support poles. Wove smaller one-inch branches between all of the vertical side poles. Finally, wove pine tree branches into the grid of vertical and horizontal poles. Also, covered the solid pole wall on north side of shelter with pine tree branches.

Final step was to complete the roof. Unsecured tarp on roof set up last night and expanded it to its full size. Green side of tarp up. Carved fourteen sixteen-inch pegs. Attached two paracord lengths to each grommet on east, west, and north sides of wall. Attached each length of paracord to a prepared peg. Stretched out the lengths of paracord as evenly as possible in all directions with some overlap of the tarp in all three directions. The overlaps extended about a foot beyond the vertical walls of the shelter. Pounded pegs into ground creating as tight a waterproof cover over the shelter as possible with a bit of air circulation as well.

Next step in completing shelter was to lay pine branches on top of roof with goal of at least a foot-thick layer of those branches in place. Final step was to complete sleeping and sitting platform. Added enough pine branches to be two feet thick. Then layered on a moving pad, which we unrolled, two sleeping bag foam ground pads, and finally the sleeping bags. Wife fabricated a rough bag for the dogs using our second moving pad and put it between our two sleeping bags. It was done. Wasn't pretty, but our best effort to protect us.

Some would ask why so much work on a shelter. Given predicted snow, wind, and much colder temperatures, we had to do all that we could to insure we could stay reasonably warm and out of as much of the snowy wet weather as possible. Add the fact that we might be hunkered down for as many as seven days, and the effort will likely pay off. We need a shelter that will give us as good a chance as any to make it through the rough weather. 3 PM arrived and had two important tasks to complete. At 3:15 PM we noticed the first light snowflakes falling outside the pine tree grove. Nothing was reaching the campsite because of canopy of pine branches above us at first. Gathering at least three nights and two days' worth of wood was of top priority at this point. Wife and dogs stayed in camp. I set out beyond pine tree grove to gather wood. Armed with bow saw and hatchet, drug two or three dozen four-to-six foot-long small logs, two-to-four inches in diameter, back to camp and built a pile just to the side of the shelter. Worked for ninety minutes, wind increasing, and snowflakes getting gradually larger. Temperature was hovering between twenty-eight and thirty degrees most likely. Did my best not to overheat and sweat, but not successful most of the time. Sawed and cut wood pile into two foot lengths. My wife hauled results and stacked under the tarp storage shelter beside the Trekker. At 5 PM called it enough for time being. Ended up with a four-foot square two feet high stack of wood. Knew wood would be a priority tomorrow morning and every day that we would be hunkered down.

One final major task for the day was to build a temporary fire reflection structure to push heat from fire toward the shelter entrance. Will have to complete a sturdier reflection structure tomorrow. No time left today and snow was getting heavier by the minute. Quickly built a frame of two-inch diameter sticks vertically and pounded into ground. Attached one of our space blankets, silver side pointing to shelter, about a foot from the south side of fire ring wife had built earlier. Will have to do until tomorrow morning. With reflector wall done, built up fire to both cook supper and allow us to hang damp clothing to dry. Was cold changing clothes but had to be done. Decided to have four-course supper and share with dogs as much as possible. Hot pasta, freeze-dried beef, rice, freeze-dried corn, and coffee. Dogs got their portion. Sure hit the spot. Changed into camping shoes and put damp boots on poles by fire to dry them out some. Surprising how damp our boots got just working.

After supper cut up small limbs left from cutting firewood into fire-starting material to be added to tinder should we have to restart our fire. Stacked in storage area. Cut kindling by LED headlamps. Dangerous work. One slip and we could have had serious medical situation on our hands. With that declared the day done. Thank the Lord no problems. Short session of radio NOAA weather report. National news still not good, with general population and attacked areas continuing to be on emergency alert. Casualties growing by the hour. Followed with scripture reading and prayers. Really bundled up for the night. Two pairs of socks on each foot, wool scarves around heads and necks, and putting socks on our hands. Decided to each pull one dog into our individual sleeping bags and cover all of us up with the moving pad that we had for them. Took a look out under the pine trees and saw it snowing heavily. Wind not too bad yet, but that could easily change. Doing our best to stay warm. Fire will be an issue in the morning. God bless us and watch over us.

The heavens are telling of the glory of God;
And their expanse is declaring the work of His hands.
(Psalm 19:1)

Day #24, February 13: Pretty cold when woke up. Probably in mid-to-high 20s. Wind had picked up considerably. Canopy above us of pine trees had protected us quite a bit from snow but if wind picks up or it warms up slightly, shower of melted snow is going to fall on us.

Hands, feet, head, and necks made it through the night. Had put boots in bottom of sleeping bags as well so they were in good shape first thing. Dogs did not move during the night. They wanted to be warm as well. Keeping them in sleeping bags with us seemed to work pretty well. Wife's joints were not doing well. Cold weather is not good for fibromyalgia. Stayed in warm sleeping bags for quite a while. Got up and was able to start good fire from embers that remained. No sounds during the night, but would imagine our little camp had been a curiosity to many four-legged critters. Boiled last of our water supply and cooked double portion of oatmeal and water for hot coffee. Smelled wonderful and tasted even better as we ate under the protection of our shelter roof.

Finally ventured out to the edge of pine tree grove. It appears we got four to five inches of snow. Still falling lightly and probably will throughout the day. Priorities for the morning were replenishing our water supply, building a more substantial fire reflector and protective covering over the fire ring, digging a trench around the shelter to run off any potential snow melt, and gather as much firewood as possible. All of that will likely take me into the early afternoon to complete. Will work on water all day long, boiling and storing additional water in the two one-gallon jugs that we had with us. Will continually fill up our canteens as we drink water during the day.

Late in afternoon boiled some extra water and took what some would call a sponge bath washing face, necks, arms, pits, bodies, and most importantly our feet. Air dry all of that washing even though it was very cold. Remembered importance of air drying bodies as much as possible.

Shortly after breakfast had started on the many tasks that still needed to be completed. Tied dogs to their long leashes, but mostly they stayed close to the fire for warmth. They didn't seem to be interested in exploring the area. **First task,** one which my wife would continue all day long, was to go to stream, haul water to camp in folding bucket we had with us, boil it, store it, and repeat process several times both in AM and PM. While she was busy, I tackled **second task** of building a more substantial fire reflection and protection structure. It took a while to complete, even though not nearly as complicated as building our sleeping shelter. Prepared two four-foot poles and sank them into ground about two feet behind the fire ring to the south. Attached noggins to both for stability. Then prepared two six-foot poles and sank them into ground a foot from the fire ring and spaced a foot wider on each side than the four-foot poles. Again, attached noggins to them for stability. Four-foot long vertical poles then spaced width of space blanket apart. Attached space blanket to these poles. Attached small horizontal cross beams to top of both four-foot and six-foot vertical poles. Attached space blanket to horizontal poles between six-foot and four-foot vertical poles, which was just far enough to protect the fire itself for the most part from falling snow or water. Last step was to gather enough right-length small diameter poles to build a reflecting wall of wood on both sides of structure to about three feet high for wind protection. Bound all poles to vertical four- and six-foot main vertical poles. Secured six two-inch diameter poles three feet long and drove them into ground as noggins to hold wall logs in place. When all finished slightly resembled home fireplace that we had in our home in TX. It did a pretty good job of radiating heat into shelter, and it allowed us to continue to cook meals, boil water, and dry clothing without being too cramped.

Just prior to preparing lunch completed **third task**, digging water runoff trench around main shelter and fire complex as well as our storage structure. Difficult at times because of tree roots, but got it done pretty quickly. Depth of about three inches and width about six inches. With natural fall of hillside, water will run off to the south and away from our location. Hauled water for cooking lunch, cooked soup, and added boiled rice to increase its bulk. Snow continued to fall all morning, fairly lightly, but even that is adding up. We are very careful to not hit tree branches above us and make snow fall on us. Heat from fire seems to be causing small amount of melting above us but we decided there is nothing we can do about that. After lunch spent three hours gathering more firewood logs, cutting it into two-foot sections, and putting it in our storage structure. When finished had four-foot square, four-foot tall stack of medium-sized fire logs. Feel pretty good about that. While collecting logs, noticed several rabbit-runs and lots of tracks from four-legged critters, especially underneath where we had hung our food supply. Decided to set out wire snares tomorrow morning in hopes of catching a rabbit or two. Also, noticed quite a few squirrels in trees around us. A priority tomorrow will be to start securing small sources of fresh meat to add to our and the dog's diets. We sense also that we need to inventory our food supplies and add to those any meat we might be able to secure. Also, need to do a bit of target practice with wife's air rifle that we had with us. At ten to fifteen feet it had the potential of killing squirrels. We got it without scope to save weight, so it will take practice to be successful. Larger 17HMR scoped rifle would give us better chance of success, but we don't need report from firing it alerting others in the vicinity. So it's the air rifle unless we get to a desperation stage.

Cooked an early supper. Soup again expanded with rice. One last water trip to stream using light from LED headlamps. Use primary flashlight very sparingly and only in middle of night if we hear anything or need to make a latrine run. So far, we have avoided any intestinal issues but we are also being very careful. Our supply of meds for such problems is not that large. Bedded down after listening to Christian music, news, and NOAA weather for about twenty minutes. Things pretty much the same as the last couple days on all fronts. Nationally there are cries for answers as to why all the recent attacks could have been possible. No answers yet but the questions are increasing. Bundled up the same way we did last night, boots in bottom of sleeping bags, head and necks wrapped in scarves, two pairs of socks on feet, one pair of socks on hands, dogs in sleeping bags with us, and fire stoked. Some heat to put us to sleep. Prayers said and scripture read. Some key tasks tomorrow but we don't have much if anything to do to complete our campsite. That is some progress. One and a half days completed into our hunker-down situation.

We will boast in the name of our Lord, our God.
(Psalm 20:7)

LARRY D. HORTON, PhD

Day #25, February 14: When we woke up around 6 AM, appeared to have snowed lightly all night. We knew we would be repeating some of the chores from yesterday again today. Wife collecting and boiling water. I would gather firewood to replace what we had burned. But as I said in journal yesterday, there were some other important tasks to undertake and complete primarily having to do with securing additional food resources in the form of meat. Shortly after breakfast of oatmeal and coffee, rice added to dogs' for more volume, headed out into cut timber areas within one-fourth mile of camp to set wire snare traps. Saw lots of rabbit tracks along a couple of runs and probably some raccoon tracks as well. Set four traps. Makes sense that rabbits will be traveling between scrap branches and logs from timber cut off. Did my best to cover up my scent on traps and using sticks to hide the snares. Glad I had my gaiters. Snow was about eight inches deep outside of pine tree grove where camp located.

Back in camp, gathered up air rifle and fifteen pellets to do some target practice. Noticed couple squirrels when out setting snare traps. Set up target, four-inch square piece of paper, paced off ten steps, and took five shots at target, hitting one-inch circle three out of five shots; other two were only one-half outside circle. That was good. Added another five paces. About fifteen yards. Had new target with one-inch circle. Hit circle one out of five. Other four shots were between one to two inches from circle. Feel good about success. Have a reasonable chance of actually hitting small critter from fairly close range. Will have to spend a lot of time sitting and being very quiet to get them close enough for a good shot.

Back to camp. Made water run to stream which was now frozen over. Hand ax to break up ice and hauled full folding bucket of water for boiling. Likely have to make three to four more water trips today. Made three before calling it a day. Lunch was rice and beans for all, hot tea for us, and water for dogs. Right after lunch made two wood gathering and cutting trips to build wood supply back up to four-foot by four-foot stack. That done, another water trip, and water boiled, wife and I started a detailed inventory of our food supplies. A two-hour detailed review of supplies resulted in the following:

1. We have enough freeze-dried food, rationing their use for three daily meals, for seventy- five days.
2. Have enough dog food for five more weeks if only used once per day.
3. Have enough rice and beans, if carefully rationed to one meal a day, for the four of us for forty more days.
4. Have enough coffee, tea, and juice powder to last seventy-five more days if only used one type once per day.
5. Still have all water purification materials, tablets, and small container of bleach. Was packed because we had been boiling all of our water. Will continue to boil water and only use other materials if no boiling possible.
6. We have not touched our extravagant treats to this point in time other than a few pieces of hard candy. Our full stock remains:
   a. Twelve 5 oz. tins of tuna in water
   b. Twelve 50 ml. bottles of vodka for medical purposes only
   c. Small container of hot chocolate mix
   d. Small bag of hard candies

If we are really careful and able to add fresh meat periodically, to the above, we can likely stretch these supplies out for around ninety more days starting with supper tonight. However, we decided to break a bit from that commitment. We needed to have a little celebration and thanksgiving for our safety and progress to date. Needless to say, we were looking forward to supper with great anticipation. The dogs seemed to sense something as well.

After making final water run and boiling it we prepared a supper of rice, tuna, and pudding. Smelled wonderful. Tasted even better. The dogs kept looking for more. We cooked double portion of rice so they got more with a few pieces of tuna mixed in. Full tummies for all. Sat by nice fire and listened to radio NOAA forecast, news, and fifteen minutes of Christian music. Forecast is for more of same. Snow flurries, winds, and temps around freezing during the day and mid-twenties at night, wind chills around twenty degrees for next twenty-four hours. National news is filled with updates on recent attacks. Cleanup has started in all locations. Hundreds were hospitalized with lung and breathing issues. Death toll across the country well over 1,000 individuals with more likely to be added to that total, given grave injuries of many victims. Country is on high alert. Citizens are arming themselves at faster rate. Multiple run ins between groups have happened with some resulting violence. Several locations have seen violence against police with resulting gunfire. National guard is on alert across the country. Regular military had canceled all leaves. New president, using executive actions, took all steps promised to take place in first 100 days in office. Opposition party and groups are up in arms due to by-passing of Congress, but could do little.

Ordinary people are screaming for answers and scared about the future. Short tempers seem to be the tone of the day. Prepper and survival companies are swamped with orders they cannot fill due to selling out all of their materials. Stores and shops are empty that sold weapons. Ammo is impossible to secure. The country is becoming an armed camp. Things are not good. If and when there are more attacks, things may possibly get much worse.

Internationally, Europe is experiencing daily bombings and individual attacks. Across the area, the military is increasingly in control. The Middle East is burning to the ground. Refugees are in the millions. Governments do not seem to have any control. Food riots happen hourly. Casualties are in the thousands. Not a good place to be. After listening to all of that we counted ourselves very lucky to be reasonably safe in our little camp. Listening to the fifteen minutes of Christian music helped give us hope. Used hand crank to charge batteries in our radio as we had not had any sun to use the solar power charging and had been too busy to use the crank to power up the radio's internal batteries earlier. Before we called it a day, planned next four days of hunker-down. Normal daily activities will continue: water and firewood collection, personal washing, washing basic clothing items, cooking meals, checking traps, and trying to secure squirrel meat if opportunity presents itself. In addition, will do some detailed writing in journal about several subjects not recorded to this point in time due to more pressing matters. Bundled up again as did last two nights and hit the sack. Good night, Lord watch over us.

Be exalted, O Lord, in Your strength;
We will sing and praise Your power.
(Psalm 21:13)

Date: February 12–18   Mileage: Hunker Down 0 mi.

Day #26, February 15: Daily routine continues: four trips to stream for water and getting it boiled, gathering and replenishing wood supply, meals according to rationing plan, wash clothing and bodies staying as warm as possible, exercising dogs as much as they are willing. Then completed inventory of clothing, made any necessary repairs to clothing, and checked batteries in all equipment. This routine will continue as long as we are hunkered down. First thing after breakfast checked snare traps. No luck. Maybe tomorrow. Constantly on alert for squirrels in trees as well. Checked snare traps again after lunch and shortly before sundown. Again, no luck.

As planned sat down after lunch and reviewed first area which had been slack in this journal because did not previously have enough time to put detail into journal. **First area, human_impact.** We have, as planned, attempted to avoid as much human contact as possible ever since we started on foot. We were lucky with the farmer and his wife during our first hunker-down. Since then we've had no direct face-to-face contact with any other humans. That said, humans continue to impact us on a daily basis. We have to deal with human structures daily, particularly fences. Luckily in this hilly country there are not large plots of cultivated farmland. However, fences were everywhere to keep livestock contained. We have lost count of the times we had to unload the Trekker and relay our stuff over a fence line. That means reloading it after by-passing the fence obstacle. No electrified fences to this point but expect that at some time.

A few run-ins with cows and bulls drove dogs nuts but weather is forcing farmers to keep animals close to barns. Lots of dogs barking as we pass during daytime have kept ours energized. Dogs barking at night in the distance keep ours restless as well. No direct run-in with dogs to this point but again we are lucky. It will happen sooner rather than later. Daytime sightings of buildings, houses, barns, and outbuildings happen repeatedly. At night, we have easily seen lighted houses, yard lights, and a few vehicles moving on roads and heard gunfire in the distance. Some was disturbing as it was obviously from semiautomatic weapons and large-clip handguns. People are practicing and preparing for anything. Shotgun reports as well for some reason every once in a while. Nearest nighttime lights from our hunker-down camp are about two miles to our south.

We figure likelihood of human contact will increase as we move further north as population centers will be closer to our path. We will be moving into flatter geography, which will mean more farms as well. Contact will happen. Prayers that it will go well. Prepared to avoid bad stuff if at all possible. Dogs great to have with us, but they are a beacon to our location and presence to anyone who wants to check on us. To bed around 9 PM, going to be a cold night. Prayers said and scripture read. Watch over us, Lord.

Upon You I was cast from birth;
You have been my God from my mother's womb.
(Psalm 22:10)

Date: February 12–18   Mileage: Hunker Down 0 mi.

Day #27, February 16: Daily routine continued: Multiple water trips, wood gathering, fire maintenance, shelter maintenance, checking food security, tending to dogs, staying warm, maintaining firearms, security checks of area around shelter, checking for signs of unfriendly creatures, staying out of sight as much as possible, and dealing with weather and snow. Higher winds brought large clumps of snow down on us from treetops which meant more work to dry things out. Did detailed check of shelter roof and added more pine branches where needed. Re-tightened supports for storage shelter and checked tarp for leaks. Where found, repaired with duct tape. All three meals were carefully rationed portions of our supplies. Maintained fluid intake to keep strength up.

Checked snare traps. We got lucky. One rabbit. Gutted and skinned the body, cut into portions, and cooked as soon as had in camp to add to our menu. Buried entrails and skin under one of the large piles of brush about 100 yards to our east. Meals by our rationing plan, with added rabbit meat, for lunch and supper. No squirrels today, but heard them in the trees chattering at the dogs. Reset and checked snare traps couple times during the day.

Second area, personal cleanliness and food preparation safety, is topic for catch-up notes today. Have noted a couple times that we did simple body cleaning. This was really a daily routine at midday while it was slightly warmer. Also, aired out boots, washed pits, and feet at minimum every other day. We check bodies for any critters on daily basis as well and treat as necessary. Multiple small cuts and dings are dealt with immediately, disinfected, and bandaged. Bandages changed daily. Use latrine religiously and bury fecal matter immediately. I urinate in a circle around our campsite, working in a circle approx. fifty feet from the camp itself. Critters don't like smell of human urine. Wash socks daily. Rest of clothing about every third day or at most every fourth day. Cleaned teeth daily using innards of paracord as floss. With my dentures, packed enough cleaning tablets to last sixty days. Clean them religiously. Rinse mouth with small bit of vodka from our medical supply daily.

Food preparation safety involves washing cooking tools after each meal in boiled water. Using small freeze-dried food containers set up three-part system. Bin #1, boiled water with bleach to rinse tools. Bin #2, very hot water with concentrated cleaning fluid. We each had 8 oz. bottle of dishwashing soap in our pack. Bin #3, hot final rinsewater. Dry cooking tools immediately and stow in packs until needed for next meal. We bury any leftover food waste at least 100 yards away from camp. We open food containers, Mylar bags, only just prior to cooking. Dog dishes are washed in the same way but separately from our plates, utensils, and pots. We never eat anything by hand except directly from plastic wrappings, candy, for example. Wash hands before and after preparation and eating of each meal. Once we had wild animal meat for our diet would never touch raw meat of animal without wearing surgical gloves. We packed lots of these. Any uneaten food or waste is immediately buried. We never let it sit around just in case.

I need to note one additional area related to cleanliness, and it is true for my wife and me as well as our 2 dogs. It has to do with ticks, spiders, and other creepy crawlies. One would think given the cold weather that these are less of a worry as when it was warmer. However, any of these creatures who withstood the cold will be looking for the warmest locations possible to keep warm. Nothing could possibly work better than human bodies and other animals. So, since the first day we started camping outdoors, beginning while we were still using our truck, and something that would be a daily activity, we search for ticks in warm body areas and on the dogs. To this point in time we had found a few on the dogs and removed them, which the dogs do not enjoy. Nothing on our persons yet but we will stay vigilant.

To bed around 9 PM again. Going to be cold again tonight. Prayers said and scripture read. Lord, protect us.

> The Lord is my shepherd, I shall not want
> He makes me lie down in green pastures;
> He leads me beside quiet waters.
> (Psalm 23:1–2)

Day #28, February 17: Daily routine continued as previous two days after a night of not much sleep. Sometime in middle of night dogs started barking very loudly. Howls came back at them and it seemed like the source was very close to the shelter. My wife grabbed the dogs as best she could. I climbed out of the shelter, weapon in hand. Grabbed flashlight as well and started to search for intruder. It didn't take long to spot two eyes glowing in light from my torch. Appeared to be a dog checking us out. I picked up a small log from our stack and threw it at the dog. Missed it but must have scared it quite a bit because it took off down the hill tail between its legs. Guessed it belonged to house couple miles away and had gotten curious. But it really sent a message to us. Be prepared and if necessary for safety don't hesitate to use a weapon to do away with any dangers of the four-footed kind.

Once we were up at sunrise, routine for day took place: multiple water trips, wood gathering, fire maintenance, shelter maintenance, checking food supplies, tending to dogs, staying warm, firearms check, burying waste materials, and ramping up our parameter security warning system. That involves piles of brush at smaller possible entrances to camp and stretching thin wire one inch above snow level with spaced pieces of metal taken from tuna can that would hit branches and send a warning. Wire is strung between 20 and 25 feet from the shelter.

Checked snare traps. No luck overnight. Rebaited those that needed it. Saw several squirrels in trees around their nest about 50 yards to our north.

Third area of catch-up related to the daily security checks concerning firearms. Just prior to leaving our home in TX both my wife and I had received our CCLs. She now carried a Sig-Sauer 9 mm small handgun for personal and family protection. I carried a Beretta 380 for the same purpose. We have packed 200 rounds of ammo for each handgun. As previously mentioned in this diary we also have two long guns. One is an un-scoped air rifle for my wife with 1,000 rounds of pellets. The air rifle has a muzzle velocity above 1,500 fps which meant it can potentially kill squirrels and even rabbits with a head or neck shot. The other is a scoped 17 HMR with 300 rounds of ammo. Our objective is never to use any of the weapons other than the air rifle unless we are forced into a situation where we have no other choice than to go up in power and effect. We pray daily that we will never have to decide to use more power.

In addition, we each carry a medium-sized spray can of pepper spray with enough force to send a steady stream to a target fifteen feet away. There are obvious human uses for this, but we carry them primarily for larger hostile critter protection like dogs, coyotes, and even bears, if need be. We think about skunks a lot as well. The pepper spray would do nicely with them. Do not want us or the dogs to get sprayed by skunks. That would be tough to live with.

We carry multiple bladed weapons and tools as well. First, my wife carries two blades, a small tactical knife with sheath, and a folding rescue knife in her pocket. I carry a small folding knife in my pants, have done that for years, with a combat knife in sheath on my hip, and a wild game preparation blade in a sheath in my pack. We also have stowed a machete in sheath on the Travel Trekker for times when we may need to hack our way through brush. In our packs, we carry materials to clean our guns, sharpen our blades, and some specialized materials, for example arrowheads, should we ever want to fabricate a more silent weapon. But we will do that only out of desperation or fear of discovery when close to population centers. We also carry other bladed tools which have a primary function but can also be used as both offensive and defensive weapons. First, a small hand ax for obvious purposes but also does well as our primary hammer. Second, a full sized one-side bladed ax, again for obvious purposes, as well as a lightweight sledge and a personal protection weapon, should that be necessary.

Prior to bugging out we had secured and prepared fairly stout walking sticks, each about twelve inches longer than we were tall. These have proved very valuable for stability in our walking to date, and we hope that is all they will be used for. But we could use them for other purposes if necessary. Listened to NOAA weather before sacking out. Weather is to break on the twentieth, so we will stay hunkered down through the nineteenth using that day to prep for hitting the road again. Temp tonight in low twenties. High tomorrow of only high twenties means we are going to have to work at staying warm. In a day or two, will moderate to high in low thirties with no snow or high winds. Bundled up as on previous nights and climbed into sleeping bags with dogs. Neither could sleep right away so we started to talk about the end times and everything that will lead up to them. We agreed that for our country at least we are in the early days of those tough times. Agreed to continue conversation tomorrow as we grew warmer and sleepier. Scripture read and prayers said, we asked for continued guidance and protection.

The earth is the Lord's, and all it contains,
The world, and those who dwell in it.
(Psalm 24:1)

Day #29, February 18: It is enough to record that daily routine stayed the same and we were disciplined in doing all that was necessary. Must report fifteen minutes of early morning excitement. We heard something walking across roof of our shelter. Grabbed handgun and air rifle and climbed out as quietly as possible just in time to see squirrel jump from roof to closest pine tree branch. Dogs were stirring so knew could not wait. Took aim and missed with first pellet. Probably nerves. Second pellet found the neck of the squirrel and it tumbled to ground. As quickly as I could I carried it away from shelter where I skinned and butchered it. Fresh meat for breakfast. Kept the heart again for the dogs. A treat. Meat made breakfast very special. Our primary task for the day was to build up fire and keep warm. Dogs stayed covered in shelter most of the morning and for a while after lunch.

Fourth, fifth, and sixth catch-up areas are medical, communication and fire. First, **medical**. We each carry an Army corpsman medical kit bag. Within each are countless items. My wife is carrying the lighter materials, I the larger and heavier stuff. We have used some of the basics to this point, small bandages, gauze pads, antibiotic cream. The following materials make up each of our bags: Redundancy was crucial.

Wife's Medical Kit	My Medical Kit
Assorted gauze pads	Assorted gauze pads
One-half of band-aids, assorted sizes	One-half of band-aids, assorted sizes
Three rolls one-half inch wide white medical tape	Three rolls one inch wide white medical tape
Sewing kit, assorted needles	Shoe repair kit, shoe goo, heavy needles
One-half roll duct tape	One roll duct tape
Bottle 81 mg. aspirin	Two bottles Aleve
Allergy medications	Sinus, allergy medications
Assorted non-stick dressings	Assorted large non-stick dressings
Two bottles, Advil and Tylenol	Stethoscope
Assorted safety pins	Assorted safety pins
One and two-inch wide Ace bandages, two each	Two and three-inch wide Ace bandages, two each
8 oz. tube of aloe gel	Blood pressure cuff
Two trauma pads	Four trauma pads
8 oz. bottle normal saline	8 oz. bottle normal saline
Assorted rubber bands	Four rubber tourniquets
100 pairs small latex surgical gloves	100 pairs large latex surgical gloves
Penlight and spare batteries	Two small tubes super glue
Bottle meat tenderizer	Bottle meat tenderizer
Medium tube of toothpaste	Four tubes denture adhesive
Four containers dental floss	Small field first-aid manual
Small bottle disinfectant gel	Small field trauma care manual
Pad of paper and two small sharpened pencils	Small natural medicines manual
Two large bandannas	Four large bandannas
One surplus army poncho	One surplus army poncho
Twenty tongue depressors	Twenty tongue depressors
Twenty-four condoms	Twenty-four condoms

LARRY D. HORTON, PhD

Each of us carries assorted specific meds for any potential problems for us or the dogs. We each carry a redundant supply of the following. For the dogs: anti-runs meds for obvious purpose, topical wound cream, cotton strips for bandages, anti-itch/flea meds., and eye inflammation meds. Typical dog antibiotics. We carry a supply of individual specific prescription meds for our personal needs related to joint pain, fibromyalgia, blood pressure, cholesterol, anti-run meds (Imodium), and a three-month supply of multiple vitamins. Lastly, I carry a small paperback field manual related to natural safe foods, their identification and preparation. Including bags my wife's bag probably weighs in at 6 or 7 lbs., mine probably at 10 to 11 lbs. Completing the above review allowed us to do an up-to-date inventory of our med. supplies.

Our **communication** resources consist of the following: personal cell phones, 24 glow sticks, a medium sized NOAA AM/FM radio with battery, solar, or crank charging with 24 spare batteries, a total weight of five pounds, which I carry on my utility belt. My wife carries a smaller version NOAA AM/FM radio with the same charging options and spare batteries on her utility belt. These radios have the capability of charging our cell phones using cords/attachments which we brought. The larger has a built-in capability to send a preprogrammed SOS strobe beacon. Both have LED flashlights as well. Our space blankets can serve as a rescue beacon if necessary.

The next area for review and inventory is items related to **fire** starting. We each carry a small Pelican box on our utility belts. Each is stocked with redundant fire starting tools and tinder fire starters. The larger supplies of some of the materials are also on our utility belts as long-term backups.

To be more specific, the following fire materials are carried in a three-level redundant fashion. We individually carry each of these.

Utility Belts	IOSs	Main Packs	Total Carried
Two Bic lighters	Two Bic lighters	Two Bic lighters	Twelve lighters
One ferro stick	One ferro stick	One ferro stick	Six ferro sticks
Waterproof matches	Waterproof matches	Waterproof matches	240 matches
Forty tampons	Twenty tampons	Sixty tampons	240 tampons
Sixty cotton-balls	Twenty cotton-balls	100 cotton-balls	360 cotton-balls
Four oz. tube Vaseline	Two oz. tube Vaseline	Four oz. tube Vaseline	Twenty oz. Vaseline

In addition, we each carry a specialized fire starting file in our main packs. As we travel, we will scrounge for appropriate tinder materials, keeping a kitchen garbage bag full of it at all times if possible and stored on the Trekker.

We also packed the following **General materials.**

Two pairs of EMT surgical scissors, one in each of our utility belts
Whetstones of assorted sizes, one small one in each IOS and one medium one in each utility belt
Assorted zip ties in my main pack
Assorted bungee cords on the Trekker
Three small 500-pound capacity "come-alongs" on the Trekker
Extra batteries, 24 each, AAA, AA, C, and D, on the Trekker
Twenty-four extra quart and gallon size Ziploc bags
Fifty feet of fine diameter rolled steel wire
1,000 feet of lightweight thread
120 alcohol wet wipes, sixty in each of our utility belts
Twenty sq. feet of plastic paint drop sheet, folded, in bottom of my pack
Four rolls, twenty-four-inch wide aluminum foil, unrolled and folded, in bottom of each main pack

All the materials and supplies reviewed and inventoried over the last couple days were packed in quart Ziploc bags to make them waterproof. When added together they create some weight, so we split the load between the two of us and the Trekker. We are prepared to cull this all down to critical elements if and when the Trekker is no longer viable. Combo of critical materials, our clothing, weapons, tools, shelter, and sleeping resources will require some careful weight planning, given time of year we are walking and our physical conditioning. More on that plan tomorrow. It was a worthwhile exercise to use the four hours to do this inventory. Having it gives us a significant decision-making leg up when we come to the point of abandoning the Trekker. It also gives us a sense of assurance that we will be able to deal with most, if not all, situations that we will encounter.

At 3 PM as I was finishing a call to the latrine I heard a small vehicle stop at the bottom of the gradual hill on which our camp is located. Immediately alert I watched as a middle-aged man started up the hill with his dog beside him. The dog looked familiar from the run in the middle of the other night. Appeared to have no weapons, so I stepped out and we spoke. He asked if we were OK. He had been hearing dogs, observed smoke from our fires, light from our LED lamps and flashlights for several days. He asked if we could talk. I agreed and invited him to the camp. Our dogs, on their long leashes, immediately became very animated. It didn't take long till all three dogs were doing their dog thing, smelling each other, and running in circles. Wife and I spent thirty minutes explaining why we were there, what our goal was, how we had traveled to this point, and where we hoped to end up—some details but not everything. He indicated that he and his wife had eighty acres. The pine tree grove we are in is on the northern edge of his land. He has six head of cows, couple pigs, couple dozen chickens, and has lived on this land most of his life. We made hot coffee and sipped it as we talked. Asked him if our being on his land is a problem. He said not at all and that we should have visited them earlier. Told him of our plan to break camp tomorrow as early as possible after policing the area making sure it's back to original as much as possible.

He then threw us a big curve. Day after tomorrow he will be driving his truck north to Frankfort OH where country Ag Agent and feed store are located. A drive of about eight miles from where we were all sitting. He offered to load us and all of our stuff into his truck early that day and tote us to the vicinity of Frankfort. We looked at each other, not believing what we were hearing. We said yes as long as it is no trouble to him. His response was that he and his wife have wanted to do something for someone, given all the trouble that has been happening and we appeared to be an answer to their prayers. That comment led us to share our faith and he the same with us.

We finished our conversation with prayers and a handshake. He told us to be at the roadside at the bottom of the hill at 9 AM day after tomorrow, and we agreed. With that he headed back to his RV, dog in tow, and we heard him drive off. Of course, our dogs wanted to go too, but we held them back. After a few minutes, we just sat and looked off into the distance. We finally looked at each other and knew how grateful we both were. It means staying hunkered down an additional day, but that will be just fine.

We decided to have a bit more special supper so dug out some of the freeze-dried chicken, cooked it with rice and beans, and the four of us had a thanksgiving meal. Temperatures were moderating a bit but we didn't even notice the cold as we climbed into our sleeping bags. Feel sleep coming easily after prayers and scripture. Thank you!

To You, O Lord, I lift up my soul,
O my God, in You I trust.
(Psalm 25:1–2)

Day #30, February 19: Good night's sleep. Day chores continued in what had become normal: shelter, water, food, and meals, more or less at same time as previous days. Spent AM completing inventory of remaining topics which follows below. PM spent in initial breaking down of the camp, getting ready to leave tomorrow. NOAA weather forecast for next seven days was for temps in the thirties, cloudy with a bit of sun, low winds, and some flurries. Snow cover from last big storm may melt a bit, creating some standing and running water. Fields and cross country walking will be much harder. We may have to bite the bullet and stick to secondary and dirt roads most of the time. We will soon know. We are anxious to get started on our way again. Tired of sitting. Grateful again for neighbor's offer to drive us a few miles to the north.

Seventh area of catch-up has to do with **clothing**. What we are carrying given the time of the year: starting our trip in January, heading north from TX into much more serious winter conditions, meant that we had to choose clothing very carefully. At the same time, we had to consider that we would not finish our trip at best until late spring or early summer. That meant a bit more complexity in our clothing planning. Our packing plan led to the following basic clothing resources for each of us.

Two pairs of blue jeans
Ten pairs of wool socks, mid-calf length
Seven days of underwear changes
Two sets of wool long-johns, aka. union suits with flaps in the back
Four long-sleeve wicking T-shirts
Three short-sleeve wicking T-shirts
Two long-sleeve flannel shirts with high button collars
One low temperature rated hooded winter coat
Two pairs of leather gloves, one lightweight and one heavy duty
One pair ankle tall camp shoes with large vibram tread
One pair heavy duty twelve-inch high leather boots with large vibram tread
One lightweight waterproof jacket
One heavy duty Army surplus poncho
One lightweight poncho
Two knit snow caps, one full face
One baseball cap
One pair denim shorts
One towel, one face cloth
One pair gaiters
One cotton hoodie
Two wool scarves
Two dog sweaters sized for our dogs
Two sets per dog paw booties for cold weather

We restricted ourselves to between 20 and 22 pounds of carried clothing due to our physical ability to carry heavy weight loads in our packs. Minimum of half weight in packs would be critical food. We did not carry any clothing items on Trekker due to their critical nature and in case we had to abandon the Trekker at a moment's notice. The preceding list would have looked quite a bit different had we begun our journey in late spring.

The eighth area of catch-up is an **inventory and plan for our food supply** moving forward. The following items are packed in our packs. Additional items are packed onto the Trekker again hoping we will be able to use the "Trekker" long-term.

Ten lbs. dry dog food, two lbs. in each pack, balance on Trekker
Fifty lbs. assorted freeze-dried food, ten lbs. wife's pack, twenty lbs. my pack, balance on Trekker
One lb. special treats like hard candy
Twenty lbs. combined rice and beans, five lbs. in each pack, ten lbs. on Trekker
300 coffee packets, 200 tea bags, three lbs. in each pack, balance on Trekker
One two lb. container iodized salt in my pack
Five lbs. sugar in one lb. splits, quart sized Ziploc bags, one in wife's pack, four in mine
Two containers of meat tenderizer and basic spices split between us
One set each, personal cooking/camping flatware, pot, cup, and small saucepan/plate combo
One set of two larger cooking pots, one quart and one gallon, carried externally on my pack
Two cooking spoons, two cooking forks, one medium kitchen knife, one small kitchen knife in my pack
One dishrag and drying towel in each pack
Each pack, one 8 oz. bottle concentrated dishwashing soap
Each pack, one salt and one pepper shaker
Two water straws each pack

Our plan, for food when combined with packed clothing, is for my wife's pack to top out at around 30 to 35 lbs. My pack will top out between 45 and 50 lbs.

The final area of catch-up is our **packing and carrying tools plan.** As we completed our inventory the last two days we then packed our backpacks accordingly. They will be ready to go tomorrow morning as if the Trekker did not exist. Again, the weight for my wife's pack will be between 30 and 35 lbs. My main pack will be between 45 and 50 lbs. We had to make some tough decisions but we made them. The Trekker is a lifesaver at this point because our plan is to place completed main packs on the Trekker and only start carrying them when absolutely necessary. We hope that day will be a long time in coming. We will only touch our main packs for clothing changes and cooking utensils on a normal day. We will use up supplies carried on the Trekker until they are gone and then begin using food from inside of our main packs.

Fully equipped for walking, we will each be carrying the following:

1. Main packs, wife's 30–35 lbs., mine 45–50 lbs.
2. One medical kit bag each
3. One utility belt each with the following materials attached or in pouches on belt
   Primary personal blade
   Hand ax on my utility belt
   Fire kits
   Personal one qt. canteen
   Stainless steel water bottle, for drinking, water for dogs, and boiling water
   NOAA radios, wife carrying small one, me the medium sized one
   Twenty rounds firearm ammo for each weapon, with me carrying the balance in the main ammo belt
   An emergency space blanket
   One machete which I will carry
4. Personal primary handgun and holster, concealed in holster in coat pocket or attached to belt at all times

5. Air rifle carried by wife, Scoped 17 HMR carried by me
6. I will carry a single bladed ax and bow saw
7. Rolled sleeping bag and foam ground pad
8. Wife will carry lightweight tarp
9. I will carry heavy duty primary shelter tarp

After completing our resources inventory, packing it all over the last two days, and then lifting the finished packs, utility belts, and attached items, it is clear that initially we will be pushing the limits of our abilities to carry it all as packed. We reviewed the packs and decided to leave the weight as it appeared to be and plan for fewer miles and more rest stops for at least a week or two, to give us the chance to build up our strength. In addition, we will be using food packets after abandoning the Trekker which will lessen the overall weight over time. Not the best plan but the only thing that makes sense to us given the trip ahead. We also decided that we will do a weekly review of our packed and carried resources. If necessary, we might have to make some tough decisions and leave some materials behind along our walking route. We are determined that we will not push our luck. Injuries could be a big problem. Add to all of this the fact that each of us will have a dog on a leash while walking will make our daily treks very interesting and likely more difficult. We accept that as reality.

We spent the last couple hours of daylight in the afternoon beginning to break down the camp as much as we could—basically, policing the area as much as possible. At last light, I went out and collected our wire snare traps. To my surprise, we had two rabbits. Cleaned them and hung them from our food pole for the night. They will be quite frozen in the morning. Plan is to give them to the neighbor who is giving us a ride in the AM, along with $50 from our cash stash. We will not take no for an answer. Warm supper for all, then turned on radio. NOAA weather forecasts a definite break tomorrow. Highs to forty degrees during next five days. Lows around freezing with light wind. Chance for a few -flurries each morning but nothing serious. Prayers said and scripture read. A lot of things done over the last two days. We feel rested and ready to start walking again. Conditions will be different with melting snow. Lots of water around but bit warmer temps. That will be appreciated.

For Your lovingkindness is before my eyes,
And I have walked in Your truth.
(Psalm 26:3)

Day #31, February 20: One month since we backed out of our driveway in TX. Parked truck on Feb. 2nd and set out on foot 18 days ago. Prior to today walked approx. 26–28 miles. With lift today, we added another 15 miles by vehicle to just south of Clarksburg OH. We then started walking and covered another 3 to 4 miles, stopping above Deer Creek about 2 miles east of Clarksburg OH. Will explain why our ride took us further than originally planned. By the end of today as we sat by the fire in our temporary camp, we had traveled on foot, plus short ride, a total of 53 to 55 miles since leaving truck. Doesn't sound like much, but given our extended hunker-down near Lattaville, we are doing OK. Still looking at between 350 and 400 miles of walking.

Our ride picked us up at 9 AM and took us further than planned. As he dropped us off, gave us a local map with side roads marked directly east to Yellowbud OH area where we could use a bridge to cross the Scioto River. We gave him the two rabbits and $50, which he did not want to accept, but we insisted.

Once unloaded, we set off on foot with the Trekker in tow. Weather was OK. Snow melting some. Probably four to five inches on the ground, so we stayed on side roads that were marked on map. It was wet. We started walking around 11:00 AM with a goal of stopping and making camp for the night around 2 PM. We were feeling pretty good from extended hunker-down. No problems with hypothermia to this point, but constantly on guard against it. Knew that once in camp we would have to set up some kind of sleeping platform to keep us off the cold ground. Stopped briefly around noon and had cold lunch. Dogs were excited that we were moving again. They had been in one place long enough. Full of energy which made pulling the Trekker an adventure.

At 2:15 PM found good place in small grove of trees to set up camp about 100 yards off the road. Scrounged for fallen logs, mostly under snow, and cut additional ones we needed. First task was to get a fire going. Used tinder we had been carrying and a couple tampons soaked in Vaseline with Bic lighter. Had collected dead branches from trees in small grove to be initial larger fuel. Knocked down a dead tree and using bow saw cut up initial logs. More wood to collect for fire once shelter built. Shelter using Trekker as base was a simple lean-to. Build sleeping platform eight feet long, six feet wide, eight inches off the ground, with short support poles and main structure connected using paracord. Added six two-inch thick cross members and wove branches into the structure. Cut branches from nearby pines to function as mattress and covered with secondary tarp. Main lean-to structure completed over sleeping platform. Tied small logs described above with paracord. Angle of roof was approx. thirty degrees. Much closer quarters than in our more sophisticated hunker-down camp, but functional. Took couple hours to get initial fire and shelter in place. We decided to try to use same design for temporary camps. We would get better at building them with practice. Biggest unknown was availability of materials at future locations.

While wife secured and boiled water from nearby stream, as well as cooking our supper, I went about gathering as much firewood as possible. When done used some of the logs as fire reflector structure and piled wet wood near fire to dry it out as much as possible. After supper listened to NOAA weather forecast and a few minutes of news. Weather is to hold for another three to five days before it turns very cold again. News both domestically and internationally about the same. Lots of uncertainty. Everyone on alert. No events since the last ones I noted earlier. Prayers said, scripture read, we bedded down about 9 PM. Bundled up. Low temp is to be around freezing.

> **The Lord is my light and my salvation;**
> **Whom shall I fear?**
> **The Lord is the defense of my life;**
> **Whom shall I dread?**
> **(Psalm 27:1)**

LARRY D. HORTON, PhD

Date: February 21   Mileage: 4 mi.

Stopped for the day approx. three miles west of Yellowbud OH. If all goes well tomorrow, should be able to cross the Scioto River and get a mile or so east of the river before setting up for the next night's camp. A bit more traffic on secondary and dirt roads that our ride had mapped out for us. Most everyone drives by us staring. A couple have slowed down to ask if we are OK, but no one to this point has given us any trouble. After breaking down camp, having breakfast of oatmeal, plus dog food for dogs, and repacking our stuff we headed out around 9 AM. Plan again was to walk four miles and stop for night around 2 PM. Weather was cooperating. As day wore on, more snow melted. Fields were mush. Glad we had a seemingly safe route on dirt and secondary roads to travel. Dogs settled down from yesterday. They were just glad to be moving. Stopped long enough at lunch to heat up some soup using our hexamine stove and fuel. Warm soup hit the spot. Dogs kept staring, so we gave them a bit even though had some spices they didn't need. Lots of rest stops watching sweating. Not too tired but cautious regarding hypothermia.

Country was pretty hilly, some up and down on roads walking. Shortly after 2 PM spotted a sheltered stand of trees in lee of small hillside. Headed there on a rutted path likely used by hunters and local farmers. Land is tough for farming but seems people are trying. Repeated build-out of shelter like yesterday. Tough finding firewood and structure logs that would work. Took longer than hoped. Things were pretty wet. Knocked down some standing small dead trees to build shelter and to cut up some firewood. Did this very carefully. Collected as much as possible on the ground. Was wet, so tried to find stuff that had been sheltered from snow and snow melt. Stacked wood near fire to help it dry out. Not sure had enough to keep fire going for night. Might be a cold one. Dampness was not helping. Hung wet clothing, socks, and boots as near to fire as possible to dry out some. After boiling water from nearby stream, washed our bodies, washed out socks, and hung them to dry. Temps pretty much the same. Probably around freezing during the night. Dogs glad to be in shelter. Dried them off as much as possible before letting them climb into sleeping bags. Didn't need their wet bodies next to us.

Boiling water, cooking supper, drying things out as much as possible, and airing out sleeping bags with dogs lying on them took up our evening. One thing we noticed was how dark it was at night. Had been that way every night, but seemed especially dark this night. Must have been cloud cover. Changed out batteries in radio and listened to news and Christian music. Reception not too good but got Circleville Bible College station and was OK. NOAA weather now predicting big cold snap in four days so we need to be planning on another short hunker-down, two to three days, until it moderates. Everyone tired from walking and setting up camp, even taking short breaks every thirty minutes today. We are feeling stronger walking and pulling the Trekker. No cross-country hiking is probably helping. Supper hit the spot. Cooked over fire pasta, freeze-dried veggies, and pudding. Dogs liked it a lot. Bundled up and hit the sack around 9 PM. Lay there listening to all the sounds around us. Critters were out and about, so kept fire going as well as possible, with weapons at hand just in case. Prayers said, scripture read, finally called it a night.

The Lord is my strength and my shield;
My heart trusts in Him, and I am helped.
(Psalm 28:7)

LARRY D. HORTON, PhD

Date: February 22   Mileage: 4 mi.

Up bright and early this morning. Lots of critter noises nosing around our camp during the night. Cows bellowing in the distance. Roosters crowing. Civilization not too far away. No real disturbances during the night. Up several times to make sure the fire was not going out. Seems like we are settling into a routine pretty quickly. No time to get bored, just staying very busy with the same chores. Breakfast of oatmeal and coffee. Dogs got dog food and oatmeal mixed together. Broke camp. Policed area. Put things back as much as possible the way we found them. Packed camp garbage into bag to load onto Trekker. Going to do that until we have to hunker down again where we can burn and bury it. Dogs were ready to get moving. Set out about 9 AM as usual with goal of getting across Scioto River and camping mile or two to the east of that crossing.

Bridge was one-lane country bridge. Pretty easy to travel. While crossing, looked to south and saw a large marsh stretching southward. How grateful we were to the one who had pointed us to the bridge. We would have had to walk along the river, slow progress, without guidance, until we found the bridge on our own. No way to cross the marsh. A valley leads from the bridge to the east with a dirt country road that we were told to use. Up and down quite a bit. Obviously not much traffic on this particular road as grass was growing along the middle. Up and down put a bit of strain on us with the Trekker. With a lot of rest stops we did make it about a mile east of the bridge crossing before starting to look for place to spend the night.

Finally found a lee side of a hill with quite a bit of pine tree cover. Was off the road about 100 yards. No path, so had to relay everything to a good site about 50 yards up a hillside. Relaying put us behind quite a bit, so not ready to set up camp until around 3 PM. Decided would go with bare minimum for the night: a fire, a simple tarp shelter, and a horizontal pole between two trees to hang up food. Not much water, but able to boil about a gallon. Gathered some firewood for the night.

Cooked supper and bedded down. Again, tried to dry things by the fire as much as possible. Simple supper of beans and rice which the dogs liked and filled us up. Hot tea, and hard candy was a treat. NOAA and local weather reports indicated cold front will move through in about 48 hours. Cold will last three days. Decided to walk for couple more days. Will stop earlier on 2nd day and get set to hunker down for three to four days until cold snap ends. Everything will freeze up big time. We will have as priorities, shelter, firewood and fire, water, and warmth. Already dark when we got camp set up. Grateful for LED headlamps. Dogs not a problem getting into the sack. Built small sleeping platform using the main tarp. Shelter cover was secondary tarp with no logs or branches added; simple. Weapons at hand. Lots of critter sign. Prayers said, scripture read, up early tomorrow.

Ascribe to the Lord the glory due to His name;
Worship the Lord in holy array.
(Psalm 29:2)

Date: February 23   Mileage: 5 mi.   Walk Total: 58–60 miles.

Goal today was to end up couple miles west of Leistville OH. We came pretty close to that. Not exactly sure how close we are, but step counting gave us approx. distance traveled. Out in the country. No real landmarks to triangulate from using compass, but can hear traffic from route 56 or 159. Should have a more exact location fix tomorrow. Temps about the same, cloudy skies, and dampness in the air. Lots of breaks today but we seemed to make good progress.

Breakfast was usual oatmeal and coffee. Dog food for dogs. Lunch quick soup cooked over hexamine stove, shared a bit with dogs. At 2 PM found grove of trees and small stream a couple hundred feet off our travel road. No fences to cross, but soggy ground made it more difficult to pull Trekker to location. Nice small cleared area amid grove of oaks and maples. No pine trees. Quite a bit of fallen timber in area looks like someone had come in and cut down some trees and left brush in small piles from the cutting. Farmhouse probably one-half mile further up the road. Didn't notice any sign of life until yard and house lights came on at dark. Barking from dogs there set our dogs off for a bit. Kept an eye open for four legged visitors coming to check us out.

Started to set up camp around 2:30 PM. Process similar to last couple nights. Using Trekker, built simple lean-to shelter. Not much snow in the clearing among trees, so decided not to build sleeping platform. Opting instead to build a couple foot thick layer of small tree branches covered with secondary tarp and our bedding to protect us from cold ground. Winds were picking up a bit so covered open ends of lean-to with branches as well. Big task of gathering firewood. Little on the ground. Luckily found couple small dead trees which I knocked down and cut up. Fire circle with crude reflector wall using space blanket set up. Was able to secure water supply, but as always boiled every drop. Filled our two gallon jugs with water for tomorrow and enough to cook supper. Supper was beans, rice, freeze-dried beef from our supplies, and hot tea. Dogs liked the beans, rice, and beef combination. They are looking a little thinner, but I imagine wife and I are as well. Couple vehicles slowed on dirt road we had been walking while eating supper. Imagine they saw smoke from our fire and were curious. Didn't stop which was good.

Know we have one more decent day to get some miles in. Day after tomorrow we will have to make serious effort to find short-term hunker-down location to sit out cold and freezing event that is coming. We will have to jump at best possible site for that, so may not travel very far. So be it. More tired this evening. Dogs pretty quiet. Lots of noises in the vicinity as we bedded down for the night. NOAA radio confirmed forecast. We spent some time checking all four of us for skin, critter, and cleanliness issues before climbing into sleeping bags. No big problems. Covered couple sore spots on feet with second skin and bandages. Prayers said, scripture read.

Hear, O Lord, and be gracious to me;
O Lord, be my helper.
(Psalm 30:10)

Date: February 24   Mileage: 5 mi.   Walk Total: 63–65 miles.

Up early. A chilly night but stayed pretty warm. Broke camp, packed up, and breakfast of oatmeal and coffee. Goal today was to travel northeast and get to point west of Tarlton OH close to Salt Creek. As near as can figure, ended up northwest of Tarlton OH near Cross Mound Park. Used dirt and secondary roads again. Snow melt stopped. A cloudy day. Before we started out on the day listened to NOAA weather and local weather. Front is to come in midday tomorrow with much colder temps, sleet, freezing rain, and slight chance of flurries. Decided our camp tonight will be next hunker-down point for four to five days to allow front to pass and temps to get a bit better. Will spend late afternoon and tomorrow morning building out a better more substantial camp to weather the storm. Finished our walk by 2 PM with short breaks and a hot lunch cooked over hexamine stove. We pushed pretty hard because we knew we needed time to prepare. Dogs were pretty good other than their wanting to go slower so they could explore. Few sightings of other humans. People mostly going about their daily business. No one paid much attention to us.

Decided on campsite within couple hundred yards of Salt Creek. Country is pretty hilly. Creek sits in a small valley headed up hill. Found pretty sheltered area on lee of good-sized hill and decided to make camp there. Creek is not very wide but inspection showed no sign of critters using it for a water source above us. Campsite on edge of wooded area. Lots of wood available. Fairly flat area to set up on. Given time frame of four to five days, built a reinforced lean-to for our shelter but otherwise very similar to our last hunker-down shelter. Sleeping platform, a small log framework with branches interwoven on shelter sides and on sleeping platform. Covered roof with primary tarp. Set up secondary shelter for Trekker and firewood supply. Wife built fire ring, got fire started, and collected couple gallons of water to boil. I set about gathering as much firewood as possible, cutting some into bigger fire logs. Initial fire was three four-foot logs placed horizontally on each other with fire started at center. Plan was to move logs into fire as center burned away. Will last quite a while built this way. We have a pretty good view out front of shelter down to road we were traveling. Last thing completed before calling it a day was to dig a trench around shelter for rain runoff. Temps dropped pretty dramatically late afternoon and into the early evening. Quite a bit of sweating given work load. Changed clothing and hung up damp stuff to dry by fire. Last thing done was to build cover and heat reflecting structure for fire using space blankets and small log walls. Seems to work pretty well. Clothing slow to dry but it is working. Humidity is high and last clouds we saw were dark and threatening. Weather looks like it will get nasty sometime tomorrow. Supper of beans, rice, and tea. Dogs devoured beans and rice. Several more projects to complete tomorrow morning before weather really goes south to batten down the hatches. Using lengths of regular rope we were carrying, tied everything down securely. Used noggins on all vertical columns to give them additional strength. Wife able to get couple gallons of water boiled. More water boiling tomorrow.

Listened to Christian music on Circleville Bible College station. Then listened to NOAA and local forecasts. Now saying by noon tomorrow weather will set in and nasty stuff will last minimum of three days. Sleet, freezing rain, wind, and temps dropping. Highs in high twenties during daytime. Lows in high teens at night. Coldest weather yet. Add in moisture and we are bound to get cold. AM tomorrow will be full time collecting wood which is damp already. Fire is going to be very important to us for time being. Said lots of prayers for safety, and read scripture. Bundled up with dogs in sleeping bags for cold night. Clothing had dried some. Put it in bottom of sleeping bags so it would use some of our body heat to keep drying. Got all rain gear out and hung from shelter beams. It will be critical for us. Last check was on food supply hanging from support pole between two trees. Covered with plastic sheeting we had packed. Hoping for a decent night's rest. Good night.

You are my hiding place;
You preserve me from trouble;
You surround me with songs of deliverance.
(Psalm 32:7)

LARRY D. HORTON, PhD

Date: February 25–28   Mileage: 0 mi.   Walk Total: 63–65 miles.

Feb. 25, Day #36:

Up early. Much colder, higher winds, and very dark clouds out of northwest. Hill sheltered us some from the winds but still was biting. Quick breakfast of oatmeal and tea. Dogs had some dog food as well. They were not excited about getting out of warm bags in the shelter. Quickly dug a latrine fifty yards to our west. Then spent the rest of the AM, three hours, collecting as much firewood as possible. By noon had three by three by three-foot stack under secondary shelter and several more four-foot logs for our horizontal fire. Placed additional wood beside part of fire pit that was sheltered under space blankets and stacked as much as possible near fire to dry it out. So glad we have been collecting tinder as we traveled. Cotton ball soaked in Vaseline is a great way to get fire started. Lunch of hot soup. Prior to cooking, built substantial structure above fire to hang cooking pots from. Makes it easier to control heat and boil water. Two thick forked sticks with a horizontal crossbeam between them. Fabricated couple hanging hooks from thick sticks to hang from crossbeam to hold cooking pots. Just like you see in the movies. Also, collected stones, as flat as possible, and built a semicircle next to fire to sit pots and water purification bottles on to allow them to get radiant heat and boil water. Whole system seems to work OK. Hung sleeping bags from front shelter horizontal support so radiant heat from fire will work on drying them. We stripped down and washed as much of our bodies as possible. Likely not do this again for a few days until weather changes.

Aired out boots, socks, and feet. Feet doing OK but pretty damp from last couple days. Wet weather is going to make it critical that we dry them out every day and evening. Forecast is a bit off. Nasty stuff didn't start until 1 PM. Cold drizzle, freezing rain, and sleet for the rest of the afternoon. Winds up a bit too, which means checking for shelter leaks constantly and reinforcing dripping areas and where we feel wind coming into shelter. Routine all afternoon was keeping warm fire going, collecting water in containers set up around the camp from light rain, keeping dogs in shelter so they won't get everything wet, hauling water, collecting wood from under trees that kept some of the rain off it, and just trying to stay as warm as possible. Ponchos are invaluable right now, keeping us reasonably dry when doing chores.

When not doing those chores, sat or lay in shelter. Nothing stirring in the woods or below us in the valley. Animals, both four legged and human, were obviously hunkered down sitting out the weather as well. Did hear something that sounded like a coyote for about five minutes, the only sound all afternoon other than our dogs. Decided not to undertake any other tasks for balance of day, as we need to just stay warm. Also, decided that tomorrow, when time is available, will pull out maps and decide on general travel plan for next thirty to forty-five days after we start out again. Very glad to have more detailed maps of each state we are traveling through. Also, know that we are heading into country that we have been in for most of our life at various times and we will be able to navigate fairly well. However, traveling off the beaten path will require constant daily adjustment of travel directions and plans. Even though familiar with general area we are heading into, know that anything could throw a curve at us, and we will just have to trust our instincts and skills. Also, rest of trip will be through some heavily populated areas which will require additional alertness. More population means more chances for danger and confrontation, and it will be much harder to stay off the grid and avoid discovery. Countryside will be much hillier with more waterways to cross and more up and down for rest of the trip.

Simple supper of soup and freeze dried veggies. Doubt we'll be able to add any game to meals. Will set out traps tomorrow, but seems critters are hunkered down as well. Our weather will be with us another forty-eight to seventy-two hours. Talked a lot about trip so far. We are OK. Bundled up, socks on hands, full face hats on, couple layers of clothing, sleeping bags zipped, and fire doing OK, we said prayers, read scripture and hugged everyone. Brrrrrrrr! Lord, protect us.

The counsel of the Lord stands forever,
The plans of His heart from generation to generation.
(Psalm 33:11)

LARRY D. HORTON, PhD

Date: February 25–28   Mileage: 0 mi.   Walk Total: 63–65 miles.

Feb. 26 Day #37:

Woke up around 6 AM. Bad night for sleeping. Very cold. Winds howling. Dogs were uncomfortable as were we. Fire had to be tended quite a bit even with the space blankets over it. Coating of ice on everything. Heard lots of deadfalls during the night around us, but nothing hit our shelter. Glad we built camp carefully, looking up for that possibility. Light snow falling. Wind blowing it through the smallest holes in our shelter walls. More work to do today to shore them up. Checked secondary wood shelter and food hanging from above ground. Covered with ice but seemed to be pretty dry. After got fire going well again, cooked oatmeal and rice for breakfast with hot cup of coffee. Dogs started to explore a bit, but as soon as they felt sleet and wind, were back on top of sleeping platform trying to stay warm. Fed them some dog food and a bit of oatmeal.

Weather forecast was right. Glad we stopped a bit early and built our temporary home. Clothing was still damp so kept it set by fire under protection. Going to take quite a while before it's reasonably dry. Spent first couple hours after breakfast tending to fire and gathering wood. Looked under overhanging trees for most of it and stacked by fire to aid it drying out. Wife very uncomfortable. Cold weather makes her fibromyalgia bad. So joint pain has increased. Dressed as warmly as we could while trying to avoid overheating and potential hypothermia. Once fire and wood situation was as good as we could make it, set out three snare traps in hopes of getting lucky and catching rabbit or maybe a squirrel. Time will tell. Lunch was hot soup and some rice. A cup of hot chocolate as well. We are becoming aware that all four of us are losing a bit of weight. Need more protein for strength and stamina. Will have to get really serious about adding meat to our diet from critters. Wish streams were not frozen over with ice. May try to cut hole in ice tomorrow on Salt Creek and see if can get lucky with that. Not too hopeful, as fish are not going to be very active in weather this cold. No real pools of water in stream as it is pretty small where we are located. But have to make the effort.

As I said yesterday did some trip planning in general terms using our maps in the early afternoon. General plan is to go straight east from current location so we can then turn north from well east of Columbus OH area. Once around Millersburg OH will turn straight east toward Dover OH crossing I-77. From there we will go NNE toward the PA line south of the Canton and Youngstown area, likely crossing into PA east of Columbiana OH. Once cross PA line will head north between Youngstown OH and Pittsburgh PA and travel east of Bessemer PA. From that point we will go NE toward Franklin PA. From there we will travel pretty much east to Leeper PA then on to Cook Forest State Park area where we will cross the Clarion River where it is shallow or at the bridge in Cooksburg, an area I am pretty familiar with. That is the plan but realize we will likely adjust it as we go due to conditions of environment and people. At least we have a go by from where we are currently located. Circumstances will dictate how close we can stick to it. Our biggest concern will be people and geography. Add those to our physical condition, and we have no idea how long it will take.

Been a very cold day. Spent most of it hunkered down in shelter near fire. Dogs didn't venture very far. Only to take care of necessities, which means having to get out and clean it up and deposit in our latrine. Other necessity is boiling water most of the afternoon to make sure we have sufficient supply. Drank quite a bit of water including couple mugs of orange drink. One thing I should also mention, which I haven't to this point, is that we daily take vitamin supplements to help us maintain strength and energy. Our attitudes have been pretty good given stress we are under. Fire and warmth have been a great help. We have been thinking about long-term weather some. We are hoping for spring to start early this year. But thaw will bring another set of challenges, rain, mud, swollen streams, storms, and wind. Given how cold it currently is we would take an early thaw and then deal with the challenges that come with it.

For supper, hot soup, freeze-dried veggies, and some pudding to add some sugar to our diet. Dogs not so hot on veggies, but they ate them. Before we bundled up and shut down for the night, listened to NOAA weather. More of the same tonight and tomorrow. Another forty-eight hours of this weather. So we may have to stay put for an extra day to make sure things get a bit better before striking out. Also, listened to news report for about fifteen minutes to catch up a bit. Seems after a month in office new president is taking some of the promised steps identified during election campaign. Lots of unhappiness in the country. Slow progress on figuring out last series of attacks that scared everyone. Internationally, Iran is getting much more belligerent. Middle East is a mess. China continues to build out situation in South Asia waters. Russia continues to defy the world in its current efforts to regain power within its geographic area and beyond. Everything brought up in election campaign seems to be happening. Our country is not just sliding down a slippery slope anymore; it is in free-fall. It is only a matter of time, probably short, until we see more attacks within our borders. Not fun things to think about, but at least we are controlling what happens to us personally as much as we can. We can't control what others do. Multiple layers of clothing, gloves, full head gear, fire stoked, and long logs added to the fire for the night. Prayers said, scripture read, we settled in to sleep as warmly as possible. Still periodic sleet and freezing rain with a few snowflakes sprinkled in. Lord, watch over us. Keep us and our families safe another night. Tomorrow will be a new day with its own unique challenges.

I sought the Lord, and He answered me,
And delivered me from all my fears.
(Psalm 34:4)

Date: February 25–28   Mileage: 0 mi.   Walk Total: 63–65 miles.

Feb. 27 Day #38:

Even colder last night than night before. Didn't get much sleep. Will have to try and catch up later today. Normal breakfast of oatmeal, rice, and coffee. Dogs a little lethargic this morning. The cold is getting to them just as it is to us. Post breakfast, collected water from Salt Creek. Had to break through ice to get to it. Ground very slippery. Glad we prepared strong walking poles many days ago. Moved some firewood close to fire to help dry it out. Fire kept going at pretty high level because it is so cold. Sky is very dark. Weather change not in the works as of this morning. Hung clothing and sleeping bags close to fire to dry out as much as possible. Changed our clothing, washed and dried feet, pits, and bodies as much as possible. Glad we have sweaters for the dogs. Washed them as well. Dog smell getting pretty strong. Checked dog's feet for cold effects. So far so good. Also glad we brought along dog booties for them. They don't fuss at all with them on. Spent hour very slowly cranking both NOAA and AM/FM radios to charge batteries. Surprising how even that can work up a sweat, so very careful. Checked our feet, hands, and faces for effects of cold. Nothing much to see, but being very cautious. Wearing two layers of socks and two layers of gloves; thin cotton ones under leather ones seem to help. But even taking them off for fifteen-minutes, hands get very cold. Checked our blood pressures and heart rates. They were both pretty normal. Cold is slowing everything down. Going to spend day resting and conserving energy other than fetching and boiling water or building up wood supply. Thank goodness there is quite a bit of dead timber and logs in the area.

Spent a good hour listening to the radio once we turned it on. Things hitting the fan all over the place. Given what I said yesterday think I should have been a person who predicted the future in the past. Not rocket science to predict what we heard this morning.

Overnight Iran fired multiple ship-to-ship rockets at two US destroyers in the Strait of Hormuz. Severe damage to one, minor to the other.

Multiple sailors killed and wounded. US military response was to fire back and sink four Iranian fast-attack boats. US warplanes were in the air but no report as of yet as to any targeting they undertook. US called for urgent session of UN Security Council today. Nothing on whether that will happen. US military on full alert in Europe and Middle East. It will get worse over there. China confronted US warships in South China Sea with jets and patrol boats. US planes responded, and there were several near misses between jets over ships on the sea. US stood its ground, and Chinese forces eventually withdrew. Japan, South Korea, Taiwan, Australia, Singapore, and Vietnam on full military alert. Chinese army forces moving to all of its borders. North Korea moved three divisions of troops to the border with South Korea. Pakistan and Afghanistan started a shooting conflict between them. Turkey declared martial law across the country and directly invaded Kurdish territory. Multiple political leaders were shot dead in the Muslim countries bordering the south of Russia, resulting in Russia going to full military alert on its southern borders.

New US president has called for calm. American diplomats said to be involved in conversations with world leaders in all of the areas where things going badly. President has verbally warned multiple countries that US will take whatever actions necessary to protect American interests and personnel overseas. Noncritical personnel being pulled from all countries where violence, military action, and expected escalation will take place in next forty-eight hours. Congressional leaders, especially those on the right, are calling for concerted military action in particular against Iran. President has ordered navy, army, and marine assets to move to full prepared status for possible action. Navy is sending two aircraft carriers into the Med and Persian Gulf.

Man-on-the-street is reacting as would be expected, wondering what this will mean for already jittery economy, oil, and financial sectors. US president has used executive power to put final rationing of fuel and food in place. It is expected that food and fuel supplies will be very limited as US prepares for the unknown, and reserves become a top priority for the near-term future. At this point no direct attacks have taken place in US homeland. I can only assume that there are those who are predicting that it will only be a matter of time before that happens. Terrorists across the world will likely see this as an opportunity to strike when US is occupied with international turmoil. My wife and I hope it doesn't happen but we are not hopeful.

Needless to say, we were quite subdued the rest of the day. Lots of conversation about the preceding events. Lunch passed as well as supper. Chores, collecting water and boiling it, collecting wood, and drying it as much as possible consumed our day. Spent most of day trying to stay warm and obviously writing in diary. No change in weather. Very cold but clouds not quite as dark. Clouds and wind still from the northwest. Hoping when we wake up in the morning we will see indicators of a break in the weather. Same routine in the evening as last night. Decided that we would do a review of our supplies tomorrow. If things continue to get worse internationally, and if there is any violence in the U.S., we will need to carefully ration our supplies, in particular food. We had prepared for this. We may be coming to a time when we have to get very serious about what stores we have. Prayers said, scripture read, multiple layers of warmth in place, fire going well, wood supply adequate for the night hopefully, and dogs bundled up and staying very close. Good night. Hope we wake up to a more positive day tomorrow.

Contend, O Lord, with those who contend with me;
Fight against those who fight against me.
(Psalm 35:1)

LARRY D. HORTON, PhD

Date: February 25–28   Mileage: 0 mi.   Walk Total: 63–65 miles.

Feb. 28 Day #39:

Fitful night's sleep. Cold combined with mind not relaxing due to yesterday's news made sleeping very hard. Up several times to tend fire. Dogs seemed to be agitated as well. Up early and heated up some cream of wheat for a change. Added some freeze-dried fruit for a special treat. Usual cup of coffee. Lunch was hot soup and pudding. Another treat. Dogs got their share along with a bit of dry dog food. Checked snare traps, nothing. Still too cold for most critters to be out and about. Fire maintenance, water boiling, and wood collecting were chores undertaken off and on. Uneventful morning at campsite.

Weather seems to be tempering a bit. Cloud layer not as dark and thick. Maybe on way out of this front. NOAA says another thirty-six hours and it will be gone. Have decided to spend one additional day here to allow front to end and warmer temps to melt some of the ice. Spent an hour crank-powering up main radio and tuned into national and local stations to check status of international events. Was not prepared for what was reported. Not prepared but not completely surprised. Spent balance of day listening periodically in between chores. Tough news. Things we had been anticipating and preparing for. When they actually became reality today was still a shock to emotions and hope. Prepared supper of pasta and freeze-dried veggies with a bit of the dried beef we had been saving. We needed something positive given the world and country that we now are facing. Spent considerable time recording events of today and impact of those events on us. Thought about, talked about, and recorded events and thoughts up until suppertime. The world that we now face is a different world.

Internationally UN has called emergency Security Council meeting, but larger members like Russia and China ignored the call for a meeting. Middle East continues to sink into full-out war. Asia on full alert. Chinese military, army and navy, mobilizing across its borders. Russia at full alert status adding military buildup on eastern European borders. European countries calling for military assistance from US on eastern borders. North Korea launched three long-range missiles at South Korean port city of Pusan. South Korea has declared war on North Korea and fully expects an invasion from the north in the next forty-eight hours. US president keeps calling for calm and diplomatic solution, but it seems that no one is listening. World is facing a three-front escalation of conflict: Asia, Middle East, and Europe.

There are obvious downstream impacts of all of this on the US and to some extent on us as we try to survive. However, those impacts involve some delay before we feel any direct impact. More immediate impact will come from events within US borders that have taken place in the last twenty-four hours since our first becoming aware of the escalating international troubles. It seems that some kind of coordinated escalation was undertaken by the bad players in the world. As I said yesterday it's only natural that it would include direct attacks on the US. Not by a formal military force but by things that had been predicted for quite some time. Silent and hidden, out in the open were very bad.

The US came under attack both conventionally and unconventionally overnight. We have been hearing for many years about cyber warfare. It is now a reality. Strategic technology capabilities were attacked using Trojan Horse programs that have likely been introduced to the US technology infrastructure over at least the last ten years. The targets did not surprise anyone. The following critical capabilities, organizations, and structures have been effectively shut down at the same time at midnight this morning: the Central Bank of the US; all global stock exchanges including Wall Street; the Federal Reserve; the Chicago commodities market; the US Internet; all TV cable systems; the IRS; and the FBI. All forms of communication across civilian and military networks have been temporarily disrupted but are coming back online fairly quickly. None of these federal and private organizations, and the problems they now face, will impact us directly in our survival mode. We decided late last year that once we bugged out we would have to be independent of all traditional societal organizations. We knew that the longer-term impact would hit us if the downtime extended for any length of time. But we have prepared for these things and won't lose much sleep over them for the time being.

The third prong of events has an impact on us even while we were listening to the report on the radio. The US has also come under violent attack from inside its borders and in one glaring event from outside its borders. We have been living with and growing our own Trojan Horse for a couple decades. It has come alive, and the cost is significant. Granted the physical damage that resulted was not large, but the economic and psychological impact is beyond measure. It will change our country and push us backward in time. It will directly impact our ability to deal with the growing international crises. It will create internal crises that we may not have the capability to overcome.

What happened? In a twelve-hour time period the following attacks occurred in what seems to have been a coordinated effort. First, the one from outside our borders. Several individuals crossed the Canadian border and bombed the key oil sands pipeline in three locations. Reports from local authorities indicate that tracks were followed from the explosion sites back north to the Canadian border. Second, multiple groups, one each in Georgia, California, and Illinois, and three in Texas, set off explosives destroying sections of key pipelines for finished and raw oil products. This effectively stopped flow of these materials to major cities and in some cases regions of the country. Third, Hoover dam came under attack, and 80 percent of its power generation turbines were disabled. Suspicions exist that some type of poison was introduced into the impoundment waters as well. This affected large parts of the southwestern US.

Fourth, multiple major refineries came under attack along the Delaware River between Philadelphia and Newark, in southern California, and in the Houston TX area. Fires were burning out of control in the facilities. Distribution pipelines were destroyed, and tank farms were burning. The fires could be seen from the Space Station circling above. Fifth, two major bridges were hit. The Golden Gate in San Francisco had one line of suspension cables destroyed, effectively shutting down the bridge. The interstate main bridge across the Mississippi river in Memphis TN was effectively shut down when sections of pavement were destroyed across all lanes by the explosion of a truck bomb. Finally, in the four largest cities in the US, hospitals were attacked by suicide bombers and armed groups of individuals, killing significant numbers of staff and patients before all the attackers were killed. Of all the attacks just mentioned, this attack on hospitals likely impacted people emotionally more than the others. In the report we listened to, first responders are working at all attack sites, but resources are overwhelmed. Commentators are trying to stay on top of all of this, but casualty and impact reports are all over the place.

The president is pleading for calm, but people are not listening. Crowds, and in some cases mobs, have taken to the streets. US political opposition leaders are going for the jugular vein of the new president. Wall Street is in the tank. We lost 75 percent of the value of our investments in the first four hours of the day. A run on all banks has led the president to declare a second banking holiday for the next week, just as was done in 1929. US economic indicators are on a crash slide into the basement. Reports are coming in of riots and violence at local grocery stores, with people fighting for anything on shelves. Some reports indicated that several deaths have resulted, primarily in larger cities. Grocery distribution warehouses have come under attack by mobs and have been eventually overrun. Bottled water is worth more than gold immediately. Production facilities have been overrun. Drug stores were looted for medications and anything else that might be valuable. Gas stations were shut down, but looters were able to activate pumps, with supplies quickly disappearing. Refineries had to put armed guards at all access points to prevent looters from trying to get to raw product before it was even distributed. And all of this happened in the first four to six hours before and after daybreak. The country was moving quickly into chaos.

One is hard pressed not to conclude that international events and domestic events are part of some hidden coordinated effort and strategy. Thirty days into the new presidency, while the new president was trying to consolidate the victory, was a prime time to strike, and that is what is happening.

So what is the national response to all these events? The new president continued to ask for calm. But average citizens took some very definite actions. A national emergency was declared, and the national guard was activated across the country to work with local law enforcement to bring order back to the streets. Travel was immediately restricted to local only. The entire interstate system was shut down to all but military and truck traffic for food and resource movement. Fuel consumption and fuel stamps were limited to 50 gallons per month per household. Electric consumption was restricted to 8 hours per household per day. Going over that amount would lead to power shut off for remaining days in the month. All firearm and ammunition sales to the public were suspended indefinitely. A national curfew applies from sunset to sunrise. Law enforcement in all locations has search and seizure authority if given any cause to believe that an imminent threat to their community exists. All schools, colleges, and universities are closed for at least the next two weeks. All public events, concerts, and sports matches are canceled for the next two weeks. Public meetings in any open or closed venue are suspended until further notice. Private meetings are required to notify local authorities of the event but may be closed if any sense of threat exists for participants. Churches are asked to cut back on their schedules to enable law enforcement to secure their safety when events are held. Print and visual media are asked to curtail programming to some degree to enable their use as communication vehicles to the public. Congress has been called into emergency session. All local governments and authorities are asked to coordinate their security efforts through local military and federal government offices.

Those are the main initial actions taken at the federal level. There will likely be much more if the internal attacks continue. Obviously local and federal authorities will be stretched to the breaking point especially if any additional events take place. It will likely take twenty-four hours for the full impact of these actions to hit the average citizen. Reaction to these steps can't be known, but as my wife and I discussed, reaction will come and fast. Tomorrow morning when we turn on the radio should be interesting and scary listening. All we can do is keep our wits, keep planning, keep surviving, keep a very low profile, and keep praying.

Our afternoon was spent making some decisions preparing for the days ahead and getting a handle on our resources. First, we decided to stay put one more day. NOAA radio indicates that the weather front will break early tomorrow afternoon and that the next week will be a bit milder, enabling us to get under way again. Second, we decided that tomorrow will be a day of reviewing our supplies, preparing our backpacks in case we have to go really dark in the days ahead, maintenance on weapons, inventorying medical supplies, maintenance on the Trekker, and general evaluation of our physical and emotional preparedness for the much more difficult days ahead. Once we made that our plan for tomorrow, we decided to have a few special treats to end the day, pudding and hot chocolate. Our last actions for the day were to wash our bodies, inspect the dogs, and bundle up for the night. We did notice, as we climbed into our bags, that it's not as cold as the last couple nights. The wind has died down some, and the sleet and drizzle have stopped. Good signs, we hope. Prayers said, scripture read, we climbed into bags for the night, hugs all around. The dogs were priceless. Good night!

How precious is Your lovingkindness, O God!
And the children of men take refuge in the shadow of Your wings.
(Psalm 36:7)

Date: March 1   Mileage: 0 mi.   Walk Total: 63–65 miles.

March 1 Day #40, Extra Hunker Down Day:

Sun peeking through clouds when we woke up this morning. Weather has broken. Wind more from the east and south. Birds in trees woke us with their singing. Not as cold during the night. Slept some better even with our minds racing after yesterday's news. Cooked rice and beans for breakfast over hexamine stove. Small fire burning. Trying to use only dead wood to cut down on smoke created. While wife cranked power up on our radio, I went for more water to boil. Once had enough power, turned on radio and got update on events and people's reaction to them overnight. Spent an hour listening to the radio, and what we heard will drive us and impact us for the rest of our journey. For that matter, it will change our life forever.

Every major city in the US is experiencing violence. Food, water, and fuel are the catalysts. Armed groups of people roaming the streets are confronting authorities in particular at grocery stores, pharmacies, gas stations, and distribution warehouses. The number of killed and wounded in the confrontations is growing by the hour. We noticed that there were no commercial planes in the sky when we first woke up. We could see fast moving military aircraft likely out of Dayton OH base. They are likely flying Combat Air Patrols around the Columbus area. It was silent in ways that reminded us of the first few days after the 9/11 attack in 2001.

Announcements make it clear that travel is very restricted. Military convoys are moving on the interstate system to take up positions at major junctions. Word had come in that paramilitary groups are emerging in the western and northern parts of the country. These groups stand between the government forces and resources in their communities. The government has seized all food production, fuel production, and distribution facilities to try to maintain some type of control over these vital supplies. The general public, when possible, is coming into the streets armed for both their own protection and for the possibility of securing needed materials. The inner cities and suburbs in every major population center across the country are in chaos. Crowds are marching in front of the national capitol and every state capitol demanding help. The official government statement again asks for calm.

Internationally the state of emergency across the world is growing, especially in Asia, Europe, and the Middle East. National governments in those regions continue to threaten and gear up for confrontation. All branches of the US military, at home and abroad, are at the highest state of alert. All leaves are canceled. The national guard mobilization is to be completed in the next three days. People have been ordered to stay off the streets but that order is being generally ignored. The new president is hunkered down with government leaders working on a ninety-day plan to try to deal with all the turmoil. A request was again made to the UN to convene but few if any countries responded. It seems that everyone is concerned only with their own well-being and safety. The last statement on the radio report was that updates on the developing situations will occur at 6 AM, noon, 6 PM, and midnight each day. With that announcement, regular programming to some extent resumed, and we got busy with all our preparations.

We first sat down by the small fire and developed our plan. We still have at least 350 miles left according to our travel plan. So we have to prepare for that. Our first priority is our backpacks, med. kits, food, weapons, and shelter/sleeping materials. We have to prioritize down to what we can carry on our backs should we lose or have to abandon the Trekker which we know is pretty likely. Once we had our plan, we quickly got about preparing. We know that the poundage we are able to carry will restrict us: for me total weight no more than 50 lbs., and for my wife no more than 30 lbs. We also noticed that the tires on the Trekker are showing the effects of the very cold weather, so we'll have to change out tires in the next couple days. Our plan is to carry all our packs and gear on the Trekker until we need to ditch the vehicle and go solely on foot. As we traveled we have reduced the total weight of our resources, primarily food, by between 20 and 30 lbs. That will help a bit as we set out. We developed specific lists of what each of us would carry and got about packing. We did stop for a few minutes to cook some freeze-dried pasta and chicken for our lunch. Needed the extra energy for the afternoon ahead. We attempted to make our preparation and final packing plan as clear as possible.

My List	Wife's List
Basic clothing for cold and warm weather	Basic clothing for cold and warm weather
Rain gear	Rain gear
Utility belt	Utility belt
Hand ax, single bladed ax	Survival knife
Survival knife	Canteen
Canteen	Handgun and ammo
Handgun and ammo	Air rifle and ammo
17 HMR and ammo	Backup medical kit and bag
Machete, bow saw	Cooking and eating kits
Main medical kit and bag	Lightweight backup tarp
Fire starting kit	Fire starting kit
Cooking pots and pans	Sleeping bag and ground pad
Primary tarp	100 ft. coiled rope
Plastic ground cover	Ten lbs. freeze-dried food
Sleeping bag and ground pad	Small backup NOAA radio and batteries
100 ft. coiled rope	150 ft. paracord
Twenty lbs. freeze-dried food	Two water straws
Dogs dry food and medications	Plastic zip ties
Plastic bags, large and small	Thread and needles
Two water straws	IOS, EDC/BOB
IOS, EDC/BOB	Aluminum foil
Fishing kit	
Emergency tool kit	
Steel wire	

We will be going dark if and when we have to rely solely on what we can carry above.

With our packs and other carry items organized we set about getting Trekker ready. Primary remaining material on Trekker is food. We have a sixty-day supply of two per day freeze-dried meals left on the Trekker. Our plan, as I said earlier, is to load packs and carried materials onto Trekker until we have to ditch it. Hopefully it will be easier to pull with the reduction in weight and better organization. We are ready to set out tomorrow. Late in the afternoon we gathered and boiled as much water as we have containers for, including our canteens. Once we ditch Trekker, our carried water supply will be reduced dramatically.

After a hot supper of pasta, freeze-dried beef, vegetables, pudding, and hot coffee we cranked up power on NOAA radio and listened in again. Weather report is much better. Bit warmer tonight. Heavy frost however. Tomorrow will be partially sunny with high just above freezing, and next five days after that temps in mid-thirties with more sunshine. Sounds wonderful to us. Long range forecast called for similar temps with light snow flurries every day. Will be cold and slippery but nothing like the past five days. So we have a pretty positive perspective on travel weather, hoping to travel 2 mph for four hours each day. We need to make progress but realize that plan might have to be adapted in view of the newscast of current events in the country.

Things are getting progressively worse across the nation. Confrontation between authorities and population and between groups of private citizens are increasing. Many casualties. Sections of major population centers in flames and under martial law. President continues to call for calm. International situation a powder keg ready to explode. Military and national guard patrolling all major interstates and conducting security searches of anyone caught out after curfews. All food, fuel, and medicines now under direct government control. No distribution taking place. All NGO disaster services taken over by government and incapable of dealing with the many needs that have surfaced. It seems as if the country has stopped in its tracks with little or no control over basic safety and survival needs of the general population. Preppers and survivalists have hunkered down in safe havens prepared ahead of time and are defending them with all means possible. It's only a matter of time before armed confrontations take place across the country. Several militias in western states have warned government authorities and forces not to venture into large geographic areas. They are not wanted or needed. Not heeding these warnings will mean those militias defending themselves by any means possible. Not what we wanted to hear but what we fully expected. We are ready to go tomorrow. We will deal with whatever we find. Prayers said, scripture read, and bundled up, we climbed into sacks ready for the new day and what it will bring. Lord, watch over us.

> **Commit your way to the Lord,**
> **Trust also in Him,**
> **And He will do it.**
> **(Psalm 37:5)**

Cross Country Diary: Day #41

Date: March 2   Mileage: 6 mi.   Walk Total: 69–71 miles.

Up early. Broke down camp after breakfast of oatmeal and coffee. Dogs had dry food with a bit of oatmeal. Tore down both shelters. Drowned fire with several gallons of water. Scattered firewood under pine trees. Folded tarps, rolled up bags, filled in latrine, collected snare traps from multiple locations. Moved food from tree hang-up and loaded everything onto Trekker. Tried our best to make sure as little sign as possible remains of our campsite and were ready to move. Weather is partial sunshine and gray clouds. Remaining ice has melted quickly. Paths are wet and a bit muddy.

Hiked to dirt country road below us and headed to the northeast from Salt Creek. Our goal was to make it six miles for the day, crossing state highway 136, and to set up overnight site a couple miles to the northeast of Oakland OH. Fairly easy walk as we were out in the country. Some up and down elevation gain and loss in the hills. Seemed to make pretty good progress. Stopped every thirty minutes or so to cool down and water for everyone. No traffic on the country road. Saw very few buildings except off at some distance. Noticed some farm homes and outbuildings. Sky still very quiet. No planes other than occasional military aircraft. We did our best to stay out of sight when we heard them coming. We knew that as we approached larger population centers aircraft traffic would increase. Also, a thought had crossed our minds that authorities might use drones to do air based flyovers to keep an eye on things. We will have to deal with that possibility when the time comes. It will be important to avoid discovery as much as possible and to know how and when to evade any seeing eyes on the ground or in the sky. With the current situation in the country, anyone out in the open like us might be, will be, immediately suspect and face questions at a minimum. We want to avoid that if at all possible.

At approx. 2 PM found a large fallen tree about fifty yards off the road and decided to build our overnight camp beside it. Things were very wet. Temps weren't bad, but nighttime will be in the twenties again.

So, using primary tarp, built a lean-to shelter for the night. Gathered as much dead firewood as possible to keep smoke down and to have a small fire all night. Decided to cook supper over hexamine stove to lessen smoke as well. We ate a cold lunch so were anxious to have warm supper. Walked into low hills around us and found small ice-covered stream in shade. Broke through ice and collected enough water for cooking and our canteens. Once we move closer to population, will likely use water straws for our drinking water and hexamine stove to boil enough water to fill canteens for the next day. Invisibility will be a key to our travels from this point forward. Covered Trekker with secondary tarp. Hung food on small log between two nearby trees and decided to hit the sack early. First day back on foot wore us out a bit. Listened to NOAA and AM/FM radio. Not much changed since yesterday. Still lots of violent incidents across the country. Listened to fifteen minutes of Christian music from Circleville. Said prayers and read scripture. Good night, Lord, keep us safe.

For I hope in You, O Lord;
You will answer, O Lord my God.
(Psalm 38:15)

Date: March 3   Mileage: 5 mi.   Walk Total: 74–76 miles.

Up early again. Was a bit warmer during the night. Broke camp after oatmeal and juice breakfast. Mixed a bit of dry dog food with some oatmeal for the dogs. Pretty simple cleanup. Triangulated our position and made decision to strike out pretty much straight east, until we are sure we have passed Newark OH, then begin traveling in a northeasterly direction. Figured it will be four or five days going east to ensure that we miss Newark. With Trekker loaded we set out for the day following country dirt and secondary roads. Had to make a few slight direction changes during the day to compensate for road direction changes. Saw a few signs of civilization, mostly farms. Things were pretty quiet in general. Stopped every thirty to forty-five minutes for a cooldown break. Hard work pulling Trekker even in the cold weather. Thank goodness elevation changes are not significant. Lunch during one of the short breaks, a treat for dogs, cold lunch for us. Did use our water straws periodically to drink from small streams we passed. Didn't taste too bad. Know they are keeping us reasonably safe from water-borne stuff. Started out the day dressed lightly because we knew would be warm with walking and toting. A couple times cool wind kicked up and on went another layer. Also, glad for compass practice, as we have a reasonable sense we are traveling in our chosen direction.

Around 1:30 PM started to look for a location to camp for the night. Took us a bit as we were walking mostly through open fields with only sporadic clumps of trees. Dirt roads were muddy and full of puddles. Knew would have to take care of boots and feet tonight. As we looked for campsite, a few snowflakes put a little pressure on us to find a good one. Finally saw a hillside covered with pine and oaks in the distance and decided that would have to be it. When we arrived, we went to side of the road into the trees about 100 yards and up a slight grade. Found a grove of pine trees and immediately started to build out overnight camp. Found couple trees about eight feet apart on fairly flat ground and cut off lower limbs of both. Rigged up a simple lean-to using cut branches for windbreaks on sides. Cut additional limbs for ground cover and sleeping area. Not worth building a serious sleeping platform. Covered Trekker with secondary tarp. Covered lean-to with primary tarp. Built a better fire than last night with space blankets as reflector. Immediately worked on boots. Hanging by fire to dry out. Boiled water from nearby stream and washed up, feet, pits, face, arms, and bodies. Felt good, especially the warm water. Supper was freeze-dried pasta and fruit. Dogs were certainly happy with pasta. Hot coffee hit the spot also. Once supper done worked on cleaning up edges on all of our cutting tools. We were all tired so once supper cleanup done, all climbed into lean-to and listened to radio and talked. Dogs were happy to have us pay attention to them as well. NOAA forecast indicated that current conditions will continue for the next week, then an early spring snowstorm will hit. Looks like we will be hunkering down again. So will plan accordingly. Couldn't bring ourselves to listen to the news. Do that in the AM before we set out. Prayers said, scripture read, hugs all around, with much thankfulness. Night!

And now, Lord, for what do I wait?
My hope is in You.
(Psalm 39:7)

Date: March 4   Mileage: 6 mi.   Walk Total: 80–82 miles.

Up early again. Quick hot breakfast and cup of coffee. Broke camp and were on our way. Nothing unusual happened between breakfast and quick lunch of cold beans and rice left over from this morning. Roads are even more muddy and wet than yesterday but made reasonable progress given that we took frequent breaks and had quite a bit of elevation up and down. Haven't mentioned crossing any water to this point. Have been lucky to find country bridges and had major passovers of large rivers and streams prior to all of the recent events in the US. We know that will likely change in the future in particular if we have to go totally cross country if significant dangers are present near towns and on roads. We do not look forward to that day. It would present a whole new series of challenges and dangers especially if the weather stays cold, exponentially increasing the danger of hypothermia. But we will deal with that when the time comes.

Made more progress through 2 PM and started to look for campsite for the night. We were traveling through small hills and valleys with lots of cover, so knew we would find a good place. Around 2:15 PM spotted a small valley to our left that went up between two hills. We headed that direction, finding a good stream and some decent outcroppings of rocks. Decided to camp at one. Built fire against rocks. Set up lean-to. Collected and boiled water supply. Washed our bodies and dried out our equipment. Had few snow flurries during the day, some cool sun and slight breeze. Once wood collected, water boiled, and washing done, cooked rice and beans again for supper. Added a bit of freeze-dried chicken to the mixture. The dogs were in heaven. Hot cup of coffee hit the spot as well. Checked all packs, critical supplies, and camp materials to see how they were handling being on the road again. No visible problems. Sat by fire with no socks or boots on to dry and warm our feet. Simple sleeping arrangements on platform of branches cut from surrounding trees. Simple tarp lean-to for protection. With the wind down, did not put up side walls to allow slight breeze to pass through. Have not mentioned to this point that when hit the sack had leashes on dogs and leads around our wrists. Did not want them running off in the middle of the night if spooked by something that approached our campsites. So far that has worked, but we had few incidents where the dogs got agitated during the night. That will likely happen sooner rather than later. Cranked up power on NOAA radio and heard that weather is going to hold for no more than five more days. Then significant blizzard and snowfall will hit us. We figure we have four more good days to walk before hunkering down again. We hope we will be able to reach Licking Creek somewhere southeast of Newark before we have to do that. Water will again be critical for a longer holdover. National news was much of the same. Chaos is slowly coming under control. Government has set up system to get food, water, and supplies to people, but the system is stretched to the limit and people are not happy. Armed confrontations continue but only periodically fall into actual violence. Reinforced uncertainty of the days ahead. Prayers said, scripture read, and hugs around, we settled down for the night.

I waited patiently for the Lord;
And He inclined to me and heard my cry.
(Psalm 40:1)

Date: March 5–6   Mileage: 10 mi.   Walk Total: 90–92 miles.

Two routine days. Up early. Breakfast, lunch and supper as usual. Camped both nights building temporary lean-to in groves of hardwood trees. Cut pine branches for sides of lean-to and for sleeping platform on the ground. Ran out of dry dog food the second night. Late camp set up on the fifth due to a small detour we had to take around a couple farms at crossroads on country road we were using. Avoided them by taking farm roads through some fields. Added a couple hours to our walk. Usual health issues, washing, and drying clothing. Brief periods of snow flurries both days. Nothing out of what has become the ordinary for us. We did hear some dogs barking and a couple roosters in the mornings, so knew we were not far from farms or small population centers. Roads, primarily country, were pretty quiet though on first evening we saw several vehicles pass by. First ones we had seen in a couple days. We obviously stayed under cover. Cooked over hexamine stove to avoid smoke, and kept fires small and used only dead wood for same smoke issue. Temperatures were about the same. Low thirties during daytime. Mid-twenties at night. Nothing we were not prepared for.

Second day walk was a bit harder as we were in more hills. More up and down. No air noise other than sporadic military jets. Listened to NOAA radio, and forecast is for big front to move in morning of the ninth. Decided that on the eighth we will look for a good site and build a substantial camp to get us through what promises to be a very heavy snowfall. Closed each day with prayers, scripture reading, and hugs all around. I spent quite a bit of time the second night awake reflecting on our journey to that point in time. Decided would do a bit of writing the second day of our next hunker-down to record thoughts on what we have been through so far. Went to sleep concerned about events in our country but grateful we were together and able to take care of ourselves reasonably well. Two more days of walking and then some downtime to rest, stay safe, warm, and plan for the next segment of our journey. Trusting that our direction of travel is still good and that we will reach the area of Licking Creek in the next two days. Good night!

March 5

As for me, You uphold me in my integrity,
and You set me in Your presence forever.
(Psalm 41:12)

March 6

As the deer pants for the water brooks,
so my soul pants for You, O God.
(Psalm 42:1)

Cross Country Diary: Day #46

Date: March 7   Mileage: 6 mi.   Walk Total: 96–98 miles.

Up early. Today will be our last full day of walking. Weather much the same, though clouds are taking on a darker look. Breakfast of oatmeal and coffee. Dogs not too happy with oatmeal. Think they are getting tired of it. More up and down today, requiring more frequent rest and cooldown stops. No planes in the sky. No traffic on the back-country roads we were using. We stopped for a hot lunch of soup cooked on hexamine stove in grove of trees just off the road. Walked until 2 PM and started to look for a suitable campsite. Once found a small distance off the road, set about setting up normal lean-to campsite. Found small stream and boiled enough water to fill canteens, cook supper, and wash body parts. Kept fire small again to avoid detection. We have become pretty efficient in setting all of this up and were able to sit down by fire, dry out our boots, and watch last five minutes of partial sunset. We are all tired and ready for a few days' rest. Grateful we still do not have to tote our stuff. Once we hunker down, going to change out Trekker tires. Current ones look like they won't last much longer in these cold temps. Supper was freeze-dried pasta with small portion of dried beef thrown in and hot cocoa. Dogs enjoyed the pasta and beef of course. Did a bit of compass triangulation and know we are in the vicinity of Licking Creek but no idea of just how far. Very ready to hit the sack. Bundled up as normal, prayers said, and scripture read. Flurries falling as we said good night. Lord, keep us safe and warm through the night.

LARRY D. HORTON, PhD

Date: March 8   Mileage: 3 mi.   Walk Total: 99–101 miles.

Up early, breakfast as usual of oatmeal and coffee, broke camp and were on our way. Seems to be a bit more civilization around us. More lights in the morning in the distance. Figured we had to be coming near a geographic landmark. We just hoped it was somewhere south of Nashport OH. Uneventful walk in the AM until we went around a bend in the road and saw a small stream below us down a slight hill. We hoped it might be Licking Creek, but weren't going to waste a lot of time at this point trying to figure out if it was or not. Went up an old logging road and sat down for lunch cooked on hexamine stove. Just soup as we wanted to get moving to find a suitable site to hunker down in. We were not going to take any chances of trying to go any further than necessary at this time. Spent fifteen minutes exploring up the old logging road and discovered lots of cut treetops. Perfect for firewood, cover for critters, and materials to build a substantial shelter. Located a reasonably flat place back toward lunch site about 100 feet and decided this would be it. Small valley to our left held small creek tributary of larger stream below us. No sign that the area had been visited by humans recently. Lots of sign that small critters were around. Multiple squirrel nests in many of the trees. Rabbit runs perfect for setting up snare traps. Some deer sign but we weren't interested in masses of deer meat. So the decision was made. We will hunker down somewhere south of Nashport OH and hopefully near Licking Creek. Invisibility is our motto.

Date: March 8–14   Mileage: 0 mi.   Walk Total: 99–101 miles.

March 8 Afternoon, Hunker Down

We have been on foot now for thirty-five days. With multiple hunker-downs our average mileage walked per day works out to about two and three-fourths miles. Not setting any land speed records, but considering we hunkered down for two long periods and that we are safe and reasonably healthy, we won't complain. Knowing this information brings us quickly to the reality that we are going to be living like this for quite some time. Something we prepared for, yet a realization that is tough to accept even as we get busy for our third hunker-down. Traveling in the winter and with spring thaw coming, we know we have bitten off a lot. But preparation has paid off to this point regardless of how slowly we're moving and what is going on in the country even as we keep moving. It is our reality and we accept it. We know that when we reach our final destination, we will look back on the entire ordeal and see it as something that changed our lives forever. Changed us for the good and made us capable of dealing with anything. With the Lord by our side we are able to deal with anything that comes our way.

Once we decided on a hunker-down site, we quickly got busy building the most substantial shelter we have undertaken on our journey to this point. NOAA weather predicts ten to twelve inches of snow, quite a bit of wind, and drifting. We have to be totally secure from the elements in our temporary home. Given the national situation, we also have to be as secure as we can make ourselves from any external threats. Lots to do before the sun sets for the night. Bad weather will be here late tomorrow morning. Clouds getting darker and wind picking up from the northwest. No animals seen. No sounds heard. No birds in the air. They know what's coming as well. Tied dogs to some trees with their twenty-foot leads so they can nose around and stay out of the way. Think they enjoy a bit more freedom.

Primary Shelter and Fire Pit: Decided to expand primary shelter to size that will hold us and the Trekker as well. Laid out grid on ground.

LARRY D. HORTON, PhD

Cleared all debris from the site. Included plan for keyhole fire pit with wood reflector lined with space blanket. Included plan for spit and cover over fire using second space blanket. Given lots of cut timber in area, was able to get multiple six foot vertical beams as well as three ten-foot three-inch diameter logs for horizontal supports for shelter. Collected five six-foot two-inch-diameter logs to build primary sleeping platform along with smaller two-foot logs to use as corners for platform to raise us a minimum of eighteen inches off the ground. Collected two-foot one inch diameter smaller logs to function as noggins for shelter and fire site. Once had all these materials collected, cut a two by two by two-foot stack of smaller logs and branches for initial fire material. Built keyhole fire pit first and got good fire going. Wife will tend it initially. First step was to set up primary vertical supports and lash horizontal supports to them. Noggins added to each vertical support. Next step was to build core support structure for the sleeping platform. While I was doing all this, wife collected water from small stream below and boiled water filling our two water jugs. Once had skeleton structure completed collected enough one-inch diameter lengthy logs to build shelter wall and internal sleeping platform structure. Lashed the smaller logs to all three walls of the primary shelter and sleeping platform. Secured several dozen pine branches from nearby trees. Wove smaller branches into primary structure walls and sleeping platform. Put primary tarp over roof and as far down each of the three sides of primary shelter as possible. Put secondary tarp over woven materials on sleeping platform. By the time all this was completed, light was fading, so pulled out LED headlamps and proceeded to cut a large supply of pine branches off nearby trees. Applied those branches as a mattress to our sleeping platform and on top of shelter on primary tarp. More fine-tuning of the primary shelter to be completed in the morning, especially on the walls. But for this first night our basic structure was completed. While I applied pine branches, wife cooked hot supper of soup and rice with hot coffee. Dogs were excited to be eating. Once supper eaten, set about securing two-inch diameter log between two of the pine trees from which I had cut branches. Secured it about eight feet in the air and hung our food supply from it covered with some of our ground plastic. Last task of the evening was to build out the fire reflection wall and the space blanket cover and reflector. We will need the reflected heat tonight, and we have to protect the fire as much as possible.

Sleeping Shelter & Trekker: Made sure had two-foot-thick layer of branches on our sleeping platform. Laid out sleeping mats and sleeping bags on top of that layer. If need be will fine-tune it tomorrow. Pulled Trekker under primary shelter and covered it with sheet of plastic. Was close to 8 PM when had all of this complete. Spent better part of six hours setting up the basics. Fine-tuning of the entire camp will happen in the AM. Set up entire camp facing to the southeast as much as possible as primary winds and storm will hit us from the northwest. We are far enough up in the trees that sight line to campsite is blocked partially by trees below us. Fire reflecting wall and fire pit are set up on the same angle to block light as much as possible from being seen from below us. The one good thing about weather forecast is that temps are not going to dip too much at night. Have to stay just below or above freezing to produce the amount of snow we will get. Decided to fix some pudding for a bedtime snack. Needed the extra energy. Boots and clothing a bit damp from snow flurries that had been falling and sweating from labors. Tried to dry them a bit by the fire and decided to put them in bottom of sleeping bags to keep drying and warmth process going. Know that we have several important tasks to complete in the morning before our campsite is done. But most are not too labor intensive and can be completed by noon if all goes well.

Bedded down all bundled up and turned on radio to check on forecast. Hasn't changed: storm to hit in earnest late in the AM and to continue for minimum of seventy-two hours. Likely a foot of wet, heavy snow to fall. Part of reason built things out as described was expectation that snowfall will be heavy and we cannot afford flimsy shelter. Prayers said, scripture read, and hugs around, we settled down for night.

O send out Your light and Your truth, let them lead me;
Let them bring me to Your holy hill and to Your dwelling places.
(Psalm 43:3)

LARRY D. HORTON, PhD

Date: March 8–14   Mileage: 0 mi.   Walk Total: 99–101 miles.

March 9 Hunker Down:

Pretty tired from long exhausting day yesterday. Sky completely gray with darker clouds blowing in from the north. We were sheltered by trees and slight slope behind our shelter, but we could still feel that the weather was going to get much worse. Cooked large breakfast of beans, rice, freeze-dried fruit, and coffee. Dogs were hungry. When finished eating, put them on long leashes again and hooked to some nearby trees. Wanted them to get rid of some of their energy before we had to get out of the weather. Snow flurries falling and putting thin white coating on everything. Will be slippery when out and about. Multiple tasks to complete before snow really starts to fall. **Task #1,** dug drainage trench around perimeter of camp shelter for eventual runoff and some melting due to our fire. **Task #2,** collected and cut all the dead wood I could in two hours to build up our wood supply, which we also located under the Trekker under primary shelter roof. Built up stack to three by three by three-foot stack. Realized daily task while hunkered down will be to keep that stack of wood up to snuff. **Task #3,** completed digging latrine fifty to sixty feet from camp shelter behind stack of treetops cut when area was logged. Built Cadillac latrine with seat, back rest, and privacy wall of branches. Better than at home. By the time this was finished, snow was falling more heavily. We were in for it.

Wife was collecting and boiling water this whole time, keeping fire going, drying out sleeping bags and clothing as best she could, keeping the dogs occupied, and in general organizing our resources within the camp. She cooked quick lunch of soup and coffee. Warmth hit the spot. Gave dogs bit of soup as they needed to stay warm as well. Had their sweaters on them. They were bright-eyed and bushy-tailed, so to speak, chasing snowflakes in the wind. Shortly after lunch we brought them in under the shelter, dried them off as best we could, and attached their short leashes to shelter supports. They stayed pretty close to the fire. They knew it was going to get nasty. Wind continued to pick up all morning. By 2 PM we were in a semi-whiteout situation and were all under the shelter. Nothing else we could really do but sit tight and wait out the snow over the next couple days.

Plan tomorrow is to set out snare traps. Should be able to pick up ground sign of rabbits and other small critters in new-fallen snow. Also, thinking seriously of taking air rifle up slope behind us and sit under tree to watch for squirrels. Maybe get lucky and get some fresh meat. Diet has become pretty routine. Need a bit of a change. Supper was hot beans and rice this evening. Dogs were happy for it, as were we. Hot cocoa really hit the spot. Can't do much more to camp until we see if need to repair leaks and wind damage. In some ways looking forward to quiet day tomorrow. No radio tonight. Need to relax a bit. Prayers said, scripture read, and bundled up. Trying to stay warm and not hear the wind blowing. A few leaks. Snow getting in a bit from sidewalls. Will have to fix them first thing tomorrow. Good night!

Rise up, be our help,
And redeem us for the sake of Your lovingkindness.
(Psalm 44:26)

LARRY D. HORTON, PhD

Date: March 8–14   Mileage: 0 mi.   Walk Total: 99–101 miles.

March 10 Hunker Down:

Cold, snowy and windy night. Fire down to embers so got it back alive when first awoke. Small piles of snow around the inside of the shelter where wind blew it in through holes in the sidewalls. While wife started fixing breakfast, quickly got about patching as many leaks in walls as I could find. Will have to watch it all day to make sure it's shored up. Breakfast of hot coffee and cream of wheat. Dogs were hungry, so fixed double batch. Decided to wait another twenty-four hours to see if snowfall lets up to set out traps. No sense in putting them out and getting them buried. Besides, critters were not moving on the ground. Did spot a few shapes moving around in the trees both above and below us on the little hillside. First task was to gather more dead wood and add it to our heat source fuel pile. Worked at that wrapped up in poncho.

About 11 AM walked up the slight hillside behind the shelter carrying the air gun to try luck at getting a squirrel. Sat down at base of large oak tree in center of grove. Snow coming down pretty heavily. Looked like we got about eight inches of snow overnight. Rate of snowfall hasn't really lessened at all this morning. Might get more than a foot if this keeps up all day. Wind slowed down a bit but if it picks up again, we could expect clumps of snow to fall out of the trees, especially the pines. Oak tree provided me with sort of a windbreak. Carried a plastic bag with me to sit on to stay drier. Told wife would be back in couple hours to get something to eat and would likely head out again for couple hours in the afternoon after lunch. Light very subdued in the snowstorm. At times, could not see more than 30 feet in front of me. Only knew where camp was from glow of campfire off of snow in the trees. Dogs barked once in a while probably wondering where I was. After ninety minutes of seeing nothing, went back to camp to eat. Hot soup hit the spot.

About 1 PM headed out again to the same tree, sat down, and waited. Snowfall got a bit lighter and I could see further and more clearly. Could actually look out in the distance and see other small hills with valleys between them. Everything was white with snow cover. Nothing moving. No sounds other than the wind. Cold finally got to me and I headed back to camp at 3 PM empty-handed. Tomorrow will come out again and set traps if snow backed off any. Took me a while to warm up back at camp. Climbed into sleeping bag and that seemed to help. Warm supper of soup and hot coffee. Dogs wanted more but we decided to conserve a bit of food until had more bulk, meat, to add to it. Hoping tomorrow will bring us a bit of success in that. After supper built fire up a bit to warm up. Not much risk of any dangers as long as the snow keeps falling. Listened to NOAA weather and snow is to lighten up a bit tomorrow. Light snow to continue for another forty-eight hours and then front will have blown itself out. Really bundled up. Fewer leaks in walls of shelter. Dogs happy to climb into bags. Prayers said, scripture read, hugs around, talked about situation, and watched snow falling in firelight.

They will be led forth with gladness and rejoicing;
They will enter into the King's palace.
(Psalm 45:15)

Date: March 8–14   Mileage: 0 mi.   Walk Total: 99–101 miles.

March 11 Hunker Down:

Snow still falling when woke up but not nearly as heavy. Another four to six inches overnight. Clouds not nearly as dark and wind not as strong. Breakfast of hot oatmeal and coffee. Dogs were hungry and cold so they stayed in shelter. Sky lighter through the trees which may be a good sign. Wife continued to collect water, boil it, and dry everything as much as possible while I headed back up hill to set out snare traps and sit at my squirrel stand. Some rabbit tracks in runs so set up snares. Good signs. Sat down at same oak tree. Four squirrel nests within fifty feet of me. Now just had to wait. Finally saw a couple squirrels running on limb about thirty feet from me. Long shot with air rifle but had to take them. Missed the first one but hit the second and it fell out of the tree still alive. Dispatched it and field-dressed it. We will have meat for supper tonight. Kept the heart to roast for dogs. They will be in doggy heaven with that. Once meat prepared headed back to camp with big smile. Hung meat beside food above ground to let it freeze. Cutting it up easier if frozen. We celebrated over soup at lunch knowing we would have fresh meat tonight. Decided to head out again in the morning now that the squirrels are moving a bit.

Spent first part of the afternoon building up our wood supply. When done back at camp, pulled out our bladed tools and put a new edge on all of them. They were getting a workout, especially using the larger ones on wood issues. Decided to head out to top of hill behind us after dark tonight to see if I can see light reflected on bottom of clouds from multiple locations; if so, will try to use compass readings from each to zero in on our location. It bothers us that we don't have a really good feel for where we are. Snow getting lighter by the hour. Late in afternoon got squirrel and carved the meat into small strips and chunks. Being frozen sure helped. Brazed the meat over the stones lining part of the keyhole fire. Once that was done, heated up some soup and added the chunks of squirrel. It sure smelled good, especially when brazing it. Did not cook it completely over fire but let it finish cooking when added to soup to keep it more tender. Also, fixed up some freeze-dried corn to give us a more complete meal. Of course, coffee was ready as well. Wife had completely refilled our water jugs and our canteens. We are trying to drink three canteens full of water each every day even when hunkered down. Eating some whole fresh meat will stress our digestive system a bit, and we need the water. We savored every bit of the soup. The squirrel was a bit gamy, but it hit the spot. Next time will add some meat tenderizer to give it more flavor.

Sat by fire on edge of sleeping platform and talked for quite a while about situation in the country. Will spend some time tomorrow trying to catch up a bit on events. Still very quiet all around us. Nothing in the sky due to storm and likely ongoing stoppage of commercial aviation. About 7:30 PM with good fire going, wife and dogs in shelter keeping warm, I headed uphill behind us to give the surrounding area a good look. Took me thirty minutes in the dark, with only LED headlamp for light, to get to top. Slipped a couple times on snow-covered logs, so took my good old time. Last thing we need is sprained ankle or messed up knee. Found a spot with few trees and line of sight in all directions and got my compass out. Small pad of paper and pencil in hand. Looked in all four directions. To the west-northwest saw significant light reflecting off of clouds. That had to be Newark OH. Glanced for second directly north and saw only slight reflections in multiple locations. To the northeast saw good reflection and took compass reading off of it, forty degrees. Continued further to the east, another good light source, it read at 100 degrees. East-southeast another good light source which read at 120 degrees. Converted readings to true north from magnetic and drew those degree #'s on piece of paper. Drew straight lines at three degree markers until they crossed that would give our best possible location. With all of this information in hand, headed slowly back to camp to interpret it by our map.

Light shining on clouds was strongest to the east and east/southeast which meant those communities were closest. One to the northeast was dimmer so further away. Once those locations are tentatively identified, can probably figure out how far east of Newark we are and decide when to head in a more northeasterly direction. We hope that will be when we break down our hunker-down camp and head out again. Also, this will hopefully tell us we are in fact on the banks of Licking Creek.

While on the hilltop I did notice one more thing. To the northeast I saw vehicle lights emerge from a small valley and travel for a couple minutes along the stream to our northeast, then turn back into another valley and disappear. People are in the area. Also, if there is a road, there might be a bridge in vicinity that we can use to cross stream rather than risk being in cold water and having to set down again to dry clothing, warm ourselves, and avoid hypothermia.

Back at camp took out information had collected and map of area we were carrying. In light of LED headlamp and flashlight held by my wife built grid and did some educated guessing. Turns out we are somewhat east-southeast of Newark OH but not as far east as we hoped. We are still south of US route 22. Stream below us is not Licking Creek but rather Jonathan Creek. We have strayed a bit further south of directly east than we had planned. Brighter lights to our east are likely Fultonham OH. Mount Perry OH is part of that light reflection as well, probably only a couple miles off in distance. Map showed OH route 668 must not be too far to our west, and it has a bridge across Jonathan Creek. If we continue on current track, we will likely run into problems of population near Zanesville OH when we turn north. We need to head for the 668 bridge and strike out directly north/northeast until we come to Dillon Lake. That will be the plan until we can get a better location fix based on proximity to a community or a route sign, water source, or other landmark.

Felt good to get ready for bed with this tentative knowledge. We were all tired. A lot more to do tomorrow. Temps pretty consistent. Snow lightly falling. Wind lessening even more. Few leaks if any in shelter walls. Decided will head upstream tomorrow to see how far we are from OH route 668 and perhaps see the bridge. Prayers said and scripture read, we went to bed with full tummies and hope in our hearts. Thank you, Lord!

God is our refuge and strength,
A very present help in trouble.
Therefore we will not fear.
(Psalm 46:1–2)

Date: March 8–14   Mileage: 0 mi.   Walk Total: 99–101 miles.

March 12 Hunker Down:

Snow was almost completely stopped when we woke up. Just light flurries and no wind. Best guesstimate is we got between 12 and 14 inches of snow total. Not much drifting where we are, but imagine worse on roads and fields. Got fire going and heated up some soup for a change. Needed energy for busy day ahead. First, I headed out to check snare traps and then hike back to the west toward OH route 668. If snares were empty, planned to do some more squirrel stuff this afternoon. Then later, check on Trekker and likely change out the tires. Could bury old tires here in logged area. Wife would maintain camp, dry our stuff, and collect and boil water. Quick look at Trekker as I headed out to check snare traps showed that I also need to shore up the frame a bit. Previous work is wearing. Will also grease up axles using tube of grease in repair kit. It was starting to run low. Will have to find substitute soon or we will have problems with its mobility.

Headed out to check the three snare traps set yesterday. First one was a mess. Had indeed caught a rabbit, but there wasn't much left of it. Larger critter had gotten to it so pulled snare and reset it at another location. With snowstorm ending lots of small hungry critters, raccoons, possums, skunks, and maybe even some larger ones will start to forage for food. We have to keep an eye on things and make sure weapons are at hand when in camp. We also have to police food prep and cooking areas and make sure we bury remains a distance away from shelter. Dogs are likely to start going crazy with scents and sightings.

Second snare trap was empty but in third hit jackpot. A rabbit. Dispatched it quickly, foot on neck, quick tug on hind feet separating head from spine, killing it instantly. Field-dressed and skinned it and immediately went back to camp after resetting snares. In camp cut up meat and cooked in same way as squirrel. Added it to prepared rice and beans, and we had a feast for lunch. Ate slowly, as bulk of meat is not something we are really used to anymore, and had to take care not to gorge ourselves and set our innards into a tailspin. Rabbit has a sweet flavor, so made the rice and beans much better. Dogs each got about one-fourth of the meat. They need the protein just as much as we do.

After lunch, after warning wife to be on lookout for foraging critters while she dried sleeping bags and clothing by fire, I set out straight west to find OH route 668. Walked as straight a line as possible along two low ridges into and out of neighboring valley. When came around point of second ridge, there was the bridge, within mile and a half of our camp. Could see intersection of country road we had been walking joining the route about 100 yards short of the bridge. Observed vehicle traffic. Three cars and one pickup in the fifteen minutes. Sat on ridge point watching. We would have to be careful and choose a good time to cross the bridge. Could not tell if any roads intersected route after bridge, but guessed and hoped we would not have far to go to get off the main drag in the area. Made my way back to camp and reported findings to wife. We are glad we won't have to find a stream crossing and relay stuff to other side.

Spent remaining daylight hours of afternoon tending to the Trekker. Changed out both tires. Took couple hours because of cold hands and rubber tires. Few dings and words not proud of. But got them on and inflated. Buried old tires. Greased axle. Spent last hour before supper reinforcing and changing out wood supports to main frame. Wire used to attach supports was rusting pretty badly so changed as much of that out as I could. Trekker was getting beaten up especially the material used to form the bed. Patched up tears and holes as best I could, using duct tape, which was difficult because of cold. Of course, had to unload it to get all of this done. Reloaded and organized when finished with repairs. Decided to do thirty-minute squirrel hunt from in front of camp in waning light, but that was futile because every time dogs saw one in trees they went nuts. If only they could climb trees. Saw first deer in days come up valley to our left. We were downwind of them so they never saw us. Again, dogs saw them, and once started barking, deer headed for different country.

Light supper of soup and coffee since had big lunch. We fixed a bit of rice and mixed in remains of lunch and gave that to the dogs. I had saved the rabbit heart until this meal so cooked it quickly on stick over fire and gave each dog half. You would have thought it was their best meal ever. They enjoyed licking my fingers to get the last bit of flavor. Once they had eaten they were satisfied to sit by the fire on their short leashes and stay warm. We had moved all of the snow we could from area between shelter and fire to cut down on mud forming and to allow us to put plastic down for dogs to lie on. They were having a hard time staying awake in the heat from the fire and from full tummies. We are so grateful for them. Unconditional love even in these tough circumstances.

Once we had prepped our sleeping area for the night we washed our bodies while boots put on end of poles by fire to dry them out a bit. Just a note about our physical condition. It is obvious to us that we have lost weight over the past few weeks. The dogs have as well. We look tougher. Less body fat. Injuries have been kept to a minimum, bruises, bumps, small burns, nicks, and cuts.

Feet are in reasonable shape. Some points of irritation and redness but covered with moleskin and runner's second skin. Those are under control. Hands show wear and tear of hard manual work both when traveling but even more from work setting up and maintaining temporary and long-term camps. Gloves are really showing wear. We will be breaking out new sets of soft cotton under gloves before too long. Leather gloves are OK, couple small holes but repaired using shoe repair needles and heavy thread. Socks and boots showing wear. Outerwear in pretty good shape. Tends to smell like smoke, but that is OK as well. Checked dogs completely. Their feet are a bit beat up but all in all in pretty good shape.

With all of that done decided it was time to hit the sack. Radio reception not good in this valley. Prayers said, scripture read, and bundled up we hit the sack.

God reigns over the nations,
God sits on His holy throne.
(Psalm 47:8)

LARRY D. HORTON, PhD

Date: March 8–14   Mileage: 0 mi.   Walk Total: 99–101 miles.

March 13 Day #52 Hunker Down:
A few beams of sunlight woke us up this morning. Flurries stopped. Breaks in the gray clouds. Wind had shifted to the east. We weathered the storm in pretty good shape. Quick breakfast of rice, soup, and coffee. First task was to listen briefly to NOAA weather update and a bit of national news. Weather is indeed changing. High pressure system moving in. Temps will stay about the same, but winds will be down. Will last for at least a week.

International and national news not good. Internationally Russia has sent patrols into eastern European countries on its borders. China has fired at some Japanese patrol boats. North Korea has sent army divisions down western and eastern borders of South Korea and appears to be trying to surround Seoul. Russian jets have bombed several Jordanian air bases. Turkish army driving toward Kurd capital city. Israel is on full war setting, though few if any attacks in last week. Just patrols and an occasional rocket launched across its borders. The US Navy is sending what ships it can to the Med and to the South China Sea. American military in South Korea is in process of preparing to defend itself from North Koreans. American air power there gives it some hope for safety. The US government and president have been in conversations with leaders in all the areas of concern but have little progress in slowing down any threats to report. All national guard has been called up to both deal with domestic issues as well as to prepare for being sent into a world trouble spot.

People are very jittery. Add to all of that the US domestic problems, and people are questioning whether the US has the leadership it needs. Far too many problems at once have stretched US capabilities beyond the breaking point. Some in the military asking for the freedom to prepare for all-out conflict have been immediately replaced with others who will toe the government line. World financial crises have calmed some. US and international banking systems are back on line and a bit of calm is restored. US stock market has recovered a bit. Main index sits at 6,400 down from the low 18,000s before the problems hit. The Fed, IRS, and other federal systems are slowly coming back on line. Communication systems holding, but outages occur in large sections of the country periodically. Electric and other power systems are also sporadic at best.

Food, fuel, and water distribution are at a complete standstill. NGO disaster groups have no supplies and few volunteers. It seems everyone is concerned with their own well-being rather than rushing to the aid of others. Armed groups of citizens are patrolling all major cities alongside police and national guard. Gunfire is the norm in all major inner cities across the country. The death toll is unknown but growing daily. All vehicle traffic on all highways is stopped except for military and police vehicles. An occasional semi tries to make a run from distribution points but is soon stopped in its tracks and looted. Reports of multiple confrontations after the mandatory evening curfew with gunfire and killings have been reported in many major cities. The countryside, the flyover states, is suffering but not nearly as badly as along both coasts. Several reports indicate that some small migrations of people have started leaving major cities and heading out into the countryside. The US is receiving no assistance from its neighbors to south and north. One final disconcerting thing is reported. Military armories and gun shops have been looted across the country. Lunch, afternoon, and supper were uneventful. Mostly resting, tending fire and boiling water. To bed early this evening, needed the rest. Lord watch over us.

The Lord is for me; I will not fear;
What can man do to me?
(Psalm 188:6)

LARRY D. HORTON, PhD

Date: March 8–14   Mileage: 0 mi.   Walk Total: 99–101 miles.

March 14 Day #53 Hunker Down:

Up early, a lot of preparation to complete as we have decided to begin moving tomorrow. Simple breakfast and got busy. Morning spent collecting firewood, boiling water, cleaning clothing, and general packing. Lunch would be simple, hot soup. Dogs could sense that things were about to change.

With all this chaos in the country on our minds, we sat and talked about our next steps. With the weather changing we cannot sit any longer. Even with the amount of snow on the ground we decided to start moving again tomorrow. Since temperatures are not going to rise much, the snow might melt slowly and roads or paths not be too bad. If the sun shone consistently, that would change, but we would deal with that. So, we decided to pull in our snares, inventory, repack everything, and break camp early tomorrow morning. I went out before lunch to see if by luck I could get some fresh meat for supper tonight. Critters would very likely be out scrounging since the weather was better. With those decisions, made my wife set about securing and boiling a supply of water, hanging bags and clothing by fire to dry, and inventory our remaining food supply on the Trekker. We know what we have in our packs, and they are ready to go.

Late in the morning I walked around the small hillside to the west and placed myself under another oak tree with two squirrel nests in sight. Could hear them chattering. Twenty minutes after sitting down I spotted one on the ground and watched as it came straight at me. It stopped on a tree trunk fifteen feet away, and that was its mistake. Nailed it in neck. Likely broke its spine. It was dead instantly. The air rifle was really good. Gutted and cleaned the animal and headed back to camp. We would have it for lunch, as warmer temps meant it probably would not freeze and stay OK until supper. Was a bit more work preparing it since it was not frozen, but brazed it on fire ring and added it to rice and soup wife had fixed. Of course, the dogs each got half of the heart. Could see them smiling. At least in our minds they were.

Weather is to be good tonight. No snow. No real wind. So, we set about camp cleanup. Burying anything we won't carry, covering over latrine, and pulling pine branches off the shelter roof. Tarp will be enough tonight and much easier to take down in AM without any of the branch mess. Left sidewalls alone. In the AM, we will unbind the whole shelter and let it fall in upon itself. In the middle of this logged out area it will look just like any other pile of rubbish from the lumbering process. Last thing done in the low afternoon sunlight was to waterproof our boots with some mink oil. Will likely repeat that process once a week until we are through the coming spring rains. Last thing we need is for our boots to quit on us. Put few things, like ponchos, back into our packs, things we will likely need on a daily basis. BOBs and med bags all ready to go. Checked weapons and positioned ammo to readily available spots on our utility belts. Canteens filled, and water jugs filled, we used last bit of boiled water to fix soup for supper. Dogs got their usual portion and looked for more. Was a busy afternoon and evening. Ready to hit the sack and get moving in the AM. Prayers said, scripture read, Lord, guide us down a safe path. Good night!

> **For such is God, our God forever and ever;**
> **He will guide us until death.**
> **(Psalm 48:14)**

LARRY D. HORTON, PhD

Date: March 15   Mileage: 4 mi.   Walk Total: 103–105 miles.

Didn't sleep much. Up early. Quick oatmeal breakfast then destroyed keyhole fire pit. Cleaned dishes in remaining boiled water after filling canteens. Packed last few things on Trekker and unlashed and knocked down the shelter. Tarp was hard to roll up due to cold. We made the best of it. Dogs knew we were moving and were full of energy. Last thing was to throw snow on top of the pile of what had been our shelter to hide it as much as possible until snow melts.

With all that done, we were ready to move very carefully. Going back down slight slope was a chore. It took both of us to hold the Trekker on line. Snow-buried logs and cut brush kept us from moving very fast as well and had to tug and pull stuff over what we could not see. After an hour, had reached the country dirt road we had been using. It was completely covered in snow. Only a few tracks left by ATVs and one likely pickup since we had camped. Moving on any road will be difficult because they have not been plowed and there's at least a foot of snow on them. Progress was slow. Lots of breaks and far too much sweating. Arrived at dirt road junction with OH route 668 by 10 AM. Could see the bridge crossing Jonathan Creek just up the road. Listened but heard no vehicles, so across we went. There were some ruts in snow on the road, but progress was slow because only one set of Trekker wheels could sit in a rut. The other set was in foot-deep snow. Trekker has been good to us, but we were struggling a bit with it and getting frustrated.

About 400 yards past bridge, found small farm path into some trees off to the right. Decided to set up there and cook hot soup lunch using hexamine stove. The break was good for us, and we backtracked a bit and set off down route 668 slowly. Another hour of huffing and puffing and we came to a dirt road heading generally north by east. We headed that direction. Wanted to stay southeast of Brownsville OH and camp a bit short of where we hoped to cross I-70 west of Zanesville. If we were able to do that, our goal tomorrow was to reach Dillon Lake and shadow the western shore of the lake until we got to a place on Licking Creek where we could cross it fairly easily.

Still lots of clouds today but periodic sun breaks were great for our spirits. We pushed a little later into the day until around 3 PM. That gave us a couple hours of reasonable sunlight to find a good location and set up our overnight lean-to shelter. Nothing fancy, just adequate to get us through the night. Eventually found location where now sitting—a grove of pine trees mixed with a few oaks. Cut hole in branches of two pines up about six feet and built lean-to and basic fire pit. Collected reasonable pile of firewood but worried it would be enough to get us through the night. Small fire. Just enough to cook supper. No real water supply nearby, so we would be conserving water and hopefully find good supply tomorrow. Supper of soup and rice. Dogs got mix of both as well. Cut pine branches and built simple two-foot thick sleeping mattress. Secondary tarp on ground underneath it. No cover other than poncho for Trekker. Prayer said, scripture read, we are bushed.

But God will redeem my soul from the power of Sheol,
For He will receive me.
(Psalm 49:15)

Date: March 16   Mileage: 5 mi.   Walk Total: 108–110 miles.

Tired when woke up. Simple breakfast of cream of wheat, a bit of cooked rice, and coffee. Dogs did not want to move. No new water, so planned to look for a source as soon as possible this morning. Headed due north to cross I-70 and US 40 east of Gratiot OH. Road was still snow covered except for a few ruts, so going was slow. Road we were on crossed over I-70 amid a grove of trees, so had good cover for the crossing. A bit of traffic, mostly authorities, as much as we could see. Very little civilian traffic. I-70 was snow covered. A bit further on came to US 40 intersection. No traffic in sight so made way through intersection as quickly as we could. Lots of rest stops to cool down as snow was causing difficulty pulling Trekker. Only one set of tracks on small road we were on north of US 40. Pulled off road about one-half mile north of US 40. Built small fire by a little stream we found. Stayed at that location until had heated up some soup and boiled a jug full of water. With that we headed out again. Still heading straight north by compass as much as possible.

About 1 PM came to an even smaller snow-covered road heading off in general northeast direction, about fifty degrees by my compass. Decided to take it as that was likely general direction of Dillon Lake. Want to hit its shoreline by tomorrow and follow western shore until we cross Licking Creek north of the lake. Really hard going until around 3 PM. No tracks or ruts on new road. Slogging through a foot of snow is very difficult. Didn't take the time to stop and fabricate snowshoes. Will do that tonight for tomorrow's walk if needed. Knew we were going very slow, but at least we seemed to be out of touch with anyone else. Hilly countryside didn't help.

Finally found a reasonable spot to bed down for the night in the lee of a hill in a small grove of trees by a frozen-over stream. We were pretty exhausted but still had to build an overnight camp. Got around to that after breaking through ice on stream so wife could get after our water supply. Couple good dead logs laying on ground covered with snow.

Gathered as much small stuff as I could for fire and built pit and got fire going. Similar shelter to last night. Simple lean-to using small log between two tree branches as main support. Fashioned some small pegs and tied down corners of primary tarp roof. Cleaned out as much snow as possible and built windbreaks on each side of lean-to with the snow. Couple small pine trees provided a minimal sleeping mattress. Rest of sleeping gear opened on it. Expect to be comfortable tonight. Wife cooked double portion of hot soup and coffee for supper. Dogs were listless. They were tired of walking through snow on their shorter legs. Made reasonable progress by our calculations in spite of the difficult walking through snow. No radio tonight. Reception was not possible in our location down in a valley. Covered Trekker with ponchos and hit the sack. We know tomorrow will be more of the same. Prayers, scripture reading, and some conversation about how to conserve our energy tomorrow. We prayed Lord would give us strength.

Call upon Me in the day of trouble;
I shall rescue you,
And you will honor Me.
(Psalm 50:15)

LARRY D. HORTON, PhD

Date: March 17   Mileage: 5 mi.   Walk Total: 113–115 miles.

Lots of strange sounds during the night kept the dogs restless. Couple times pairs of eyes close to camp got them all stirred up, but their barking made whatever visitors leave pretty quickly. Wife fixed hot oatmeal and coffee while I broke down our temporary camp. Pushed snow back into small indent in cover we had made. When breakfast done, covered fire pit with snow as well. Left our tracks. Too many to mess with. Buried some small items near stream. Canteens and jugs were filled last night. More sunshine this morning. Temps around freezing. Might get to mid-thirties today which means lots of snowmelt and messy traveling. Decided we might spend couple nights by lakeside, if we were able to get that far today, to rest a bit. Pushing and really tired right now. Cautious of slippery conditions.

Around 8:30 AM moved out and stayed on same road until quick lunch stop around 11 AM. Again, quite a few breaks to cool down and rest. Pushed on until shortly before 3 PM on top of a small ridge, and we could see Dillon Lake in the distance. Probably another mile or so. Road appeared to be heading downhill slowly to the lakeside. Agreed to look for campsite that would be good for a couple nights to our right or left within sight of the lake but far enough away, in a small side valley if possible, to avoid others. Took us thirty minutes to go about 300 yards in the deep snow on the road, and we spotted a small valley to our left and pulled Trekker about 100 feet off the road into it. Saw small stream back across the road that was headed to lake and knew we had water source. Same process as yesterday. Built fire ring, collected initial wood for cooking supper and boiling water, and got fire started. Wife busy collecting water carefully after I broke ice on stream. She then fixed us pasta and veggie supper with hot cocoa.

I took time to eat quickly as it was taking a bit of time to build a two-night shelter. Basic lean-to with cut branches from pine trees for sides and for sleeping area. Built up sides with snow scooped out from under sleeping area. Pretty sheltered in this little valley so no wind to speak of. As sun set pretty early we were able to see stars and moon. Gave us a little bit more light to move around by. Also, heard squirrels chattering in trees on both sides of the road. Tomorrow will get out air rifle and try to get us some fresh meat. Will set out couple of snare traps first thing tomorrow and hope to have rabbit as well by evening. Lots of noise in the trees around us. Critters are starting to come out in force with weather change. Able to collect enough wood to enable us to keep decent fire going all night. Most were three to four feet long so decided to use Indian star fire construction for nighttime fire. Less hard work but would mean up couple times in night to tend it. Lots to try to accomplish tomorrow on our rest day, but we need some protein badly because of difficulty moving in snow. Dogs need something more than carbs as well. No radio again tonight. No other lights in any direction other than our reflected light from our fire. Not much talk as we settled down. Wife's fibromyalgia kicking up pretty badly in damp cold conditions. Prayer said, scripture read, a fitful rest tonight. Decided at last minute to keep moving tomorrow.

The sacrifices of God are a broken spirit;
A broken and a contrite heart, O God,
You will not despise.
(Psalm 51:17)

Date: March 18   Mileage: 4 mi.   Walk Total: 117–119 miles.

Slept a bit better but kind of cold during the night. Fire was only embers by the time we got up. Hot oatmeal and coffee for breakfast. Packed up sleeping stuff and pulled down tarp and packed it. We pushed snow back over our campsite and were ready to move out. Downhill to get closer to lake. Road ended at lake, but we discovered a hiking trail going around lake to west and north we so took it. Not quite as much snow on path due to tree cover and fact that weather had begun to melt it some. Was messy, slushy, and slow going. Slippery as well. Looked across lake to what must have been a campground and saw several columns of smoke rising into the sky. Some people were obviously camping getting away from all the mess in larger population areas. We stayed under cover as best we could. Saw a few small critters out as well. Lots of squirrels in the trees. Slow progress until lunchtime but we could see that we were getting close to the northern end of the lake. Just hoped hiking trail continued and had a bridge across Licking Creek. Stopped for quick lunch of rice and beans cooked on portable hexamine stove to avoid detection. Water supply OK for now. Multiple stops when we overheated.

After lunch moved on and we did find a small walking bridge across the creek, but it was not wide enough to pull Trekker across. Had to relay all equipment and dogs across. After that, wrestled Trekker across folded up. Took the two of us a bit of time to do that. Lots of grunting and not so nice language. But we did it and repacked it and set off down the trail again, this time to the southeast. Took trail all the way to the entrance road to the campground. No one in sight, so we hurried and moved to OH route 146. Headed northwest on that route about a mile until we came to another country road heading to the northeast. We took that country road. Didn't go too far on it and looked for a site to camp. Took a bit but lots of cover in the valleys and hills around us. Had to have gotten to the mid-thirties in the afternoon, which felt like a heat wave to us. Shed all heavy outer clothing and were able to control overheating somewhat. By the time we pulled off the road into a grove of trees by a small stream that was headed for the lake, the sun had set behind a hill to our west, and it cooled off pretty quickly. Glad to stop for the day.

Moved into tree grove off the road and pretty quickly set up temporary camp just like last night's. Gathered sufficient fire wood plus 50 percent to get us through the night. Wife fixed hot supper while I was busy with wood. We had decided late last night not to spend second night on the other side of the lake when we saw evidence of campfires on the far side of the lake. We were tired when we finally stopped and settled tonight. Decided to push on to Muskingum River Parkway State Park and spend couple nights there instead. Tired but satisfied with progress. To bed early so we could get an early start. Dogs tired as well. No fussing tonight. Prayers said, scripture read, we just lay in our bags listening to the sounds around us as we waited for sleep. Good night!

Why do you boast in evil, O mighty man?
The lovingkindness of God endures all day long.
(Psalm 52:1)

LARRY D. HORTON, PhD

Date: March 19   Mileage: 5 mi.   Walk Total: 122–124 miles.

Slept pretty well. Quick oatmeal start. Dogs were very hungry so did double portion. Broke down as had done yesterday. Water we collected and boiled last night in jugs on Trekker and in canteens. Won't have to be quite as careful with it today. Trekker loaded we headed out on the country road we had found heading northeast. Reached OH route 60 before lunch and our road crossed it, so we kept going in same direction. Assumed we were heading towards the next state park. Road had been traveled a bit more, so its surface was showing once in a while through the melting snow. Mud getting worse. Lots of water on the road. But progress was steady with the usual breaks to cool down. Not much for lunch today. Felt like we were making good progress towards park so pushed a bit to get to it. Around 2 PM saw wisps of smoke at distance in direction we were traveling. Had to be campground at state park. Had to be Muskingham Lake. But only saw one pillar of smoke, so hoped would not be too many people.

Crested last little ridge and could see where the smoke was located. Road we were on seemed to turn to the east a bit, so we stayed on it to avoid any contact again. Crossed a small stream below the campground and looked for safe place to spend two nights. Small valley to our right. Decided to head that direction. Had to walk up the valley a bit to check it out as there was no path or road heading into it. Found reasonable location and headed back to relay everything to the site, after which pulled Trekker to the site. Went back to road and covered our tracks with snow to keep our location as unknown as possible. Hoped nighttime would make it hard to see evidence of our passage.

Set up temporary camp as had done previous two nights, but made it a bit more stable because of our plan to spend two nights here. Supper was rice, beans, and pudding. Gathered wood in darkness to get us through the night. Would have to get quite a bit more in the morning. Stream is a good 200 yards from us, so took some time toting water for cooking and boiling as well. Dogs interested in all the brush around us. Had a feeling we might have some visitors tonight. And we did. Around 7 PM spotted a raccoon coming towards our location. Stood up on its hind legs about 15 feet from fire. Dogs went nuts. Made a quick decision to secure some meat for the dogs. Air rifle not powerful enough. So took risk and used 17 HMR to put slug into critter's neck just above shoulders. It flew 5 feet when slug hit it. Was dead before it hit the ground. Gutted and skinned it. Buried pelt. Wife and I could not bring ourselves to consider eating any of it, but cut up and roasted pieces over our fire. Dogs were beside themselves. Once roasted completely cut up a hindquarter for each dog and fed them. First real meat they had had in days. Washed everything, including our hands, twice after messing with and cooking the critter. Buried the remaining meat with the pelt. Didn't need dogs overeating and getting sick. For the next couple hours, we went as silent as possible listening for any sign that the rifle shot had brought any curious individuals in our direction.

No traffic on the country road. Lots of moonlight tonight, as high pressure system seems to be right over us. Will be a chilly night. Tried to get some reception on our radio but it was not very good yet. Need to get out from among all the hills. Hope we can do that in the next couple days. Did talk about what we would do if another storm forecast. Probably hunker down again.

Planned inventory of resources for tomorrow, gathering firewood, boiling water, getting some rest, and trying to get us a squirrel for supper. If time available will attempt to do a bit of reflecting on our latest part of the trip just to note our feelings and perspectives on the journey. Prayers said, scripture read, hugged each other and the dogs, and crawled into bags for the night.

God has looked down from heaven and the sons of men
To see if there is anyone who understands,
Who seeks after God.
(Psalm 53:2)

Date: March 20   Mileage: 0 mi.   Walk Total: 122–124 miles.

Fairly quiet night. Had another visitor in middle of night. Dogs alerted us to it. Saw another set of eyes sitting about ten feet from the embers of our fire, a raccoon. Used air rifle to put a pellet in its hind end, and it took off in a flash. No other disturbances during the night. Quite a few tasks to complete today before we head out again tomorrow. Cream of wheat, rice, and coffee for breakfast. Dogs not too hungry after their raccoon feast of last night. They were just contented. Gathered water for boiling, then plenty of firewood, dead stuff, for the day and night. Checked shelter and tightened it up a bit. White fluffy clouds. A good weather sign.

Got about doing our inventory check. Everything seems OK. A bit damp but that was to be expected. Changed clothes and dried day wear out by fire. This is our normal practice when we have time. We had sleeping clothing and traveling clothing. Would save sleeping clothing to use for traveling when other stuff started to show a lot of wear and tear and could not be repaired. Did detailed food inventory. Twelve to fifteen days of freeze-dried stuff left on Trekker and a few pounds of rice and beans. Food stores in backpacks not touched since last inventory. Likely twenty to twenty-five lbs. left in packs depending on how much meat we are able to secure and use to expand that food supply. We can safely go another sixty days on what we have on hand. Then we will really have to start living off the land even more. If we could get a supply of fresh meat every other day and combine that with rice, we could go a few more days. Really important for the thaw to start so we can add fish when available to our diet. That will help a lot also. All in all we seem to be in OK shape for now.

After lunch of rice and beans charged up crank radio and we walked up to top of small hill behind us to see if we could get any reception. Success! NOAA forecast said another front will move in from northwest in about five days. Will last only three days with snowfall likely much less than last big storm. Temps will be below freezing. Indicated weather would start to get a bit milder after the next front, so best we can hope for is beginning of thaw in seven to ten days.

National news has not gotten any better. More instances of violence across the country. Groups of people migrating out of the cities. International situation is in a lull at least for the time being. Walked back to campsite and spent rest of afternoon resting, all four of us. Gathered and boiled water supply and cooked supper of freeze-dried pasta with dried chicken chunks. Fruit juice to drink. Staying light a bit later each day. We sat in camp and just relaxed. Did a quick cleaning of our firearms and checked edges on all of our blades and sharpened, as necessary. When hiking clothing was reasonably dry, did a few sewing repairs to them. Checked for any new nicks, cuts, and bruises and dealt with them. Last thing was to wash our bodies as best we could. Warm water, cold temps, it didn't take long to get that done. Couple irritated points on our legs and arms from carrying some of our gear, but that was to be expected. We looked at each other and grinned. We were pretty lean compared to when we started out. Muscles no longer sore, and they seemed to be much stronger than before. When all that done, said our prayers, read scripture, and thanked the Lord we were still safe. Good night!

Behold, God is my helper;
The Lord is the sustainer of my soul.
(Psalm 54:4)

Reflections:

Wrote these reflections as we rested during the afternoon on March 20th. Looking back to the day when we bugged out from our home in Houston, January 21st, thanked the good Lord we had moved out when events around us indicated it was clearly the thing to do. We wondered what people would think of us then, so we told no one of our plans. That morning our lives left that environment and headed out into an unknown future. We wondered about our friends there and across the nation. How were they surviving in all the chaos?

More importantly we wondered about our immediate families. Our daughter and son-in-law in Indiana had a couple bug-out locations identified. Hopefully they reached one and were able to deal with everything there safely. No word from our two sons and their wives on the west coast. One lived somewhat off the grid to begin with, away from large centers of population. They had been preparing to be self-sufficient since they moved there. The other, living in a suburb of a large city, would have to be dealing with a totally different situation. They were in our prayers daily. Our hope was that they were safe, but we had put them in the Lord's hands.

Our brothers and their wives were scattered. All living in population centers in Indiana, Texas, and Ohio. We have no idea of how some might have prepared themselves. We had had no word from any of them. As with our kids we had put them in the Lord's hands. We were safe and away from much of the conflict so far. That might change in the days ahead. Our decision to bug out had proved to be the right one.

Cross Country Diary: Day #60

Date: March 21   Mileage: 5 mi.   Walk Total: 127–129 miles.

Woke up early after day of resting. Much of our former world no longer existed. Our little camp here in Ohio was our world now. We trusted the Lord for the future. We would walk into it cautiously but with faith. Temps pretty decent during night. Light fluffy clouds and sunshine again this morning. Packed everything, loaded the Trekker, broke down the camp, and headed out to the northeast. Objective today and tomorrow is to end up a mile or so north of Otsego OH and south of Willis Creek Lake. Breakfast of oatmeal and coffee. Dogs seem to be getting tired of oatmeal. Followed couple country roads today winding through some small hills and valleys. Saw no traffic, and road was starting to melt free of snow. Only couple inches left to hinder our walking. Lunch was quiet just off the roadside. Was nice to see the sun and a few clouds. Able to shed couple layers of clothing yet even with that had to stop periodically for cooldowns.

Kept walking at a pretty good pace during the afternoon and by 2:30 PM were ready to look for our night campsite. Pretty good place found 50 feet off the road back in a sheltered little cove of trees. Small stream a short walk away. No sign of critters using it. Wife worked on fire pit while I put up our normal tarp shelter in the tree grove. Getting to point where can set it up in about thirty minutes if have poles to function as framework or trees that are close to use rope to build primary support cross member. Fire started, though harder than some. Wood very wet. Thank goodness, we have a good supply of fire starters, cotton balls, and Vaseline. Had to look for some dry bark under trees to provide kindling. With everything being so wet, took a bit to get fire going. Piled as much brush and firewood as could collect next to fire to start drying it out. Again, using Indian star wood formation for main fire.

Wife started supper of pasta, veggies, and coffee while I kept looking for more reasonably dry firewood. Ate around 7 PM, then dried hiking clothes by fire. Wife had an irritated spot from her boot on her foot, so fixed that with moleskin. We sat for a while after supper and just listened to noises around us. Heard some gunfire off in the distance. We hoped that it was some hunters out getting fresh meat. We did not want to deal with any alternative to that. Dogs on alert. Smaller one was afraid a bit. Put them on their long leads so they could snoop around campsite. They have been so good. Losing a bit of weight, but so far nothing has really spooked them. They just want to get into the woods and chase something.

No radio tonight. Reception not good. That made us think of the fact that we have had no contact with anyone, face-to-face or by phone, for weeks. Would like to call family, but no reception and to be honest don't want a record of phone call made that could be used to triangulate our location. Abundance of caution in everything. Prayers, scripture and hugs, good night!

> **I said, "Oh, that I had wings like a dove!**
> **I would fly away and be at rest."**
> **(Psalm 55:6)**

Cross Country Diary: Day #61

Date: March 22   Mileage: 6 mi.   Walk Total: 128–130 miles.

For some reason seemed to have a bit more energy when we woke up this morning after a quiet night. Same morning routine. Breakfast, made sure had water supply filled, broke down temporary shelter, packed up Trekker, made sure dogs were satisfied, policed camp area, and then set off down the road in the same northeasterly direction. Good pace walking. Road pretty clear. Lots of standing water, but that didn't seem to hinder us. We could sense that Mills Lake was off to our left as we traveled down a road that seemed to be going around the lake. Lunch uneventful. Heated up some soup on hexamine stove. Dogs got their last Milkbone dog biscuit, but they were happy. Set out under partly sunny skies after lunch. Had our first encounter with other humans shortly after 1 PM. First direct contact in weeks. Couple of hunters walking up the road. We passed with a few greetings. Asked how hunting was going and tried to just be about our business. The rest of the afternoon passed with us stopping periodically to listen for human sounds and to look behind us to see if we were being followed. Knew would have to get a bit further back off the road tonight and keep our fire very small and sheltered. There were two legged critters in the area, and we didn't want to take any chances with them. Especially with ones who were carrying high-powered hunting rifles. We slowly calmed down as time passed.

Continued to progress until around 3 PM, when we saw what was likely a farmer's road. Two ruts going out through a field to our left. We decided to take it and find a camp between the two hills we saw about a quarter mile from our traveling road. We sensed that potential for human contact was going to increase. We had observed lots of small paths and roads heading off from our travel roads over the past weeks. Given the number of critters that would be in the countryside we guessed a lot of those paths and roads led to hunting camps. Luckily, we had not run into anyone until today. Found a small valley on side of one of the hills and pushed back as far as we could into it. Site not as ideal as some others we've had, but we would be concealed quite a bit.

LARRY D. HORTON, PhD

Routine set up. Wife fixed hot soup and rice for supper. Dogs liked it. Orange drink for dessert. Gathered quite a bit of wood. Little site had not seen total snow of other places, protected by overhead canopy of pine trees and oaks. Quite a bit of deer sign and rabbit trails. By time got shelter set up and ate, was too late to look for any critters for meal. Maybe tomorrow. We sat down by small firelight and looked at map to plan travel for next few days.

We are still pretty much on track we set days ago. Geography is not too much of a problem. Weather has made it easier, and leftover snow is rapidly going away. Tomorrow will cross OH routes 662 and 541 and head toward Newcomerstown OH area. Hoped to get another ten miles total in next two days. We actually sang couple Christian hymns tonight. Dogs looked at us kind of funny. Lots of prayers said, scripture read, and hugs all around. Lord, continue to watch over us. We love you.

**In God I have put my trust,
I shall not be afraid.
What can man do to me?
(Psalm 56:11)**

Cross Country Diary: Day #62

Date: March 23   Mileage: 5 mi.   Walk Total: 133–135 miles.

Didn't sleep well. Too worried about human contact from yesterday. Low profile breakfast. Hot soup on hexamine stove. Dogs shared it with us. They seemed to be hungry. Quiet breakdown of camp and got on our way as quickly as we could. We had no idea where the hunters came from yesterday and wanted to get out of the area. Crossed over OH route 662 and found an isolated dirt road heading in general direction we wanted to travel. By lunchtime had crossed OH route 541 on that same dirt road, which continued northeast. Heard more gunfire in the distance, so were very careful to stay in cover as much as we could. Had to travel through a couple open fields, and we did not waste any time. Sweating a lot, but temps were OK and sun kept us warm. Would really have to wash and dry clothing tonight. A good hound could have smelled us from three miles away.

Sat under canopy of trees by roadside and fixed a bit of lunch. Nothing fancy. Mixed up some flour and salt and made flatbread. Need the carbs for energy. Dogs thought was greatest thing since one of their store-bought treats. Kept moving. More rest stops. Sweating a lot. Always worried about hypothermia. Wife's foot is some better. Her joint pain in warmer temps is not as bad. I am getting tired of pulling Trekker, but it has been a lifesaver to this point in our journey.

By midafternoon we sensed we were getting closer to Newcomerstown. Heard traffic noises in the distance through the valleys that were all around us. Still no commercial air traffic above. Country really must have shut down. By compass dead reckoning around 3 PM figured we were a couple miles to the southwest of Newcomerstown. Time to find shelter for the night and deal with some roads tomorrow that are likely to have some traffic. Newcomerstown is the biggest community we will have been around in last couple weeks. Might get indications of a lot of peoples as we skirt the town. We have to cross a pretty significant stream tomorrow, the Tuscarawas; are prepared to deal with it as best we can even if we have to ford it relaying everything across.

LARRY D. HORTON, PhD

We're beginning to wonder how much more valuable the Trekker will be for us. With supplies on it dwindling and the fact that we will run into more civilization, wonder if we might have to go with packs only and travel off road for the remaining distance ahead of us. Next few days will help us make that decision. Roads, with weather changing, will become more dangerous. Found semi-hidden camping site off the road around 3:30 PM. Evening routine the same. Two primary tasks, gather firewood for concealed fire with as little smoke as possible, and replenish water supply. No real streams near us, but a pond is in a nearby field. Water not the best, but filled up using water straws, filtered water through sock filter, and then boiled. Will be on the lookout for a better water source all day tomorrow. What we have can be used in emergency, but don't want to take any chances on it. Quick supper of soup and rice. Same meal but tasted good. Dogs seem to sense we are getting closer to people. To bed early, prayers, and scripture. Hard time getting to sleep again.

I will cry to God Most High,
To God who accomplishes all things for me.
(Psalm 57:2)

Date: March 24   Mileage: 5 mi.   Walk Total: 138–140 miles.

Up early. Did some map planning while wife boiled water and cooked some rice and beans. Plan was to head in more northerly direction toward Stone Creek OH where we will then cross I-77 on the third day. Then try to get a few miles east of I-77 and hunker down for the next cold front. Breakfast eaten, we broke camp and headed out. A small country road was our pathway. Lots of ruts and puddles. Looked like it was primarily used by farmers in area and maybe some loggers. Pretty clear day with wind blowing at us from the east. Because of that we could hear some traffic sounds from there, guessed from US route 36 and the later in the day we guessed might be from I-77. Either way we knew we were getting nearer people. Hills not quite as big as last few weeks. More open farm fields, mostly dairy cattle and what probably were cornfields. Noticed geese flying north during the day. A good sign. As we get closer to end of month, hoping old tale of March coming in like lion and going out like a lamb turns out to be true this year. We have at least one snow event coming and lots of cold or chilly days yet to come, but hoping worst of winter is past. Spring equinox behind us, so we're hopeful.

Lunch done quickly. Hot soup and orange drink. Afternoon of good progress. Tired and sweating, so more rest stops. Just glad we still had country roads to rely on. Saw couple farmers out in their fields moving some dairy cattle around. As the day wore on, could hear the milk cows bellowing to be let back into the barn. Painful udders were probably not a good thing. All in all, more life stirring around us. It is only a matter of time before we have more human contact. Found decent place to set up our camp in a section of woods that our road cut through. Pulled Trekker about 100 yards off the road. Very wet and muddy. Did find a small stream for water. We had stopped for lunch by another small stream and had taken the time to boil enough water to fill our extra water jug and canteens. That little delay meant that we did not get about setting up camp until around 4 PM. Normal setting up camp routine. I gathered firewood and water while wife got fire pit built and fire going.

While she was fixing our soup, rice, and some freeze-dried beef for supper, I got about and finished putting up our tarp shelter for the night.

Supper hit the spot. After eating, gathered some firewood. Knocked down a couple small standing dead trees. Cut up into four-foot logs and built Indian star fire. We washed our filthy, stinky bodies and our socks. Dried feet and socks by the fire. When about ready to hit the sack, hung hiking clothes by the fire to dry a bit. Last thing done before climbing into sleeping bags was to take those clothes down and put them in bottom of sleeping bags to keep them as dry and warm as possible. While all of this campsite stuff was going on, put dogs on their long leads and let them snoop around. They were more than ready to hit the sack when it was time. Day after tomorrow will start looking for next hunker-down site. Prayers said, scripture read, and sang a few songs again. We are so blessed to be safe and with each other; thank you, Lord.

All men will say, "Surely there is a reward for the righteous;
Surely there is a God who judges on earth!"
(Psalm 58:11)

Cross Country Diary: Day #64

Date: March 25   Mileage: 5 mi.   Walk Total: 143–145 miles.

Slept in a bit this morning trying to conserve energy. Another partly sunny morning, but more nip in the air. Tomorrow we will start watching the weather looking for signs that the next front from the northwest is approaching. There is a good chance that tomorrow evening we will once again be hunkering down to wait out the storm.

Routine breakfast. Made sure had enough water boiled for the day. Policed campsite and tore down our tarp shelter. Repacked the Trekker and were on our way by 9 AM. Moved very cautiously down our country road. If all went well, would cross OH route 751 and camp just west of Stone Creek. Likely to see more humans around as there is an I-77 interchange at this town. So evading contact is again on our minds. Uneventful morning through lunch just off the roadside.

Just before we set off again, heard the sound of a tractor coming up the road toward us. Quickly cut some branches and did best to cover the Trekker. We went a little further off the road into a small ravine with the dogs. Did not want them to see disturbance and give us away. Tried our best to keep them occupied. Looking back to road watched two tractors go by pulling wagons loaded down with round bales of hay. Likely headed out to a pasture where some cows were located. Disconcerting thing about seeing them was fact that drivers on both tractors had rifles slung over their shoulders. Obviously, they were not taking any chances with strangers that they might encounter.

As we got closer to Stone Creek, could hear some semi-truck traffic probably on I-77. Confirmed our earlier thoughts that we were getting closer to concentrations of other humans. Bore a little further to the west than planned crossing OH route 751. Walked until 3:30 PM due to our late start this morning. Looked for some serious cover for the night and found a farm road that curved around a point of a hill and headed up a small valley. Decided that was best we could do, and hoped

LARRY D. HORTON, PhD

that nothing would come down the road in the valley as we set up our camp and spent the night.

Again, normal camp setup activities. Wife collected water from nearby stream now not frozen over. Was cold water. Would have tasted good if we did not have to boil it. She also built another fire pit big enough to put three four foot logs in horizontal fashion in it to build a fire. I first collected what we thought would be enough firewood for the night. It was a bit dryer due to sunshine and slight breeze. Still evidence of the last big snow, but far easier to find logs and wood for both the fire and the basic tarp lean-to shelter. Wife prepared rice and freeze-dried beef with coffee for supper. As soon as finished eating completed shelter and bedding. Once everything unrolled and in place, we sat by the fire and talked about what might be going on out in the rest of the world. We were getting close enough to New Philadelphia OH that we figured would be able to get a bit of news on radio from there tomorrow evening. Dogs tired. They just wanted to stretch out by the fire. A long day ahead tomorrow with weather likely starting to change. To bed, prayers, scripture, and hugs for everyone.

But as for me, I shall sing of Your strength;
Yes, I shall joyfully sing of Your lovingkindness in the morning.
(Psalm 59:16)

Cross Country Diary: Day #65

Date: March 26   Mileage: 5 mi.   Walk Total: 148–150 miles.

Up early as we wanted to get another five miles in, which we did, and still have enough time to build a serious shelter tonight before the weather starts to change. Same morning routine. Breakfast, boil bit of water, break down camp, police camp, load up the Trekker, and set off for the day. Food pretty much the same. About seven days left in the Trekker. If need be could load that into our packs and abandon the Trekker, but we hope that won't be necessary. Back on a country road we found heading north by northwest. Five miles on this country road should take us toward our next landmark, Ragersville OH. Kept moving with periodic breaks. Wind increasing a bit from northwest and gray clouds started to show up about 1 PM shortly after we stopped for lunch. While eating turned on NOAA weather and report said storm is in the Akron OH area and front will pass New Philadelphia sometime tonight. That was all we needed to hear.

Pushed on not seeing or hearing anything other than birds and the occasional dog barking in the distance. Lots of dirt driveways we assumed heading off the road in many places back into the hills. Hoped they were to unoccupied hunting camps, but also knew might be headed to homes with people living in them. As the afternoon wore on, we got more anxious about finding suitable hunker-down site. At 2 PM we decided to follow one of those small two-rut roads west. There was no sign that it had been used recently, so we felt that was our best bet. Followed it three-fourths of a mile until we came upon a broken-down camp on one side of the path and a thick grove of pine trees on the other side. We chose the pine grove as next hunker-down site.

Took a while to get the Trekker under the trees. Went back into the grove about thirty yards to a location where the overhanging pine branches kept undergrowth at a minimum and had laid down a nice carpet of pine needles. We were home for now once again. Looked for water source and found very small stream about 100 yards distant. We will have to be very careful with our fire in this location with so

LARRY D. HORTON, PhD

much dead and dry material lying around. Pine needles, sticks, and dead wood were great fire materials because of their sap, but they also present a large fire hazard if our fire gets out of hand. Caution again. First task was to get shelter built. Pine cover above us simplified hunker-down shelter a bit. Built same sleeping platform and shelter structure as before but only covered the roof with a tarp. Pine trees will protect us somewhat from large amounts of snow, at least until any wind sends it all down on us. Tarp was stretched very tight in a lean-to configuration. Cut lots of pine branches for flooring and sidewalls of shelter. Wove sidewalls together as best we could.

While I started to collect firewood, almost all pine, of which there was a lot, wife laid out a keyhole fire pit. With those jobs done I put up a reflector wall and a space blanket roof over the fire pit. Covered Trekker with secondary tarp. Was pretty dark by the time this was done, so we took break and fixed something to eat. Pasta, dried veggies, and orange drink. Of course, dogs liked the pasta, the veggies not so much. After eating finished basic campsite by digging drainage ditch around shelter and digging small latrine some distance from the shelter. With that we were done. Given weather report, two to four inches of snow, we hope we've done a good enough job preparing. Will do a complete check of it in the AM.

One more quick listen to NOAA radio after cranking up battery to confirm tomorrow's weather. It will soon start getting colder and snow starts after midnight. We were right to set up hunker-down site this afternoon and evening. Feel secure even though we know that could change any minute. Closed the day with prayer and scriptures as we do every night. Special thanks to the Lord for His protection in our prayers tonight. Everyone in bags as warm and cozy as possible. Looking up through pine branches, we see that stars are all hidden. Cloud cover has moved in and winds picking up a bit. Zipped up bags. Settled the dogs down and waited for sleep.

O give us help against the adversary,
For deliverance by man is in vain.
(Psalm 60:11)

Date: March 27   Mileage: 0 mi.   Walk Total: 148–150 miles.

Last night noticed lights reflecting off clouds to our southwest. Assume that is Ragersville. We made good progress yesterday. No need to get up early this morning so took our time getting breakfast. Once that was done, I got about gathering couple days of fire wood and covered stack with our secondary tarp. Also, decided to build up a sleeping platform to keep us off the cold, damp ground. Wife hauled water for boiling while I was doing my chores and had it boiling on fire. Wanted to fill up our spare water jug. Light snow falling as we worked. Wind blowing out of northwest. Wind chill was cold when out from under canopy of trees in our grove. Rechecked all weapons and blades. Maintenance of critical stuff.

We changed into our stay-put clothing and hung hiking clothes under shelter cover where reflected heat from fire would dry them out some. Did body hygiene late morning, washed up, and air-dried all parts washed. That was a brisk process but absolutely necessary. Checked status of wife's foot irritation, and it looks much better. Put dogs on their long leads and let them snoop around. They have too much energy to just sit by the fire. Decided to take air rifle after lunch and head to a grove of oaks and maples across way on another hill for a couple hours sitting and waiting for a potential shot at a squirrel. Lunch was hot soup. Double portion so dogs got their share. Once lunch finished gathered up rifle and water canteen. Dressed warmer because of falling snow and wind. I would be sitting and likely to feel the cold more. Took thirty minutes to get to the grove of trees across the way. Found a good oak to sit against. Saw several squirrel nests in area. Sat down and waited. After about ninety minutes was getting really cold and about to head back to camp. Saw squirrel coming toward my location and went motionless. Took shot when about twenty feet above me and it almost hit me as it fell out of the tree. Field-dressed and skinned it.

Headed back to campsite with supper. Once back in camp washed carcass and skewered it on a hand-held spit. Would cook this one by hand so we could have meat as our main course for supper. Pot of soup cooking at the same time. The dogs were going nuts. All they could smell was the roasting squirrel. Took a good twenty minutes to make sure it was cooked enough. Quartered the cooked meat. Each dog got a quarter. Wife and I each had a quarter along with soup and hot coffee. Was a feast. Full tummies do wonders for the emotions. Doesn't take much to fill us up right now. Rationed meals have gotten us used to going with just three basic meals of sufficient quantity to give us energy throughout the day. We do not miss any of the sweets or snacks that were so much a part of our diet before, which is good.

Washed up supper dishes. Snowing lightly. About an inch of new snow on the ground. Put dogs on short leads, and they lay by fire on sheet of ground plastic covered with small blanket we had brought along for them. They were snoring quite a bit. Full tummies and warmth has a way of doing that. One more water run to boil and make sure we have supply for tomorrow. Drying some wood by the fire. Space blanket reflector really works well. Had to do a bit of duct tape repair on the one space blanket. Had a couple small tears in it.

Decided to turn on radio and catch up on events. Most situations still the same; however, Russia has given countries on its western border twenty-four hours to accept Russian protection or face being overrun forcibly. By end of day tomorrow Europe could be in bad way. Middle East and Asia basically unchanged. North Korean invasion of South Korea has bogged down a bit in winter weather. A new hot spot has surfaced in northern South America and in parts of Central America. Venezuela and Colombia are angry with each other. One thing that was very clear. All of these situations are beginning to create the largest humanitarian crisis the world has ever seen.

US domestic situation is more of the same. Roving bands of armed individuals, confrontations with national guard and police, people leaving cities in droves, small communities and countryside faced with threats from all of the people movement and armed groups. Several incidents where individuals have died trying to protect their homes and land from these groups. Police and national guard stretched to the limit of what they can do. In fact, in many cases they seemingly could not respond and people were left to their own means to protect themselves. We know we will face these threats as we travel.

With that, turned on NOAA weather and heard that snow will be ending tomorrow afternoon late, and next day will just be cloudy and cold. We will head out again day after tomorrow. We had a little praise service before getting ready for bed. Some singing and a lot of prayers for many things—family, friends, country, safety, wisdom, patience, and good old street smarts. Played with dogs a bit. They are the best companions. Unconditional love given so freely. A big adventure for them, and so far they had been really all that we could ask them to be. Wife and I thankful for each other. We have our daily chores and know that we need each other. Prayers said, scripture read, lots of hugs. Thank you, Lord, for the day.

From the end of the earth I call to You when my heart is faint;
Lead me to the rock that is higher than I.
(Psalm 61:2)

LARRY D. HORTON, PhD

Date: March 28   Mileage: 0 mi.   Walk Total: 148–150 miles.

Lots of critter noises during the night. Saw couple sets of eyes glaring in the distance, but dogs barking sent them running. First things first. Got fire going and carried water from stream to be boiled. Wife fixed simple cream of wheat and coffee breakfast. Only a couple more days of food left on the Trekker. Gathered a bit more firewood just in case. Light snow falling. Looks to be up to about three inches out in the open. Not as much at our camp. Decided to go back to hunting site for couple hours; might get lucky again. Time will tell. We also decided to stick close to camp and do inventory of supplies and more maintenance on equipment. Hung stuff up to dry. Washed feet and socks. Top priority with walking ahead of us tomorrow. Air dried feet again. It was cold.

Headed out late AM to sit under hunting tree again. Very cold after sixty minutes, and saw and heard nothing around me, so headed back to camp. Dogs were up and about when got back anticipating another hot piece of meat. Was tough to disappoint them. Lunch of hot soup and coffee. Hit the spot. Decided to go back to tree and hunt for another hour. Came back empty-handed again. Afternoon spent resting under the shelter, doing maintenance to equipment, and checking our physical status. We actually took a short nap, the dogs with us. Woke up when we heard some shots in the distance. Again, hoping was hunter or someone shooting target. Seemed strange that someone would shoot target given fact that ammo supplies and sales had been stopped weeks ago by the new president when things started to get dangerous within the country.

Spent later afternoon packing as much as possible for travel tomorrow. Keep camp shutdown in AM as simple as possible. Collected and boiled water. Made sure jugs and canteens were full and had enough to use in cooking supper. On days like this not much really goes on other than to get as much rest as possible while doing basic chores and ongoing preparations of equipment. Didn't listen to the radio this evening; figured would find out status of everything tomorrow.

Objective tomorrow is to head straight north, cross US route 39, and find camp a few miles west of Dover OH. Population concentration growing. We are not that far from the Youngstown/Canton/Massilon area. From traveling through there in the past know what we will be heading into. We were ready to hit the sack tonight so with prayers said and scripture read we did exactly that. Good night!

Trust in Him at all times, O people;
Pour out your heart before Him; God is a refuge for us.
(Psalm 62:8)

Date: March 29   Mileage: 7 mi.   Walk Total: 155–157 miles.

Quick breakfast of hot oatmeal and coffee. Broke down camp, policed area, filled in latrine, spread pine needles to cover our sign, packed sleeping gear, and headed out. AM uneventful other than having to zig and zag quite a bit on small country roads to maintain our basic northerly direction. Probably only traveled five miles as the crow flies but likely about seven miles due to changes in direction. Periodic compass checks when we came to intersections to try and decide which road to take. Snow, three inches, on roads didn't melt much. Cloudy day, no sun, so progress impeded a bit. Slippery. Pulled off road around noon. Hot soup cooked over hexamine stove and then hit the road again. Simple camp planned tonight to get early start tomorrow.

Quite a bit of civilization ahead of us tomorrow. Crossing I-77 again. Population between Dover OH and Parral OH. Thank goodness mostly farming communities, but still must be very careful. Finally came to a good place to spend the night about 3:30 PM and built out camp. Same look as on many other nights. Lean-to shelter, pine branches for flooring and sleeping, sleeping mats and bags, branches as windbreaks on sides of shelter, simple fire pit with space blanket reflector and roof, and secondary tarp cover for Trekker. Wood gathering for cooking and the night, but no really good water source, so will have to take care of that as we travel tomorrow. Supper of pasta, dried chicken, pudding, and orange drink. Dogs of course loved the chicken and pasta.

After supper spent some time studying map for tomorrow's travel. Will head east-northeast and try to camp a couple miles east of Parral OH. Will first head north toward Winfield OH and strike out pretty much to the east. Try to keep on a twenty-degree compass setting as much as possible. Likely have to do more zigzagging, as there are lots of short country roads and intersections in the area. Today wore us out with the new snow on the ground. All of us were glad when we finally were off the road and sitting in front of our small fire in our shelter.

Turned on radio and heard that Russia has indeed moved into eastern European countries. Has also moved forces into all of the "stan" countries on its southern border. Georgia has put up a fight, but it won't last long. Turkey is in full invasion mode toward Syria. India and Pakistan are lobbing shells and rockets back and forth at each other. China has posted forces on border with North Vietnam. Large numbers of people fleeing south across the Mexican border. Canada has declared state of emergency and closed its borders. NATO and ASEAN holding emergency meetings. US leadership trying to talk world leaders out of all the aggression.

US domestic situation violent. Economy in shambles. Increasing number of armed incidents across the country. US military totally unprepared for both international and domestic situation. Several state governors telling federal government to stay out of their territory. Media talking solutions even as they are totally messed up themselves. Sounds like the 1920s and 1930s all over again. Not much good news to go to sleep on, but we had to rest. A stressful day tomorrow. Prayers said, scripture read, night!

**O God, You are my God; I shall seek You earnestly;
My soul thirsts for You, my flesh yearns for You,
In a dry and weary land where there is no water.
(Psalm 63:1)**

LARRY D. HORTON, PhD

Date: March 30   Mileage: 6 mi.   Walk Total: 161–163 miles.

Up and at 'em. Risky day today. Going to do our best to say out of eyesight. Regular breakfast and camp breakdown. On road by 8 AM. Temps not too bad. New snow not too much of a problem. Sky gray and a slight breeze blowing. As the day wore on gray clouds gave way to lighter, thinner clouds. Hoping weather is changing for the better. We are about due for cold rains to start in days ahead rather than snow. But prepared for late snowstorm that seems to be the routine every year in this part of the country. Crazy lake effect from Great Lakes.

By late AM had crossed OH route 516 and quickly approached I-77. Two exits were in the area, and we planned on crossing I-77 somewhere halfway between the two exits then turn slightly north toward Parral OH. Seemed to be some traffic on I-77. So started looking for a covered area where we would be able to stay out of sight as much as possible. After looking to south a bit where small valley emptied into larger valley containing the interstate we discovered a culvert under the road used by a stream. Was pretty large. Probably six-feet high. Only way through it was to relay everything. So I got about doing that. First packs, then stuff on Trekker, then Trekker, then me carrying larger dog, and finally wife carrying smaller dog. I went back to help her to make sure there were no accidents as she made her way through the eighty-foot culvert. Successfully completed relay.

Repacked Trekker and headed up to find road on other side. Some tough going as we had to navigate across a few hundred yards of field and stands of wood but within thirty minutes came to a small country road headed north paralleling I-77 about three-fourths mile to the west. Some traffic but we decided to follow it for a bit to see if we could find another road heading more out into the country. We did. Made quick turn onto it. Late lunch around 1:30 PM. Soup on hexamine stove. By 2 PM we were on our way again. Road was pretty windy but headed generally in a northeast direction. By 3:30 we had had it for the day with walking. We guessed we were pretty much to the east of Parral OH.

Had avoided any troubles near I-77 though a few people in pickups and cars did eyeball us when they spotted us. No authorities so we just kept on walking as if we were not seen. Imagine people were seeing all kinds of things along the roads given domestic situation. I would be cautious if I were them as well. Taking no chances.

Took us another thirty minutes to find suitable spot to spend the night just off the country road about fifteen yards up a small ridge. A reasonably flat spot under a canopy of oaks, maples, and a few pine trees. This was it. First priority, firewood. Wife went up small valley by ridge and found a small stream covered with thin ice. Broke through and started to haul water. Fire pit built and fire started quickly. Normal tarp lean-to. Cut what pine branches I could reach for bedding. Covered Trekker with secondary tarp. Supper cooked on small fire, water boiled. Heat reflector working OK. Going to be chilly night. We were all tired from walking and stress of the day. Got to bed early as possible. Prayers, scripture, and hugs. Watch over us, Lord!

The righteous man will be glad in the Lord
And will take refuge in Him;
And all the upright in heart will glory.
(Psalm 64:10)

LARRY D. HORTON, PhD

Date: March 31   Mileage: 4 mi.   Walk Total: 165–167 miles.

Tired when we woke up. Backed off a bit on how far we planned to go during the day. Set objective to walk northeast to point south of Zoar OH and set up camp a bit early to get more rest. Oatmeal, rice, and hot cup of coffee. Broke camp. Same routine. Packed Trekker and got on our way around 9 AM. Zigged and zagged all morning. Small country roads through valleys with few fields between the hills. Road did not evidence much traffic. Heard some gunfire off to our south at one point. Hoping as usual that it was hunters. Around 11:30 AM stopped for hot soup lunch and water. Constantly drinking water even when cold. Temp probably just above freezing during the afternoon. We are cold and tired. Guess been doing this long enough now that we want to see an end in sight. That is a long time coming yet. Just have to keep going and not lose hope and faith.

2 PM and we had had it for the day. Came to the stream we had seen on map in vicinity of Zoar OH. Not sure how far it was from us but not to worry about that. Will look tonight after sun sets to see if we can see town lights reflecting off clouds in right general direction. Tired but set about looking for overnight sight. Had to be as safe as possible. Can't let our guard down even when we are tired. Took a bit but found a nice stand of pine trees on the crest of a small hill above Sandy Creek. Good sources of water nearby, and good cover under the pine trees. Set up basic shelter and fire pit. Gathered as much dry wood as possible and knocked down a standing dead hardwood. It splintered when it hit the ground. Cut five three-foot sections of four-inch thick trunk. Plan was to build an Indian star fire. A lot of work during the night. Trekker covered, packs under ponchos hung from a tree, hiking clothes hanging to dry by fire, and fire reflector set up. Dogs didn't have much energy; just lay near the fire. Supper cooked, eaten, and cleaned up by 6 PM. Spent the rest of the evening either sitting by fire or lying on top of sleeping bags. Did personal hygiene check and wash. Checked dog's coats for ticks and other problems, and nothing found. Still too cold for insects to be out and about much. No radio tonight. Too tired to listen.

Around 8 PM climbed into bags and just lay there for sleep after prayers and scripture. Hope to have more energy tomorrow. Night!

By awesome deeds You answer us in righteousness,
O God of our salvation,
You who are the trust of all the ends of the earth
And of the farthest sea.
(Psalm 65:5)

Date: April 1   Mileage: 4 mi.   Walk Total: 169–171 miles.

Not quite as tired when opened eyes in the morning. But knew we would have to take it a bit easier today and settle down early again this afternoon. Slow work preparing breakfast, filling up second jug and canteens with water, breaking down camp, policing the area, and packing everything on Trekker and into our packs. Got started headed almost directly east by compass. Objective was to cross stream and then OH routes 212 and 600 and camp a bit east of Mineral City OH. That would be pushing it a bit today, but would do the best we could. Broken clouds as we started out. Some sunshine but nothing to drive temps up very far. Stream crossing was not too hard. Could see a small country road on the other side. Relayed everything across ten-foot wide shallow water then repacked on other side.

Up a slight grade and we were on the country road. It had quite a few turns and twists in it as it traveled through some small valleys, but overall we were headed east. Road immediately crossed OH route 212, and we entered a pretty wide valley with several farmhouses on either side. When we were just past the last farmhouse, we had our first potentially violent animal contact. Two very large dogs likely from the last farm we passed. They approached to within thirty feet of us and bared their fangs. We talked later and thought they were probably eying our two dogs. I grabbed the air rifle from my wife's shoulder and put two pellets into each dog's haunches. Would not break their skin but it sure scared the daylights out of them. They took off howling headed back home. We hoped that would be the last we would see of them, but kept a watch behind us to see if they got a fresh infusion of courage later. That didn't happen.

We continued on our way and eventually crossed OH route 600. At that point we had another late lunch cooked on hexamine stove. Chicken noodle soup really hit the spot. Gave a bit to the dogs as a treat and they obviously wanted more. We decided to walk for another hour and then look to set up our camp for the night. Two priorities. First, find a good water source. Second, find as safe and out-of-sight a location as possible. We knew we were north of Somerdale OH and southeast of the larger town of Mineral City. We would look for light reflecting on the clouds to confirm the likelihood of our location.

Finally found a small farmer's field road heading off into two small hills to our north. Walking a couple hundred yards up the road, I reached a small grove of trees. My wife stayed with dogs and our gear, air rifle at the ready should she need to use it. Found a clear stream, little if any ice, heading toward the road we had been using. Trusted that water would be better further up the little valley. Found a wonderful flat spot among some medium-sized oaks and maples. No leaves obviously, but site could not be seen from road below. Went back to wife and gear and we all moved to the good site, one of the best we have found to date. Quickly set up camp, gathered wood, hauled water, built tarp lean-to, changed into camp clothing so we could dry hiking clothes, and built fire reflector.

Supper was simple tonight, rice, beans, pudding, and orange drink. Dogs ate their fill. Shook out sleeping bags as we did every night to make sure we had no creepy crawlies in bed with us. Boots on stakes near fire to dry out. Personal hygiene taken care off. Spent fifteen minutes rubbing dogs' shoulders as we did every night. They really enjoyed that and were ready to doze off afterward. No interest in listening to news tonight. We are kind of pessimistic about the whole thing from a human perspective. Nothing is happening that should surprise any of us. The saddest thing is that our country is so very different from the country we grew up in during the 1950s and 1960s. We ultimately have no one to blame but ourselves. Most sadly the country will continue to slip down a very steep slope into having little or no relevance. With those wonderful thoughts (not), we bedded down for the night. Prayers said, scripture read, and the dogs one last rub on the shoulders. Good night!

**Come and hear, all who fear God,
And I will tell of what He has done for my soul.
(Psalm 66:16)**

LARRY D. HORTON, PhD

Cross Country Diary: Day #72

Date: April 2   Mileage: 7 mi.   Walk Total: 176–178 miles.

A bit more rested when we woke up with the sun peeking out from behind a hill to our southeast. Temp seems to have moderated a bit. Maybe March did go out like a lamb. Plan today is to travel straight east cross OH route 542 and camp somewhere north of Atwood Lake. We will be out in the country, hills, valleys, and likely some farms. But people should be few, considering what is going on. Figure we will be about 50 miles south of Canton OH by then. Quickly broke camp, boiled last of water supply, quick breakfast, packed up, and we were on our way. Continued on same country road we used yesterday until it turned more northerly at a junction with another country road that appeared to head off to the east, our direction. Both roads zigged and zagged through the hills and valleys of the countryside. A couple farmhouses and other dwellings along the way. Dogs at each location, but they stayed close to home and just barked at us. Got our dogs all exercised, and they wanted to run to the sound. Making some progress. Bit warmer weather is helping. Roads still wet and muddy so have to be careful. Stopped just off the road to have soup and juice for lunch warmed up on hexamine stove. Once that was done headed out again.

Crossed OH route 562 shortly before 2 PM. Decided to keep going until around 3:30 when we would set up for the night. Lots of curves and some up and down on the road. No sight of any other humans. Still no commercial air traffic. Has been several weeks now. Still seems strange. About 3:15 PM began to seriously look for stopping point. Saw a logging road or natural gas road off to our right that curved behind a small bluff covered in trees. That would seem to be safe. After going few hundred yards up the unused road, we found a spot under some trees about 25 feet off the road in a little cove in the hill. That would be it. Stream across the way about 100 yards, so had water source. Went through normal camp setup routine. Didn't take too long. Spent most of my time building lean-to and fire pit and then gathering wood. Simple supper of soup, veggies, fruit, and coffee. Dogs liked soup and tolerated veggies. They seemed to be doing OK and had settled down from encounter with distant dogs earlier.

Once supper dishes, pots and utensils cleaned, sleeping bags shaken out, hiking clothes and boots hung up to dry, personal hygiene done, and changed into camping clothes, we settled down to relax a bit. Did some equipment maintenance and plan for tomorrow. Pulled out our two primary fire kits and backup materials to inventory them. Still have six unused Bic lighters, couple hundred cotton balls, three-quarters small jar of Vaseline, all of our waterproof matches, two small tins of char cloth, two unused fire cans in our basic fire kits with two spare ones in our backpacks, and four ferro sticks, lightly used so far. Also, we have small waterproof tinder bag for emergencies like starting a fire in the rain. Have two small backup pen knives just in case. Half supply of tampons still left as well. All in all, we are in pretty good shape. Once spring rains start in earnest, know we will be using these more often. Also, knew that within next couple of weeks when we pass between Youngstown OH and Pittsburgh PA area, with all of the population concentrated there, we will have to go very dark, and some of these materials, like the fire cans, will take on more importance.

Repacked all the fire prep stuff and pulled out map to begin next few days of planning. Reading by LED headlamp has become the norm. Tomorrow we will head east again and try to cover four to five miles as the crow flies, a straight line. Know we will actually walk farther than that. We have a good sense of how far we can travel in an hour on winding roads with some elevation changes. We have figured out a step count per mile for each of us as well. We paced ourselves and measured distance by how many steps my wife took. Her shorter steps, and my step count model was hit and miss while I pulled the Trekker. Objective tomorrow is to continue straight east as much as possible and camp tomorrow night a couple miles west of Carrollton OH in the hills somewhat north of US route 39. The next day we will head in a more northeasterly direction, forty degrees on compass, and continue on that heading for as many days as necessary, with slight adjustments due to geography and human contact, toward Lisbon OH. Once in Lisbon area will be about 50 miles from crossing into PA.

With equipment checking and map planning done by 8 PM, we pulled out primary radio. Crank charged it and turned on weather and news. One other check made at this point was to pull out our small backup radio, open up the tin we were carrying it in, breaking the lead tape seals we had wrapped around tin, to check whether it was still watertight. It was. Retaped the tin, covering it completely in lead tape. Why lead tape? We wanted to make sure we had a workable radio should all our other electronics fail us. We are carrying our cell phones in the same protective way. We have not used phones in weeks but want to make sure they are viable should something happen. Given world situation, who can say that some nutcase might not explode something high over the US? The resulting EMP would shut everything down. We aren't willing to take the chance of not being prepared for that.

The dogs sat looking at us expecting their nightly rubdown, which they got of course. Had a little songfest, very quietly, read scripture, and said our prayers. We are so thankful that we have traveled all these miles with very little threat to our safety. We hope it will continue. Weather is to become rainy with some sleet over the next couple days, but temps will moderate a bit more after that. Reports of violent spring storms and tornadoes south of us. Only a matter of time before conflict between cold and warm fronts moves over us and we get some nasty weather.

Not much has changed on international front. A lot of posturing and testosterone being exhibited. Shooting conflicts contained to a few small areas but potential for much more could only be minutes away. Domestic scene is much the same as well. Isolated rioting, looting, shootings, and confrontations. Economic infrastructure still in very bad shape. Disaster relief agencies have no money or supplies to feed the tens of millions of people who are getting more desperate each day. Safety authorities are exhausted and only able to respond to about 40 percent of calls for help. Small petty crime is ignored. Reports surfacing that hospitals and medical centers are running out of supplies. Lots more, but we certainly get the point of the newscast: things are rapidly descending into uncontrolled chaos with not many people believing it can be turned around soon, if ever. The US government seems incapable of managing the situation. The thousands of government workers who should have been working on the issues are just like anyone else: looking for someone or something to fix it all and to provide what they as individuals and families need to survive.

There is a bit of positive out of all this. Churches are filling up with people looking for answers there. Some are making real changes in their lives. Others, only the Lord knows the end result. We have seen this type of thing before at times of disaster or danger. We just hope good comes of it. Quite a conversation for over an hour. We finally realized what time it was and knew we had to hit the sack. The dogs were already asleep at our feet. With prayers said and scripture read, we turned in, knowing morning will be here soon. Night!

**God blesses us,
That all the ends of the earth may fear Him.
(Psalm 67:7)**

LARRY D. HORTON, PhD

Date: April 3   Mileage: 5 mi.   Walk Total: 181–183 miles.

Up and a bit slow this morning. Slept hard, pretty tired, but ready to go. Normal camp breakdown. Added bit of boiled water to our canteens for the day. Quick breakfast of cream of wheat, rice, juice. Dogs seemed ready to go as well. Had day planned and after repacking headed out. Back on same road we had been traveling yesterday. Had to change roads three times during the day to stay as close to compass reading as possible. Traveling in valleys between larger hills. Country getting a bit rougher. Lot more trees. Fewer farms for first couple miles. Lunch on the roadside.

Shortly after lunch had the most dangerous encounter with another animal that we had had to date. Two dogs, seemingly bent on attacking our dogs, came running at us from out of the woods to our left. We heard their barking while they were still in the trees. When they came into view, it was obvious to us that they had no good intentions. I pulled out my Beretta 380 and my wife pulled her Sig Sauer 9mm. Firing our weapons would definitely be a last resort, likely giving away our position and bringing possible others curious about the shots. But we had no alternative than to protect ourselves in this moment of danger. When the dogs were about thirty yards from us we opened up on them. Two slugs from my weapon in the lead dog into its shoulders knocked it down. The second dog hesitated briefly. My wife fired off one shot and I let go two more shots. Two of the three hit the second dog. The first was dead on the spot. The second still breathing, so I put a third slug into the back of its head.

Our dogs were going nuts, the smaller one cringing in fear from the gunshots, and the larger wanting to inspect the downed animals. I very carefully poked each downed animal with my walking stick, and they were obviously finished. As much as we love dogs, it was hard to do, but in the moment, we could only think of our safety and be grateful that we had finished the task at hand. Pulled out my folding shovel and dug two graves. Looked for any tags and collars before covering up dead dogs in the graves but found none. We sat for a few minutes reflecting on what had just happened. A few tears of release after the stress. Our dogs were very agitated and it took a bit for them to calm down. We looked and listened to see if the shots had brought out any who might be curious. Maybe we were lucky that there were others out hunting for food and the shots had been taken just as other hunters. We would be on the lookout all day just in case. To be honest we were pretty shook-up. Will have to clean the guns tonight before sacking out. But they have been trustworthy and kept us safe. For that we are grateful.

After giving thanks and praying for safety, we got on our way again. Very quiet walk the rest of the afternoon. Around 3 PM started looking for a bed-down site for the night. Road was cut through some significant forest north of Atwood Lake, so there was lots of cover. We found a decent old logging road again and set off slightly to the north, up a small valley with a clear stream. Finding piles of cut tree tops we chose one to build our nightly camp behind. Lots of firewood available. Not much cutting necessary. Set up regular camp, gathered wood, hauled water for boiling, and built fire reflector. Temps continue to be OK just north of freezing tonight. Tomorrow supposed to warm up to around forty degrees. Will feel like a heat wave. Quiet camp tonight after today's incident. We were all emotionally spent so to bed early. Prayers said and scripture read. We prayed that we will not face any similar situations for some time. It was a tough day. Thank you, Lord, for safety.

Blessed be the Lord,
Who daily bears our burden,
The God who is our salvation.
(Psalm 68:19)

Date: April 4   Mileage: 5 mi.   Walk Total: 181–183 miles.

No disturbances during the night. Neither of us slept well after yesterday. Woke up pretty early and had breakfast and broke camp. Nothing much said as we headed back to the country road and got on our way. Sun and clouds during the AM with temperature warming. By the time we finished lunch, we could see gray clouds moving in from the south and the wind increasing. Figured that was the rain that we had heard about on the radio and that we might be facing a wet and chilly night tonight. We didn't see much as we walked today. Road headed in general direction we wanted to be going. Crossed over a couple bigger roads, US 9/43 and OH route 171. Saw a few vehicles so that slowed us a bit waiting for all clear. After crossing 171 we found road on our map that we followed to the end of the day. We are headed in the general direction of Pattersonville OH as near as we can figure. Will pass there tomorrow and cross Still Fork Creek headed toward Augusta OH for our next night. Figure it will take us a while tomorrow especially if we are having a cold rain and wind.

Lunch was simple, hot soup. We knew we were making slow progress but just couldn't push too hard. By 2 PM we had had it for the day and started to look for a place to spend the night. We have lost much of the tree cover around Atwood Lake but were able to find some stands of trees that looked promising. We finally landed on one just to the west of our travel route. No direct path to it, and had to cross a marshy, very wet field. So relayed everything to a decent spot among some trees and set up for the night. We are still feeling the effects of our run-in with the dogs yesterday. Slow camp set up. While out gathering wood, it started to rain lightly and did not stop. Dry wood will be hard to come by later, so worked hard at collecting it even before starting our lean-to shelter. Wife worked on fire pit and gathered materials to cover sides of eventual lean-to. Used rope we had been carrying to set up roof support for tarp. No really good longer small logs available. We tried to keep our spirits up. Supper was hot pasta and veggies as well as coffee. Dogs could sense we were a bit under the weather. Rain was not helping. Could not bring ourselves to turn on the radio tonight. Sat by small fire and just held and petted our dogs. Will be hard to sleep again tonight. Prayers said and scripture read, we knew sleep would come eventually.

But as for me, my prayer is to You,
O Lord, at an acceptable time;
O God, in the greatness of Your lovingkindness,
Answer me with Your saving truth.
(Psalm 69:13)

Date: April 5   Mileage: 6 mi.   Walk Total: 187–189 miles.

Feeling better this morning. Rest has a way of helping. Overcast and drizzling. Breaking out the ponchos today. Breakfast of cream of wheat and veggies. Coffee as well. Camp broken and policed. Things packed up and we were on our way. Relayed things back to the road, which was a pain but necessary. Goal today was to camp along OH route 9 a bit north of Augusta OH. Only real obstacle other than rain, windy road, mud, cold, and wind was crossing Still Fork Creek. Pretty secluded walk for the most part. Able to make progress on road.

Ponchos did a reasonable job. Trekker covered with secondary tarp to keep gear and remaining supplies dry. Dogs were soaked, of course. We would have to dry them really well tonight. We had packed a couple small towels just for that purpose. We didn't need them getting sick. Same was true for us. In some way, much easier to hike in snow than in rain. Felt cold. Walking helped us stay warm, and stopped less often to cool down.

Lunch of hot soup and coffee hit the spot. Gave dogs a bit of the soup to warm them up as well. We are needing more protein again. Soon will have to make a serious effort to secure some. Walked slowly. It was close to 2:30 PM before we started looking for a site for the night. Dry firewood was really going to be a problem. Still drizzling and as temp started to drop felt a bit of sleet hitting us. Sounded like little pellets hitting our ponchos. Walked slowly for another hour and spotted an abandoned structure off to our right in a small valley. It looked like some kind of shelter for cows or horses to enable them to get out of the weather. On one side of the main building was a small lean-to roof and it looked very inviting, especially with the drizzle falling. The only drawback was the fence we had to get over. A potential hindrance if we had to leave in a hurry. Going against our plan, we relayed everything over the fence and headed down to the building on an obvious tractor path.

Nothing was stirring. The drizzle and cold helped us make our decision, which seemed like a good one when we arrived. The little roof shelter on the side was over some grass, with no real evidence of animals. The inside of the main building minus one wall had obviously been used by animals but probably not since early last fall. Their droppings had dried and frozen, so the smell was manageable. We found a couple of old bales of straw under the main roof and used them to build a floor under the lean-to roof. With that done, realized there was no wood for a fire. It was really going to be cold. Parked and covered Trekker on side where wind was blowing in. Supper cooked over hexamine stove, soup and coffee. There was a water trough to one side, but the pump was frozen, so no water supply to boil. Priority tomorrow is to find water. About 9 PM drizzle stopped. Still chilly wind blowing, but we just layered on more clothing and climbed into sack. First thing in AM will plan out next stage of our travels. Prayers said and scripture read with aid of LED headlamps. Hugs all around, brrrrrrr, good night!

O God, hasten to deliver me;
O Lord, hasten to my help.
(Psalm 70:1)

Date: April 6   Mileage: 4 mi.   Walk Total: 185–187 miles.

Up pretty early. While wife fixed breakfast of oatmeal and coffee, looked at map and figured out next three general camp areas we would like to achieve. Drizzle had stopped overnight. Still chilly and damp. The kind of damp that goes right through you. Did a quick check on remaining food supplies in the Trekker, and we have enough there for three more days. By the time we reach our third site over next few days, we will have used it up. We'll have to decide then whether to keep moving with the Trekker.

Broke camp quickly from under the lean-to roof at the small building in the field. Gathered up as much as possible of the straw we had used and spread it in the main part of the cattle shelter. Tried to get rid of any signs that we had been there. Packed and moved back to fence where we relayed everything over it again. Back to road and on our way. Dogs didn't really want to move in the chilly weather, but they eventually got the idea that we were moving on. A couple hours along, passed a few more farmhouses off to the side of the road. Few people in sight. They waved, as did we, and then they went on with their work. Seems like people in the country, though cautious, are just trying to keep up some kind of semi-normal routine.

Lunch by the roadside again. At least we stayed near the road hidden behind a small growth of brush, bushes, and trees. Soup and hot coffee. Water supply getting a little low. Would be on lookout this afternoon for a campsite with a decent water source even if that meant stopping a bit early against our plan of travel. Saw a couple small groups of deer in the distance through the early afternoon. They had come out from under their cover once the drizzle stopped. Gray clouds all afternoon threatening more rain, but it didn't happen. Moving slowly as road was windy, and we entered more up and down even when the road stayed in valleys. Lots of mud and puddles on the road as well. Pretty slippery if we weren't careful. By 2:15 PM looking hard for place to spend the night. Not as much progress as we had hoped for but that was OK.

Eventually spotted good stand of pine trees off to our left with small two rut path heading into it. Probably an old camping or farm path. Took it into the grove of pines. Found small stream as water source, and pulled off into a thick part of the trees. Shelter from wind and possible rain. Cut area of branches away. Used for sides of lean-to and set up camp. Took a while, as we were tired and dogs were acting up. There must be some critters in the area. Water, firewood, and shelter were priorities. Eventually got it all done, boiled water, and cooked pasta and veggies for supper. After cleanup a quick listen to NOAA weather. Next few days will be chilly, but rain is done, at least for now. Glad we were able to get some reception. Spent quite a while just paying attention to the dogs, petting and wrapping them up in sleeping bags. Nothing exciting today, which was good. Hope for same tomorrow. Clothes drying by fire, we settled down for the night. Another day on the road tomorrow. Prayers said, scripture read, and bundled up, night!

In You, O Lord, I have taken refuge;
Let me never be ashamed.
(Psalm 71:1)

LARRY D. HORTON, PhD

Date: April 7   Mileage: 4 mi.   Walk Total: 189–191 miles.

We crossed US route 30 yesterday and hoped to cross OH route 644 today north of Millport OH. Up pretty early for quick breakfast. Made sure had enough water, broke camp, restored as much as possible to original state, repacked, headed back to road, and were on our way. Gray skies again this morning, though didn't seem quite as chilly. Wind blowing slightly from the south. Traveling winding road through pretty good-sized hills. Not much sign of civilization other than a few camps and a couple small homes along the way. Lights on in the homes, but camps were all dark. Critters not moving in this weather, and large game season is done. Given food situation in country, we doubt official hunting seasons mean much anymore. Survival is the name of the game now, and people will do what they must to put food on their tables.

Noticed a few flyovers going north to south. Military jets doing something. We are close enough to Youngstown OH, Pittsburgh PA, and maybe Columbus OH that something may be going on there. Will check on that tonight on radio if we can get reception. Slow going. Up and down elevation gains as road was wet, slippery, and muddy. Trekker was not nearly as heavy now, so tends to lose traction more easily. Had to be very careful. Dogs kept getting in the way as well. Tough keeping their leads from getting tangled in the wheels of the Trekker. Rested for about an hour while eating hot soup for lunch. Needed it. Weather was making it hard to walk on the roads. Took our normal rest stops as well to cool down, so progress was a bit slow. Crossed OH route 644 near 1 PM and decided to camp no later than 3 PM. While walking through narrow valley between two hills, noticed a small secondary road heading off to the south. Took it, and a few hundred yards further on found a pretty recent gas line road. Really muddy, but we took it. A few yards further on found piles of treetops cut when gas well area had been cleared in distance. Perfect blind to build our night shelter next to. Lots of potential drier fire material under the piles of brush. Also, and important, potential area where we might see a small critter or two. Meat for supper.

Set up camp. Pretty simple. Gathered firewood and started fire. As always, tried to get dead wood to burn. Walked further up valley, and found a small spring coming out of the hillside. Took thirty minutes to haul water back for boiling to replenish our water supply. Saw very small green plants starting to push up through leaves and sticks on the ground. That is a good sign of changing weather. We will have to be on the lookout in coming days for edibles like dandelions along our travel path. Young leaves, a bit of flour, salt, and water, and we could have fresh veggies. Looking forward to that. Also, collected small bag full of acorns. Will start boiling them tomorrow to take out tannins. A good energy snack. No radio reception back in the secluded area we were in, so will have to wait to catch up tomorrow. Ready to hit the sack early, so we did. Prayers, scripture, hugs for the dogs, some solo reflecting time, and down to sleep.

For he will deliver the needy when he cries for help,
The afflicted also, and him who has no helper.
(Psalm 72:12)

Cross Country Diary: Day #78

Date: April 8   Mileage: 6 mi.   Walk Total: 195–197 miles.

Normal morning camp breakdown and breakfast. Knew we had some challenges today to get by. Since we were not making as much progress as planned. knew we would only get to a point today that would require us to cross some major highways the next day, OH route 11 being the major one. Today would mean crossing Little Beaver River and one major secondary road. Likely to see more humans today than before. Day after tomorrow would mean a lot more potential contact as well.

A bit of sun poking through the gray clouds this morning. Slight breeze from the south. Hoping that we were headed into a period of clearer skies, high pressure, and a bit warmer weather. Time would tell. Back on secondary road after slipping and sliding down from the small hillside we had camped on, and we were on our way. Few more birds in the sky, and actually saw a flock of geese heading north. Another good sign. Reached Little Beaver River. Hardly a river at this point, but knew it becomes larger as it gets closer to Pittsburgh. Only about fifteen feet wide at this point. Luckily, road we were on crossed using an old one-lane bridge. We were down in a valley obviously surrounded by pretty significant hills. Because of hills, chance of sunshine was cut down by a few hours.

Crossed bridge and picked up smell of smoke coming up the valley toward us. Smelled like a campfire, so we knew there were other humans in the vicinity. Kept moving to get away from it. Stopped for lunch by a small stream that probably emptied into the Little Beaver. Took enough time to replenish water. Used hexamine stove to boil enough water for canteens. Dogs got a bit of our lunch as well. Headed back uphill out of the Little Beaver area and crested a small ridge. Could see out through the trees that we were definitely moving into a riskier area. Could see indications of Lisbon OH to our north, and that meant US route 45 and US route 11 were not too far off. Once off that ridge and back in valley below, started to look for a suitable campsite for the night. Given that we knew we were close to large civilization risks and that food on

Trekker would be finished tonight we decided to spend two nights at next site to rest and prepare for abandoning Trekker and going fully on foot from that point forward.

Weather continued to get a bit better throughout the afternoon. Temps would not be so bad tonight hopefully. 2:30 PM and we started to look for campsite. Sun was already behind hills behind us. Surrounded by trees on both sides of road. Smell of smoke coming from our north by the time site was chosen. Pulled off road about 50 yards behind clump of bushes and small trees. Camp set up as usual. Collected firewood for the night. More of that tomorrow as well as other preparations. Boiled water to fill canteens and one extra water jug. We will try to carry the extra water jug if possible. Going dark tonight. Too much evidence from smell of smoke that others are around. Bundled up to sleep. Supper on hexamine stove. Soup, veggies, fruit, and orange juice. Last of the foodstuffs on the Trekker. No radio reception in this secluded area. Lots to do tomorrow, so to bed pretty early. Prayers, scripture, and attention for dogs. Night!

**With Your counsel You will guide me,
And afterward receive me to glory.
(Psalm 73:24)**

Date: April 9   Mileage: 0 mi.   Walk Total: 195–197 miles.

Good night's rest. Still periodically smelling smoke from somewhere. Lots to do today. First things first, replenish water for cooking for the day. Second, gather enough firewood to get us through tonight. Put dogs on long leads so they could explore a bit and stay out of the way. Breakfast of oatmeal and fruit along with hot coffee. Once dishes cleaned, got about the tasks of the day. Unpacked Trekker completely, putting our stuff under our lean-to shelter for protection. Fewer clouds this morning. More sun once it crested hills surrounding us. Temps moving up slightly. May have made low forties during sunny part of the day. Once Trekker completely unpacked, broke it down and stacked it off to side of camp. Cut quite a few pine branches and covered it completely. Removed anything that might be useful to us on the rest of our trip, all bindings, tires, etc. Took time to cut up half of one of the tires into strips that could be used in an emergency to help with fire. Would be dangerous because of smoke that it would create, but in a pinch, would do it. Once Trekker completely hidden set about packing our backpacks and other gear we would carry. Rolled tarps bound with cord. Would add them to packs when ready. We already were carrying rolled-up sleeping bags and ground pads, but now they would be attached to backpacks when moving. Meant each of us will have three rolls of stuff to carry.

Will ditch one water jug with Trekker in the morning. Also, will attach weapons, large ax, and machete to our packs in the morning along with rolled-up sections of rope. Large cooking pots attached as well. Stuffed couple remaining packets of orange drink into spots in packs. While doing all of this, had hot chicken noodle soup for lunch with orange drink. Dogs like the soup. They were content to snoop around, nap, and watch us most of the day. Shortly after lunch spotted couple squirrels in trees off in the distance. Grabbed air rifle and quietly snuck up on them. A lucky shot from about 30 yards knocked one out of tree. Not dead when hit ground but stunned. Dispatched it quickly, field-dressed, and brought back to camp. Wife cooked it on hand-held skewer while

I continued to work on packs. We would have a midafternoon meal and light supper as a result. The dogs could smell it and were licking their lips. All cooked, I took time to cut critter heart in half, roast, and feed to the dogs. Bright eyes and wanting more. The meat hit the spot obviously and gave us a spurt of energy.

Once all this prep was done, we rested under our lean-to until it was time to fix small supper. Was able to nap for a short time. In many ways, glad to be done with Trekker. It served us well, but given surroundings to come, we needed to go even more dark than up to this point. To be honest, I was tired of pulling it. Travel could be more efficient maybe, and we would not be constrained by needing to follow roads. Cross-country travel had more potential for avoiding contact with others. Supper of fruit, veggies, and coffee. Dogs got last bit of squirrel meat left from earlier meal. Knew tomorrow was going to be stressful, so to bed early. Dogs very contented and fell asleep quickly. Prayers, scripture, and request of the Lord to grant us safety in the dangerous days ahead.

How long, O God, will the adversary revile,
And the enemy spurn Your name forever.
(Psalm 74:10)

Date: April 10   Mileage: 6 mi.   Walk Total: 201–203 miles.

Very few clouds in sky when we woke up, at least from what we could see then in the subdued light. Would enjoy the sun when it peeked over tops of hills. A new day. A new way of traveling lay ahead. Risk would go up exponentially, but we could get further off the beaten path when and if necessary. Breakfast was simple and quick. Broke camp, packed and rolled up sleeping gear, policed campsite, and we were off. Packs were heavy of course. Stuffed to the gills. Three months ago, would not have even tried to carry them this heavy, but we are in much better physical condition now. Though it will be a tough slough for a few weeks as we use up food supplies, will gradually get better. We walked slow using walking sticks a lot for support. Each of us had a dog on leash that we were also trying to control and lead. Everything we needed instantly was within easy reach. Am sure we were a sight. Each with pack and attached weapons, axes, our rifles slung over our shoulders, our med bags hanging from our necks, our utility belts strapped around us, and me with my basic BOB bag as well. All in green or coyote brown. One good thing is that we were traveling without putting on heavy winter coats that were draped over our packs. Need to do personal hygiene against sweat and human smell tonight.

Stayed on road for first couple miles, but as we drew closer to US route 45 and shortly after that US route 11, a four-lane road, we headed off cross country. That will be our MO from now on: following route of country and secondary roads but walking between 50 and 100 yards off to the side of the road. Walked along ridgelines when possible. Trying to angle up and down hillsides to reduce elevation up and down. This means we won't be walking in straight lines but instead depending even more on compass readings to keep us going in the right direction. Took our time to get our toting feet under us. Difficult at times with dogs as we had to walk around obstacles constantly. Lunch in sight of US route 45. Much larger highway. Interesting sight as we observed other individuals, under packs, heading south. We were not the only ones who had bugged out. Sadly, most of what we saw were people who had not prepared as much as we had.

Able to cross US route 45 in a narrow valley where we could cross very quickly and be under cover immediately. Another mile and we could see US route 11. More difficult crossing but we found section where four lanes were separated by stands of trees. A few vehicles moving each direction. A few more people walking, again heading south. A few waves from one couple walking south, but we didn't hesitate and moved into woods on other side of northbound lanes. Lunch quickly. Hot soup and water to drink. Moved quickly to the east and by 3 PM, by compass triangulation, figured we were a couple miles south of Elkton OH. Easy to find campsite as we just choose a location on our walking direction. Set up low lean-to under some pines. Cooked supper of soup, veggies, and coffee. Few branches for bedding, bags set out, very tired. Prayers, scripture, no radio, no fire. Temps bit better. Good night!

But as for me, I will declare it forever;
I will sing praises to the God of Jacob.
(Psalm 75:9)

Date: April 11   Mileage: 4 mi.   Walk Total: 205–207 miles.

Woke up very stiff. The effect of carrying all of our equipment. Plan today was to bear slightly to the northeast and camp tonight in the hills south of Rogers OH. Not quite as far as yesterday, but tired from walking and carrying yesterday, so hopefully a realistic objective. Easy camp breakdown this morning. Hot cream of wheat and tea. Dogs enjoyed hot meal as did we. Repacked camping clothing. Hiking clothing back on after we took care of personal hygiene. We needed that. Set direction by compass. Hills just as big. No roads really in sight so we are truly going to be going cross country. Crossed several small creeks that likely were headed to Little Beaver Creek.

Had to cross OH route 7 around noon. Again, saw individuals and small groups walking to the south. Seems like some had given up on cities. We hoped they had someplace to go. We stayed hidden as much as possible, taking no chances on confrontations with desperate people. Stopped for an hour to rest, eat some lunch, give weary shoulders and legs a break. Wife struggling a bit walking on hillsides and ridges with balance. I finally took both dog leads to allow her more stability when walking. Lunch eaten and cleaned up we moved on. Only wanted to go another mile or so east of route 7 and would set up camp. We realized that we had set goal of four miles for the day but likely walked at least 20 percent more than that with all the weaving and direction changes. Checked compass periodically and we were able to stay pretty much on track we had set in the A.M. Hoped we would see lights tonight from Rogers OH.

By 1:30 PM we had had enough for the day and started looking for suitable campsite. Took 45 minutes, but we found a good spot with a small stream just below us. Weather had warmed up a bit more, maybe into the high forties, as we walked in the afternoon. If this is indeed the beginning of the spring thaw, we know we have some issues to deal with. First, when it rains, streams will be up. It will rain a lot over next 30 to 45 days, so creek and stream crossings could be a challenge.

Second, with rising temps, critters, both four-legged and those that crawl, will be coming out. We assume we are in bear country. No way we want to run into a hungry bear or a sow with new cubs. Lots of caution there. Snakes will be another big issue. Given hills increasing in number and height, we will likely see rattlesnakes sooner rather than later. Will require lots of care in foot steps and collecting wood. One other danger, which will probably be more common, especially since we will be near lots of civilization, is single or small groups of domesticated dogs. They are prone to attack rather than run away. We have to be prepared for that at any time.

Finding reasonable campsite, we prepared for another night. Simple lean-to in grove of oaks. Gathered firewood for small fire. Lots of acorns lying around, so collected them as well. Hexamine stove fire for cooking dinner. Soup, veggies, and pudding, tea as well. Tired again. No radio tonight, no reception. Early to bed, prayers, scripture, and hugs around. Good night!

You caused judgment to be heard from heaven;
The earth feared and was still.
(Psalm 76:8)

LARRY D. HORTON, PhD

Date: April 12   Mileage: 5 mi.   Walk Total: 210–212 miles.

Up pretty early this morning. Broke camp. Repacked our backpacks. Knew we would likely be doing some serious hill walking today, so were prepared to stop a little early to conserve our energy. Oatmeal and fruit for breakfast. Haven't really mentioned much about daily supplements that we take every day, multivitamins, vitamin C, and a dietary supplement of vegetable powders. Trying to make sure we get enough of those things, especially since we have been traveling during winter months when it is much more difficult to get edible wild greens. Seems to be working so far. Don't really believe we are deficient in anything.

Took our time all morning walking up and down elevation gains and losses at angles. Tried not to get into any straight up and downs. Were able to follow some small streams in valleys as long as we were headed in the general northeasterly direction we had decided on. Hot soup for lunch and lots of water. Temps seem to be up a bit so short stops to cool down as well. Not quite as worried about hypothermia as before, but nighttime will still have to watch carefully, especially when sun disappears behind hills to the west. Same walking pace after lunch. Dogs seem to be finding more scents to drive them crazy. Small critters out a lot. Saw a few squirrels, and kicked up our first game birds in some time after lunch. Looked like grouse. Those would be good for fresh meat but really difficult to find. Maybe we might get lucky.

Saw wisps of smoke in the distance several times today. More than likely from homes tucked back into the hills. A few military planes around as well. We think we are not too far from the Pittsburgh airport. One air ambulance helicopter as well heading straight east at a good clip. By 2 PM we had had it for the day, and since we were off road we didn't have too much trouble finding a place to camp. Came over a small crest and spotted a little valley ahead with what looked to be a nice stream and some flat spots above it. Chose the first one we came to, maybe thirty feet square, with some pine trees on the edge, and got about setting up camp. No rain for past couple days, but things were still very wet. Knocked down a small dead tree and cut it up into some firewood. No big fire tonight; staying pretty dark, but needed it to boil some water. Would cook pasta and veggies on hexamine stove. Tarp lean-to put up pretty fast. Packs hung in tree to protect food. Dishes cleaned after eating.

Nice to have some time to rest. Cranked up power on NOAA radio and listened to weather forecast. Bit warmer for next three days then low pressure will move in and bring rain. High temps in high forties, lows in mid-thirties, so things are changing. News out of Pittsburgh wasn't any better; in fact, getting worse on both international and domestic fronts. Hope to get fuller report tomorrow. Bedded down by 9 PM. Looked at stars through break in the trees above us. Did one final compass check for direction of travel tomorrow. Prayers said, scripture read, hugs all around, we enjoyed the silence of the late evening. Good night!

I will remember the deeds of the Lord;
Surely I will remember Your wonders of old.
(Psalm 77:11)

Date: April 13   Mileage: 5 mi.   Walk Total: 215–217 miles.

Up around our usual time. Quick, simple breakfast of oatmeal and orange drink. Fixed enough for the dogs as well. Camp breakdown pretty simple and routine. Everything packed into or attached to our backpacks. Headed off cross country. Really hilly, so clearly progress would be slow. Plan to walk until around 3 PM. Quite a bit of short up and downs as we tried to stay on as level a walking path as possible. At one point dropped down into a valley where we were able to follow a stream for a distance but had to go back up hill eventually. The plan today was to cross OH route 517 east of East Palestine OH and then enter PA, crossing US route 51 where it's still a two-lane highway. We would set up camp for the night just south of PA route 351.

The day went pretty smoothly. A few stops to rest and cool down. Sunshine and clouds. Temps probably approaching 50 degrees in direct sunlight. When in woods or valleys felt quite a bit cooler. Spring was indeed starting. At least by all signs. Had a brief scare from a couple snakes sunning themselves on rocks just before we broke for lunch. Did not want to get too close, but assumed they were not friendly kind in the woods. Dogs didn't sense them, which was good. Forty-five-minute lunch break, dropped packs, soup and coffee on hexamine stove. A bit of soup for dogs but not much. Drinking quite a bit of water because of the warmer weather. Will have to find a good water source tonight. We had planned on stopping around 3 PM, but progress had been slow, so pushed on until around 4 PM. Found a decent campsite located about 50 feet above a small stream water source. As we were dropping our packs noticed a squirrel at about eye level down side of hill we were on. Short shot. Air rifle came through again. While I fetched and field-dressed it, wife built simple fire pit and gathered enough wood to quickly cook something to eat. Squirrel in soup with coffee. Collected dead wood. Wanted to have fire going before got too dark to remain hidden. Would let it die down considerably as it got darker. Built three-sided reflector with roof out of space blankets to prevent light from flames from being seen as much as possible. Cooked whole squirrel on hand-held skewer.

Also, cooked heart and liver for the dogs. Dogs were in seventh heaven when gave them to them. Supper was good. Needed the protein. Drank quite a bit of water. Meat needed more water in our systems to digest well. Meant hauling water after supper and made sure our one jug and both canteens were full before hitting the sack.

Listened to radio briefly as it got darker. Should mention it gets really dark in woods at night. Lots of sounds and noises around us. Residents were out and about. Radio report said things getting very tense around the world. US almost helpless to deal with so many things. Domestically violence continues in some sections. Mainly in major cities. Food crisis is growing. Large groups of people are moving away from the violence and population centers. Tomorrow objective is to get north of PA turnpike before setting up camp. Prayers, scripture, and thanksgiving service. Good night!

But He led forth His own people like sheep
And guided them in the wilderness like a flock.
(Psalm 78:52)

Date: April 14   Mileage: 5 mi.   Walk Total: 220–222 miles.

Pretty good night of rest. Silence all around us other than occasional citizen of the woods. A few owls and dogs in the distance. At least hoped were dogs and not coyotes. Dogs were not ready to get up from full tummies last night. Rousted them finally. Fixed cream of wheat and coffee over hexamine stove. Quick and dirty. After cleanup packed up and hit the path, so to speak. Plan today was to head almost directly north, cross PA turnpike, and then bear a bit east until able to cross PA 351. Would shadow PA 351 from short distance and get as far north as possible before camping. Had a funny thought as we were walking. Taxes are due to the IRS tomorrow. Don't think they will be getting any from us this year. Guess we will be fugitives once they figure out we haven't paid our taxes. So be it. Another interesting thought related to our abandoned truck. We wondered what had happened to it but not for very long. That was the past.

Same procedure for walking. Along sides of hills with as little up and down as possible. Into valleys when we had no other choice but back onto hillsides as soon as possible. Did not venture on roads at all other than to cross them when they were in front of us. Stayed pretty much on direction. Around noon came to the PA turnpike. Walked northwest along southbound lanes out of sight until we found a section split in the middle by a strip of land and trees. By finding that, we were able to only have to cross two lanes at a time and would have cover more quickly in the middle strip of land. Made it across southbound lanes. No traffic moving. However, had to spend about an hour hidden in the middle strip because of what we saw on northbound lanes.

Could hear rumble of something coming from the south as we sat in middle strip resting. Saw a convoy coming our way. Definitely military and not letting anything slow it down. It was moving. Seemed to be with a purpose. Multiple vehicles. A couple lead units with 30 cals. on top. Then what appeared to be a command car. Followed quickly by two larger vehicles with 50 cals. mounted on top. Then six deuce and a half trucks. Followed by two more larger armored vehicles with 50 cals. and two lighter vehicles with 30 cals. mounted. They were armed to the teeth. Something was definitely happening to our west. After that convoy passed, there was no traffic to be seen, so we hurried across the northbound turnpike lanes. Didn't stop until almost 2 PM to have a quick bite to eat. We wanted to get away from what we had seen. Once back on our way, crossed PA route 351 and shadowed it for another mile or so. Then started to look for a good site to spend the night with good water potential.

Set up camp quickly. Lean-to, fire pit, and fire wood. Boiled water from spring in hillside above us. Tired and stressed. Military convoy had disturbed us a bit. Sat in camp and listened to radio. No report of any significant troubles to our west. Planned tomorrow's journey segment. Target is to get close to US route 224. Prayers said, scripture read, dogs needed attention, then we're off to sleep. Hope better day tomorrow, good night!

Pour out Your wrath upon the nations which do not know You,
And upon the kingdoms which do not call upon Your name.
(Psalm 79:6)

LARRY D. HORTON, PhD

Cross Country Diary: Day #85

Date: April 15   Mileage: 0 mi.   Walk Total: 220–222 miles.

Hardly any sleep last night; too much unknown going on. Shortly after midnight we were awakened by what sounded like explosions in the distance. We looked to the northwest and southeast and saw a red glow in the sky in multiple locations in both directions. Sitting just east of PA route 351, we knew we were reasonably close to both Youngstown OH and Pittsburgh PA. Being flip we wondered if there were celebrations starting early about tax-day today. Over a period of ten to fifteen minutes we probably saw eight to ten of these same events but then nothing but silence. We turned on the radio, and there was nothing, no signal of any kind. We wondered if it was because of our location down the side of a valley. We would have to walk to the top of the ridge in the AM and see if we could get a signal. Back to bed but little if any sleep.

Finally, up and fixed normal breakfast. Worked on water supply as well. Everything cleaned up, we put dogs on their leashes and walked to top of ridge. Charged radio and heard nothing. Tried for a good thirty minutes and absolutely nothing. Walked back to camp and got smaller backup radio out, took it out of lead tape sealed container, and went back up the short walk to hill crest. Reception immediately but nothing on Pittsburgh stations. Found national emergency frequency and listened in shock. Will add details of what we heard after quick review of the rest of the day.

After coming to grips with the radio report we decided to stay put today and just try to listen and catch up on what was going on. After lunch spent an hour sitting by a tree away from camp with the air rifle thinking and hoping we could get some fresh meat. No luck. Our world has changed dramatically. After simple, very quiet supper we tried to get more on the radio, but very little was reported. We went to bed tonight with very mixed thoughts. Our world had changed dramatically. There will be no going back to what was. There is only the unknown that lies ahead of us. Hard to settle in for sleep; too many things running through our minds. Much prayer for guidance. Pored over scripture for guidance as well. We called it a night pretty early but found it hard to sleep. Dogs were restless as well. We thought we had gone dark, but we now will go truly dark for the duration of our travels. Lord, grant us your protection.

O God of hosts, restore us
And cause Your face to shine upon us,
And we will be saved.
(Psalm 80:7)

1800 Restart: Listening to the smaller and less powerful radio today, we heard the following. At midnight eastern time, on April fifteenth, what appeared to be a coordinated attack took place on the US and western Europe. Explosions in three satellites, one over the eastern half of the US, one over the western half, and one over western Europe, likely Russian satellites with Trojan horse bombs aboard, created EMPs. Immediately all technologically based capabilities were rendered useless in the targeted areas. Instantly the historical Western powers were rendered defenseless and helpless. In a second of time large sections of the world were sent back into the early preindustrial realities of AD 1800. Everything tied to any kind of technology came to a screeching halt. Totally silent. Totally useless.

We now have a better idea of what last night's events were, bright red glows in the distance rumbling like thunder. More than likely these events were explosions of aircraft that fell from the sky when all their internal systems shut down. Our only thought was that the pilots had been able to eject before their aircraft hit the ground. As we stood on the top of the hill last night we could see nothing. Where we saw reflections of lights the previous night, there was only darkness. No sounds could be heard except for those made by animals.

Our large radio is now useless. Thank goodness we had the foresight to secure the smaller radio and one cell phone in containers wrapped in lead tape. Our analog watches still work OK. Digital watches are useless.

Our compass was not affected. We had little technology loss other than the bigger radio. We listen to the news periodically on an emergency band and can get a small picture of the impact of the EMP on the US. As I said earlier, anything tied to technology, microchips, computers, and electronic switches was dead. Our society was totally wired before midnight. It is now totally silent and blind. Taken-for-granted systems are fried. All communication systems, all financial systems, banks, all medical systems, all military and defense systems, all economic systems, everything is gone. No vehicle traffic of any kind is possible. All air traffic is gone. All motors, with countless computer connections, are silent. All power systems and grids are dark. There will be no semi-trailer truck deliveries of food and water, the so-called necessities of life. All TV and radio broadcasts are silent other than those that had been hardened by the government for such an event. Only emergency broadcasts are happening on government-controlled frequencies. All postal deliveries are done. Any communication beyond what the government broadcasts are only by those who can set up basic Morse code messaging on CB or short-wave radios. Most of the US military equipment, dependent on computers and technology, is useless. State and federal government have come to a standstill. No messages are coming from our new president, Congress, or governors. Pipelines delivering home heating fuel, vehicle fuel, and water are not working. Factories are silent. Only equipment at least 50 years old is working and only then partially. Harvesting of crops is at a standstill. Ships in ports delivering goods sit unemptied.

I could go on-and-on, but the point is made. The twenty-first century has instantly become the early nineteenth century. What will the short-term and long-term impact be on people? Violence? Desperation? Starvation? Collapsed government? Panic? At this point one can only imagine a worst-case scenario. People could roll over and surrender to these things, or they could think, plan, and react with common sense and skills to survive in the new world. We made the choice to keep moving into the future. We had prepared for tough times. The times just got tougher. Our preparations will be the same now. Plan, stay safe, avoid dangers, live for tomorrow, have a specific goal, and trust the Lord to guide and protect us in our journey.

Date: April 16   Mileage: 6 mi.   Walk Total: 226–228 miles.

Tough night of fitful sleep again. Up at 6 AM and decided we had to keep moving. We could do nothing to change the circumstances around us. Planned to try to stop this afternoon just south of US route 224 somewhere along the banks of the Mahoning Creek. That would put us west of the I-376 bypass. New Castle PA will be to our northeast. Bessemer PA will be to our southwest. Edinburg PA will be slightly east, more than likely. We needed to cross PA routes 551 and 317. We would cross lots of smaller roads and streams traveling through hills and valleys and be near significant populated areas. Caution would be the word for the day.

We made some key decisions for the rest of our trip. Only small fires for cooking protected from sight by reflecting walls. Cooking on hexamine stove only for the next twenty days. Camp light only from fire tins that we have prepared for that same twenty-day period. We will reevaluate that strategy after those twenty days when we have a better sense of how people are dealing with our new realty. We will listen to backup radio only every other day to conserve its capabilities and to keep silent. We will in no circumstance walk on roads but stick to wooded cover when at all possible. If we have to cross fields, we will walk along fence lines offering some cover because of unmown weeds, grass, and brush growing along them. We will avoid all farmhouses and hunting camps. We will cross major streams or rivers using bridges only when we have no other choice. We will hunker down as necessary due to weather or human dangers. As we are finally in PA, we will take no chances on something bad happening to us in any haste that might drive us to make stupid decisions. Safety and common sense will now be our mantra.

With all that, we made slow but steady progress during the day. Hot lunch of soup off to the side of one of the small roads we crossed. Temps were getting a bit warmer, probably 50 for a high today. Felt again like a heat wave. Quite a few breaks to cool down, especially when we were close to any signs of significant population. We sat and listened in silence for sounds of humans or animals before we took any risks like crossing a road. We prayed constantly that the dogs would behave and not bark too much. All the while as we were walking we kept an eye out for nonhuman threats like snakes. At 4 PM after what seemed a long day we pulled up to a nice covered, secluded camping spot about one-half mile south of US route 224. We quickly set up camp, collected water for boiling, covered our tracks to the campsite, and cooked supper over hexamine stove. Once water boiled, we put out main fire. Temps are to be in mid-forties tonight. We can deal with that.

Stayed light until around 6:30 PM. Sat on slope of nearby hill from which could see US route 224. Saw individuals and some small groups walking in both directions on the road. Where were they going? They had deserted larger cities. But they looked to be unprepared for what they now faced, at least from a distance. Watched until grew too dark to see. Hit sack by 9 PM, prayers, scripture, and long conversation about our plan forward. We knew that some of the dangers from people we had imagined were now a real possibility. Dogs sensed that something had changed. Many prayers for guidance and safety. Good night!

You called in trouble and I rescued you.
(Psalm 81:7)

Cross Country Diary: Day #87

Date: April 17   Mileage: 4 mi.   Walk Total: 230–232 miles.

Woke up pretty early this morning with what we hoped were realistic goals for the day. We knew we had to cross US route 224, another major four-lane highway. Sometime mid-afternoon we hoped to camp just south of US route 422—once more a four-lane major highway. That would put us somewhere southeast of Villa Maria PA. Once that is achieved, we will start to bend our path toward the northeast, past New Wilmington PA, and then on to the Mercer PA area, where we will cross I-80. We agreed that we would slow our pace to be more cautious. Having been in this area quite a bit over the years, we know that it is pockmarked with small communities and that lots of secondary roads here don't show up on our map. That requires extra caution. The geography is hilly with lots of woods and open fields. Given events of past 48 hours, we have no idea how people are reacting to those events, thus raising our caution levels significantly. It is likely still pretty early to run into any really bad stuff, but we are not going to take any chances.

Breakfast passed quickly. Repacked, and we were on our way by 8:30 AM. Stayed concealed along tree-lines and in wooded areas as much as possible. Had to cross a couple major open field areas in the morning, so did that very carefully. Obviously, no vehicle traffic on roads we had to cross. Route 224 crossing went OK. When we did see buildings or homes, we noticed people out and about on their property doing whatever, but didn't notice much if any foot traffic on any of the minor roads. After crossing 224, stopped for lunch and to replenish our water. Temps in low fifties by early afternoon. Not much need to layer clothing at least when the sun was still above the hillsides. Will cool down tonight. We have been so lucky on this trip to find reasonable water sources, partly due to luck and partly due to the sort of country we have been traveling in. Water is, as always, our number-one priority. Ice was gone from all streams and creeks. Plan to try luck at fishing tonight if we come to a decent water flow.

LARRY D. HORTON, PhD

By 2 PM started to look for campsite for the night. Land not quite as hilly, in elevation that is, but still very rolling. Dotted with lots of farms. Water in streams up a bit due to snowmelt. With coming rain we expect rivers and creeks to be running high, which could be an obstacle for us requiring we slow down even more at major crossings and wait for the flow to diminish. Time will tell. Decent campsite found within sight of US route 422 just to our north. As we set up camp, kept an eye on the road; nothing to see but empty pavement. Once camp up I collected water from a reasonable stream nearby.

While wife boiled it over small fire I fashioned a small hoop net to see if I could strain some small fish from water for supper. After frustrating empty-handed efforts, I built a stone walled enclosure on the bank of the stream. One way in for the fish, no way out. Will check it in the AM. Back to camp, supper eaten and cleaned up, water boiled, fire put out, with no light except for brief fire-tin flame. Prayers said, scripture read, settled down in bags for the night. Watched stars through treetops. Dogs pretty quiet. Good night! Lord, watch over us. Happy twenty-fourth anniversary!

Rescue the weak and needy;
Deliver them out of the hand of the wicked.
(Psalm 82:4)

Date: April 18   Mileage: 4 mi.   Walk Total: 234–236 miles.

Heard a couple gunshots during the night, another indicator that we needed to be very alert no matter what was behind the shots. While wife prepared breakfast of oatmeal and coffee over hexamine stove, I took my homemade hoop net down to the small stream to see if we had any fish. Surprise, surprise. Five small, what we used to call "creek chubs," and a couple of crayfish. Crawdads to you Southerners. Gutted the fish. Cut off heads. Too small to filet so would cut them up into small pieces and put in some water to create a broth for lunch. Bones way too small and soft to worry about other than spine, which I removed from each one. Meat from tails of crayfish pulled out and thrown in as well. Smelled good as it was boiling. Poured off some water. Dogs wanted that but no way. Put meat in small plastic bag. Would add to soup for lunch a few hours from now. Since cooked, it would be OK for the morning but not beyond that.

Broke camp as usual, repacked, policed area, and we were on our way. First major task: cross US route 422 safely. In this area road was a major east-to-west route. Seemed funny to come up to it and to see it completely deserted. At least at first, we thought it was deserted. We stopped and looked carefully and could see a group of about fifteen people walking eastward to our right. We crossed over route 422 after waiting for thirty minutes to make sure that no one else was on the road. That done we continued on our way with rest stops often. Temps in low to mid-fifties with some sunshine. Noticed some building clouds to the south which was a sign of coming rain. Lots of small streams forded but not very deep. We carefully looked for places with signs of shallow water. Low banks to enable us to enter and exit easily. Walking sticks kept us steady. Carried both dogs across after relaying packs to the other side of each stream.

Lunch was soup with the fish from this morning added. Dogs really enjoyed it as did we. A different flavor. Not too many calories, but the difference it made was worth the effort if only in taste. Lunch done, we moved on. One major stream crossed in afternoon, the Shenango River. Walked upstream and came upon a small concrete bridge. Watched and listened for a bit then hurried across. Got to other side and up an embankment when we heard voices. Laid low and watched couple of men walk across going other direction carrying side-arms and hunting rifles. A near miss. Dogs were quiet. With that behind us we pushed on until we came in sight of I-376 and looked for a campsite. Set up camp overlooking I-376 and built small fire to boil water and cook supper of rice and beans. Dogs were hungry, as were we.

Fire out we turned on radio after charging to catch up a bit. Cities are in a mess. Military and national guard as well as local police in major cities have lost control. Countryside left to its own devices. No good news but no surprises. Fire-tin lit for a brief time to read scripture, then out and sat just listening and thinking. More clouds moving in. Rain sure to come. Dried clothing and boots as best we could. Prayers, scripture, and hit the sack. Another risky day tomorrow. Good night!

O God, do not remain quiet;
Do not be silent and,
O God, do not be still.
(Psalm 83:1)

Cross Country Diary: Day #89

Date: April 19   Mileage: 5 mi.   Walk Total: 239–241 miles.

Light rain started to fall in the middle of the night. Fog and low clouds made it very dark when we woke up. Thank goodness, we were less dependent on an open fire, as all wood was wet. Dogs did not want to get up. They wanted to stay dry. Broke out ponchos and worked at cooking. Boiled enough water for canteens over hexamine cubes and then broke camp. We were hoping weather would keep others from being out and about. We were not that lucky.

On our way about 8:30 AM. Gray light and cooler because of the rain and overcast. I-376 was deserted when we first looked down on it but could hear noises in the distance coming toward us. Back under cover, we watched as three small groups of people walked past heading north. They seemed to ignore each other so we hoped they would ignore us as well when we crossed the highway. Found a large culvert to use to cross under the road. Meant relaying the stuff, but that was OK. Not quite as large as previous culverts, so had to bend over quite a bit as we walked through. Was hard and back was yelling at me when we were finally done. Rested for at least thirty minutes on far side to let back settle down. Dogs just explored and were content. Lots of scents in the culvert for them to smell. Was probably major critter highway in the culvert to avoid the road as well.

Once rested, moved on. Rain coming down harder by the hour. When we stopped for lunch, was more than just a drizzle. It looked like it was going to set in for a while. Crossed PA route 208 after lunch. I remember that road from my days at Grove City College many years ago. Where has time gone, and what a different world now. As the afternoon passed we had to zig and zag quite a bit to stay under cover. A couple of open fields crossed, but nothing major. By 3 PM we were tired. Ground and grass under foot was increasingly slippery and starting to get muddy. If this keeps up, we will tire out each day pretty early. Thank goodness, we prepared for wet weather. Temps never got to fifty today. Damp and chilly, so layered a bit more than the last few days. As the

LARRY D. HORTON, PhD

afternoon wore on, took more and more breaks. We were both worn out by the time we found a decent campsite under some evergreens below the crest of a hill.

Set up camp as best as we could to stay dry. Dug trench around shelter to keep ground water away from us. Supper cooked over hexamine stove was beans and rice. Added some of the last dried chicken we had to give us a bit of protein. Dogs seemed really hungry tonight. Once supper cleaned up, we did some planning for the days ahead. If rain continues to fall, we need to be realistic about what we can accomplish. With all the zigging and sagging, we know we are walking quite a bit further than the miles covered as a crow flies. That is our reality. Planned out next five days to cover four miles in straight line but likely five to six miles of actual walking. Went to bed. Everything was damp but could do nothing about that. Aren't going to chance a real fire until we get north of I-80. Prayers, scripture, and hugs all around tonight. Lots of yawning. Listened to rain on our tarp roof as our lullaby. Good night!

O Lord God of hosts,
Hear my prayer;
Give ear, O God of Jacob.
(Psalm 84:8)

Date: April 20   Mileage: 5 mi.   Walk Total: 244–246 miles.

Three months since we pulled out of our driveway in Houston TX. So much has happened in these ninety days. We have been walking for 79 days to this point, and our average mileage covered per day is about three miles. Progress. Much more than we could imagine, but we are still a significant distance from our objective.

Rain was coming down even harder when we woke up. Thank goodness had built trench around lean-to last night. Breakfast of oatmeal and coffee. Lots of coffee left; oatmeal getting a little short. Decided to open up one of the tins of tuna we've been hoarding for supper tonight. Had to cross PA route 18 later this morning but after that we would be pretty much out in the countryside for the rest of the day. No major obstacles that we knew of. Dogs ate a full portion of breakfast. Camp broken down. Everything wet. It will have to stay that way. Packs up, ponchos on, dogs on short leashes, and we set out for the day.

Crossed PA route 18 about an hour later. No other human beings in sight. Rain a steady shower. Walking on very slippery leaves and along hillsides. Had to be very careful. Walking sticks really were important. We slipped occasionally and had to sit for a few minutes to get our feet under us again. Luckily no twisted ankles or wrenched knees. Out in the countryside now. Hills, small fields, and farms. Lots of streams to ford. Luckily the rain had not added too much water to the streams. Really careful walking on stream bottoms. Rocks were very slippery as well. Carried dogs over each stream. The bigger one was a load but we managed. Put up tarp quickly to cover us while we fixed lunch. Sat for about an hour just to stay out of the rain.

By compass bearing we head about forty degrees to the northeast now and for the next few days, then head east-northeast toward Franklin PA. Lots of hills. Avoided up and down as much as we could. On slippery ground, could not do much else. Getting a bit muddy when we were out in the open. Couple fields crossed were pretty large and always had fences to navigate. That meant relaying things over the fences before we could move on. Temps OK, just damp and chilly. Very gray skies. This will be with us a while. Around 3 PM started to look for a campsite. We were probably within a mile or so of I-80 but really out in the country. Found grove of trees, pines mostly, to give us some cover, and set up camp. No campfire tonight. No really dry wood. Water would be boiled on hexamine stove. Supply of fuel for that stove starting to get a little low. Probably have another eight to ten days left if we're careful. Supper of rice, beans, and tuna with coffee. Dogs really were hungry. The tuna was a big hit with them. Radio charged to get weather report from NOAA, if still on air. It was. Rain to continue for another couple days, then warm up a bit and be dry for the next five to six days. Tired after the tough walk today. Inventoried food. Enough freeze-dried stuff for another twenty to twenty-five days and maybe a bit longer if we can get some meat. Prayers, scripture, yawns, and to bed. Damp but OK.

I will hear what God the Lord will say;
For He will speak peace to His people, to His godly ones;
But let them not turn back to folly.
(Psalm 85:8)

Date: April 21   Mileage: 6 mi.   Walk Total: 250–252 miles.

Still raining lightly when we woke up. Really chilly with the rain. Everything very wet. Breakfast done and camp broken down, we were on our way by 8 AM. Kind of out in the sticks, which is good for our safety. Slow going on wet surfaces. Staying away from roads. Crossed a few small streams and runs, as they are called here, before lunch. Ponchos working OK, just glad wind is not up. Dogs looked miserable. Several breaks to try to get out of the rain, but not much success. Big obstacle today was crossing of I-80. Again, paralleled I-80 until we found a spot with east- and westbound lanes separated by a piece of land. No traffic of any kind, so decided to cross them directly. Stopped in middle wooded area to make sure nothing going westbound. Got across without incident. Stopped for a rest after crossing I-80 and had a quick lunch of soup. Opened a can of tuna for the dogs. They needed the energy. They wolfed it down and wanted more.

Back to walking. Rain pretty heavy at times. By 1 PM came to PA route 318. Saw some foot traffic on it headed east toward Mercer PA. We kept going pretty much north. Our plan was to look for campsite about a mile north of route 318. As we were walking, had to cross a small country road. We were had. A man about our age stepped out of some trees just in front of us. He was obviously hunting or trying to protect his land. He approached us. Dogs wanted to run to him and were barking. He came up to us and stuck out his hand to shake ours. Asked what we were up to. Quickly told him we were on our way east and had left Houston TX three months ago. He stood in shock; couldn't believe we had come this far. We were obviously very wet and pretty cold as he asked us if we had been walking in the rain. Our story of camping every night, cooking and eating in the wild, our run-ins with people and critters, and the fact that we had another 100 miles to go must have struck a nerve. He could see we were armed, and we explained why. Hearing all this, he asked if we would like to take shelter in his barn tonight to get out of the rain. In fact, he offered us the shelter for as long as it was still raining. We hesitated just for a second and then agreed. He did not seem to be a threat to us. He said his house and buildings were another half mile up the road to the right, and we could walk with him. We just looked at each other, hoping we had made the right decision.

Arriving, he led us into his barn where he had a half dozen cows, some farm machinery, and lots of bales of straw. He broke up several of the bales and helped us fix a place to sit and lie down tonight. At that point his wife came out to the barn. Introductions were made and our story repeated. She then invited us to join them for a warm home-cooked evening meal in their house. Our dogs were invited. Said they had a Lab that would make good friends with them. We accepted. She also said to come a bit early and we could take a hot shower and clean ourselves up a bit. We must have been a sight. We removed our packs and hung up everything that was wet to dry in the sweet smell of the barn. The dogs did some exploring but only as far as their long leashes would let them.

At 5 PM, after resting a bit, we loaded up extra clothing and the dogs and headed to the farmhouse. They told us supper would be ready at 6 PM so we had an hour to clean up. A hot shower never felt so good. After weeks of cleaning ourselves with a washcloth in certain areas every night the fact that we had not had a true shower in months came home to us. We were in heaven I guess. We were in their kitchen, right at 6 PM. The husband had prepared a full meal for the dogs as well. Dry food mixed with what appeared to be some kind of jerky, with a small bit of milk to add some moisture to the whole thing. Haven't seen dogs eat like that in weeks. They had been so good.

Sitting down to eat we were fed fried chicken, mashed potatoes, canned green beans and tomatoes, homemade bread, butter, and jam. Dessert was a fresh apple pie all washed down with real brewed coffee. It took us a long time to eat, and we could not eat that much, as we had been on short rations for so long. But every bite was worth eating slowly. My wife and the farmer's wife cleaned up the table and washed the dishes. The farmer and I went out to check on his cows in the barn and had a long conversation about what was going on in the country. We were of like mind in almost everything. He said all the people in their area had banded together into a mutual protection and safety group. He said all of them would have taken us in just as he and his wife had done.

They had a shortwave radio in the house and he said they got daily updates on what was going on in the world and in our country. It was not good. Anarchy has spread all across Europe and across the 48 contiguous states. The US is rapidly dividing up into regional control areas, each with extreme violence in some locations. The US government as a whole is no longer viable. Several regions are surfacing as control areas, mostly in the hands of state and local governments. The east coast, the Midwest, the Southeast, the Southwest and the Pacific coast have become pseudo-independent areas, each dominated by one or two ethnic groups. Fighting among those groups is escalating daily. We sat for a while and just reflected on what we were talking about. Western PA, the area we are in and where we will settle, has been able to avoid significant violence to this point, but in some confrontations, several have died.

With all that said, we went back to the farmhouse. We told them we have to be on our way in the morning but will be eternally grateful for their help. With that they shocked us again. They told us when we're leaving in the AM to stop by the farmhouse, and they will have something for us. We protested but they insisted. With that we headed to the barn, dogs in tow, to a dry night's rest. They were full of energy after having a good meal. We arrived back in the barn and spread our sleeping bags on the warm straw. We leashed the dogs to a nearby post and spread out straw for them. We sat and reflected on what had just happened to us in the last few hours. Again, the Lord had been watching out for us. Three times now kind people have helped us during our travels. We concluded that in spite of what is going on there are truly good people still left in the world. We just had to sit and have a praise service right there in the barn. Lots of tears as well. Lots of prayers of thanksgiving and scripture, and we settled down for the night. Praise God for His mercy, grace, and forgiveness. Good night!

**There is no one like You among the gods,
O Lord,
Nor are there any works like Yours.
(Psalm 86:8)**

LARRY D. HORTON, PhD

Date: April 22   Mileage: 5 mi.   Walk Total: 255–257 miles.

The best night's sleep we've had in weeks. The smell of straw permeated everything. Brought back a lot of childhood memories. Woke as sun was just coming up. Very light drizzle falling. Clouds were a lot lighter than before. About 7 AM farmer asked us to come up to the house for breakfast and some things they wanted to provide for us before we left. Dressed, with dogs in tow, we headed that way. Dogs had another big meal just like last night. We sat down to fried eggs, bacon, toast, and coffee. It was wonderful. After eating we were ready to get on our way. Rain had stopped, but was going to be muddy and chilly. High today around fifty, but colder than that when we were ready to go. Dampness went right through us.

Our hosts presented us with two pounds of jerky, three pounds dried dog food, enough dried eggs for a week of breakfasts, and a loaf of homemade bread. We protested, but it didn't do any good. We joined them in a prayer giving thanks and asking travel safety and were on our way to the barn to get our stuff and set out. We knew we had been blessed and that our travel route had brought us to this wonderful couple. Gifts loaded, packs on backs, we set out waving at the couple as we headed down their lane.

By noon we had crossed PA route 318 without incident and were at the side of US route 62. Observed a few people walking toward Mercer PA, so waited until they were out of sight before we crossed route 62. Again, without incident. Not raining but our path through the woods and an occasional field was wet and muddy in some places. Crossed multiple small creeks and streams which showed effect of the rain. Got wet but that was OK. Stopped each time, dried feet, and put on dry socks. Would have to dry all of that stuff by our fire tonight. We knew when we crossed PA route 258 that we were getting close to our night's campsite. Not a soul in sight. We did hear some gunfire in the distance and hoped it was someone out getting some fresh meat and nothing more.

About a mile after we crossed route 258 we found a reasonable spot to set up camp. Had spent the day walking gradually up and down hills trying our best to keep elevation gains and losses to a minimum. Zigged and zagged a bit but stayed pretty close to our planned compass heading all day. Took a few minutes to set up camp located in a small grove of pine trees which provided additional shelter. Some firewood under trees that wasn't too wet. Did find couple small dead trees which I knocked down. Would burn a bit hotter. We decided to chance a small fire to dry our clothing, boil water from nearby stream, and cook our supper. Supper was beans, with pieces of gift jerky, rice, and coffee. Dogs got jerky stirred into some of the dry dog food we had been given. Lean-to set up, pine branches for mattress, trench dug around shelter, we settled in and rested. Dogs were pretty satisfied. Full tummies. Will let fire burn out overnight. Bundled up, prayers said, scripture read, and hugs all around, we'll soon be asleep. Lord, protect us tomorrow. Thank You for watching over us.

Then those who sing as well as those who play the flutes shall say,
"All my springs of joy are in you."
Psalm 87:7

Date: April 23   Mileage: 6 mi.   Walk Total: 261–263 miles.

Cool when we woke up. Probably in the low forties. Very damp but some sun peeking through the clouds, so rain was likely over for the time being. Breakfast of oatmeal, jerky, and coffee to warm up. Broke down camp, cleaned up area, and filled canteens and one water jug. Dogs on short leashes were ready to go. Plan for the day was to cross US route 19, a four-lane highway, then cross Neshannock Creek and camp about a mile on the east side of the creek. Knew would have hills and valleys and quite a few small swollen creeks to cross. Would take our time and of course do our best to avoid any contact with other humans.

The morning passed pretty quietly. Came to route 19 and used our normal process of crossing. Found area where we could use a culvert. Relayed everything to the east side. Reloaded and were on our way. As we approached Neshannock Creek, we had the first real accident of our trip. We were walking along a slope above a small valley which was the pathway for the creek. My wife, trying to get one of the dogs around a downed tree, slipped on some wet leaves and twisted her ankle. We stopped immediately to check on ankle damage. The sprain wasn't too bad, but it did swell up a bit pretty quickly. Put one of our packed ankle braces on it and tied her boot on pretty tightly. We walked a bit further but realized it was going to stop us. Sat her down with dogs, dropped my pack, and walked on a bit further to find campsite. Once found went back and relayed both packs to the site. Then back to get her and the dogs.

Arrived at site shortly, sat her down with dogs on long leashes, and I started to build camp. We then realized we hadn't eaten lunch, so got small fire started and fixed some soup and coffee for us. That done and cleaned up, saw that had about three hours of sunlight left so got to camp building. We knew walking for a day or two was out of the question so built a bit more substantial camp as we would be in place until wife's ankle was better. Lean-to built in grove of hardwoods in semi-flat location looking down on stream. Fire pit built, small fire started, I set out to get water for boiling and supper. Collected as much firewood as I could that would burn reasonably well.

Wrapped wife's foot in packed ace bandage and brace, then did some looking around the creek. Found a great pool where there had to be some fish. Decided first thing in morning would set out lines to try and give us some fresh meat. Hunkering down for a couple days would possibly give me the chance to add to our food by catching some fresh fish. Stream was swollen from rains, so sitting for couple days would possibly allow it to go down a bit as well. With all that planned, back at camp, fixed light supper of soup and some jerky. Dogs got some of each as well. We were going to have to be very careful with wife's foot and figure out how to enable her to carry pack, have one dog on lead, and use a walking pole to move forward. We were going to have to slow down a bit obviously. After eating, carried folding bucket of cold stream water to camp, and she soaked her foot in it. Did that three times before calling it a night. Ankle will be swollen in the AM. Some pain meds help as well. Prayers, scripture, we then bedded down for the night. Not as cold. Temps better.

Let my prayer come before You;
Incline Your ear to my cry.
(Psalm 88:2)

Date: April 24   Mileage: 0 mi.   Walk Total: 261–263 miles.

Restless night for my wife. Ankle hurting some. Dogs knew something was wrong. Woke up to more sunshine coming down through trees. Temps up a bit, maybe mid-forties at sunrise. Going to feel good later, getting into mid-fifties today. First things first, wrapped her ankle. Then I got about fixing breakfast, oatmeal with jerky, and coffee. Dogs got dry food and jerky. That all done, hauled water and boiled it. Next was gathering wood for a small fire. Most of cooking from this point forward would be on hexamine stove with fire only for boiling water. Heard some gunfire east of us. Again, hoped was people out getting fresh meat. Official hunting season was long over, but with current conditions seasons were meaningless.

Spent quite a bit of time preparing multiple line fishing gear, a mini-trot line. At stream, set it in small pool. Would check it late in afternoon to see if had any luck. Used jerky as bait. That would put a good attraction smell in the water on the multiple hooks. After lines set, got about moving a bunch of rocks to form a pool on side of bank. Hopefully fish would move into shelter of bank. Then when water went down, would be trapped in the pool with no way out. Would check that tomorrow during the day to see if it worked. By time got all this done, was getting late in the AM, so headed back to camp. On way saw several squirrel nests not too far from camp and not too high in hardwoods. Would come back after lunch and stake out the nests with the air rifle. Might get lucky that way for fresh meat as well. Lunch was soup and orange drink.

Given weather changes, backtracked a bit after lunch to a couple small fields passed through yesterday. Walked fence lines and was able to find a small quantity of new dandelion plants. Gathered leaves and planned on fixing them with bit of flour and salt for supper tonight. Likely would look again tomorrow morning for these fresh greens as well. Back to camp. Hauled multiple buckets of cold stream water to camp, and wife soaked ankle repeatedly. Some swelling. Will get black and blue as well, but all-in-all could have been a lot worse. Tomorrow afternoon will know if we can start out again the following day or will have to stay in place a bit longer to let her heal as much as possible.

Around 4 PM went down to check on trot-line, and a couple of the lines were taut. Pulled them in and had two four- to five-inch rainbow trout on them. Fresh meat for supper. Gutted and cleaned them and rebaited hooks with their innards. Then back in water. Big smile on face when got back to camp. Prepared fish. Started small wood fire and cooked fish whole on skewers. Smell was wonderful. Could see the dogs licking their lips. Fixed some rice as well. When all done, we sat down to a hot rice and fish meal. Dogs wolfed theirs down and wanted more. Cleaned up dishes and washed our socks. Hung up sleeping bags to air out. Could still smell straw aroma on them from night in barn recently. Was wonderful. Washed our body areas as well. Last thing was to haul enough water to fill canteens and one water jug before we rested.

That all done, we cranked up battery power on small radio. Signal was weak, but we could hear it. Sat down to listen to NOAA radio and national news. Things are pretty much the same as when we were at the last farm. Internationally, three large military conflicts happening, one in Korea, one in eastern Europe, and of course in the Middle East. In the US, things had gotten even worse than three days ago. The national government has put all domestic armed forces, primarily the army and marines, into major cities to try and maintain some semblance of control. New York City, Washington, Boston, Atlanta, Miami, Chicago, St. Louis, Houston, Denver, Phoenix, Los Angeles, San Francisco, and Seattle. All other areas in what was called flyover country have been put in the hands of local authorities. The government has no choice but to try and provide some safety in the larger population centers due to the lawlessness in every location. The countryside, small cities, towns, and rural areas are left to the locals. In many, local safety committees and militias are trying to maintain some type of control.

Movement of food, water, supplies, and fuel is nonexistent. Armed confrontations and conflict are springing up all over the country.

Armed groups forage around the countryside trying to find what is needed. Commercial ground and air traffic have ground to a halt. Power services, communication services, and electronic services do not exist. The recent EMPs shut down all technology. Banking and financial services are stopped. Stock market results have moved lower than during the Great Depression of the 1930s by percentage.

The US overseas military is in effect cut off completely from domestic control and supply. Military aircraft still patrol the country's borders but do not exist elsewhere. All major highways are being patrolled by national and local authorities. Checkpoints at all major bridges in an attempt to control the movement of out-of-control groups. Radio broadcasts now under the control of the federal government and only used on an emergency basis. Underground communication, radio and shortwave, is trying to keep people informed of situations on a more local basis. Medical services outside major cities are nonexistent. In reality it would appear that people are taking care of themselves with little interest in keeping the country on a steady footing. Food and water supplies in many parts of the country are depleted completely. Food and water riots are taking place hourly all across the country. The US has ceased, for all intents and purposes, to be a functioning nation.

Needless to say, we are depressed to hear all this but in many ways not surprised at all. It does make us wonder about the status of our house in Texas and our abandoned truck in southern Ohio, but only for a minute. We can do nothing about those things. One final check of wife's ankle, rewrapped, and we settled down for the night. Lots of prayers for safety, of course. Scripture reading. We decided to break into the hot chocolate supply for a special nightcap. Petted the dogs and hugged them as we settled down for the night. Lord, continue to protect and watch over us. We are totally in your hands at this point. Good night!

**I will sing of the lovingkindness of the Lord forever;
To all generations I will make known Your
faithfulness with my mouth.
(Psalm 89:1)**

Date: April 25   Mileage: 0 mi.   Walk Total: 261–263 miles.

Up with sunrise. Wife's ankle only slightly swollen but pretty black-and-blue. Sunshine down through trees around us. A bit warmer. Per last night's NOAA radio broadcast, into mid-fifties again today. Dogs full of energy. Put them on long leashes to let them explore. Started small fire, cooked breakfast of cream-of-wheat, jerky, dried fruit, and coffee. Dogs were hungry as were we. Cleaned up dishes, gathered firewood, and hauled water for boiling. Then to creek to check on trot line and fish trap. Water down just a bit so making progress. By tomorrow if all goes well, will have fish in trap. No luck overnight on trot line. Will check it again late this afternoon. Thought I saw a couple of fish in the trap this morning but not sure. Hauled cold water back to camp for wife to soak ankle in again. Seems to be helping. But we know progress for next few days will be slow. Decided to stay in place one more full day before trying to cross stream and be on our way slowly.

Late morning spent an hour with air rifle watching for squirrels. No luck. Will try again late this afternoon. Cold lunch of jerky and orange drink. After lunch carried cold water up from stream for wife to soak ankle. Hung sleeping bags in sunlight to dry as much as possible. Changed into camping clothing and hung up hiking clothing to dry in the same way. Camp looked pretty cluttered. Good thing no one stumbled upon us. Heard more gunshots off to our east. Same hope as before: hunters. Things still pretty damp but a bit easier to find wood that would burn OK. After cleaning up from lunch, headed back out with air rifle. Sat for couple hours underneath big oak tree while wife and dogs napped.

Back to camp around 3 PM, and all were up and about. Wife walking pretty well. A slight limp, but will not restrict our travel significantly for next few days. Decided to spend one more day hunkered down to let it heal as much as possible. Late afternoon hauled more water for soaking, for boiling to fill water canteens and jug, and to prepare supper. Trot line had one four-inch trout. Dogs will get that tonight. Cleaned and gutted it. Headed back to camp. Hopefully by tomorrow afternoon creek will be down enough that we have fish for supper then. Time will tell.

Supper was rice and beans for us. Rice and a bit of fish for the dogs. Again, cooked on skewer over fire. Coffee to drink. Dogs went nuts again when they smelled the fish cooking. Cleanup for supper done hauled cold water from creek a couple times for wife to soak her ankle. Had hung up sleeping bags and clothing earlier in the day, so by bedtime they were reasonably dry. Took dogs for a short walk down to creek at dusk to check on fish trap one more time today. Water continues to recede each hour. No desire to listen to radio again tonight. Our guess it that news will be much the same, and we want to stay as positive and upbeat as possible. Usual bedtime routine, prayers, scripture, and petting the dogs who were just glad to be with us. Thank you, Lord, for a good day.

Lord, You have been our dwelling place in all generations.
Before the mountains were born or You gave
birth to the earth and the world,
Even from everlasting to everlasting, You are God.
(Psalm 90:1–2)

Date: April 26   Mileage: 0 mi.   Walk Total: 261–263 miles.

Up again at sunrise. Night was not as cold. Sun shining through the trees. Wife's ankle had little to no swelling. Brace put on and boot. She will walk around camp today to see how it handles the walking. Also, soak in cold water from creek as well. If all goes well today, will set out tomorrow and try to cover a few miles until she needs to stop. Dogs on long leashes. For some reason, they seem excited today. Breakfast cooked and eaten. Hauled several loads of water, and wife will boil it all while I am checking on fish and trying to get a squirrel. As soon as breakfast dishes cleaned, headed down to creek to check on fish trap and trot line. Trot line had a couple small trout on it; gutted and cleaned, and will have for lunch. Creek almost back to normal, so inspected trap pool I created. A couple more fish in it who couldn't get out. Altogether had four fish. Not very big but combined would give us a good lunch. Rebaited trot line. Try for fish for supper.

Back to camp with fish. Gathered firewood for one more night. Clothing down to long-sleeve shirt and jeans. Warmer today. Lunch of beans, rice, and chunks of fish all cooked in broth. Dogs got lunch as well. Not usual but today had extra. Lunch cleanup finished, hauled more water for boiling. Then headed out with air rifle. Lots of squirrels making noise in trees, but none close enough for a decent shot. Back at camp, cleaned weapons. Hung sleeping bags, clothing, and socks in sunlight to dry. Did inventory on food and all other supplies. Repacked backpacks. Transferred some from wife's pack to mine to help her walk. With the supplies that farmer had given us, my pack pretty close to where it had been when we had left the Trekker behind. What we had received replaced all the freeze-dried food we had eaten since then.

Took some time to gather more firewood and haul water. Want to start out tomorrow with full water containers. Did a few minor repairs on packs where branches had snagged. Glad we had packed heavy-duty thread and some large needles. Made the job a bit easier. Repacked my med kit as stuff for wife's ankle had been taken out of it. Took dogs for a walk down to the stream. Once back and dogs on leashes, I set out to walk upstream and downstream on creek to find the best location for us to attempt a crossing should we set out tomorrow. Walked upstream for thirty minutes and found one possible site, but it had two deep pools in it. Easy access and egress on both sides. Then back to starting point and headed downstream. Fifteen minutes into walk found an even better place. Straight creek-bed with small pool on far side. Will be a bit deeper, but can manage that. Current not too fast. Most of crossing will be in two feet of water. With hiking poles, we can manage our balance. Will require me to relay everything across. Will have safety rope anchored to starting side in case I slip. Second rope will then be anchored on far side and brought back to starting side so wife can hang on to it going across. Carrying dogs will be the hardest part of the relay. Cannot afford to drop them into water. Sun getting low, so headed back with a plan. Simple supper, pasta for us, dog food for dogs. To bed around 9 PM, prayers, and scripture. Hoping for successful crossing tomorrow. Thank you, Lord, for giving us knowledge and common sense.

He who dwells in the shelter of the Most High
Will abide in the shadow of the Almighty.
(Psalm 91:1)

Date: April 27   Mileage: 3 mi.   Walk Total: 264–266 miles.

Again, up at sunrise. Would be long slow day, so wanted early start. Wife's ankle seemed OK. Put on brace and boot, and she did not have any real discomfort. A slight limp was all, as expected. Quick breakfast of cream-of-wheat and coffee. Dog food for dogs. Camp broken, we loaded up packs, descended slowly to creek, and headed south couple hundred yards to crossing point I'd found. Water was cold but manageable. I tied myself off to tree on bank and in order relayed stuff across, my backpack, wife's backpack, med kits, BOBs, weapons, and then dogs. Then one final trip to help my wife across. I had hooked up second rope on my first return crossing. After she was across, I went back and unhooked second rope and re-crossed creek for last time. We both used walking poles to steady ourselves. I hooked my belt onto her belt when I crossed with her in case she slipped. There were minor slips, but ropes and walking poles kept us upright. We were both pretty cold and numb by time we were done.

We set up on opposite bank. Built a decent fire after I gathered wood to dry both clothing and our bodies. We changed into dry extra clothing including socks. Boots were put by fire, and we decided to let them dry a bit for an hour while we fixed lunch. Took about 45 minutes to complete the crossing, so with hour to eat and dry out, it was close to noon before we set out from far side of creek. Followed small tributary valley between two hills. Elevation went upward very gradually. As we went, we decided to walk until 3 PM if possible. Rate of travel very slow. We would be lucky to cover three miles, which is exactly what we did cover for the day. But it was progress. No sign of any other humans. Lots of critter signs, birds, and squirrels. When we decided best for wife to stop for the day, we were probably a couple miles from US route 62 somewhere south of Stoneboro PA. Took us couple days to cover what we had been covering in one day but we didn't care.

Wife's ankle was throbbing when we finally stopped for the day at a reasonable campsite by a small stream about halfway up a little valley

LARRY D. HORTON, PhD

between two fair-sized hills. We were definitely getting into the first low foothills of the Allegheny mountain range. We had eaten lunch of jerky and juice on the move. Set up camp as usual. Hauled water for boiling. Gathered firewood and built decent fire again. Wood dryer than last week. Still smoked a bit as was hard to find any really good deadfall wood. Since we were back in the sticks, we took risk of a bigger fire. Hauled quite a bit of water for boiling and cooking, as well as for wife to soak ankle. With boot and brace off, massaged her ankle lightly after she soaked it. Was going to be sore, but no new swelling. Plan again tomorrow is to walk as far as she can comfortably and then camp for night.

Supper was rice, jerky, veggies, pudding, and coffee. Dogs got rice and jerky. They were happy. Hung up clothing, boots, and socks to dry some more. Dried eggs for breakfast tomorrow, double portion. Dogs love eggs. Sounds good. Bags unrolled, dogs petted and spoiled, prayers, and scripture, then to bed we went. Tired but grateful we had made progress. The Lord is merciful.

It is good to give thanks to the Lord
And to sing praises to Your name, O Most High.
(Psalm 92:1)

Date: April 28   Mileage: 4 mi.   Walk Total: 268–270 miles.

Up with the sun still shining though some clouds. Seemed to be moving in from the southeast. Signs of rain to come probably. Dogs up and alert. Cooked scrambled eggs for all and coffee on hexamine stove. Water canteens and one jug full. Cleaned up, broke camp, and we were on our way. Plan was to cross US route 62 and camp south of Sandy Lake PA just short of PA route 173.

Took our time. Wife seemed to be doing OK. Her biggest issue was smaller dog wanting to go faster and pulling on leash. With wife's balance issues, we had to be very careful. I took both dogs for some of the time. Approached route 62 about 10 AM. Looked OK, so we started across. As we got to far side heard someone calling; looked north, and saw three men and three women coming toward us. We stopped. Checked on handgun availability and waited till they got to us. Very carefully observed what appeared to be three couples, one older, two younger. Carrying backpacks and visible weapons, we greeted each other cautiously. Stories shared. They had left Hermitage PA five days ago, when gangs from Youngstown OH showed up and caused problems, confrontations, and theft. Were headed south of Pittsburgh into the western mountains of Maryland where they had other family. We shared our story as well. They were surprised we had traveled so far already and were envious that we were getting close to our final goal. They told us they'd had little contact with others traveling by foot up to this point. Were glad to see that they were not totally alone and that we seemed to be safe. They loved the dogs and the dogs ate up all of the attention.

With wishes for good luck both ways, we watched them set off south. For the rest of the day we were constantly looking backward to check if anyone was following us. That did not happen. About an hour later we stopped to fix lunch of jerky and orange drink. Didn't want to chance a fire of any kind. We rested for about 45 minutes after lunch. Checked wife's ankle and set off again. Topography was getting increasingly hilly.

Hills getting higher. Lots of small streams crossed, but didn't get very wet at any time. More clouds moving in by the hour. Would listen to NOAA weather tonight and hopefully get official forecast. If not, we would rely on scoping out types of clouds we saw, wind direction, and temperature changes, if any, to give us an idea of what was going to happen. We walked slowly until 4 PM and looked for campsite. That found, we set up lean-to, small fire pit, and hung up clothing and boots to air dry. No wood fire today after run-in with other people. Wanted to be invisible as much as possible. Had ten-minute walk to stream to haul water for cooking and boiling on hexamine stove. Three trips for that took better part of an hour. Checked and rewrapped wife's ankle. Seemed to be doing OK, but very sore. Supper of mac-and-cheese, veggies, and orange drink. Dogs loved pasta with some dry food mixed in. No radio tonight. Seemed very dark without fire. Didn't even use LED headlamps to stay invisible. Figured we are about a mile west of PA route 173. Prayers, scripture, hugs, and fuss with dogs a bit. To bed and sleep. Pretty tired and stressed after human contact today.

> **Your testimonies are fully confirmed;**
> **Holiness befits Your house,**
> **O Lord, forevermore.**
> **(Psalm 93:5)**

Date: April 29   Mileage: 4 mi.   Walk Total: 272–274 miles.

Up with the sun even though didn't see it much. Too many clouds. Temps warming up. Warm front moving in from south and that likely means more rain. Quick breakfast of scrambled eggs and orange drink. Dogs were ready to go after breakfast. Rewrapped wife's ankle, broke camp, checked water supply, picked up packs and bags. We were on our way. Plan today was to follow Sandy Creek east until we were just east of Raymilton PA. Small farms, some open fields, lot of small streams and creeks, some elevation gain and loss, but for most part walked along ridges, always adjusting direction of travel to compass reading. Sandy Creek actually followed a small valley through the hills, so we stayed close along its banks quite a bit. Very little sign of civilization a lot of the time.

Shortly before lunch we did come upon a beaver dam on the creek. Lots of downed small trees. Pretty good sized impoundment behind dam. These had been busy little beavers. Any other time would have been fun to put a line into pond to see if could catch anything but not today. Also, came upon an abandoned structure further downstream. More than likely an old hunting camp that hasn't been used in decades. Sad to see, but nothing to be found of worth there. Just kept moving. We did fix our lunch near abandoned building. No open fire, just jerky and orange drink. Needed the protein at least. Rested a bit. Attention to dogs and we then moved on. The dogs had lots to smell at the abandoned building. We had to drag them away. Imagine lots of critters used that building as their home. Footing for walking not too bad. Had to move uphill a few times when underbrush by the creek became too thick. Not worth hacking our way through all that. Temps not bad. Guess around sixty with slight breeze. Still sweat a lot, which meant several cooldown breaks. We smelled burning wood several times during the day. More than likely people burning wood to stay warm. Lots of natural gas wells in the area but doubt few if anyone had that connected to their homes. With no power, there would be no electric heat and no pumps to push natural gas into homes. Imagine they were no warmer at night than we were. 3:30 PM we figured we were couple miles west of Raymilton PA, so decided to stop and camp for the night. Moved uphill away from creek in case there was a flash flood during the night. Found flat spot, at least fairly flat, in grove of oaks and maples. Leaves were starting to come out on the trees. We also noticed some wildflowers poking up through the ground. At least some sign that spring had started.

Camp set up, lean-to built with tarp, some firewood collected, multiple trips to bring water from creek to camp for boiling, cooking, and cleaning. Washed body parts and checked feet for sores. Couple spots on my feet got second skin covering. We had been walking in water and partially wet boots for quite a few days. Not surprised that feet were a bit irritated. Supper of pasta and jerky. Dogs got pasta and bit of dry dog food. Hung clothing and boots to dry. Tired this evening. To bed pretty early, prayers, scripture, and some general conversation. Hit the sack, good night!

For the Lord will not abandon His people,
Nor will He forsake His inheritance.
(Psalm 94:14)

Cross Country Diary: Day #100

Date: April 30   Mileage: 4 mi.   Walk Total: 276–278 miles.

Up again with the sun. Two major crossings today, Sandy Creek and PA route 353, one of the main roads through the area in the vicinity of Raymilton PA. Breakfast of oatmeal and orange drink. A bit of jerky for the dogs with their dry dog food. Camp broken, wife's ankle wrapped, and we were on our way. Didn't take us too long to get to route 353. No vehicle or foot traffic in sight, so we crossed pretty quickly. Almost immediately we came to Sandy Creek. Found reasonable place to ford, and repeated the same process we had used to cross creek a few days ago. Relaying everything, ropes for safety, and last across was wife, with me beside her to make sure she didn't slip and hurt ankle again or worse. Took about an hour to complete the crossing. Rested on other side. Put on dry socks. Let boots air dry for about thirty minutes. Made sure feet were OK before we set out again.

Looking at map we decided to follow north side of Sandy Creek just south of Polk PA around big bend in creek until we reached planned campsite for tonight about three miles just southeast of Polk itself. We didn't want to risk crossing Sandy Creek again today so avoided that event. Our campsite was south of the small airport in the area as well. Away from any possible prying eyes. Stopped for cold lunch of jerky and orange drink. Wife doing much better. Ankle still sore and only limping slightly. We found what appeared to be an old gas line or logging road through most of the forested areas north of Sandy Creek, and followed it until it headed off in a direction that led away from our compass heading. Our progress was steady but slow after that. Again, sticking to as much cover as we could find.

Smelled smoke from the south, and heard a few gunshots to our north. Each time we heard shots we got under cover and waited for a bit to make sure that it was not repeated or if so was not getting closer to us. We were lucky again. The known was not too much of a worry for us. It was the unknown that we really had to be careful of. Given situation in country, we could not afford to take any chances. By 4 PM it was time

LARRY D. HORTON, PhD

to look for a good overnight site which took us a bit. We had to cross an open fence-lined field to get to what looked like a good stand of trees.

Temps were even better today probably close to sixty. No new rain yet just lots of heavy gray clouds. We were betting it would start raining tonight. We also noticed that leaves were really coming out on trees. Along last fence lines, on last field crossed, we collected new dandelion leaves again for a bit of salad with tonight's supper. 4:30 PM and we were at our site. Lean-to set up. No fire wood gathered. Not going to take that risk. I hauled water for boiling about 100 yards from small stream. Only going to use hexamine stove for boiling water and cooking. Only light when it got dark was previously used fire-tin. This would be last time to use this particular one but still had three left.

Supper of rice and jerky. Enough for the dogs as well. Pudding for desert. Even a nibble for the dogs. Settled down for a dark night. Just after we hit the sack, light rain started to fall. We would get wet tomorrow but had our gear. Ongoing prayers for safety and wisdom, scripture, and hugged our dogs. They were very quiet. Lots of critter noises but nothing too serious. Dogs barking way off in distance. Good night!

Let us come before His presence with thanksgiving,
Let us shout joyfully to Him with psalms.
(Psalm 95:2)

Cross Country Diary: Day #101

Date: May 1   Mileage: 4 mi.   Walk Total: 280–282 miles

Realized when woke up that today was our 90th day of walking. At end of day today averaging three miles per day of walking. Had a hard time accepting fact that had been on foot for ninety days and at the same time felt like we had been walking forever. Jan. 21st to May 1st was a significant length of time. Yet we had traveled, by truck and on foot, approximately 1,175 miles by truck and 275 on foot. A total of 1450 miles. Hard to believe. Still had between 60 and 80 miles to go, but were not going to throw caution to the wind just because we were getting close to our goal. Talked about that as we ate our breakfast of oatmeal, jerky, and coffee. Dogs got dry food and jerky. Plan today was to try and go a little further. End up somewhere close to Bully Hill PA to our east. Light rain falling, so we will see how far we get. Camp broken down and we were on our way.

Heard some dogs barking in the distance. They didn't get too close. Didn't need that threat. Things turning green pretty quickly. Picked dandelion plants as we walked for supper tonight. Mostly walked in woods and small fields during the AM. Hills getting bigger. Lots of small valleys, which meant quite a few small streams to cross. Rest stops periodically as temps were higher and we were sweating a lot. With higher temperatures, not quite as worried about hypothermia but we needed the rest breaks to make sure wife's ankle was OK. Ground was slippery. Light rain fell all morning. Ponchos kept us pretty dry. Dogs looked like drowned rats, but they didn't seem to mind. They were mostly interested in smelling things.

Lunch was cold jerky and orange drink. Early afternoon came to another major highway obstacle, US route 8 south of Franklin PA. Followed usual process of sitting above road, watching and listening. Nothing detected, so we quickly crossed over to the other side into wooded area that provided cover. On other side of route 8 found a power line access road underneath high tension power lines. Decided to follow it as long as it headed in our general compass direction. Some inherent dangers

LARRY D. HORTON, PhD

with all of the thick brush that grew up on both sides. We were really getting into bear country and they would definitely be out now that weather had broken. But we decided worth risk. Weapons in hand the whole way and we were able to follow the little roadway for about a mile before it went off in a different direction. Turned straight east into the woods again, and made slow progress.

By 3 PM we were pooped and started looking for a good campsite. Finding one with plenty of tree cover we stopped for the night. Given we were so close to Franklin PA, decided to stay dark again tonight. Supper of beans, rice, jerky, and coffee cooked on hexamine stove. Dogs got good portion of dry food and jerky. Once lean-to set up and supper eaten, I went downhill a bit to a small stream and carried several loads of water up to camp for boiling. Listened to NOAA weather. Light rain to continue tomorrow, then following 5 days are to be warmer and partially sunny. The food given us by the last farmer was really helping. Lots of protein. Dandelions cooked tonight hit the spot as well. Prayers said and scripture read. Petting dogs we settled down for the night.

Let the heavens be glad, and let the earth rejoice;
Let the sea roar, and all it contains.
(Psalm 96:11)

Date: May 2   Mileage: 6 mi.   Walk Total: 286–288 miles

Up early as usual. While breakfast of cream-of-wheat and coffee heating up, did planning for the day. Would have to cross Sandy Creek again below where French Creek joined it. Means it will be a bit bigger stream and with rain might present some difficulty crossing. Shortly afterward we would cross US route 322. Breakfast done, dishes done, water supply ready, broke down camp and headed out for the day. Within an hour came to Sandy Creek. Had to go downhill quite a bit until we arrived at its banks. Wife and dogs rested there while I searched up and downstream for a good place to cross. Light rain falling all the time. Glad not heavy rain last couple days. The creek was not much higher than normal by our guess. About 300 yards upstream from where we arrived at creek found reasonable place to cross. Returned for wife, dogs, and packs and headed to crossing. Water running very slowly, but still used roping process to provide safety when crossing. Used relay system again. Made my way across to attach second safety rope with primary rope around me as well. That done, brought second safety rope back across and started to relay everything to other side. Packs first, then dogs, then helped my wife. Last trip for me was to go back and release second safety rope on original side and made my way back across a final time. We sat on bank, changed our socks, dried dogs as much as we could, and decided to eat bit of lunch before setting out again.

Cold lunch again but it hit the spot. Once done loaded up and headed toward route 322. Arrived there about noon. Normal observation process. Saw signs that someone else had camped near the road recently but today saw nothing. We had heard that all bridges were being guarded by locals to prevent unwanted individuals from hitting their towns. They were also patrolling major roads in and out of their communities. But we saw none of that today and hurried across the road and into the woods. Uphill climb after that until we got a bit of distance between us and the road. Then resumed our zigzag walking process on the hills and valleys. Because of all that, we knew we would only travel around four straight miles today but more like six miles of actual walking. Our pace count, time pace, was really out of whack but we had walked enough to know approximately how far we could walk in the topography we were in the middle of. Passed several empty hunting camps during the afternoon. We used their outdoor facilities a couple times, doubting anyone would know. Just nice to get out of the light rain for necessities.

Around 3:30 PM found a good spot to spend the night. Light rain had stopped. All wood was very wet, so we would be using hexamine stove and fire tin tonight. Supper of hot pasta, jerky, dandelions, and coffee. Dogs had pasta and jerky. Water boiling process as usual. Did enough to enable us to take care of personal hygiene. Canteens full. Water jug full. Didn't take long to set up tarp. Had to repair a tear but beyond that went up quickly. Talked about journey as we sat in lean-to. Tired. Prayers, scripture, messed with dogs, and hit the sack. Thank you, Lord!

The heavens declare His righteousness,
And all the peoples have seen His glory.
(Psalm 97:6)

Date: May 3   Mileage: 6 mi.   Walk Total: 292–294 miles

Rain stopped during the night. A bit of sunshine poking through clouds once got above hilltops. Plan for day was the same. One road obstacle to cross, PA route 257, and we would stop just east of Seneca PA about two miles north of Cranberry PA. That town had good memories for me. My uncle had been the Methodist minister there as well as Rockland PA further to the south. That is where I gave my life to the Lord during a revival in his church. Breakfast cooked and eaten, water bottles full, camp broken down, dogs fed, and we headed out.

Lots of hills and more open fields than we had seen for a while. More farms in this area. Mostly hardscrabble farming with dairy cattle, chickens, and pigs. Was pretty quiet. An occasional dog barking which got our dogs excited but not much else. Traveling through countryside, crossing lots of farm roads, secondary roads, small streams, and a bit of up and down. Did our best to walk on our compass heading. Some zigging and zagging of course. Wife's ankle appears to be OK. Ground underfoot still wet from recent rain, so we were careful. Glad again we had our walking poles to steady us. Temps approaching sixty, so light clothing on. Still sweating a lot. Thank goodness, no wind to speak of. Around 11 AM stopped and ate cold lunch per usual the last week or so. Once that was done sat for about thirty minutes. Headed out again. We had learned that sitting for more than thirty minutes led to a lot of stiffness so we were careful not to overdo the rest times. Just took more of them. Usually fifteen minutes out of every hour.

Afternoon passed quietly. Lots of critter sign, lots of critter scat, rabbits, deer, and something bigger, which we didn't want to think much on but were really on alert the entire time. Woods very heavy between open fields. Walked fence lines in fields. At each fence crossing had to relay everything over the fence which took a bit of time. Have done it enough times to have a good routine to get it done. Midafternoon came to PA route 257. Usually a busy rural road in this area, but very quiet today. Crossed quickly. On east side of road saw quite a few hunting camps back in the woods. Avoided them which cost us a bit of time. One had vehicle sitting in front of it. Smoke coming out of chimney. So we gave it a wide berth. Could smell smoke in the air likely from Seneca. With electric-power down and natural gas not being pumped, as far as we knew, a lot of people likely burning wood for cooking and heat. Camp tonight would be in the dark again. Just too close to civilization.

4 PM soon arrived, and we were at our next camp. It was on brow of hill where we could look out through trees at the terrain that faced us tomorrow. Lots of hills and valleys for as far as we could see. We were now south of Oil City PA so there were people all around us. Lean-to set up in grove of pine trees. Nice bed of pine branches to sleep on. As usual, after supper cooked, we hung packs on branch of tree about eight feet off the ground 30 to 40 feet from lean-to. Walked 100 yards to small stream and hauled several loads of water for boiling. That done, we settled down for the night. Dogs seemed anxious. We wondered if there were critters in the area. Prayers and scripture. Good night!

The Lord has made known His salvation;
He has revealed His righteousness in the sight of the nations.
(Psalm 98:2)

Date: May 4   Mileage: 5 mi.   Walk Total: 297–299 miles

Up early. Plan for the day was to back off on distance a bit. We would be traveling through lots of woods, hills, and valleys today. Likely a few farms but we were gradually getting closer to the Allegheny National Forest to our northeast. Land was getting wilder by the day. Breakfast of oatmeal and jerky for all, water bottles filled, packs repacked, dishes cleaned, camp broken, we set out for the day. Plan for the day was to head east in the general direction of Coal Hill PA. Hopefully get halfway there today. Lots of old logging roads in the forested areas we walked through. At times this made walking easier, at times harder. It all depended on how well the loggers cleaned up their mess when they were felling trees.

Lots of piles of downed treetops. Good cover for critters. Good firewood source and as always containing some danger. We saw our first rattlesnake today sunning itself on a log by the roadside. We stayed far away from it. The dogs of course wanted to take after it, and their barking spooked the snake and it vanished into the brush. No stepping over logs today. Walked around anything that was in our path. We did not need to have to deal with snakebite for any of us. More deer sign. We actually saw a buck, two does, and a couple fawns in the distance. They spooked of course when the dogs started barking. Logging roads took us in pretty good direction most of the time. They tended to follow ridge lines, which meant our elevation up and down was kept to a minimum as much as possible.

Stopped for lunch around 11:30 AM in a small clearing on a hilltop where it seemed loggers had piled logs prior to loading on trucks. There were still some logs stacked there. Had been left behind. Cooked hot lunch today. Soup and jerky. We all enjoyed some. Temps likely in low sixties during the afternoon. With sunshine seemed so warm compared to the cold, snowy weather we had experienced over the past few months. We were grateful for it. We actually saw a couple of jet contrails above us as we ate lunch. Had to be military. Have not seen or heard any commercial air traffic for weeks.

Afternoon passed pretty quietly. Occasional dog barking in distance. Passed several deserted hunting cabins. More deer sign. Lots of squirrels in trees. Planned on trying to get squirrel after we had set up camp. By 3 PM found good spot to camp again in small natural clearing on hillside with good squirrel sign in the trees. Water source a good 200 yards down the side of hill, but that would work. Lean-to set up and fire ring built. Would have wood fire tonight. Firewood gathered and water boiled. I left camp and went downhill a bit to watch for possible squirrel shot. As got closer to dusk they would be out feeding, so good time to have the air rifle in hand. Was getting pretty dusky, around 5 PM, and saw squirrel working way toward me. At thirty feet took shot above me and we would have fresh meat for supper. Field-dressed, gutted, heart in hand for dogs, then back to camp. Excited dogs of course. Seared squirrel over fire. Added to soup, veggies and coffee. We had a feast.

Tired from day. Temp tonight around fifty. Rested, talked, sang, prayers, and scripture reading. It was to bed. Dogs were happy. A good day. Hard not to get excited as we knew we were getting closer to goal. Good night!

Exalt the Lord our God and worship at His holy hill,
For holy is the Lord our God.
(Psalm 99:9)

Date: May 5   Mileage: 5 mi.   Walk Total: 302–304 miles

Planned for day after getting up early. Camp tonight a bit southeast of Coal Hill PA along PA route 157. Wild country ahead of us. Breakfast, water filled, repacked, dogs fed, camp broken, and we were on our way. No logging roads, so struck out cross country through the woods. Periodic open fields but no real farms in the area we were walking through. Again, lots of critter sign. Saw several deer. Some dogs barking in the distance. Sunny morning warmed up quickly, probably near 60. Nice to not have layers of clothing on. Sweating a lot. Imagine we smell a lot. As always, will do personal hygiene and washing tonight. By late morning approached PA route 338. Pretty isolated area, so crossing of road done with no incidents. Walked about one-half mile east of route 338 and broke for cold lunch of jerky and orange drink. Thirty-minute break and we were on our way again. Came upon more logging roads and followed them as before. Zigging and zagging a bit but staying on overall easterly compass direction. Warmed up a lot in the afternoon probably well into the sixties.

By 3:30 PM started to look for site to camp tonight. Ended up in wooded area that had been logged. Lots of firewood to be had. Lean-to built in grove of pine trees. Rest of camp setup procedure same as usual. Short walk to water source down a slight hill into a little valley. Hauled multiple loads and boiled for cooking and containers. Took dogs down to stream so they could drink cold water. On our way back saw couple more snakes. Also, dogs spooked a couple grouse from a pile of brush. No weapons with me. Impossible shots anyway. Back at camp settled in for restful evening. Supper of pasta, veggies, and coffee. Dogs had dry food and jerky. Did inventory of our food stores; if we ration things carefully have about 10 more days left. Would be better if I could get us some fresh meat. Time will tell.

Evening passed quietly. Sun setting around 7 PM now, so had lots of good light to see. Hung all damp stuff up to dry. Food and packs hung in nearby trees out of reach of critters. Had fun laughing at some chipmunks while the dogs barked at them. Pretty mundane day and glad for that. Tired but feeling pretty good. Will listen to radio tomorrow to get update on events. Need to get updated weather forecast as well. Prayers said, scripture read, and attention to dogs before we climbed into bags to sleep. Calmest day of the trip so far, even though hard walk at times.

> Shout joyfully to the Lord, all the earth.
> Serve the Lord with gladness;
> Come before Him with joyful singing.
> Know that the Lord Himself is God;
> It is He who has made us, and not we ourselves;
> We are His people and the sheep of His pasture.
> Enter His gates with thanksgiving
> And His courts with praise.
> Give thanks to Him, bless His name.
> For the Lord is good;
> His lovingkindness is everlasting
> and faithfulness to all generations.
> (Psalm 100:1–5)

Date: May 6   Mileage: 6 mi.   Walk Total: 308–310 miles

Chattering of squirrels in trees in dim early morning light woke us up. Before we prepared breakfast and broke camp, planned the day: Shadow PA route 157 for several miles before crossing it. Once across, head east and camp just northeast of Venus PA. Breakfast of oatmeal, jerky, and coffee. Dogs had dry food and jerky. Dogs have another three or four days of dry food left. Cleaned up, made sure water containers full, repacked, and broke camp. Again, area ahead of us was heavily wooded.

Closing in on Allegheny National Forest. Couple hours into the morning we saw a black bear on ridge across valley from us as it crossed an open field. Dogs did not see it, but they smelled something. Got very agitated but no barking. We watched the bear move until it was out of sight to our southwest. With one in the area, might see others, so on double alert from now on. Passed multiple hunting cabins, several with vehicles in front with flickering light inside buildings. Smoke again rising from them as well. We tried to stay out of sight and detoured around them. For sure, there would be weapons in each of them. People had moved into the woods to get away from the mess in areas of population. Likely hunkering down for a long time. We did not want to be seen as a threat to them and have to face unwanted confrontations. This added some distance to our walk today and quite a bit of time, but it was worth it.

Lunch in the middle of a large brush thicket. Followed critter trails around it to the backside where we felt a bit safer. No fire; only cold lunch of jerky and juice. Moved on pretty quickly. Afternoon full of critter sign. Several camps again. None occupied, as best we could see, and some heavy elevation gain and loss. We were getting pretty tired after we had traveled a bit over five miles for the day. Started looking for campsite. Took us another 45 minutes and probably three-quarter mile of walking before we found a good secluded spot down in a little valley. Found a spring above us for fresh water. We would be going dark tonight again. With sun setting later, we did not heat up our supper; again, only cold jerky and juice. Dogs got dry dog food. No fire-tin light tonight either. We figured going without flame, even the smallest one, was better than being discovered and risking situation we did not want to face. Did crank up power on radio to get quick NOAA weather update. Weak signal out here in the sticks. Got enough info to know that we have two more days of decent warm weather before a heavy-front hits, bringing couple days of very heavy rainfall. Not good news, as we have some major creeks and the Clarion River to cross soon. Not much we can do. If it rains significantly, we will likely hunker down for a few days to let water flow downstream and then cross those obstacles.

We took care of our personal hygiene tonight as we did at least every other night. Checked out dogs for ticks as we were in heavily populated deer area. Found nothing. Did a quick body check on all four of us for nicks, cuts, anything that might bring on a dangerous infection. Found nothing. Second skin put on couple spots on our feet that were irritated. Red sunset tonight through the trees. Prayers, scripture, and we were to bed. Tiring, somewhat stressful day. On to tomorrow.

I will sing of lovingkindness and justice,
To You, O Lord, I will sing praises.
(Psalm 101:1)

Date: May 7   Mileage: 5 mi.   Walk Total: 313–315 miles

Lots of sunshine over the hills when we woke up this morning. Going to be a beautiful day. Much warmer. Things gradually drying out from recent rain. We all seemed to sleep well. Lots of birds singing this morning. Truly a sign of spring. Leaves on trees, especially some, filling out. Beautiful green fresh smell in the air. Wonderful time of the year.

As I sit and write tonight at our campsite, might include a few reflections on things in general as we approach the last few days of our journey. Physically we have held up pretty well. Lost quite a bit of weight but in much better shape as to strength and stamina. No serious physical injuries during entire trip other than wife's recent ankle sprain. Dogs have lost some weight as well but they are good to go. The woods are their element. Lots of nicks and small cuts which we have treated immediately. So, no infections. Bruises of course, with all the physical work we have had to do. Sore muscles and shoulders from pulling Trekker earlier and from carrying backpacks and bags. Nothing that wasn't expected.

Equipment has held up really well. Of course, minor repairs all the time to tarps, packs, boots, clothing. Food has held out much better than we could have imagined. Fresh meat has been lacking some of the time, but always seems we got some when it was necessary. Water has not been too much of a problem. Given countryside we have been traveling through there have been sources available on a daily basis. Great care taken to purify it, 95 percent of the time by boiling. Only used other means like purification tablets when had no other choice. We have been able to avoid almost all potential confrontations with other human beings by avoiding contact, staying dark when necessary, and staying off the beaten path especially after last month's national events.

Shelter has not been too much of a problem. Have gotten wet a few times and cold, of course. Our journey has taken place during the worst weather time of the year and was a constant worry for us. Shelter has been adequate, but we would sure like to be in a real building sooner rather than later. Constantly inventorying our supplies. If things continue to go as they are, we should have enough freeze-dried and dry food to get us to final destination. Adding fresh meat to that will make it much easier. Looks like it will be primarily through fishing from this point forward. Given our food supply, we haven't had to rely on scrounging for other food from the land. For that we are grateful.

We have had no communication with family through technology for weeks. That will not change. Our radio is virtually useless to us due to topography we are traveling through and the complete breakdown of normal audio capabilities across the country. As I have said earlier we have taken a complete step back 200 years in time. We will rely on reading nature's signs for our weather until we complete the journey. Emotionally we have had our ups and downs. Rainy weather being the most depressing times. Cold and snow was fine since we were able to stay reasonably warm. Faithfulness of the Lord to watch over us has brought us through many things. The driving force, reaching friends, has given us daily motivation to work through anything that came our way. Our love for each other has been the glue of our little family. The dogs have provided joy, comfort, love, and frustration. At the same time the dogs have meant slower travel, more potential danger, and security threats, but they were worth the risks.

In camp tonight planned out the rest of our walking path. The weather will determine whether or not we can finish as planned. We will adapt and adjust as necessary. We are not going to rush at all in these last few days. Haste towards the end of the journey might spell disaster, and we have worked too hard to get this close to our goal to have something happen.

Now to events of the day. Wish every day could have been as uneventful as today was. Breakfast and broke camp and were on our way by 8 AM. Traveling in mostly wooded areas with a few small fenced fields. Only had one major man-made obstacle in our way today, PA route 157. Crossed it without incident early in our walk and got back into wooded cover quickly. Lots of critter sign and noises, including dogs barking in distance. Saw several deer shortly after we started. Dogs spooked them quickly with their barking. Multiple short rest stops during the morning. Wife's ankle giving her no problem at all. Things have dried out enough that underfoot was dry. Didn't hurry but we moved along at a good pace. Cold lunch of jerky and water. Dogs had a couple bites as well.

By 2 PM we had covered our planned distance, and by our estimation and compass checking, we were just north of Venus PA. Decided to stop and not push on. Needed to do an inventory of our supplies and check and repair equipment if needed. We also wanted to pull out any damp clothing and dry it in the sun. Late in the day we noticed some clouds starting to move in from the south and figure we might have one more reasonably dry day tomorrow followed in all likelihood by rain. We need to prepare for it. Camp setup pretty simple. Lean-to in place and small fire pit. We were going to have a small real wood fire tonight. Gathered enough wood to cook evening meal as well as breakfast in the AM. Had to tote water a couple hundred yards from stream to our north, so that took some time. Boiled water supply before we set about fixing supper.

Good meal, beans, rice, jerky, and coffee. Dogs got a good helping along with some of their dry dog food. Everyone had full tummies. After eating we sat by our small fire and watched the sun set in the west. No red sunset tonight. Remembered old saying, red at night, sailors' delight. We had no red sunset, so had a good idea weather was going to change. When moon was visible, we saw a ring around it, which was another sign of moisture in the air and probable rain. Spent a lot of time in prayer and scripture reading tonight. We realized how much we are missing talking to other people as well. That will happen soon enough at our goal. Dogs seemed especially contented tonight and settled down pretty easily. Another day tomorrow. One more day closer to our final destination. Thank you, Lord!

But You are the same,
And Your years will not come to an end.
The children of Your servants will continue,
And their descendants will be established before You.
(Psalm 102:27–28)

LARRY D. HORTON, PhD

Date: May 8   Mileage: 5 mi.   Walk Total: 318–320 miles

Woke up to gray skies and pretty warm temperatures. Wind coming from the south. Darker clouds lower in sky in the distance. Decided we needed to get moving pretty early to avoid as much of the coming rain as possible. Cold breakfast of jerky and orange drink. Dogs had dry dog food and a few pieces of jerky as well. Water supply checked, and jug full. Broke down lean-to and packed it. Repacked everything we had hung out to dry. Picked up packs and we were on our way by 7:30AM.

Plan was to go completely cross country mostly through woods today. No major man-made obstacles in our way. Of course, secondary roads, fences around fields we had to cross, multiple likely streams, but those had all become normal. As we progressed, we discovered an increasing number of hunting cabins. Like I have said before, this is prime deer and to some degree bear country. Several of the cabins were occupied as before, so we detoured around them. Quite a number of large hills around us, so lots of zigging and zagging to keep walking on as level a plane as we could. Several breaks during the morning. Lunch again was cold jerky and juice. We planned on stopping by 2 PM at the latest to enable us to build a substantial shelter for the rain we assumed was coming.

At 2:15 PM we found a decent site in a grove of hardwoods with a few pines thrown in. First things first, we built reinforced lean-to. Cut pine branches for the external walls for protection from any windblown rain. Checked for any potential deadfalls as well. Lean-to finished, gathered enough wood for cooking and boiling water for several days and placed in tarp lean-to. Pine branches for mattress with secondary tarp as waterproofing on top of branches followed by sleeping bags. Fire pit with reflector wall built and space blanket roof over it. Started small fire. Next task completed was to collect and haul water for boiling and cooking. Some distance to closest stream but got enough. No good place to fish nearby. All of this done by 4:45 PM.

At 5:00 PM sharp, drizzle started, and wind picked up a lot. Warm breeze, but it started to make treetops really move. We cooked supper quickly. Pasta, veggies, pudding, and tuna for the dogs. They got a bit of pasta as well. Rain increasing in intensity the entire time we ate supper. Could see reflection of lighting and hear distant thunder as the minutes passed. We battened down the hatches as best we could for what might be a very wet and noisy night. We had set up campsite partway down a hillside. Didn't want to be anywhere near the summit if lightning was in the area during the night. Read scripture, said prayers, and huddled together under our shelter. Glad had dug trench around shelter and that we had set up sleeping area with our heads higher than our feet. Dogs could sense things were changing. Smaller dog was scared, her normal response to any thunder and loud noises. Rain increasing. Knew we would likely not get much rest tonight. Lord, please watch over us.

As far as the east is from the west,
So far has He removed our transgressions from us.
(Psalm 103:12)

Date: May 9   Mileage: 0 mi.   Walk Total: 318–320 miles

Virtually no sleep last night. Lightning, thunder, and heavy rain all night. Had to get up multiple times to add additional tiedown to lean-to tarp. Several of the pegs we had used to anchor it into ground with rope pulled out in heavy winds. Had to pound several back into the ground more than once. Dogs were scared. We got a good soaking during the night. All of our sleeping equipment was soaked. Winds were howling through the trees above and around us. By the time the sun had come up, we decided that we weren't going to move at all today. Too many dangers out there. Slipping, falling branches, lightning, and just overall miserableness from the falling rain. We didn't need any of that. Impossible to start a wood fire in all of the wind and rain. Didn't want to waste fire-starting materials and just get frustrated. One good thing: it was warm rain and wind. General storm direction was away from open end of our shelter. Glad had put ponchos over our packs hung in trees, but wind blowing them around a lot, and knew they would still get pretty wet. Will likely require some time to dry things. One very wise thing we had done in our preparations was to put everything in plastic bags in our packs. We just hoped none had sprung any leaks.

Breakfast of jerky and water. Dogs got dog food. After that we just hunkered down, sheltered in place, and prepared for ongoing storm. Dogs just stuck to us like glue. Lunch of jerky and cold water again. Storm let up periodically during the day but then came back in full force. We heard branches falling out of trees and crashing to the ground. There were no critter noises all day. They were smart and had hunkered down as well. Just dark gray day interrupted by bolts of lightning. By late afternoon water everywhere. Ground was completely wet. Lots of water running downhill to any nearby stream. Pulled out hexamine stove and heated up some soup and rice for supper. We needed a warm meal at least once today. Dark gray sky. Could not tell when sun sank below hilltops to our west.

Intensity of storm seemed to lessen some as evening arrived, but rain still falling steadily. Remembered this kind of storm from when I was a kid growing up in the area. Given cloud sign while still light enough to see, it looked like rain would continue far into the night. As we said our prayers and read scripture, another bolt of lightning and thunder passed. The Lord was really fired up tonight. All the dogs wanted to do was get as close to us as possible. We pulled out remaining main poncho and the two-flimsy backup ponchos and tried to cover up as best we could. Tough climbing into our bags when they were very damp. No dry clothing for us to sleep in. Didn't want to just get another dry set of clothes all wet. Just more to dry. Temp likely into mid-fifties tonight so we will survive being damp. Expecting a hard time getting to sleep tonight. We hoped for a few hours' sleep after prayers and scripture.

He established the earth upon its foundations,
So that it will not totter forever and ever.
(Psalm 104:5)

Date: May 10   Mileage: 0 mi.   Walk Total: 318–320 miles

Too much noise and dampness for sleep, and the dogs very restless. Very dark except for occasional lightning. Felt like the whole world closing in on us. Sometime during night rain slowed. Not raining as hard when light appeared in sky. Clouds not quite as dark. Winds down a lot. Everything was wet. Although we got more sleep than night before, still pretty tired as we set about getting our breakfast ready. Used hexamine stove again to prepare some hot soup. We needed hot food to help us warm up. Dogs got their share as well with some dog food mixed in.

By time we had finished eating, clouds were getting lighter, and rain had slowed to a drizzle. Figured worst had passed. But even with that we decided to spend another day tomorrow not moving. Ground will be saturated. Streams and creeks will likely be at the tops of their banks for a couple days before they start to go down. As the rain decreased and the clouds got lighter during the late morning, did our best to hang up wet stuff under the lean-to to start the drying process. Slight breeze blowing helped some, but it will take another twenty-four hours, with some sun and wind, to get things dried out a bit. When things are wet, even damp, the added weight to our packs is a royal pain.

Collected water from containers we had set out around camp to collect rain water and boiled it. Also, hiked to near-by stream and hauled multiple loads of water to boil. Lunch was again hot soup with jerky to keep warming process going. Dogs got full portion as well. Was able to start a decent fire using wood we had kept somewhat dry under the lean-to during the rain. Fire did wonders for our emotions. It also was warmth. Dogs curled up on some pine branches as close to the fire as possible and napped under the front roof covering of the lean-to. Rain pretty much stopped by 2 PM, and we caught glimpses of the sun low in the clouds to the south of us. A good sign for tomorrow, we hoped. Once we had done all the chores we could or needed to do, we all just lay in the lean-to trying to rest. We were all bushed from two nights of little sleep.

Around 5:30 PM prepared and cooked supper over open fire. Hot soup with chunks of freeze-dried chicken, hot veggies, pudding, and coffee. Dogs got some along with some jerky. Supper cleaned up, we talked about setting out tomorrow and decided against that. We seem to be reasonably safe where we are. The weather shows signs of improving tomorrow. We have a lot of things to dry out and preparations to make before setting out, so we decided that it will be best to spend a day resting, preparing, and waiting for the impact of the storm to stabilize in streams, roads, and the path we have to walk. With that decision made we felt better. Yes, we are anxious to keep moving, but we also know we have to stay smart. From the very beginning of this entire process, a full year before we actually bugged out, we have made preparation our number-one priority. We are not going to move until we feel reasonably prepared. That means another day hunkered down where we are. With that agreed to, read scripture, said prayers, hugged dogs, and settled down into another night hopefully dryer than the previous two.

Oh give thanks to the Lord,
Call upon His name;
Make known His deeds among the peoples.
(Psalm 105:1)

Date: May 11   Mileage: 0 mi.   Walk Total: 318–320 miles

Woke up to broken clouds with sunshine drifting down through the trees around us. Temp warm, likely in high fifties. It was a good decision to stay put another day. Quick breakfast of oatmeal and jerky all around. Then got busy at the many tasks for the day. First was to hang sleeping bags, wet clothing, and boots in as much sunlight as possible to dry. Gentle breeze blowing would help with that. Then gathered multiple buckets of water, built small fire, and boiled as much as we could to fill up canteens, our jug, and cooking pots for use in fixing supper tonight. Went out with air rifle looking for squirrels or anything else that might help with our meals. After an hour came back to camp with two squirrels field-dressed and gutted. We had an early lunch to keep meat as fresh as possible. Cooked well and added to portion of rice for all of us. Each of the dogs got a complete heart. We ate until we couldn't eat anymore. Cleaned up cooking tools.

Cleaned weapons, checked ammo, did another inventory of food, and repacked backpacks with everything other than what we will wear tomorrow. Hung up packs, ponchos, and secondary tarp to dry as much as possible. Killed fire after eating. Didn't want any more smoke than necessary. Sharpened all knives and cutting tools. Checked med kits, BOBs, utility belts, and ropes. Made sure everything was in good shape for our final push to goal. Once all that prep work done, began to plan out our final days of walking. Used compass, maps, and my knowledge of the area to identify what we hoped would be the safest path forward. Planned in as much detail as possible other than not knowing absolutely what kind of topography or obstacles we would run into. In a nutshell, will try to move five or six miles a day by step count. Probably only four to five miles as the crow flies. But we will progress steadily if weather cooperates and we can avoid any confrontations.

Our goal details beginning tomorrow: Day #1, south of Tylersburg PA; Day #2, north of Leeper PA; Day #3, northern part of Cook Forest state park; Day #4, two-thirds of way south through state park; Day #5, cross

Clarion River east of Cooksburg PA; Day #6, northwest of Sigel PA; Day #7, east-northeast of Sigel, PA; Day #8, approach PA route 949; Day #9, cross 949 to northeast ; Day #10, northeast toward Portland Mills PA; Day #11, friends' farm near Portland Mills PA; Day #12 cross Clarion River to north; Day #13, north toward Sackett PA; and Day #14, reach our final goal on the east bank of Bear Creek. Probably a total of approximately seventy more miles of zigzag, up and down walking, and we will be at our new home. That is possible if everything goes just right. We know odds are against us that it will work perfectly, but we are excited to see how much is left.

Supper was fixed. A bit of leftover squirrel for dogs. Wife and I had special pasta dish we had been saving, lasagna, and orange drink. Dogs seemed to sense the positive mood we were in. Tried to listen to radio. Absolutely nothing but static. Lit fire-tin when it got dark. To bed early, but excitement of our plan made us wakeful. Prayers said, read scripture, hugged the dogs, and hit the sack looking at stars through the treetops. God is good!

**Blessed be the Lord, the God of Israel, From
everlasting even to everlasting.
And let all the people say, Amen. Praise the Lord.
(Psalm 106:48)**

Date: May 12   Mileage: 5 mi.   Walk Total: 323–325 miles

Up before the rooster crowed. Too excited to sleep. Anxious to get on our way. Cold breakfast of jerky and orange drink. Dogs had the last of the dry dog food the farmer gave us, with a bit of jerky as well. Packed remaining stuff, primarily sleeping stuff, broke camp, checked water supply one final time, hefted packs onto shoulders, and we were on our way. Could tell it was going to warm up today, more than likely into the low to mid-sixties. Dogs were champing at the bit to get going.

Hills getting bigger, farm fields fewer, and larger stands of trees as we progressed. Heard more dogs, so knew we would have to be careful. Saw large group of deer staring at us from edge of woods as we started out. Quite a sight in the thin fog that covered the land. As we draw closer to Clarion River, with sun shining and temps going up each day, the fog will get thicker until we have crossed to the other side. In some ways, that is good, providing more cover. In some ways, not so good because it will provide cover for critters and other humans we don't want to run into.

Made steady progress. Footing pretty slippery from all the recent rain. Saw quite a few trees that blew over during the heavy winds of recent storm. Lots of downed branches as well. Glad we did a really good job of scouting out deadfalls when we set up our last camp. In these hills the weather can change in a minute, so constantly on guard for signs of weather changes. Lunch was quick, jerky and some water. Knew it would take us to late afternoon to reach our day's objective south of Tylersburg PA because we were being so careful with footfalls, line of walking, and quite a few breaks in this now warm weather.

Around 2 PM we had to cross PA route 208, a heavily used local road in what were normal times. We actually had to stop for about 45 minutes as we saw two groups of people on foot heading south separated by about ten minutes from each other. Dogs let out a couple barks, but people were intent on their walking and paid no attention. After the second group passed, we waited at least fifteen minutes until they were out of earshot and we felt confident that no one else was coming before we crossed route 208. We had only gone about 100 yards after crossing when we heard a third group heading south on the road. We again hunkered down and waited until we could not hear them anymore.

By 3:30 PM we started looking for campsite. We will be going dark until after we cross the Clarion River and are six to eight miles beyond it because of all the small towns and hunting camps in the area we'll be passing through. Set up camp on the side of a small hill partially cleared and with some cows in a field to the west. Pine grove, so had really good cover and a larger stand within a short distance if we had to disappear quickly. Camp set up. Supper on hexamine stove. Hung everything up to continue drying process. We were tired after much up and down today. Sat in lean-to, listened to critter sounds of spring, and watched stars and moon through trees. To bed early after prayers, scripture reading, and hugs. A good day. Hoping for same tomorrow.

He changes the wilderness into a pool of water
And a dry land into springs of water;
And there He makes the hungry to dwell,
So that they may establish an inhabited city.
(Psalm 107:35–36)

Cross Country Diary: Day #113

Date: May 13   Mileage: 5 mi.   Walk Total: 328–330 miles

Up pretty early this morning. Birds in trees woke us up. Quick breakfast, repacked, broke down camp, checked water supply, and we were quickly on our way. Headed southeast today toward Leeper PA. Had one major road to cross, US route 66. Plan was to camp for the night north of Leeper, somewhere close to the boundary of Cook Forest State Park. Really hilly. Lots of cleared fields as we neared Leeper, but woods would be thick and dark soon. Morning was pretty uneventful. Did see quite a few cows in fields as we neared population. Not much else. Couple dogs barking.

Leeper PA had good memories. My uncle, the minister, lived there when he had one of his multi-church charges. Had visited a few times, so knew area a bit. Also, lots of memories from the days of raising support for us prior to going to Taiwan to teach Old Testament in the Central Taiwan Theological College. Had spoken in many of the small churches in this area. Not quite as much up and down during the morning. The Leeper area contained a lot of small farms so a lot less woods as well. Still progress was slow. Temps in the mid-sixties probably. Sweating, rested periodically, and just took our time moving. Dogs had to bark at everything they saw and every scent. Lots of rabbit runs and droppings so they had to inspect each and every one of them.

Stopped for lunch around 11:30 AM. Cold lunch of jerky and orange drink. Rested a bit and on way again. Decided to head a bit north of Leeper, which meant we had to cross US route 36 before we got to route 66. Route 36 is the main east-to-west road in the area. Found wooded areas on both sides of road to provide cover. Waited and listened and finally were able to cross the road. Did not see anything traveling either direction. About an hour later came to route 66 and went through the same process. Heard some noise in the distance, but it turned out to be nothing. Crossed quickly and headed southeast.

Found reasonable campsite south of Crown PA in what appeared to be the beginnings of Cook Forest State Park. All kinds of very large trees. Located site at the top of a small gully that headed down to what we assumed would eventually be the Clarion River. Lots of open areas among the trees so we were able to find comfortable spot. Set up lean-to, built small fire ring, collected wood, and hung everything that needed to be hung in trees. Walked down gully a bit and found a spring coming out of hillside. Hauled plenty of water and wife started the boiling process. Took air rifle back to stand of oaks and maples behind us and sat down to see if any squirrels showed up. After 45 minutes headed back to camp with one in the bag, field-dressed and gutted. As soon as back at camp cooked up the squirrel. Heated up some soup and added squirrel. Of course, dogs each got half of the cooked heart. Everything tasted really good. Put out fire after dishes cleaned and water boiled for our containers. Then we sat and rested. Going to be warmer tonight. We are safe, warm, and dry, which is all good. Prayer said, scripture read, and hugs around. Tomorrow basically will be downhill walk until we reach the river. Lord, protect us.

Through God we will do valiantly,
And it is He who shall tread down our adversaries.
(Psalm 108:13)

Cross Country Diary: Day #114

Date: May 14   Mileage: 4 mi.   Walk Total: 332–334 miles

Nice warm night last night. We saw a lot of eyes out in the trees staring at us. Couple times had to shine flashlight in their direction to make sure they stayed away. Fired couple of pellets from air rifle as well. Must have been effective because we heard a yelp from one hit and weren't bothered any more during the night. The smells in the woods were wonderful when we were so close to such a large forest. Breakfast, oatmeal, and coffee fixed on hexamine stove. Double portion so dogs got their share as well. Packed, loaded, camp broken, water checked, we headed out.

After about an hour we entered a much larger darker forest, the state park. Surprising how dark it was under the large trees even with the sun shining above us. Cover under the trees was far less than in other wooded areas, so able to walk without too much trouble. Lots of old timber lying on ground. Moss on everything, squirrels in the trees, deer sign, and footing was pretty good as things had dried out quite a bit. Forests like this are really quiet as well except for birds. No sign of any other humans having walked the path that we were following. Likely only hunters had been in this area before us. We were constantly on the lookout for signs of people possibly hunting. The last thing we needed was to be a mistaken target. Dogs enjoyed the easier walk and of course were smelling everything they came to. Lots of chipmunks to try to chase even though dogs were on short leashes. Around 11:45 AM stopped for a cold lunch of jerky and water. Only enough jerky to last us through tomorrow. We have been rationing it very carefully. Once rested a bit, we set out.

Walked another mile or so and our day and plan changed dramatically. We heard a loud scream down hillside below us, followed by more screams and shouts. Wife and dogs stayed put. I dropped my pack and as quietly as possible headed downhill to see what was going on. Doing that went against our tactic of avoiding contact, but this sounded serious. A half-mile down the hill I spotted two people: a man and what appeared to be a young teenage boy lying on the ground rolling around in pain. I slowly approached them, called out, and they responded guardedly. They had no visible weapons, so I continued to move closer to them. The man, whose hunting rifle was leaning up against a nearby tree, stood beside the young teenager looking scared and very worried. Got to them, shook hands and quickly was told what had happened.

The two, with woman and young girl, a small family, were trying to get to northern West Virginia and had become stranded at Cook Forest campground. More on that later. First things first, the man, the father, was really shaken up. What had started out as a quick trip into the trees to try to get some fresh meat had taken a bad turn. The young boy, in far too much of a hurry after seeing a squirrel, had stepped into a critter hole and hurt his leg. He was in a great deal of pain. I asked if I could help. Needed to look at the leg to see if I could figure out how bad injury was. That agreed to, I carefully felt his lower leg. I then cut jeans up to his knee. There was no bone sticking out through his skin but about half way down his shin I could sense that the bone was not right. Just to touch put him into agony and screams. My best guess was that he had broken his lower leg. I immediately set about to immobilize it. His dad found two small straight logs, two inches in diameter. Using the boy's belt with his dad's and my own, we fashioned a splint as best we could.

I then told the two of them to sit tight while I went to get my wife, better materials to make a splint, and some strong pain meds from our kit. I told the father to keep his son awake so he wouldn't go into shock. It took about 40 minutes for me go and return with wife, dogs, and packs. Had the boy take the pain meds and then fashioned a much better splint. Removing the temporary one we tore up a couple shirts and padded his leg where the new splint would rest on his leg. Then we cut lengths of rope and tied the same small logs round his leg to form a stable splint. That done I asked his father to find two longer poles about the same diameter. We took our secondary tarp, doubled and tripled over, and built a litter. His father and I would then have to carry him the mile or so downhill to the campground. Putting him on the litter was painful, but he took it as well as possible. With that done, I hung my pack up in a tree. We picked up the litter, and our little group, wife, dogs, and father and I carrying the litter, started downhill to the campground.

Forty-five minutes later we arrived and met the wife and younger daughter. We made the boy as comfortable as possible, laying litter on a picnic table. I then asked father to go to campground office and see if they could contact a park ranger while I trekked back uphill for my pack. Took about an hour for me to return. I found the family huddled around the boy with a woman, who I found out was a nurse, and a park ranger working with them. The nurse said the boy's leg was likely broken as I had concluded and that we had done everything right. The boy was still awake. The pain pills seemed to have helped. The ranger said they had no vehicles to transport the boy the 30 miles to the nearest medical facility, but they were trying to contact state police to see if they could help.

As we sat waiting for a possible response from the state police, we talked about how the family had ended up in their current location. They left the Youngstown OH area, fourteen days ago, heading for their family farm in northern West Virginia, traveling secondary roads to avoid confronting the many dangers that existed. Arriving at Cook Forest, they had planned on camping overnight and then heading further south. The EMP hit them while they were camped, making their vehicle useless. They were now stranded, running out of food, and scared. The father and son had set out this morning into the woods to try to get some kind of fresh meat for their meals when the accident happened. The rest of their story we were now part of. We told them our story, and they were astounded that we had traveled so far especially on foot. The father just stood there shaking his head when we told them how we had prepared for months, had traveled first by vehicle, then over 300 miles on foot.

After an hour or so the ranger got a call on his radio saying state police were sending a fire emergency vehicle from Sigel PA. It was at least thirty years old, and had not been disabled by the EMP. They would pick up the boy and take him to the Clarion hospital. Two hours later it arrived. The boy was loaded, and the entire family piled into it with him. There were tears of thanks and hugs from all. We told them we would leave them a bit of food to help them get through. With that they were off, and we stood there with the nurse, also trying to get to another location, and the park ranger. The nurse again said we were a miracle coming along when we did and that we had done quite well in handling the situation. She left to tend to her family, and we talked to the ranger for a few minutes explaining that we had planned on walking east along the river after crossing it and then heading northeast. He looked at us and just shook his head. He said he would accompany us across the bridge so we had no problems. We exchanged names and phone numbers should we ever be able to use them again. We had filled water bottles in the campground and reloaded our packs, so we were ready to go.

After crossing the bridge, we shook hands with the ranger and struck out east along the southern bank of the Clarion River. We were going on pure adrenaline, and it didn't take long for that to end. Our energy was spent after we had walked no more than a mile. It was also very late. Just inside the park boundary we found a good campsite about 50 feet above the river. We had had hardly noticed skipping lunch, so we were pretty hungry. Since the ranger knew where we would likely be, we felt reasonably comfortable building a fire. Tarp lean-to set up, wood gathered, we boiled water and cooked a fairly large supper of pasta, jerky, veggies, pudding, and coffee. The dogs had been so good. We gave them as much food as they wanted. After hanging up packs we settled down to rest looking out at the river below is.

How grateful we were for the Lord's provision. The river was really high and running fast from all the recent rain. If we had continued as we planned, we would have had to hunker down for an unknown number of days to allow the river to go down rather than being escorted across it. The Lord had really been looking out for us, timing our arrival in the forest at a time when we could bring healing and peace to a needy family and providing us positive human contact and support. We had our own little praise service right there in our lean-to. Emotionally and physically exhausted, we were ready for sleep very early. Would be another nice warm night. Many prayers of thanksgiving said, scripture read, and hugs all around we settled down watching the moon and stars over the river and drifted off to sleep. Praise you, Lord.

I must add these final comments to what we experienced today. We have given our entire effort over to the Lord to guide us, protect us, and use us as He saw fit. He in turn did what He had promised us. We wonder how many people who've found themselves in the same type of situation we are in have the kind of peace and security we have. Add hope and trust in the Lord to it all, and we hold a great advantage over many others. Our lives have changed and are changing with each day. Our faith and trust are growing each day. We are indeed blessed beyond measure.

With my mouth I will give thanks abundantly to the Lord;
And in the midst of many I will praise Him.
(Psalm 109:30)

Date: May 15   Mileage: 4 mi.   Walk Total: 336–338 miles

We were pretty tired when we woke up as well as emotionally and physically drained. Plan was to take it easy today. Long uphill climb out of the Clarion River valley. We had to cross US route 36 again today. Our goal was to get as close to Sigel PA as we could and stop fairly early to rest as much as possible. Weather seemed to be cooperating. With the sweaty, hot, long climb out of the valley, we would make plenty of stops. Glad we had filled up water containers. Simple breakfast for energy, cream of wheat, pudding, coffee, and orange drink. Since we did not have any dry dog food or jerky left, dogs got same even though pudding not good for them. They needed the energy it would give as well.

Packed up, camp broken, water checked, we started our trudge uphill. Took ninety minutes to get to what seemed to be the top; lots of rest stops, and sweating a lot. Rested quite a bit once reached the top and were out of state forest. We had to detour around quite a few hunting camps just outside state park. Progressed slowly under sunny skies. Summer was just around the corner. Quick lunch of soup and water and back on our way. Stayed inside tree-lines all day when possible. Only had to cross one open field and relay stuff over two fence rows. We finally came to route 36 and following practice stopped, waited, and listened. Smelled smoke in the light breeze that was blowing off to our south. Eventually were able to cross route 36 and back into the woods.

Lots of deer sign again. Squirrels all over the place. We also saw some larger scat and did not want to run into the owner. Saw several fields off to our south with dairy cattle eating grass and resting in the hot afternoon. About 3 PM saw a couple squirrels playing in trees in front of us. Dogs didn't see them until after I had the air rifle out. Approached closer with dogs and of course they went nuts. Their barking made the squirrels hesitate and that was their big mistake. Both came down quickly. Had to run to keep dogs from tearing them apart. Let the dogs get a good smell of the two bodies. Field-dressed and gutted them,

LARRY D. HORTON, PhD

keeping dogs away from that stuff. Knew we would have to camp soon and cook the meat before it started to go bad in the heat.

By 3 PM we were bushed. Found a good tree-line on hillside and decided to camp there. Packs hung, got about cooking squirrel over hexamine stove. Dogs were going nuts smelling it. Did hearts first and gave each dog one. All that did was make them want more. Heated up some soup, parceled up meat into four equal parts, and we sat down to a good hot protein meal. Then got about setting up tarp lean-to shelter. No fire tonight. Too many potential prying eyes around. Fire-tin would be only light. Was a nice evening. Warm with a slight breeze. Dogs relaxing in the shelter when they weren't exploring. When we put them on long leashes, they had a ball smelling every nook and cranny where we were. Wife and I just sat and rested. Watched moonrise and clouds. Marveled at how dark it got without ambient artificial light. Prayers said and scripture read, we were ready for sleep. Thank you, Lord, for a good day.

The Lord has sworn and will not change His mind.
(Psalm 110:4)

Date: May 16   Mileage: 4 mi.   Walk Total: 340–342 miles

Good night's sleep after a stressful few days. We took our time getting ready this morning. Breakfast of oatmeal, rice, beans, and coffee. Needed the extra energy to perk us up. Dogs ate like they had never eaten before. Packed up, cleaned up, checked on water supply boiled from nearby stream last night, camp cleaned up and policed. Finally, on our way around 9 AM.

Did not hurry. Only planned on covering around four miles today. Had to cross PA route 949. We were headed in a general northeasterly direction into the country south of Clear Creek State Park. Less woods today. More fields to cross. Had to relay stuff over fence rows several times during the morning. Many country and secondary roads to cross safely as well. After about an hour came to route 949, followed by normal waiting and listening. Nothing seen or heard. Crossed, rested for a bit, and were on our way. Another hour and we had a simple lunch of soup and water. That done, we headed further into the countryside. For first time in days we saw several men walking, hunting rifles in hand, headed to the north. We hunkered down under some pines and just waited. Took better part of thirty minutes for us to believe they were out of earshot so we could keep moving.

That done, we walked for another ninety minutes and started to look for campsite. Dogs spooked couple rabbits and some grouse as we were crossing an open field. Good thing we had them on leashes, or they would have chased the critters clear back to Texas. As it was, they made quite a bit of noise with their barking. Partially dragging them, we moved on as best we could. Again, spotted some dairy cows in adjacent field. What I would have given for a cold glass of milk and some chocolate chip cookies. A dream now. At 2:45 PM we came upon a small valley situated between two small hills with a good grove of spruce pine trees. A good campsite. Put up tarp lean-to and cut multiple tree branches and made a nice mattress to sleep on. Again, staying dark, ate supper around 6 PM of soup and orange drink. While waiting to cook supper, explored for water source and found small stream in next small valley to our east. Hauled enough water to cook with and boil for our canteens. That done, did an equipment check, food inventory, checked dogs for ticks as we were in heavy deer country, and repaired any tears in materials. We put on our camping shoes and put our boots up to dry out. Sleeping bags hung to let breeze and sunlight dry them out some as well.

Finally prepared and ate supper. Surprising how emotionally spent we still were from Cook Forest event. We talked about and reflected on it again, marveling at the Lord's guidance and provision. Charged and turned on radio for first time in days. On top of hill were able to get weak NOAA national signal. Weather will change day after tomorrow, light rain, clouds, and warmer. That will last a couple days, then turns sunny again. We will walk as long as rain is not too heavy. No other radio signals could be picked up. Watched sunset, stars came out, and had prayers, scripture, and a lot of small talk. Need another good night's sleep.

Great are the works of the Lord;
They are studied by all who delight in them.
(Psalm 111:2)

Date: May 17   Mileage: 5 mi.   Walk Total: 345–347 miles

Felt more rested when woke up. Plan today is to camp just south of PA route 949. No major roadways to cross. No key secondary roads to cross. More than likely a lot of country or dirt roads, but we would be careful with those as always. Land would be very hilly with only sporadic open farm fields to deal with. Fixed last of cream of wheat for breakfast with next-to-last packet of orange drink. Dogs got a good portion and water. Would try for some more fresh meat as we walked today. Camp broken down, repacked, check of water supply, and we were ready to go.

Decided to push a bit further today. We have more sunlight in the evenings, so could walk until 4 PM before settling down for the night. Morning passed quickly and without any incidents. Did relay stuff across fences around a couple fields, but stayed mostly in tree-lines and hardwood sections of woods. Lots of pine trees around as well. Lunch of hot soup and water cooked over hexamine stove. We have four packets of soup left and will use them for only one meal each day. Our freeze-dried food stores are almost gone. Need to have fresh meat about every other day until we are done traveling. Hope luck and my aim are with us on that.

Rested a bit longer than usual while eating lunch. No need to be crazy and push too hard in these last days. Again, lots of rabbit sign and a few spots of deer scat. Quite a bit of zigging and zagging on our route as the hills got bigger and the valleys steeper. We had done a fairly good job of avoiding any real up and down for quite a few weeks now, even though it added a mile or more each day to our actual walking. We also had to detour around quite a few hunting cabins. When in the woods, we found a lot of what were likely gas drilling and logging roads. Over the past 25 years those resource efforts had increased a lot in the area. Prior to that it was mainly coal strip-mining that had dominated the area. We knew that kind of road through the woods would be the norm right up until the end of our journey. We slowed down even more in the afternoon as it was warm, probably mid-seventies, and we did not want to dehydrate.

Water would be important if these temps continued. Noticed during midafternoon that clouds were building from the south and coming our way. Likely the light rain that we had heard about on the radio.

By 3:30 PM knew it was time to be stopping. Noticed wooded area tucked in between two hills in a valley in the distance. Headed that way and found a good water source and some reasonably level ground a few yards up one of the slopes from the stream. Lots of good cover so we set up camp. The usual process, tarp lean-to, no fire ring (still going dark), hung up packs, cut pine branches for mattress, and laid out sleeping bags. Hauled multiple loads of water and boiled it. Then fixed next-to-last can of tuna, rice, and beans for supper. Fixed quite a bit so dogs could have a good share as well. Next-to-last packet of hot chocolate mix tasted good. That relaxed us a lot. Clouds moving in quickly so we covered everything with ponchos and had prayers and scripture and then watched as weather changed. Will be a damp night and wet day tomorrow.

**Praise the Lord! How blessed is the man who fears the Lord,
Who greatly delights in His commandments.
(Psalm 112:1)**

Cross Country Diary: Day #118

Date: May 18   Mileage: 5 mi.   Walk Total: 350–352 miles

A little tired when woke up. Had some four-legged visitors during the night, raccoons, chipmunks, squirrels, and one skunk. The skunk made a mistake by getting close. Taking no chances, took out 17 HMR, and with wife holding light from flashlight on it, I dispatched it quickly. Head-on shot at base of neck. It went down quickly. Used wooden stick to pick it up and carry it further into the woods. Dogs of course went nuts, but we weren't going to mess with a skunk. Just hoped rifle report in middle of night did not bring any other unwanted visitors. Slept with one eye open the rest of the night. At least it felt like that.

Light rain when we finally rousted out from under lean-to. Ponchos out immediately. Didn't look like we would have heavy rain; just enough to be a pain in the neck. Plan today was to travel cross country and arrive either at our friends' farm or very close to it. Simple breakfast of next-to-last packet of oatmeal, some rice mixed in, and coffee. Still staying dark, so used hexamine stove. Fuel for it was getting low. Enough left only for boiling water in an emergency. Will have to risk small wood fires from now on. After inventory, we have enough for five more hot meals in our supply. Definitely need some meat to help with food issues. We have rationed carefully. So far, it's worked well.

Done eating, packed up, broke and policed camp, checked water supply, and we were walking. Land was pretty rough to walk. Hills getting larger again. We were really in the foothills of the Allegheny Mountains now. Progress slow and steady during the morning. Light rain fell constantly, but more of a pain than anything else. We were able to stay pretty dry. With ponchos covering us, sweating was an issue. By midafternoon our carried water was gone. Would need a good water source tonight. Last couple water stops in the afternoon we used our water straws to drink from a couple small streams we had to cross. Funny taste, but it was purified, and we needed the water. Knew we had to cross Clarion River soon after spending a night at our friends' farm. Today followed multiple logging and gas line roads through woods. Can

LARRY D. HORTON, PhD

always tell when approaching gas well by the slight smell of gas in the air. Didn't want to camp too close to any of them.

Was fast approaching 4 PM when we started to seriously look for campsite. Took a few minutes. After a quarter-mile we found a decent place among a grove of hardwoods. Beginning to notice lots of vines in the trees as well. All the wild berry bushes were starting to bloom as well. In three months, there will be a lot to harvest. Camp set up as usual. Priority was to secure and boil as much water as we could. Set out some containers to collect rainwater as well. Supper quickly fixed, last of pasta and coffee. Dogs wanted more, but we were watching the supply. Felt damp, but we didn't have any real problems with rain. Spent evening under lean-to trying to stay dry. Grayness and rain made us sleepy, so shut down pretty early. Prayers, scripture, and just general resting before sleep. Good night!

Blessed be the name of the Lord
From this time forth and forever.
(Psalm 113:2)

Date: May 19   Mileage: 4 mi.   Walk Total: 354–356 miles

Still raining lightly when we woke up. Clouds were thick enough to guess that rain will not end today. Knew we were in vicinity of friends' farm from how they had described the area. All this immediate area was new to me. Knew that once crossed north of the Clarion River, only civilization we would probably see would be hunting camps. With rain, footing was going to be worse, so tried to set realistic goal for the day. We warmed up one of final packs of oatmeal and had water to drink. Dogs got some as well, but as usual they wanted more. We were all getting a little tired of the same diet that we had been eating for weeks. Repacked damp stuff, broke camp, checked water as usual, policed area, and we started out.

Slower going this morning as it was wet. The ground was a bit muddy, and leaves underfoot were very slippery. We were able to use an old logging road quite a bit until it veered off in the wrong direction. We were committed to follow our compass readings as best we could. We had to cross several fence lines during the AM which really slowed us down. Dogs were getting tired of that as well. Trying to stay upbeat in the weather, but a little tough. We talked last night about how close we are to our goal and that we don't want that excitement to get us to push faster and be unsafe. Absolute caution and common sense at this point in our journey. Lunch consisted of some rice and beans cooked on hexamine stove. Just enough to take feelings of hunger away and to add a little protein to our efforts.

By 2:30 PM we could sense we were getting close to friends' farm as saw more open fields. They had told us they lived in a valley a couple miles south of Clarion River. Very careful walking downhill into the valley. We stopped on a little flat area above the river for a break. It looked pretty normal, the water level that is. We were not going to make it to friends' farm today. Too tired to keep going. As we set up camp light rain became a drizzle and then stopped completely. Still totally clouded over, but winds from northwest we hoped would blow weather out of the area. Tired setting up camp. Same profile as most other nights. Hung what we could up to dry under lean-to. Packs hung in trees with poncho over them. Dogs seemed tired of the rain as well. They just wanted to lie under the lean-to and try to stay as dry as possible. I walked couple hundred yards to a small stream and hauled quite a bit of water. Boiled water and filled containers. Once that was done we had supper of freeze-dried veggies, fruit, and coffee. Dogs were not too excited about food, but eventually ate their shares just out of pure hunger.

When drizzle stopped, birds and other critters started to come out. Life got active again. Planned out remaining meals for the next few days. Figured I need to get some fresh meat again tomorrow. Changed into dry clothing and sat under lean-to listening to water drip from trees all around us. Dampness brought out frogs and crickets, so it was a noisy evening. We were all ready to sleep, so didn't sit up too long tonight. Prayers said, scripture read, lay and listened to all of the sounds around us. Hoping for a dry day tomorrow. Good night!

Tremble, O earth, before the Lord,
Before the God of Jacob.
(Psalm 114:7)

Date: May 20   Mileage: 4 mi.   Walk Total: 358–360 miles

Very damp when we woke up, but the rain had stopped. Saw a few rays of sun to the east, so knew clouds were likely breaking up and weather was changing. Breakfast of cream of wheat and orange drink. Fixed enough for the dogs to have some as well. Repacked damp stuff, checked water supply, and broke camp.

Was going to be a slow walk today. Lots of hills and footing was not good so we took our time. Forty-five minutes after breaking camp we came to friends' farm. They welcomed us with open arms. Offered warm shower, which we accepted gladly. While we cleaned up, they prepared a hot lunch of beef, potatoes, corn, and coffee. Dogs got some of the beef as well. As we were eating, talked at length about final location that made sense to them. Told us that five to seven miles to northeast, along Bear Creek, we could find a location to set up our new home. Few if any camps in the area. No roads other than dirt and logging roads. That sounded good to us. They insisted that we spend the night with them, and we did not argue one bit. Spent the afternoon resting and checking all our gear.

They surprised us one more time before supper. For the past week, they had been preparing a supply of food for us. It was all dried or in cans. Somehow, they knew we would be running out of food when we got there. What could we do? We knew we could not refuse it but we put up a good front trying to. We were just very appreciative, and we let them know it. They insisted we nap while they fixed us a warm supper, watched the dogs, and fed them. Once again, the Lord was watching over us. We were awakened from our naps with the smell of fried chicken, mashed potatoes, gravy, cornbread, and a pie that was pulled from the wood burning oven. Nothing had ever smelled so good. Our only regret was that our stomachs had shrunk so much that we were full too soon. They said they would prepare the leftover chicken and we could take it with us in the morning. Great conversation around the supper table. But even that had to end early. We just could not keep our eyes open. One thing they made us promise before we headed to a real bed for the night was to stay in touch once we were settled in our new home. It might take us a few hours to walk to see them again, but we promised to do that when we could. They promised to visit us before the summer ended to see how we were doing. Prayers and scripture shared with them. With that, the dogs following behind us, we hit the sack. We were asleep as soon as our heads hit the pillows.

Temps to moderate more each night. Going to be warm tomorrow so plan on being realistic about how far we will walk. Excited that we are so close to goal. Thank you, Lord!

Not to us, O Lord, not to us,
But to Your name give glory
Because of Your lovingkindness, because of Your truth.
(Psalm 115:1)

Date: May 21   Mileage: 4 mi.   Walk Total: 362–364 miles

First thought on waking up was that today makes it four months since we set out in the truck from our house in Texas. Another ten days and we will have walked for four months in total. The time has gone both quickly and slowly, good and bad days, joy and trepidation. Today was a new day, however. We were up early. Breakfast was already on the stove when we walked into the kitchen. Scrambled eggs, bacon, home fries, and hot fresh coffee. Dogs had as much eggs and bacon as their tummies could hold. They curled up by stove when done eating.

We noticed a big pile of stuff on kitchen counter, and friends said it was all for us. We just stared. It had to be about 40 pounds of supplies. Told us 10 pounds of dried beef, five pounds of powdered eggs, five pounds of bacon, one pound of sugar, some salt, small tins of tuna, three pounds of powdered milk, two pounds of coffee, couple dozen tea bags, and a dozen assorted canned veggies. We tried to tell them it was too much, but they would hear none of that. Over breakfast they told us that 5 to 7 miles north along Bear Creek, they knew of an abandoned farmstead; might even call it a homestead. As far as they knew it had been abandoned years ago. Thought that might be a good place for us to settle in. Only potential humans will be hunters and that was only for few months a year. With current situation in the country, might see more hunters, but most would not want to stay in that area. Knew we would be living there illegally without a permit. But given situation in country, figured no one will make an issue of that as well. That is our new target goal.

Loaded all the gifts into our packs. Almost back to the same weight as when we first started out on foot so many weeks earlier. Good meals and good night's rest gave us hope that we could handle them. With packs loaded we were ready. Friends told us to stay couple miles west of Portland Mills. There was a country bridge that crossed over the Clarion River that they suggested we use. With grateful thanks and a prayer, we set out for the last days of our walk into the future. Took us

LARRY D. HORTON, PhD

about two hours of slow going before we came to the bridge over the river. Same procedure as so many times before. Sat out of sight and made sure no one was coming. Only took couple minutes to cross bridge, and we were back into the woods away from road. Set compass direction to travel north on a Forest service road today. Will start out the same way tomorrow, then late morning head straight east. Lunch by a small creek of some of the fried chicken. Peeled off the skin on some and let the dogs have the meat. Lunch done, headed out again.

Walked until 3 PM and found good campsite in grove of oak trees. Not a sound around us. Simple lean-to as before and a small fire ring. Collected wood and started small fire. Heated up the last of the fried chicken. Once done, walked couple hundred yards to small stream. Hauled multiple buckets of water. Boiled to clean dishes, wash ourselves, water for dogs and to fill our canteens and jug. Then put fire out. Going to be warm tonight. Used fire-tin for a bit of light before sleeping. Didn't take us long to get to bed. Prayers said, scripture read, we again praised and thanked the Lord for His mercy and care. Good night!

I love the Lord because He hears
My voice and my supplications.
(Psalm 116:1)

Date: May 22   Mileage: 4 mi.   Walk Total: 366–368 miles

Woke up with our friends' directions in our memory. Said go four miles straight north from bridge, then make 90 degree turn to east. Said we should arrive at Bear Creek after another two- to three-mile walk. Breakfast cooked over small fire. Scrambled eggs. Dogs got their fill as well. Made sure all water containers were full. Dishes cleaned and repacked packs. Broke down camp, tarp rolled and put on top of my pack. All of that is now automatic, a skill that is burned into our capabilities.

Set direction with compass to true north and headed out. Dogs on their leashes excited and exploring everything. Warmed up quickly as we walked. Really into some big hills—mountains, as they are called here. Completely wooded. Part of the national forest. Not much undergrowth due to tree canopy above, so walking was not too difficult. Lots of old dead logs, moss, and ferns around. Lots of critter sign. Squirrels in trees and deer scat on the ground. Crossed over quite a few runs and streams during the morning. Rather than use carried water, we used water straws, always careful to look to see if any sign of critter use of water in the area.

Stopped for lunch around noon, portion of dried beef and water. Dogs got couple pieces of the beef as well. Then back on the service road. As always tried to follow ridges as long as compass said we were headed in right general direction. Couple times had to dip into some small valleys where hills ran east and west. Only way to keep on direction was to do that. Slowed us a bit, but took plenty of rest stops. Could feel the additional weight in our packs. Found reasonable spot to set up lean-to. Water close by. On lee of hill, so decided to build a good fire. First can of tuna out, mixed with scrambled eggs. Enough for the four of us. Dogs on long leashes exploring everything. Last thing done was to cut enough pine branches to build up a good sleeping mattress for the night.

As the last sliver of the sun sank below the hills to the west I looked into the dancing orange yellow flames of the last open fire I would sit in front of, at the end of our four-month 1,500-mile journey. My wife, Jude, sitting beside me, our two dogs lying beside us near the fire smelling the lingering scents of our just completed hot meal, the weariness of the day set in quickly. Knowing that no more than two or three miles remained to arrive at our final destination, an overwhelming sense of relief mixed with grateful exhaustion that our journey filled with unimagined challenges would soon end. We sat under the lean-to, and I put out our final fire. No current dangers, we settled down early to rest for tomorrow. Prayers, scripture, and much thanks, we said good night!

Praise the Lord, all nations; Laud Him, all peoples!
For His lovingkindness is great toward us,
And the truth of the Lord is everlasting
Praise the Lord!
(Psalm 117)

Cross Country Diary: Day #123 The Last Day, We Are Home, Part One

Date: May 23   Mileage: 2 mi.   Walk Total: 368–370 miles

We didn't sleep much last night. Our excitement of being so close to our goal kept our minds working full-time during the night. The dogs sensed something different about this morning as well. Splurged on breakfast. Good fire built, cooked eggs and bacon. A full breakfast. The dogs got more excited as we ate. Broke camp, carefully repacked our packs, checked all gear one last time, and made sure we had enough water for the day. Was going to be sunny and warm. Probably in the mid-seventies with a breeze. Off we went.

Decided to turn directly east now. Would set up temporary camp when we reached Bear Creek, and I would scout upstream and down for the old farmstead. We were in new country. There was no sign that anyone had been in the same area for a long time. We were ready to be at our new home. We went slowly so we wouldn't take any stupid steps. Checked compass every ten minutes. Lots of deer sign, squirrels in the trees, and lots of birds singing in the trees. We scared up a flock of grouse shortly after beginning our walk. Oh, for a shotgun. A mistake not to bring one. Good progress throughout the morning, slow but steady. Lunch of beef again with water. A few brief rest stops throughout the walk but only five minutes each. We were close, and we wanted the journey to end safely. We were almost at our new home.

About 1 PM came around a point on ridge we had been following and saw Bear Creek several hundred yards below us. Caution was important. Even though we wanted to hurry down off the ridge, we took our sweet time angling downhill until at last we came to a nice grove of pine trees about 100 feet above the creek. Looked like a good spot to set up temporary camp until I was able to find the farmstead here in these wonderful woods. By 3 PM had lean-to in place and small fire going with enough wood to cook supper and breakfast in the morning. We might decide to stay here a couple more days as well. Once found any buildings would likely spend a day or two scoping them out to make sure we could make them into a reasonable home. The more we talked about that, the better the idea sounded. No sense running off with everything in tow and finding out the prospective buildings were not worth the effort. We would have to make other decisions if that proved true. Hauled water up the hill from Bear Creek, boiled some, and made sure had another bucket ready to boil. Dogs on long leashes hooked to a couple trees ignored us as they explored, smelled, and eventually lay down to rest.

Wife and I made sure we had our emergency whistle signals in mind. I was going to spend a couple hours going north along creek and then south to see if I could find the abandoned buildings. Wanted to be back by dusk, as we saw several squirrel nests close by. Maybe some fresh meat We decided to eat around 6 PM so I would gear my search to be back before that. Dogs wanted to go with me, but they had to stay behind. Could hear them barking for quite a while once I headed upstream. At least they would be a good alarm for my wife as she waited for me at lean-to.

Cross Country Diary: Day #123 The Last Day, We Are Home, Part Two

Date: May 23   Mileage: 2 mi.   Walk Total: 368–370 miles

Headed north along the creek first. It was about ten feet wide where we had found it. As I walked north, it slowly started to narrow. Saw some critter sign. A couple places were probably used as watering holes by everything in the neighborhood. Within thirty minutes, with uphill slope increasing, the creek had shrunk to just a couple feet wide. Figured headed to a dead end and as it was moving uphill, figured abandoned buildings not in this direction. Turned around and backtracked. Did my best to be quiet when passing our little camp. Didn't want the dogs to get excited again. Looked like everyone was resting, so I kept going.

Creek went around a small ridge that stuck out from hill we were camped on about a half-mile downstream. Could see the outline of something that wasn't a tree another hundred yards on. Was this it? Slowed down and approached very slowly. The jackpot if you could call it that. Obviously at some point in the past quite an area had been cleared. The years had overgrown all that work. What I saw was a small log cabin with several small outbuildings. Those smaller buildings had more or less collapsed in on themselves. But the cabin didn't look to be in bad shape. Moss covered the roof. A couple windowpanes were broken out. The door had fallen off the hinges. Likely rusted through. I peered inside, and it looked to be about 24 by 24 feet. Not much furniture, but what was there had likely been used within the last two or three years. Would have to keep that in mind.

Had seen enough, and it was almost 5 PM when I started back to camp. Dogs saw me coming from a distance, and they started barking. Wife had fire going and was ready for us to cook supper. Warmed up beef and some scrambled eggs. While it was cooking, I hauled couple buckets of water up from creek above where I had seen critter watering hole, and we started boiling it while cooking food. Dogs were really hungry. We were too. As we ate, gave my wife quick description of what I had found. The cabin looks pretty reasonable given the passage of time with

LARRY D. HORTON, PhD

no care. The location will need a lot of clearing and cleaning up. The outbuildings are likely useless beyond maybe being a supply of materials. The cabin is located about thirty feet above the creek bank, so danger of flash flooding is minimal. I saw some areas south of the cabin that have likely been cleared in the past and might be good for planting a garden. The creek itself can supply emergency water if there is no working water pump in the cabin. I suggested that we spend another night where we are and then all go to look at the site very carefully tomorrow. I was honest when I told her it will take a lot of work to get it in shape. But I also said it is much better than starting from scratch and trying to build a new structure. Time will tell if I'm right.

As the sun was setting over the ridge above us we had a season of prayer asking for wisdom as to what to do. We are together. We have our two-loving little four-legged girls. We have our health, and we are safe. The Lord has indeed been good to us over the past four months. We will soon begin the next chapter of our new life Scriptures read and hugs for the dogs, we climbed into our sleeping bags. Watch over us, Lord. We have put ourselves in the hands of the Lord, and He has watched over us, provided for us, kept us safe, and given us the common sense to bring us to our final destination.

Give thanks to the Lord, for He is good;
For His lovingkindness is everlasting.
(Psalm 118:1)

THE FINAL JOURNEY

Reflections

Reflections

In the days and weeks that followed our arrival at our final destination, our home for the rest of our lives, we spent much time reflecting on the four-month physical journey that we had completed as well as the earlier twelve months of preparing to undertake the impossible. The following notes, comments, and thoughts are but a small example of the many things we pondered. Answers to some questions. Changes we would have made had we had more experience. Many unanswered questions as well. Questions that will remain unanswered until we stand before the Lord and He explains why all of it had happened. Our thoughts are shared for anyone who might read this diary, to help them prepare for their own future journey.

We do so realizing that without the Lord as one's guide and protector, human effort alone might have done what we were able to accomplish. But with the Lord's guidance and protection, we gain a greater understanding of what life is really about, why trials must be faced, why mankind really does not control their own destiny, why history is the one great teacher we ignore to our own peril, why power and greed only lead to failure and destruction, what the ultimate purpose of life is, how family is the underpinning of purpose in life, and how all of creation groans and suffers when it stands outside the will of God.

Our strength, as humans, comes not from the world's answers to these questions. Our strength comes through surrender, faith, trust, and obedience to the one great reason for life itself. Other than the unbounded love of God for us, whom He created, nothing else matters ultimately. If our journey over hundreds of miles taught us anything, it taught us that in and of ourselves, we are as a breeze blowing across the land—now here, and then gone. Without the hand of God creating the breeze and directing it toward His plan for it, His ultimate goal, the breeze is only the wind. Life is more than just a breeze. It is the ultimate sign of God. To God be the glory, forever and ever, Amen!

To God be the glory, great things He hath done,
So loved He the world that He gave us His Son,
Who yielded His life our redemption to win,
And opened the life-gate that all may go in.
Praise the Lord, praise the Lord,
Let the earth hear His voice;
Praise the Lord, praise the Lord,
Let the people rejoice;
Oh, come to the Father, through Jesus the Son,
And give Him the glory; great things He hath done.
Charles Wesley, published 1738

LARRY D. HORTON, PhD

Reflections

Preparation and Planning (P&P)

There is no substitute for preparation and planning to give one the best chance of surviving any drastic change in one's circumstances. Whether those changes are brought about by a natural disaster or, as illustrated in our journey, through human activities, a lack of preparation and planning leads to great struggles, suffering, and ultimately the possibility of failure. We started our P&P processes more than a year prior to our actually beginning our journey. Combining knowledge through reading and research, hours and hours of practicing skills, purchasing and collecting all the equipment we could potentially need, organizing those materials into portable packs, and mapping out multiple routes of escape, we did all that was humanly possible to prepare for what might happen.

After the journey started, P&P was a daily discipline which we followed religiously. We did our best to anticipate any and all situations we might find ourselves in. We studied the areas that we would be traveling through. We studied roads, rivers, bridges, and topography to help in our decision process. We evaluated our equipment and materials using a decision tree that told us which would meet the most potential situations effectively. Anything that did not meet multiple potential needs and uses was discarded. Ultimately, we knew that this P&P, combined with common sense and logical thought, would give us the best chance to survive.

At the same time, we knew that we could not anticipate every potential situation we might face. We realized that we would have to adapt and adjust even the best laid-out plans. We tested our equipment, our food, and each piece of material that we would use multiple times. We prepared materials to repair, rebuild, and fabricate anything that we might need. Ultimately, we cut everything down to a few categories: shelter, water, fire, food, protection, and a few nice-to-haves. We knew that we could survive with what we could carry on our backs if need be. The final criterion was always what we would need to survive our travels and what we would need after we reached our goal to help us in the new life that waited there for us. Only when an item passed muster for both situations was it included in our kit. It had to have long-term use for us beyond the end of our physical survival journey.

Even as we were involved in the travel itself, we took the time each day to map out our route, to plan and ration our food, to scrounge for materials that might come in handy, to adjust our travel goal for each day depending on weather, our physical health, avoiding danger and confrontation, and to find and build shelter that would protect us for more than just a few hours. We lost track of how many times we detoured around obstacles that we had not planned for. At times, we changed our plan hourly. And when we changed our plan for any reason, we took the time to adjust that plan and move forward. We set realistic goals within our plan. We knew that those goals would keep us moving forward. And we didn't lose hope or get frustrated when we had to change our plans. We remained disciplined in even the very smallest details of each day. We went to sleep at night knowing that when we woke up we might have to change our plans for the new day. It was never easy to stay that disciplined. However, we knew without any doubt that to fail to adapt and adjust, to prepare and plan, even down to the hour, we would not be successful in our ultimate goal: surviving and finding the best chance to have a future. Don't cut corners on your preparation and planning.

Getting from Point A to Point B

We had planned for our journey of approximately 1,500 miles to take in the neighborhood of six months. The time depended largely on how much we could cover in our truck and how much we would actually be on foot. The miles were a best guess based on map study and having previously driven the entire way in the past. In the end, it took 123 days, just over four months. Total mileage was 1,175 by truck and 370 on foot. The miles walked are an approximation, as we had no way to determine actual miles walked once we were traveling cross country off road. In total, we covered around 1,550 miles, give or take a little. We had not planned on covering that much by truck. We had carried enough fuel for an emergency, and only through the kindness of a farm family in Kentucky were we able to. Our truck, eventually abandoned for lack of fuel availability, served us well.

The Trekker, home-built with a specific purpose, abandoned eventually as well, performed far better than we had planned. It was a lifesaver, so to speak. It worked well on the country roads and lanes we used off grid. When forced to go off road, it proved less useful. Once the external situation shifted to circa 1800s and we went off road, it was not worth the effort. The design would require significant alterations to prove useful in such an off-road situation.

Walking proved to be difficult yet not impossible. Our mind-set, physical abilities, and realistic daily objectives made it possible. Had we been forced to start walking cross country much sooner, without the Trekker, our progress would have slowed. We built up the needed strength and stamina in stages, which helped us a great deal. Traveling off the main highways was another smart part of our plan. As circumstances around us grew steadily worse, the fact that we stayed away from traffic and people kept us reasonably safe and secure. Roads in fact were eventually obstacles to our progress. We avoided them, other than to cross them quickly once we were totally on foot.

We learned that the better plan you have in place, the better your chances for success. Adjusting, detouring, adapting, all were part of that plan. As well, we learned that having more than one possible route worked to our advantage. Discipline and adaptability were critical to our traveling from one location to another. We are all given a path to walk in life. How disciplined and adaptable we are on that life path transfers easily to the survival trip that we have shared.

One final thought relates to our transportation and travel preparations. Don't shortchange any spare parts or tools that you need to take. You may not think you will need something, but think long and hard before you put it aside. Here's a guarantee: If something is mechanical it will break down. When it does, be ready.

Shelter

Thinking back on what we carried—both a primary and a secondary tarp, 300 feet of paracord, 200 hundred feet of 600-pound strength rope, a hand ax, a regular single bladed ax, a bow saw, a machete, duct tape, strong thread, and large needles—we believe we had all that was necessary to build required shelters. Those items, when combined with natural materials—logs, tree branches, and mud for calking—gave us the ability to handle most conditions requiring good shelter. We were able to deal with heavy snowfall, heavy rain, winds, and cover for any open fire we had to build. The materials were bulky and added quite a bit of weight to what we packed, but every pound was worth it in the end.

We found space blankets to be of extreme value for two reasons. One is obvious, the need for warmth when necessary, but even more useful for building and covering our fire reflection systems. If we had to choose between regular tarps and space blankets, the tarps might have been left behind. The tarps did prove invaluable when we had to put up and take down overnight shelters, especially when we were carrying our packs on foot cross country. They were easy to repair with duct tape. The tape was bulky and heavy but proved also to be well worth the effort to carry it. We learned very quickly to use nature's shelters as well—in particular, heavy thick groves of pine trees which provided cover from snow and rain, as well as protection from wind. Locating our shelters on the lee of hills, with the opening directed away from primary wind conditions, proved wise as well. Sheltering in covered areas provided added security from other threats, both critters and humans alike.

When we had to hunker down for extended periods, building a sleeping platform probably saved us from cold and moisture. The added comfort of using pine branches as bedding, though not without a few jabs and bumps, was wise as well. With sleep and rest being critical to so much of what we were trying to do, the extra effort to use branch mattresses, whether just for one night or for several, made a major difference. Thinking back on the entire experience, we would change little if anything on the shelters we used, the processes we used to build them, or the ease with which we could tear them down, repack, and be on our way.

Water

The Rule of Threes, as everyone knows, says in part that three days is the longest one can survive safely without a supply of drinkable water. We had prepared for every situation we could anticipate. Our basic water purification kit included purification tablets, water straws, and multiple containers to carry drinking water. Boiling was our primary means of water purification for the entire journey. Water for cooking, for drinking, and for cleaning our bodies was all boiled. We used the tablets and straws sparingly and were probably better for it. The countryside we traveled through had good water supplies. We were able to camp within a short distance of water every night. Carefully scoping out water sources upstream for contamination each day likely kept us from dangerous sickness.

We would probably add one or two more collapsible buckets to our kit in the future. We would also probably add a couple of larger pots, two- or three-quarts in size, to boil water in. The small pots we carried did the job, but with a small volume, we used quite a bit of our hexamine fuel at times for a small return in boiled water. We learned quickly even in the coldest weather that we needed to drink three or four canteens of water each day. When the temperatures rose in the latter half of our journey it became five or six canteens per day. Several times we had to stop by a stream and use our water straws until we were camped at night and could boil larger supplies of drinkable water. The plastic army surplus canteens proved effective, with one drawback. Had they been metal, we could have put them in coals from open fires and used them to boil water as well. In the future, we will change out the plastic canteens for stainless steel ones and deal with the added weight of those containers. But given the circumstances we found ourselves in, our water systems worked well.

Safety

Physical and emotional safety play a vital role in surviving what we went through. Each of the other four critical survival elements—shelter, water, food, and communication—add together to build an environment of perceived and actual safety. Walking slowly in dangerous ground conditions, fording streams with safety ropes, having a fire to keep unwanted visitors at a distance, carrying personal protection weapons, building shelters out of flash flood danger, avoiding human contact at all costs (especially within the scenario which we progressed through), taking care to treat even the smallest cuts and scrapes to avoid infection, getting enough rest to keep our minds clear and our bodies able to deal with the physical stresses experienced, and many other small things we did added to our sense of overall safety. Knowing, until radio reception ended, what was going on around us enabled us to anticipate potential problems and to avoid them. Having each other to depend on when things got tough added a feeling that we were not alone. Our dogs, even though they were a pain at times, were invaluable as an early warning system to any dangers that might be around us.

Taken together, coupled with survival knowledge, skills, and equipment, these measures gave us a reasonably constant sense of safety. Even when real dangers threatened us we knew we had prepared for what might come. And yes, ultimately our common sense brought all of these together into a sense of well-being. Add our faith in the Lord's guidance and protection, and we would not change anything we did related to our safety. Even when we took great risk in helping the father and son with the broken leg in the woods at Cook Forest State Park, we had an inner sense of peace that we would be safe even as we broke one of our cardinal survival rules: no contact with other human beings. We trusted the decision that we made to become involved and the Lord's protection to be used to help others who were not prepared and facing a desperate need.

We will be eternally grateful that we trusted our safety into the Lord's hands and that He honored that trust and faith. Real safety does not rest in the methods or ways of men but in God alone.

LARRY D. HORTON, PhD

Food

One area where we would make a few changes in our preparation, planning, and execution lay in the area of our food. For a short while, we hauled—and then carried while we were physically the only means of transport—enough food to last between four and five months if we carefully rationed it. Most was freeze-dried with a shelf life of twenty-five years. We carried additional food in more traditional forms such as beans, rice, flour, sugar, spices, canned meats, but only enough to add minimal variety to our diet. We carried enough dry dog food for one meal per day for approximately thirty days. We knew we would have to add fresh meat through killing of game as we traveled. That turned out to bring in less protein than we had hoped for. Sharing some of our own rations with the dogs also decreased the overall amounts of vitamins, minerals, and freeze-dried protein that we had for ourselves. The weight and bulk of all this was probably 50 percent of the total weight we carried. We could not have carried any more.

We learned to change what we carried. To add some of the needed nutrients that were in short supply we would have packed more freeze-dried protein, fewer freeze-dried fruits, more beans, less pasta, less coffee, and more powdered energy drinks. We should not have packed spices. We should have packed half as much salt and sugar. The other foods we had would provide enough of those in our diet. We would have made sure we had sufficient vitamin supplement tablets. As it was, we ran out of those a couple weeks before the end of the journey. We would pack more bouillon cubes to add to watery meals, even just to water itself, to add flavor and variety. Even these cubes would bring vital nourishment. We would have spent more time and effort adding natural plants to our diet even in the dead of winter which we experienced. And most important, would have made sure we spent enough time securing fresh meat for protein and energy even at the expense of traveling a set distance on any given day.

As we neared the end of our journey, we noticed a definite lessening of our energy levels. That is the one great lesson we learned about food even after reading manual after manual that told us not to shortchange our physical strength by scrimping a bit on food. We thank the Lord that at several points in our journey others took it upon themselves to provide wonderful meals and supplies of protein, jerky to be specific. Those gifts were a godsend, and we know the important role they all played in our success. Most experts say that a person can survive for at least three weeks with minimal food. We learned that it was critical to have the right kind of food rather than just bulk. This does not mean that our planning was wrong. It would just need to be adjusted a bit if we ever find ourselves having to make the same effort again in the future. Looking back, we had what we needed. It got us through. Our lack of a few things made the undertaking a bit more difficult but did not mean that we failed. Learning from life, we will live our lives differently in the future when it comes to food. We lost weight, but we gained a future much wiser and aware of making it better.

Communication

We had prepared from the very beginning to be able to communicate to family through the use of our cell phones. We had also secured devices that would enable us to stay up to date on events that happened around us in the areas we were passing through. Those devices, with NOAA and AM/FM capabilities, would also keep us linked to national and international happenings. The devices were rechargeable by solar and by hand crank. They also had the ability to provide recharging for our phones. We kept a written record of each day we traveled as you have seen in this diary. Also, we kept additional records to track our inventory of supplies. We did our best to leave no signs of our presence in any location so as not to communicate that we were traveling through an area. We carried emergency equipment in case we found ourselves in a dire health situation and had to seek help. We were prepared to send out signals using multiple tools but only as a last resort, a life-or-death situation. Looking back now, thinking about our losing the larger radio capabilities to the EMP, we would do a better job of protecting it in the future. We had the foresight to protect the backup radio and our cell phones.

Given the difficulty of securing signal strength because of the topography of the land we traveled through and the eventual shutdown of all communication capabilities due to circumstances beyond our control, we did our best. If we were to change anything, we would probably try to communicate at least once a week with family. The ability to communicate and listen proved valuable in our decision processes. Just hearing another human voice, even if electronic, was important to our psychological well-being. On the other hand, we had prepared so well related to reading weather signs that when we could no longer get forecasts, we were able to prepare for weather changes and dangers.

We really can't think of much we would do differently related to communication if given the chance. Far too much was out of our control. We did have each other to talk things through. Attempting such a journey alone would have been a far different experience. We could talk to our dogs and they listened most of the time. Just their attention to our words, with no understanding, was helpful. And most importantly we had our daily communication with the Lord in prayer and through reading of scripture. That was our anchor.

Equipment

At some point during the entire journey, we used every piece of equipment we had prepared and packed, some on a daily basis, others only as needed. We repaired many things, some multiple times. Only when we were tired and frustrated did we ever think about the what-ifs of things we had not packed. That didn't last long because we were forced to improvise, and that worked okay. A few pieces of cooking equipment were worn out when we were done. We would probably secure more substantial pots and small nested frying pans in the future. But everything survived and served us well. We learned the wisdom of what we had learned in spending a bit extra for high quality equipment. I am grateful to my father for that life lesson.

Quite a bit of our equipment was in good enough shape to continue to serve us. We would use the same lessons we learned, primarily that there is no one standard equipment kit that everyone should have. Rather one should consider extensive lists of options. Thinking through the areas one will travel; the specific personal needs that one may have related to health, physical capabilities, knowledge, and experience in the use of equipment; and the weight-to-value ratio of carrying any item, one should do their best to anticipate every possible situation and pack those things that make the most sense to carry in that environment.

One example illustrates this very well: clothing. We learned that one does not have to carry a half-dozen changes in clothing. Only underwear and socks are required in multiple sets. Other than that, one likely will only need three days of clothing, one set for camp wear and two sets for actual travel. Warmth, dryness, and comfort are key criteria to use in choosing the right clothing. Total weight also enters into the equation. Given that we traveled through the worst of the winter, the right thermal gear was critical, in particular the ability to layer clothing, with a waterproof, hooded outer coat. We also learned that gloves, both for protection from the cold and elements and for protection when using sharp tools and working with fire, were key items. Lastly, we had carefully chosen our boots and camp shoes. Lightweight day-hiking shoes worked well around camp. Breathable waterproof twelve-inch hiking boots were critical to our ability to walk safely and comfortably on the trail. We will never again cut costs on footwear. The expense we incurred was well worth it. Ultimately, equipment is a very personal thing. We had made good choices. They all served us well. We would likely do nothing different in the future.

Weapons, Knives, Camp Tools

The one regret during our journey was that we did not carry a shotgun as part of our kit. It would have been extremely useful in securing fresh protein more easily that the processes we used, the air rifle, 17 HMR, and wire snares. But we had to make some difficult choices in our preparations, and we chose to carry the air rifle for small game and the 17 HMR for larger critters and our protection.

In the end, they all worked well. We might reconsider carrying a third long gun the next time but would think long and hard concerning the extra weight of the weapon itself and the needed ammo. We doubt we would choose any differently than we did originally. Thankfully we only had to use our handguns once to deal with two attacking dogs. It was reassuring to have them. We would not have left them out of our kit for any reason. Our ammo held up well. At the end of our journey we had 80 percent of the air rifle pellets left, 95 percent of the 17 HMR ammo, all the handgun ammo except the three or four rounds we expended for each of them. We had packed knowing that the ammo we carried would have to last us long after we reached our final destination. Our knives had been functional. The only change that would be considered would be to change out the one large knife for a strong but lighter survival knife. Having backups for each of them was important as well. Carrying whetstones was also a good decision.

We had practiced using our weapons prior to our journey, but hindsight tells us we should have practiced even more. We learned at several roadblocks in southern Ohio that carrying the right documents for the weapons was important as well. Our camp tools, primarily for cooking, cutting, eating, and for making repairs, all were good choices. Keeping them functional did not prove to be too difficult. We believed we had made the right choices and that they would continue to serve us well into the future.

Our Girls

We could not have left Sadie and Sophie behind. Some would say we were crazy to attempt such a journey with two dogs. But we would argue long and hard that even with the periodic problems they presented, we would have not made the trip as well without them. One thing we would do differently is train them to be off leash and to walk with us. The leashes slowed us down many times, but reflecting on that we believe that may have been for the better. At times, going more slowly probably enabled us to keep up our strength and our eventual motivation to keep going. Their unconditional love, their brown eyes staring at us, their barking at things in the night, their wagging tails when they got rewarded with the hearts of small game we killed and ate, and their warmth in our sleeping bags all added up to say to us that without them we would not have been so much at peace as we were. Little did we know when we rescued them a few years earlier what an important role they would play in our survival, both physically and emotionally. One change we would make in our preparations would be to pack more food specifically for them. Sharing some of our rations with them toward the end of our travels did put a strain on us, but we would do it again as needed.

Human Contact, Threats, Dangers, Confrontation

From day one of our journey we were committed to avoiding all human contact. We believe we succeeded. Human threats, dangers, and confrontation were almost nonexistent once we were on foot. We dealt with humans as reasonably and safely as possible when we were initially traveling in our truck. The few direct face-to-face dealings with other humans were all positive in their outcome. We received invaluable help several times from people in the countryside who took us in, provided for a few needs, and shared our faith and common belief that the future will be very different than the past. We had developed multiple strategies for being on the lookout for situations that could present danger: bypassing dwellings and camps, carefully crossing every road, and traveling off the grid—in the dark, so to speak—the great majority of the time. The location of our campsites, cooking without wood smoke, listening to the sounds around us, waiting for perhaps longer than necessary to cross roads to avoid other travelers … all these tactics and more kept us true to our planned strategy. We were risk-averse in all things human. We must admit that the lack of human contact was very difficult at times, but in the end, it proved to be a wise plan. As I said previously, we talked more to each other and to the Lord for the entire four months. Because of that we grew closer than we had ever been before. Human contact avoidance continues to be our mantra as we move into the unknown future. Only with care will we make contact with others. That is the stark reality that we now face.

Health, Medications, Physical Strength

As mentioned earlier, my wife and I started our journey with some definite physical and health challenges. We were not young anymore. In that light, we prepared carefully for any eventuality we might face. Packing required medications for four months, we learned to carefully use those at times in half-dose increments. The physical strength we gained from the exertion of traveling more than likely helped with our overall health. The medications became a precaution rather than an absolute requirement. We were able to stretch the meds until we did arrive at our goal.

Other meds, vitamin supplements, various strengths of pain meds, and our medical kits as a whole proved to be effective. We would likely make no changes to what we had prepared and packed other than to maybe add a few more of each item to give us some wiggle room when used. We were lucky to get through the entire journey with only one injury that required more than immediate care, the sprained ankle. We experienced countless nicks, small cuts, bruises, and scrapes but were prepared to deal with them, and we dealt with them at once. We suffered no infections and only a few days of sniffles. Our allergies were normal but not bad until it turned to spring. We had no major cut injuries, which reinforced the importance of taking great care with bladed tools.

Our physical strength increased as the days passed as long as we were able to eat full rations of food. As we neared the end of the journey, we noticed that our strength was lessening due to reduced rations and the long duration of our travel on foot. We had learned a lot about field first aid and had put it into practice. We knew that the future will be much the same. We will remain committed to the same care and safety measures that we used on the journey. With time our overall strength and stamina will come back. Living each day ahead will also call on us to have new strength. We will run out of medications, supplements, and store-bought medical supplies. Learning natural medicines, fashioning homemade medical devices, avoiding accidents, and knowing how to deal with accidents that do happen will be based on the lessons we learned during our journey.

External Events

Our new world was transformed as a result of all that happened in the first four to six months of the new presidency. Our country has fallen apart. The world is at war in many places. All of the conveniences of our former life are no longer available to us.

Keeping up on events was certainly useful for our safety. But more important, our ability to read the signs and events had made our decision to bug-out an easy decision. We now are faced with living the way people lived 200 years ago. The skills, experience, and knowledge we had gained through our journey are now our life skills.

The external world is totally out of our ability to control or influence it. Our world now consists of a ten-square-mile area around our final destination. Sadly, we cannot be concerned about world events or even events within our country. Our continued survival hinges on our ability to live and survive effectively in the little section of land in western PA that is now home. We will continue to pray for our country, for other people striving to survive, for their eternal souls, for the church worldwide, and of course for the Lord to bring peace to our fallen world. Life is now to be lived as the Lord had given us. We will work daily to prove worthy of His trust and love, never forgetting that it was He who brought us safely to our earthly destination.

Our Emotions

We experienced the full range of human emotions during our travels, from joy to sadness, from fear to peace, from frustration to control, from loneliness to friendship, from being absolutely worn out to having unlimited strength and energy, from emptiness to spiritual fullness. Every human emotion had been ours. If we had made the attempt without some key assets, we would have failed miserably. Our dogs of course were our joy. Their wagging tails and bright eyes, their need for attention and their physical closeness for warmth and security, gave us something we would have missed very much. My wife and I talking and facing each challenge and every mundane task together; helping to carry each other's loads; providing mutual support and safety when crossing streams, cooking meals, securing meat, washing dishes, and building shelters; sharing the warmth of our sleeping bags with each other and the dogs; sitting at a rest break and just observing nature; watching in hiding for threats that came our way; protecting each other by killing the most dangerous threats we faced together, the hugs, smiles, and touches we shared day after day were beyond price. Our shared spiritual faith is the glue that held all of that together. Our lives and our marriage changed. We would change nothing in hindsight. We will share many more tough days ahead, but we have an emotional strength together that gives us a good chance of surviving whatever comes our way.

We will never again keep our emotions from each other. Life is too short and too difficult to keep all of that within oneself. It must be shared with the person that the Lord has put in your life.

Spiritual Journey

My wife and I have been Christians most of our lives. She at one time considered going into full-time missionary service. I did serve as a missionary in Taiwan, teaching Old Testament as a professor training Chinese ministers and Christian education workers. We were active in multiple churches, teaching Sunday school and serving on committees. We were involved. But the worries and cares of the world had gradually lessened our involvement and our commitment.

Failed marriages, the death of a young child, the death of a husband, had tested us, and we lost some of our zeal. We started to question, and with the questions came some doubts. When we decided to start our journey together, we put the task in the Lord's hands but withheld some commitment and gave it rather to human capabilities. As the world changed around us, we knew that we humanly could not cope with the changes, and we turned over more and more of our future to the Lord.

Early in our travels we stopped and made a full commitment to the Lord's guidance, protection, and love, renewing our faith and our trust. Daily scripture reading, prayer, and waiting on the Lord's guidance became the most important things we did every day. As we traveled, we saw the Lord's hand move in every facet of our lives. We know that we will never be the same again. Our relationship with the Lord will never be the same. Human strength is important in doing what He leads us to do. But we will never rely on human strength and wisdom alone again. We are committed to trusting the Lord in all things as we move into the future. We are committed to sharing that with everyone around us in the hope that they will also come to that same commitment. We have turned back to scripture for the words that will be our guide forward.

Be anxious for nothing,
But in everything by prayer and supplication with thanksgiving
Let your requests be made known to God.
And the peace of God,
Which surpasses all comprehension,
Will guard our hearts and your minds in Christ Jesus.
(Philippians 4:6–7)

What about You?

It is our prayer for you that you will never have to face the trials that we faced in this journey. But deep inside we know that you or your children, or possibly your grandchildren, will face such a situation. How will you or they deal with it? Only in your human strength? Or in the strength, love, guidance, and provision of the Lord Jesus Christ?

You face a decision today—a decision that will change your life whether the world continues on as it has for years or whether it is turned upside down. It is a decision that only you can make for yourself. You cannot make it for your children or your grandchildren. But your decision will testify to your kids and grandkids about the importance of their making the same decision. So, we ask you today to choose to surrender your life to the Giver of life, to the one who will watch over you and yours for eternity. Give your life to Christ, and live your life in ways that will end in eternal life for you in the presence of God, your Father. Amen!

LARRY D. HORTON, PhD

AUTHOR'S NOTE

A Picture of hills of Pennsylvania

FINAL THOUGHTS

Today you do not face the challenges faced in this fictional diary. Hopefully you never will. But odds are that in your lifetime you will be challenged to survive in a world that differs greatly from the world you know today. Will you survive? What will be the underlying foundation of your hope and faith? Will you lose everything to the world? How will your life story close? What will be written in the final chapter of your life?

We do not know what the future holds. As I write, in 48 hours our country will make one of the most important decisions it has made or will make in its history. The results of the election will determine the future you will face. The diary in these pages depicts one possible scenario. Many other scenarios are possible. Are you prepared? Have you thought through what will be required of you, based on the results of the election and events that are happening across the world and that will happen in the future? Events will determine what happens to you to a great degree.

But you do not have to roll over and accept those events and how they play out as the determiner of your life. You can take control of how you respond. You can prepare and plan and possibly face conditions like those that form the backdrop of this story. You can also choose to do nothing. Are you prepared for the implications to you and your family should you choose to do nothing? My wife, Jude, and I hope not. The choice is yours. Please trust the Lord, and make the right choice. Once that choice is made—the right one, we trust—then begin working today to secure your future, one that will be very different than the past but full of hope and opportunity. Choose to survive, not fail!

Larry D. Horton, Ph. D.
November 6, 2016

JUST THE BEGINNING

The Final Journey: *A Diary of Survival* is the first book of a trilogy that follows the survival journey of our couple and their two dogs. This initial diary will soon be followed by two more diaries of their ongoing journey.

The Final Journey: *A Diary of Building a New Life*
(Arriving in Winter 2017)

In the second volume, a couple chooses not to succumb to their uncontrolled world, their fractured society, and the dangers that are now a part of everyday life. After a 1,500-mile survival journey our couple finds themselves facing the daunting task of building a new life in a world that now resembles the year 1800 rather than the early twenty-first century. Survival is now not just a short-term task. It is a daily, weekly, monthly, yearly challenge to build a life using their own **survival common sense** to accomplish seven critical priorities:

- Securing and maintaining livable shelter;
- Protecting themselves from all dangers;
- Building and maintaining the capability to feed themselves and secure a safe water supply;
- Creating sufficient energy;
- Using fire for warmth;
- Using natural resources without modern methodologies; and
- Integrating themselves when necessary into safe social and support structures that are not a direct threat to their long-term survival.

What will their new world be like? The daily, weekly, monthly, and yearly journey they face will transform them as no other challenge has ever done. In their shoes, what would you do? Their diary will help you when you possibly face such a world. Will you be up to the challenge?

The Final Journey: *A Diary of a Journey Finished*
(Appearing in Winter 2018)

The trilogy closes our couple's story, now living simply and independently, as they share with us the story of their ultimate hope and faith. Hope and faith that have guided and protected them. Hope and faith that have enabled them to survive in a world of chaos and uncertainty. Answering a call on their lives, they discover their new role in that world. Constantly vigilant to continue to survive, they now understand why they did in fact survive. They survived to serve others and to become a beacon set on a hill to shine the light of God's truth to a world wandering in darkness. A new day with a new purpose has dawned in their lives. Join us as we look at the final chapter of the story of a couple who choose to survive and move on to their life's final purpose.

BIBLIOGRAPHY

BIBLIOGRAPHY

The following are the key resources used as background for this book. There are countless other resources available to the reader in hard copy print and online. Use the few resources listed below as your initial resource base, and then build upon it. Good luck!

Angier, Bradford. *How to Stay Alive in The Woods.* New York NY: Black Dog & Leventhal, 1956, 2001.

Dvorchak, George E. Jr., M.D. *The Pocket First-Aid Field Guide.* New York NY: Skyhorse Publishing, 2010.

Hawke, Mykel. *Hawke's Special Forces Survival Handbook.* Philadelphia, PA.: Running Press Book Publishers, 2011.

Kruger, Anna. *The Pocket Guide to Herbs.* London: Parkgate Books Ltd., 1998.

MacWelch, Tim, & Owen, Weldon. *Prepare for Anything Survival Manual.* New York NY: Outdoor Life, 2014.

Peterson, Lee Allen. *Edible Wild Plants: Eastern/Central North America.* New York NY: Houghton Mifflin Company, 1977.

Stilwell, Alexander. *Special Forces Survival Techniques.* London: Apple Press, 2014.

Towell, Colin. *The Survival Handbook: Essential Skills for Outdoor Adventure.* New York NY: DK Publishing, 2012.

Online resources and articles exist in abundance. One need only to enter simple search terms such as *survival, wilderness survival, surviving in the wilderness, camping skills,* or anything similar, and you will have years of reading ahead of you, much more than anyone could complete. Good luck!

Printed in the United States
By Bookmasters